KM

Millie sucked [in a startled] breath and clutched at the broom handle. Somebody was sneaking into *her* classroom. Not waiting for the door to be closed, she stepped forward and brought the broom down across the culprit's shoulders. "Get out of my classroom! What do you think you are doing?"

"Millie! Whoa, dammit!" Forrest croaked in surprise and pain. With a reflexive arm movement, he grabbed the broom and encircled her slender arm with an iron grip. "What in hell do you think you're doing out of bed in your night-clothes and taking on anybody who might be prowling about?"

Millie swallowed convulsively. "I asked you first, Forrest Sanders. Let go of my arm!"

She was so close that he could see what looked like fear in her eyes. Was Millie a little afraid, now that her plan to punish a supposed thief had failed and she was the one entrapped? Maybe, Forrest thought wryly when he caught a whiff of jasmine and felt a stinging warmth in his groin, he should teach her a lesson.

"What if I don't care to let you go?" Forrest asked softly and with unquestionable insinuation.

Also by Myra Rowe

Cajun Rose
Treasure's Golden Dream
Riverboat Fever*

PUBLISHED BY
WARNER BOOKS   *forthcoming

A Splendid Yearning

Myra Rowe

WARNER BOOKS

A Warner Communications Company

This book is a work of fiction, and no reference whatever is intended to any living person. Even when names of places or events are real, they are used fictitiously.

To Louise Conlin, my beloved friend who believed in me long before I believed in myself.

Acknowledgment

Much credit for the setting of this romance goes to my parents. In southern Arkansas "way back when," my mother attended a one-room school. During her final year there, a new teacher—a tall, dark, handsome man —arrived. My mother left the community to pursue her own career as a schoolmarm in a one-room school. Before her first year ended, she eloped with her former teacher, the man who in time became my father.

Fond recollections of talk over the years between my parents about their experiences in one-room schools and small communities have provided me with a storehouse of warm memories blended with fancy. Thanks, Mother, for sharing so generously with me. And thanks to you, Daddy, though you are no longer here to read these words. Love you both!

WESTERN CENTRAL ARKANSAS
1911 – As conceived for fictional work

Arkansas River

OUACHITA MTS.

Little Rock

Mt. Ida

Sampson

Hot Springs

Dierks

Freeman

Elmwood

Cossatot River

Murfreesboro

Texarkana

The Yearning

Croon low the song of yearning,
With limpid, rueful tones.
Insert a note of bravery
For tendering of the heart.

A new tune soon comes tripping.
Hark to sweet strains of promise.
Hum what the heart first whispers;
Then sing out with joyful sound.

Love songs limp before they soar.
'Twas then; 'tis now; forevermore.

Myra Rowe

Part One

A redhead waltzes down from the city
With her nose in the air—what a pity!
A mountain man takes in her measure,
Can't say that she's much of a treasure.
The two meet with forceful clashes
And part with vulnerable gashes.

· Chapter One ·

"What in tarnation did you do to your hair!" thundered Reverend Tate when he caught up with the young woman marching from the train toward the depot. The steam engine hissed then and puffed away his next words.

Millicent Monroe, her traveling skirt belling out above her high-buttoned shoes, turned to see the flushed face of the Methodist minister, a family friend as long as she could remember.

"Uncle Fred," she said with affection, "I was afraid you hadn't gotten my letter asking you to meet me today." To calm him and reassure herself, Millicent leaned over and kissed him on his fat cheek. "Did Aunt Phoebe come?" She searched the faces of the small group gathered around the daily train from Hot Springs, but did not see the sprightly old woman. "She is well, I hope."

"She's well, thank you, but she stayed at the parsonage to cook supper for us," replied Fred Tate, still shocked at the young woman's appearance. When he had seen her at her father's funeral last year in Little Rock, she'd had the same air of independence, the same slender build, but her hair—"What have you done to your hair?" His eyes shot up to the red curls barely showing underneath her wide-brimmed hat, and he grimaced. What Millicent had done was next door to a sin.

"I cut it." Her eyes met those of the older man straight on. Hers were brown and twinkly. His were gray and serious.

"Why did you do a fool thing like that?"

In a flash Reverend Fred Tate wondered if it had been a mistake to meddle in Millicent Monroe's life—and those of the people who lived in the nearby Ouachita Mountains, as

3

well. Now that Fred thought about it, he realized that Millicent always had seemed to step to a different tune.

It was too late to backtrack, but Fred suspected that the mountain people might not take kindly to an unconventional female. That hillfolk liked to stomp their own snakes was a saying that Fred had come to respect. More than the average Arkansan, the well-traveled preacher knew that though it was 1911, hillfolk thereabout clung to customs dating back at least fifty years: Men controlled their women far more closely than the men in urban areas did, and the women went along without open protest.

"You made it clear in your letter that an unmarried woman would never be hired—knowingly." Millicent's hand touched the riotous red curls clinging to the back of her head, and she smiled, a movement that, unknown to her, lighted up her face and transformed it into one of even greater beauty.

Lifting her chin, the tall, slender young woman continued. "After that little bit about disguising my name worked, I decided to make myself over and get a really fresh start. A new life, a new look." She swallowed hard, then let the smile dazzle again. "I need the job, Uncle Fred, in the worst possible way. Don't let me down, please."

Fred Tate succumbed to the smile, but the logic of the beautiful young woman cutting her red hair eluded him. Scissors and women's hair were strangers in the society that he knew. Though the September afternoon was cool, he removed his hat and mopped at his bald head with his handkerchief.

Millicent was evidently as strong-willed as when she was a child visiting his wife and him in past summertimes, Fred reminded himself. Here she was—she must be twenty-five or so by now, he mused—still defying convention. But, his thoughts ran on, he was fond of her and she was alone in the world, and ministers needed to look after the families of their departed brothers.

Fred Tate well knew that Millicent's father's final years of illness had depleted the aged minister's savings and that she truly had to work to support herself. An earlier letter from Millicent to his wife, Phoebe, had mentioned that her longtime engagement to a lawyer had been broken and that she no longer had plans to marry.

The clunk of baggage being set onto the station platform jarred Fred into action. Baggage he could handle.

"I'm sorry I was never able to visit Aunt Phoebe and you after you moved to Elmwood several years ago," Millicent said once they got her trunk and boxes loaded onto the back of his dilapidated buggy and started off for the parsonage.

Millicent eyed the several stores lining the main road to Hot Springs, wondering how it might be to live in such a small place after having called Little Rock home for the latter half of her twenty-six years. Behind the slow-moving buggy, the puffing train began moving southward toward Texarkana. She waited for the sounds of the great blasts of steam and the shrill whistle to fade before going on.

"Uncle Fred, you wrote that Freeman is sixteen miles from here. Is it larger than Elmwood?" Millicent held her breath for his answer, crossing her fingers hidden beneath the folds of her long brown skirt. The town was not shown on the old map she had consulted.

"Nope. Smaller." Fred concentrated on handling his horse. The danged critter never was going to get used to the train's hissing and whistle-tooting, he reflected with uncharacteristic irritation. "Not much town there at the crossroads, even if it does go by the name Freeman. A few bauxite mines started up awhile back, but most of the workers are farmers living in the valleys. The company man operating the mines lives here in Elmwood. Wagons haul the ore here for the trains to take it east to the factories." He indicated several huge piles of gray rock lying close to the railroad tracks.

After hearing the word she awaited, Millicent paid scant attention to Fred's other comments. Resuming breathing and uncrossing her fingers, she let her whirling thoughts take over. Smaller? Freeman was even smaller than Elmwood? Double damn! How could it be smaller? What had she gotten herself into?

Listen, girl, Millicent pointed out mentally to her protesting self, *the facts are that it's 1911, you are twenty-six, unmarried, and plan to stay that way. You've no choice but to seek a new life wherever you can support yourself. You gave up your job in Little Rock at the end of spring term because you didn't think you could stay where Luther and his bride are living. Once you came to your senses and realized you no longer wanted or needed an emotional attachment to any man, someone had taken your slot. Freeman is the only place needing a teacher.*

"I'll bet I'll find Freeman charming, Uncle Fred," Millicent announced in her cultured voice. She lifted her smooth face and called up a cheerful mien. "Tell me all about what Aunt Phoebe and you have been doing."

And he did, in glowing detail.

When they reached the neat white parsonage sitting two blocks behind the line of stores, Aunt Phoebe added her complaints about the unheard-of cropped hair, then launched into her version of community happenings. Between the preacher and his wife, no local event seemed to have passed without notice or comment. All they had needed, their guest decided with fondness, was an audience.

"I loved your fried chicken," Millicent said while the two women tidied up the kitchen after supper. The kerosene lamp sputtered companionably. "You seem to find cooking easy."

"After thirty years of marriage, I find it is," the energetic little woman replied with her nice smile. "Sakes alive, girl, you've cooked and kept house for your dad ever since your mother died. I suspect you find it easy after all these years, too."

Phoebe glanced affectionately at her tall, red-haired guest before she stepped out onto the back porch to slosh the dishwater onto the ground underneath a squat chinaberry tree. The screen door popped shut with a loud splat when she returned and put away the dishpan. "If I'd ever had children, I would've wanted them to be like you, Millicent. You've turned out to be so efficient, so levelheaded."

"But I'm not those things, really," denied Millicent, removing the apron Phoebe had tied around her waist to "save" her traveling outfit and returning it to its wooden peg near the black cast-iron cookstove. "You just think I am because you choose to see me that way. Uncle Fred wouldn't agree with you—now that I've cut my hair."

With a sigh Millicent spread out the drying cloth on the back of a chair and, after the older woman blew out the flame in the lamp and adjusted the wick, she followed her hostess into the parlor. No one ever seemed to listen to her when she talked about her inner thoughts, she reflected without rancor. Forced into the role of doer at thirteen after the untimely death of her mother, she sometimes suspected that inside she was no more than a young dreamer awaiting a happy ending.

Not until later, after Millicent had gone to bed and lay listening to the cicadas and tree frogs calling in the September darkness, did she allow herself to dwell upon what lay ahead on the following day. Nothing must prevent her from earning the rather generous salary offered by the Freeman School Board.

Not until last month, Millicent mused, had she been able to make the final payment on her father's funeral of last year. Buying the train ticket from Little Rock had left a terrible dent in her bank account. Her body temperature raced from up to down and back up again as her thoughts plagued her.

One month ago, as Ezekial M. Monroe, she had signed the teaching contract Uncle Fred had sent her on behalf of the Freeman School Board. Never having taught anything other than upper-level English in a private school for girls in Little Rock, Millicent had no idea how she would handle a one-room school with pupils of both sexes and varying ages. Merciful heavens! Who would have thought that she would be taking such drastic steps to forge a new life for herself?

Millicent flopped from her back to her stomach and stared out the eye-level window at the blinking fireflies. The bed springs screaked with her every movement, a fitting accompaniment to her discordant mood, she decided.

When the Freeman School Board chairman came for her tomorrow morning, what would he say when he saw that his teacher was a woman? She recalled the neat print on the contract above his scrawled signature—Forrest Obediah Sanders.

Rolling onto her back, the restless young woman tried to listen to a distant mockingbird's serenade but could not hold back her troubling thoughts. True, she assured the threatening, faceless Mr. Sanders crowding her thoughts, she was a woman but she was as capable of performing the duties of a teacher in his new school as a man.

Millicent's fingers slid through her hair, a testing forefinger and thumb telling her what she already knew: No curl stretched out longer than two inches. If a woman's long hair was truly her "crowning glory," she thought with a kind of pride in her daring, then she had rid herself of hers the night before and dumped it in a trash can.

With a fist jabbing her pillow, Millicent flipped to her stomach. Her thoughts swerved back to Mr. Sanders. When he came for her tomorrow to transport her to Freeman, what *would* he say?

"What the hell is going on!" said Chairman Forrest Obediah Sanders when he hurried into the parsonage the next morning and met the new teacher. Glaring at Millicent as though she had seven-year itch, he stood with his black coat unbuttoned and one hand rammed in a pocket of his hip-hugging breeches. The red-striped scarf falling down the front of his white shirt might well have been a flag signifying trouble. He made no attempt to apologize for his language, and the bald-headed man whom he addressed showed no surprise. "How could you, a man of the cloth, lie to me, Brother Tate? I figured you for a better friend than this."

The man's fiery blue eyes pounced upon the red-faced preacher before returning to rake over the tall young woman seated demurely on the sofa in the living room of the parsonage. "I plainly told you that I wanted a man for the first teacher of our new school. You never once told me Ezekial M. Monroe was a *female*!" His loud deep voice pronounced the last word as if it in itself were an abomination.

"Calm down, Forrest," Fred replied. "You know how you're sometimes a man of impulse and usually regret letting off steam."

"What does that have to do with this . . . this trickery?" Forrest asked with enough force to be called a yell.

Fred went on with an apologetic smile. "When I received no other applications to the ad you had me place in the Arkansas papers, I thought I was doing both Miss Monroe and you a favor." Fred was usually comfortable in the role of peacemaker, but he felt sweat beading on his bald head. "This young lady is unmarried and in need of a position. You had one nobody else seemed to want. I didn't look upon it as lying, just sort a withholding all of the truth."

In the sudden silence, Fred glanced at Millicent, sitting stiffly on the sofa with eyes downcast and hands clasped in her lap. Two spots of color on her lightly freckled cheeks vied with the brief red cap of curls for attention. "Millicent Monroe is a qualified, experienced teacher, as the ad called for. She also fills your other requirement in that she is dependable."

"Why couldn't you find a man?" Forrest Sanders growled before plopping onto the chair Fred offered and slapping his black hat onto the side table with a loud smack. The graceful parlor chair groaned from the weight of a man over six feet tall and as lean and muscled as an athlete. "A woman teacher is not what I had in mind." He shook his head and tightened his lips, then raked back his black hair with an impatient hand. Damnit to hell! For over a year he had been getting ready for this September, and now his carefully laid plans seemed impossible. "A woman teacher won't do!"

As if I wasn't even in the room, thought Millicent. *At least I've been promoted from "female" to "woman."* Righteous indignation threatened to unseal the very lips that she had promised Uncle Fred would remain closed until the matter was settled. She watched Forrest Sanders openly then. He had burst into the parsonage like a wild animal let out of a cage—or, she reconsidered, was it more like one being forced from the wilds into a cage? He appeared tamer now that he was sitting, Millicent conceded, but an eerie tension still permeated the room.

A heavy black mustache above a grim mouth led Millicent into thinking of a picture on a wanted poster she had seen in the post office last month in Little Rock. An outlaw? Yes, Board Chairman Forrest Sanders could pass easily for an outlaw with his present sardonic expression and baleful eyes.

But the cleft in the man's chin threw his tanned face into a class all its own, somehow softening the chiseled face, easing the planes of his high cheekbones, and working in harmony with intelligent blue eyes edged on the outer sides with laugh lines. Not that she was likely to see those come into play, Millicent admitted. Her vivid imagination painted an instant picture of the man smiling, and she realized that Mr. Sanders was downright handsome—and extremely well put together. In her best "parlor" voice, Millicent asked, "Why are you so sure that a woman can't do the job?"

"For one thing, Freeman is just a wide place at a crossroads, Miss Monroe, and not somewhere a woman from our capital city is likely to fit in." One of Forrest's boot heels scraped against the oiled wooden floor as he stacked one long leg across the other knee and narrowed his eyes at her. "Especially one who is . . . unmarried."

When Millicent continued gazing at him with no change in her unreadable expression, Forrest went on. "We're just mountain folks, and we figured on having a man teacher, maybe one with a wife, who could fit in." He shifted his weight and cleared his throat. Was this a staring contest? he wondered crossly, giving it his all in case it was meant to be. She never even blinked.

"I assure you that I can fit in anywhere I've a mind to," Millicent replied. "And you don't have to speak to me in that manner. I'm not deaf, and I'm not stupid." The man obviously was accustomed to being in charge and having his own way, she thought. He was not going to oust her from the job, not without a fight. Charm was not moving him. He likely would not recognize it if he saw it. Logic might. "What are your other objections to having a woman teacher?"

Millicent's remark about his speaking to her in "that manner" stung Forrest to the quick. Whatever did she mean? He was mad as hell, sure, but he was not talking any differently from the way he ever did. Was she looking down her educated nose at him? She is as brassy as her hair, Forrest thought now that he had calmed a little and was really looking at her. Why in the devil did she have to be so uncommonly pretty? he wondered as his eyes roved from her full lips to her brown eyes to her—Good Lord! What had she done to her hair?

"I was tricked. Bamboozled," Forrest accused loudly in his deepest voice. If he could not reason with her, maybe he could scare her off. He paused to see if his tone might have frightened her a little. Apparently it had not, so he went on in a less ominous way, one more in keeping with his usual self. "You didn't sign the contract with your real name." He had her there. One of his black eyebrows shot up a degree in imagined victory. Hope surged behind the initial disappointment fueling his anger.

"My name is exactly as signed: My first name is Ezekial, the middle Millicent. Men sign their first names and use the middle initial. Why can't a woman?" Millicent had not missed the mocking black eyebrow, and she watched it settle down level with the other one as her words sank in.

Though Millicent never had spent much time in the company of any man but her father, she still was surprised at the defensiveness stirring inside. Her chin shot up daringly. Let him answer her question . . . in his god-awfully loud voice. Had he been raised in a barn?

"Women just don't sign their names that way, that's why," Forrest muttered, taken aback at her words and manner. By damn, she was sharp. And apparently not scared of the devil. Never before had he seen any woman stand up for herself so belligerently. Hope wavered. He seldom lost his temper, and almost never with women. Already, as Brother Tate had predicted, he was regretting his uncharacteristic outburst. Forrest ran a long finger on the inside of the stiff white collar imprisoning his neck. Why had he bothered to put on his Sunday best?

By design Millicent's next words were syrupy enough to sweeten a whole pitcher of lemonade. "Then we have no quarrel about the validity of our contract, do we, Mr. Sanders?"

Millicent glanced at the silent but watchful Uncle Fred sitting beside her before leaning forward to add, "If you're determined not to honor it because of my sex"—from the

corner of her eye, she saw Uncle Fred fidget and redden at
her use of the word "sex"—"you should talk with a lawyer
since the contract makes no specifications one way or the
other. Should you refuse to allow me to stay, I believe
you're committed to paying me the yearly salary, since I've
come in good faith to honor my part of the bargain." She
watched Forrest's black eyebrows form a straight line above
his eyes, narrowed now in seeming disbelief.

Millicent's earlier sugary tone might have been a figment
of his imagination, Forrest noted with awe, so completely
was it hidden by steel during her last remarks. Damnation!
Was she a lawyer as well as a schoolmarm? For one of the
few times in his thirty-five years, he was at a loss for words.

Mr. Sanders looked as if thunder has crept up behind him
and rattled him, Millicent thought. Good. Let him see that
she was not afraid to stand up for herself against overbearing
men. She did not know what his stakes were, but she knew
what hers were: survival. She leaned back against the sofa,
strangely spent. Round one.

"Are you threatening me?" Forrest's bass voice was as
dark and vibrant as his hair and his handlebar mustache—
and he was not even trying to sound gruff that time. The
nerve of the woman! But, he warned himself, he should not
have been surprised. Any woman fool enough to cut off her
hair could not be trusted to act normal.

"Come, you two," Fred intervened, reaching over to pat
Millicent's hand in silent warning. He hoped no one outside
was walking near enough to the parsonage to hear the quarrelsome sounds coming from the parlor. "There's no need
for tempers to rule here. I believe you'll find Miss Monroe is
just the one for your new school, Forrest. She's alone in the
world, dedicated only to teaching."

Fred paused, remembering the way Millicent had blurted
out the word "sex" so brazenly. Did he really know the
young woman with the bobbed hair well enough to be so
expansive? He moved to safer ground. "Her father was a
preacher, a friend of mine since seminary days, and the family moved around during her growing-up years. She won't
find it hard to make a place for herself in Freeman. Millicent
Monroe can handle the job."

"Seems I have no choice but to take your word, now that September is here," Forrest replied after reviewing his options. Hope that his oft-dreamed plan could work now rolled over and died, along with his flaring anger at having been duped, however well meant it might have been on the minister's part.

Since Forrest, as chairman of Freeman's school board, had agreed to donate half the new teacher's salary this first year, he could see that he might end up paying his carefully hoarded money, along with that of his neighbors, and still have no teacher in the building only recently finished. He might have lost what he had hoped to gain personally from the expertise of an instructor, but there was no sense in depriving the youngsters of a chance to attend school close to their homes.

Forrest Sanders had not lived nearly all of his thirty-five years in the Ouachita Mountains of Arkansas without recognizing a trap when he saw it. He was hog-tied, good and proper.

In the silence, Forrest mused on. Maybe Miss Monroe would not like Freeman, once she got there, and would leave on her own. And just maybe he could help her make that decision—without her catching on, of course. She obviously believed that she could manage her affairs without outside help. Forrest found himself being thankful that the world wasn't full of Millicent Monroes. There was something unnaturally upsetting about her.

"I came in a wagon so as to haul the new teacher and *his* things," he said to Freeman's new schoolmarm, surprised to see more speculation than gloating in her bright eyes. "We'd best be going. Sixteen miles in a wagon is a long way, especially for somebody used to city ways." He cleared his throat, aware that Millicent jumped at the sound. Was she unaccustomed to being around men and hearing such everyday noises?

As heavenly smells floated in with her, Phoebe saved the day by coming in then from the kitchen and insisting all sample the pound cake she had just baked.

Afterward, while the men loaded Millicent's trunk and boxes, the women said their farewells.

"We come to Freeman every first Sunday for preaching," Phoebe assured Millicent, "so we'll be keeping in touch. A passenger buggy runs between here and there twice a week, so you won't be completely stranded. Folks from over there send messages with the driver if we're needed. You can, too."

"Thank you for everything, Aunt Phoebe. I hope my being here won't make Uncle Fred and you late for church today." Millicent looked down at the wicker basket the older woman was pressing into her hands. "I'm sure Mr. Sanders and I will enjoy the lunch you packed."

Inside, Millicent knew that she lied through her teeth. There was nothing she would enjoy sharing with the noisy, bigoted man waiting outside to drive her to Freeman in the foothills of the Ouachita Mountains.

· *Chapter Two* ·

Millicent could have sworn that a raincloud seemed to hover about Forrest Sander's face for the first mile or two out of Elmwood. She heard him give an occasional deep-voiced command to the team of mules, but he seemed oblivious to the woman sitting stiffly beside him on the hard wagon seat. After he appeared disinterested in her halfhearted efforts, she gave up trying to make conversation. Plainly, Millicent reflected, the two had nothing in common.

The purple hills in the distance seemed less hostile to the young woman from Little Rock as the sun climbed higher and gilded them with golden light. The vee springs beneath the barely padded wagon seat did little to ease the jolting ride over the rocky road, and she found her wide-brimmed hat sliding from one side of her head to the other. Even with two extra-long hatpins, the hat couldn't be attached firmly to her short hair.

"How long have you been teaching, Miss Monroe?" Forrest asked, having to clear his throat before the words would slip out. He sent a sidewise look her way. She hadn't jumped that time when he cleared his throat.

"I thought the cat had your tongue, Mr. Sanders," Millicent quipped, turning to look at him. Her hat made a half spin, and she grabbed at it with both hands. While repinning it, she noted he hadn't taken to her teasing. His angular face was solid solemn as he watched her quick movements with open interest. "I've been teaching for four years." She suspected that he was laughing secretly at the problems she was having with the sliding hat. Something was sparking those blue eyes set beneath the heavy black eyebrows.

"You've been living in Little Rock, if what Brother Tate told me is the truth." Forrest turned back to watching the team of mules, for they were edging the wagon into the underbrush alongside the road. He made a clacking sound with his tongue and his teeth before calling out: "Haw, Caesar! Cleopatra! Come up, there!" With a fluid movement, he thumbed his black hat off his forehead to rest at a rakish angle on the back of his head after the mules once more traveled in the center of the dirt and gravel road.

"Everything on my application is correct, Mr. Sanders," Millicent informed him. Her voice hid her resentment at his implication that he had been told lies. "Perhaps if you had read it more closely, you would have seen that I taught formerly at a girls' school. You might have surmised that I could be a woman."

Surprised upon seeing a pained expression claim his angular face before he looked away, Millicent swallowed any further comments and gazed at the mountains up ahead again. Was he still so angry about her not being a man? Apparently her new employer was not in the habit of losing even small battles.

"This is a good place to water the mules at the creek up ahead," Forrest said after another long spell of no talk.

Lost in thought again, Millicent started. The man's deep voice didn't seem overly loud now that they were out in the open, she reflected. All she had heard for miles was the clatter of the wheels on the rocky road, the rattle of harness,

the screak of the wagon seat, and the occasional call of a
darting bird. They had passed few houses and had met only
one other wagon.

Forrest guided the mules off the road into a shady grove
of trees running alongside it. "We're more than halfway
there." A hint of kindness softened his voice as he added,
"I'll come help you down after I unhitch the team." He was
on the ground in one leap, his lean body moving with careless ease.

"That won't be necessary, Mr. Sanders," Millicent called,
vowing silently not to cause problems because of her sex.
She had no wish to get the man riled again. Already she had
wondered how his wife stood him when things didn't suit
him.

Carefully Millicent gathered up her long skirt in one hand
and, holding on to the wagon seat with the other, backed up
enough to put one foot over the side onto the step. Her foot
searched blindly for the narrow ledge but failed to find it.
Standing with one foot inside the wagon and the other flail-
ing around outside, she tried to look over her shoulder. The
wagon lurched just then, and she fell backward onto the
ground with a decidedly unladylike swoosh and splat.

"Double damn!" Millicent yelled on her way down. Once
there, she couldn't move or breathe.

"Are you hurt, Miss Monroe?" Forrest asked, rushing to
her side. That the fool woman hadn't waited in the wagon as
he had told her to surprised and angered him, but he had to
grin when he recalled her "Double damn!" "I was coming to
help you after I unhitched the team. Most folks would've
figured the wagon might roll a bit when I let down the
tongue. You should have waited," he scolded.

Forrest looked down at the crumpled young woman lying
on her back fighting desperately for breath. Her hat lay tilted
across the upper half of her reddening face, and her skirt
revealed more leg and petticoat than it covered. He leaned
over and extended his hands, his mouth spread into a wide
smile. Gone was the poised schoolmarm.

Miss Monroe was as riled and rumpled as a Tom turkey
when a rooster dared enter his territory, Forrest reflected.
Suddenly he began thinking of her as Millicent. He guessed

he should be grateful she hadn't burst into tears as most of the young women that he knew would have done. The thought sobered him. Millicent had spunk, no doubt about it.

"And you, sir, should have told me that the wagon might move," Millicent replied testily, once she caught her breath. Refusing to take his proffered hands, she propped herself up on her elbows and let the hat fall onto her still-heaving breasts. She didn't look up at him, but she was acutely aware of the long black-clad legs looming before her.

Millicent sat all the way up and took a deep breath before flinging the despised hat onto a grassy spot and yanking down her skirts. Now the pesky man had probably seen that she didn't wear long drawers. There was no telling what he would be telling his wife about the new schoolteacher. Had her skirt shot up enough to reveal the shortened drawers that she had altered to suit herself? Mercy's sakes! How would she ever regain her dignity?

"Do you plan to keep sitting there?" Forrest asked in that drawling, deep-timbred way peculiarly his own. Who would have thought that the schoolmarm—and a preacher's daughter, at that—wore red satin garters beneath her long, somber skirt? Not that it made any sense, but he realized that he had not felt so lighthearted in a good while.

Millicent could hear laughter plumping out his words. She reckoned that she knew why, too, and almost let out a giggle before she caught herself. "Yes, Mr. Sanders, I think I'll stay right where I am. I believe this is as good a place as any to eat the basket lunch Aunt Phoebe gave us, don't you? I guess I was a bit too eager to get started." Irony flavored her voice. Both of her hands went to fluff debris from her red curls, and she lifted her face to his for the first time since her fall. Seeing the amusement dancing back in his eyes and recognizing the absurdity of her situation, Millicent smiled.

Why, Forrest mused, Millicent Monroe was a sight prettier than he had thought at first—she was a beauty. Her straight little nose went just right with her oval face. Didn't that beat all, the way he hadn't noticed before how lively her brown eyes were, or what even, pretty teeth she had behind her full, pink lips? And with her slender neck arched back and her cap of curls glinting in the dappled sunlight, he could not say for sure that cropped hair was a total mistake.

"Want me to fetch the basket?" Forrest asked, wondering why his words came out sounding far away and unusually slow.

"Why not? I'm starved."

While Forrest got the mules settled down by the creek, Millicent moved to a shadier spot away from the wagon. At least he hadn't laughed at her any more than she deserved, she mused while brushing at the twigs in her hair and on her clothing. Maybe he wasn't as difficult as she first had thought.

"That's like Aunt Phoebe to include a damp washcloth," Millicent said when she removed the small tablecloth covering the contents of the basket. After wiping off her hands and passing the washcloth to Forrest, she expertly popped the cloth and laid it in one smooth movement on the grass between them. "I hope you like fried chicken, Mr. Sanders." She peeled back the paper bag and revealed a platter of golden brown pieces. On impulse she held it toward him to share the tantalizing aroma. His audible sniff and bass "Um-m-m!" pleased her, and they exchanged grins like conspirators.

Under Forrest's appreciative gaze, Millicent then set out several fruit jars of varied sizes. One held potato salad; another, deviled eggs; a third, peach pickles; and another, sliced cucumbers in peppered vinegar. Jubilantly she lifted a loaf of fragrant yeast bread wrapped in a snowy dish towel and still warm from its morning stint in Aunt Phoebe's oven. "I don't know about you, Mr. Sanders, but I have a weakness for freshly baked bread."

"Do you think you could call me Forrest—or maybe Woods?" Forrest asked long before they were ready for the hunks of pound cake that Millicent had found in the very bottom of the basket. "Folks hereabouts don't take to much ceremony."

They sat on the ground across the small tablecloth from each other, eating hungrily from loaded tin plates in between bits of polite conversation. Overhead in the trees, bluejays twittered and complained during the spells of companionable silence, as if the delicious smells of the picnic lunch might be taunting them that their own diets offered nothing so scrumptious. Forrest wiped his mouth and mustache with his napkin before he took a swig from the fruit jar of water designated as his.

"Woods?" Millicent repeated, her eyes crinkling and her mouth pursing in thought. In the social circles of Little Rock familiar to her, Millicent mused, Forrest's suggestion never would have been made so soon after a first meeting. If she meant to fit in at Freeman, though—"I thought I heard Uncle Fred call you Forrest." She bit into a second piece of crunchy chicken, munching and watching him while awaiting his answer.

"Most folks around home call me Woods. Others stick to Forrest." Millicent's appetite astounded him. How could one slender woman eat so much? Except for the very young unmarried girls, most of the women around Freeman were far more rounded than Millicent Monroe. Suddenly the vision of her exposed legs and thighs flashed to mind, reminding him that there was far more to the new schoolmarm than met the eye of the casual observer.

Her dark skirt was so full that Forrest couldn't be sure how Millicent was sitting. Cross-legged, as he was? Surely not. Unladylike. Her long mutton-sleeved blouse cupped high around her neck, but he detected womanly curves pushing against the crisp white fabric in all the right places. And underneath that prim exterior.... Forrest grinned. Red garters. And drawers way above her knees.

"Perhaps I should call you Mr. Sanders since you're my employer," Millicent replied, her eyes solemn.

When he shook his head in emphatic dismissal, she watched an amused look hover about his mouth and found herself marking how his lips were downright sensuous. He seemed terribly pleased with himself about something private. Was the roguish glint in his eyes caused only by the little game about names? "I gather 'Woods' resulted from someone choosing to be witty about 'Forrest.'"

The idea intrigued her, and she smiled. Now that his face was not clouded with anger, she saw that she had been right in suspecting the man truly was handsome. "I think I can go along with 'Woods,' but please, let's not follow that with 'Trees.'"

"You've got a quick mind, lady," Woods admitted, glad to have the business of his name settled. He noticed again how pretty and girlish she looked when she smiled—all bright and bouncy like the sun peeking over the mountains in the mornings.

Yes, Woods thought as he ate, Millicent Monroe was different—and not just because of her shorn hair and war-horse ways. He had not set out to ignore her during the morning's ride, but he'd had a powerful lot of thinking to do about the way her arrival had shot all of his plans to hell and back. No matter that he was preoccupied, he had been rude to shut her out. But here she was, laughing and talking as though he had been nice all day. Woods Sanders admired gumption, whether in a man or a woman. And look at the way she had taken that fall and come up laughing.

Woods's thoughts veered sharply in a direction they had not visited in years. Wonder why a woman as beautiful as Millicent had not already married? She must have had dozens of suitors, probably still did in a place as large as Little Rock where young folks did not marry quite so early in life as mountain people.

"If I'm to call you Woods, then you may call me Millicent." Reaching for another peach pickle, she sank her teeth into its tart firmness. She herself might have a quick mind, she reflected, but there was no moss on Forrest—no, not on Woods Sanders either. He was one of a kind—and not just because of the arresting cleft in his chin and his biased attitude toward women teachers. Because he was serving as chairman of a school board, he must be married with a large family. Millicent's next thought shook her up a tad: Maybe Woods's wife wasn't such an unlucky woman after all.

"Why not Ezekial, like on the contract?" Woods drawled in his lazy way, tearing off a piece of bread and plopping it into his mouth. He watched a drop of peach pickle juice linger at the corner of her full lips and felt cheated, somehow, when she dabbed at it with her napkin. The pink on pink had fascinated him. His tongue wet his lips before he continued in a teasing tone. "I kinda like Ezekial. Sorta sneaky to name a girl that, wouldn't you say? It could lead to all kinds of wrong conclusions."

"I've always been called Millicent." Instantly on guard, she sat up straighter. She wasn't going to cross swords with him again over the signature on the contract, she warned the part of her that wanted to rise to the bait. She hooked a secretive glance his way. How in the world did the man shave so closely with that cleft in his chin?

"Never Millie?" Woods's mustache wriggled as he chewed a crisp cucumber slice and assessed the schoolmarm from behind half-closed black lashes. Deviltry lurked deep within his blue eyes. When she shook her head and set her cap of curls into a brief dance, but kept on eating, he asked, "You've never been called Zeke either?"

Millicent's laughter exploded then, and she tossed her head back in enjoyment. She hadn't had a lot to laugh about over the past several months.

"Never," she replied when she sobered.

There was little doubt left in Millicent's mind by then that Woods Sanders was an original. Now that he had removed his hat, coat, and tie, she could see that his shoulders were unusually broad and muscular, just as she had thought back at the parsonage. She had tried not to stare at the masses of black chest curls peeking from the unbuttoned top part of his white shirt. Never before had she seen a man expose his neck and chest that way. She liked it.

Her eyes squinting a bit in thought, Millicent found herself picturing Woods as one of the pioneering mountain men of the Old West. Strong. Fearless. A born leader.

"Guess it wouldn't do for folks to hear the new teacher called Zeke, would it?" Woods didn't look at her while he ladled the last of the potato salad into his mouth and chewed it with obvious relish. "I think Millie suits you better than Millicent, though. Would your folks be mad if I hung a new name on you?"

"My mother died thirteen years ago, and I lost my father last year. Since I'm an only child, there's no one you have to answer to—except me." She became interested in a crumb of chicken crust on her thumb and popped it into her mouth. It must be the dark musical quality of his voice that made it unique, Millicent mused. Almost a vibrato of soothing bass tones, now that she was used to hearing it. Strange how she had at first labeled it as being too loud. It fit the man.

"I'm sorry about your folks."

"I'm used to the idea of being alone." Her tone told him of her acceptance. "What about you? Do you have a family? A wife and children?"

Millicent had seen few men so at ease with themselves or with just-met women as Woods seemed to be. And, when she overlooked his brash behavior earlier in the day, she admitted that she liked a lot about him. She summed up his good looks as being natural and virile, the kind a mountain man of the West would possess.

Recalling that Uncle Fred had called Woods a man of impulse, Millicent tried to connect that quality with what she was learning about him. He possessed what she termed, for lack of a better phrase, an easy charm, one she assumed came from living a simple life in the Ouachita Mountains in the central, western part of Arkansas. He was not at all like the young men she had known—and certainly not like the dapper Luther Osgood who had jilted her only a few months ago. Millicent's lips firmed at that humiliating final thought.

Woods finished his food before replying, "I've no wife and children, but I do have a family. My pa died back when I was six. I live with my mama and her sister in the house Pa built when they came here from Georgia after the Civil War and homesteaded." Setting down his empty plate and brushing his hands together to rid them of crumbs, he went on. "I'm the youngest after five girls, so I'm a man with lots of family."

Millicent let the unexpected news that Woods was not married find a nesting place way back in her mind. She was not ready to examine it.

"That must be fun," Millicent said. When Woods looked puzzled, she finished her thought. "To be part of a big family, I mean. I always thought they had such fun, those people fortunate enought to grow up with lots of brothers and sisters."

Millicent passed the plate of cake to Woods then, smiling to herself when he took the largest piece. He probably was spoiled, what with his being the baby brother of five girls, but he was easy to talk with now that he seemingly had resolved the problem of accepting her as the new teacher. And he seemed to listen, really listen to her. For some reason, she found that extremely flattering. A little breeze stirred up the aroma of Aunt Phoebe's almond-flavored pound cake and permeated the small space between them with its piquancy.

Millicent surprised herself by confessing, "I used to think that if I married and had at least five children, I'd be able to catch up on all the fun I missed."

Picking up on a sad note of longing in her voice, Woods asked, "You don't think that anymore, Millie?" He watched her forkful of cake stop in midair. The jaybirds and sparrows overhead in the trees hushed, as if they, too, awaited her answer. The smell of the warm cake was blending now with the heady fragrances of the trees and late-summer grass and had become one with nature. In the deep shade, Millicent's hair was a rich auburn. He remembered well how it had shone like copper in the full sun . . . what little had showed underneath the wagon wheel of a hat that she kept battling to keep on her pretty head.

"I have my students now," Millicent replied coolly, bringing the fork up to her mouth and fixing Woods with a brown stare. She noted that his name for her fell easily on her ears. Millie. It did seem to fit her new self better than Millicent.

Somehow, though, Millicent wished that she hadn't been quite so frank. Whatever had she been thinking of, to be so talky with a man she had just met; the man who had scrawled his name so carelessly across the bottom of her teaching contract as to be almost illegible, the man who only a few hours ago had upbraided her for "tricking" him into hiring her? Millicent swallowed more than cake and sat up straighter. A stitch in her back reminded her of her ignominious fall.

"The sun is telling me it's time to get back on the road," Woods said after polishing off the cake and squinting up through the tree branches.

It came to Woods as he rose and started toward the creek to fetch the mules that his earlier plan to coerce Millie into leaving Freeman on her own had lost its initial appeal. Long accustomed to dealing with disappointments, on the ride from Elmwood he had come to terms with his new one about having his private plans squashed by the appearance of a woman teacher. If what he had hoped to accomplish was meant to be, he reasoned, something would work out.

What bothered Woods as he led the mules toward the wagon was his wondering what had happened to the carefree young woman with whom he had been enjoying the tasty food and light conversation. He hoped she'd not vanished into thin air simply because he had let on that he realized that she had no plans to marry.

Questions nagged at Woods while he hitched up the mules to the wagon, but he soon put them aside. From what he had already learned about Millie, it was plain to him that she must be unmarried because she wanted it that way. Why, a woman like Millie Monroe could have her pick of men—if she wanted one. The only thing that truly puzzled him was why she had apparently chosen to remain single. Had she, perhaps, turned her back on marriage because she had been stabbed fatally in the heart, as he had?

Once Woods sneaked a look at Millie while she was re-packing the picnic basket, and he thought he saw a frown marring her pretty forehead beneath the short, saucy curls.

"I was wondering if there were any houses on this road," Millie said, craning her slender neck to see the pale shape up ahead. She had decided to keep the nickname that Woods had given her. If she was going to take on a new way of life, she might as well take on a new name as well.

The rocky road had climbed steadily ever since their stop for lunch, and neither Millie nor Woods had worked to re-capture the easy mood settling upon them while they ate. Both seemed intent on private thoughts as the wagon creaked its monotonous way toward Freeman.

Millie recognized almost all of the trees bordering the reddish road. Broad-based oaks, beeches, slender gums, and curly cedars sometimes prevented a view of the foothills ahead. She admired the red leaves on the sweet gum trees as they fluttered in the occasional breezes and foretold the coming season. All day she had been smelling the peculiarly dry autumn scents of the top-heavy goldenrod and dying brownish weeds alongside the road.

"What a peaceful scene," Millie murmured, gazing at the whitewashed house coming into sight. Several horses in a rock-dotted pasture stopped grazing to lift graceful necks and eye the travelers.

"That's the Milstead place," Woods explained. "Lucas has two boys, Ransom and Steve, who'll be coming to school."

"How old are they?" She should have already been asking about her future pupils instead of woolgathering, Millie realized guiltily. But everything was so new, so different— especially the unsettling man riding with her in the wagon.

"Guess they're about fifteen and nine, or so." He watched her take in the well-tended place and nod her approval as they passed directly in front.

"We must be getting close to Freeman, if they're to attend school there," she said.

"A couple of hours yet." At her puzzled look, he said, "The boys will be staying during the week with their grandpa and aunt in Freeman. He owns the general store there."

"That seems an awfully long time for a nine-year-old to be away from his mother," Millie remarked, fighting down the little spurt of nervousness at the thought of dealing with the two unknown boys. They were probably terrors.

"Their mother died six years ago." His voice sounded mechanical, its usual musical tones flat.

"How awful!" Millie's mouth and eyes softened. The boys probably needed a woman's touch. "Does their father care for them himself, or has he remarried?" She saw a muscle in Woods's cheek twitch before he answered.

"Lucas hasn't married again. A Mexican couple live on the place. Maria, the wife, cooks and helps out with the boys when their Aunt Annabelle isn't around."

"Then they do have some mothering," Millie replied with approval. She re-pinned her hat and stuck her feet up to rest on the footboard. As unobtrusively as possible, she eased her hands to soothe the ache in the small of her back. She had noticed how Woods propped one foot upon the board and leaned forward in a relaxed way, allowing his lean body to sway with the bumps. If it wouldn't look so unladylike, she. . . .

"I told you sixteen miles was a long ride in a wagon." Woods said, amused at her efforts to hide her discomfort. "You don't have to sit so straight against the backrest, you know."

"Am I complaining?" Millie tossed her head and glared at him while she readjusted her hat. "Just because I'm a woman doesn't mean I can't take a few unpleasantries."

"In Little Rock, though, you would probably be riding on a trolley or in an auto—or certainly in a buggy."

"If I had preferred Little Rock, I would have stayed there." He wasn't going to get her dander up. Probably nothing would make him happier than to see her become dissatisfied with her new life in Freeman and break the contract. "Anyway, I doubt a car or a light buggy could travel this primitive road." A rear wheel rolled over the edge of a large rock just then, the wheel bumping noisily as it dropped back to dirt and jostled the passengers.

"You're wrong there. Clive Durham, the manager of the bauxite mines, drives his Model-T to Freeman almost every week. And sometimes a salesman calls in one, although most use buggies." Woods's blue eyes lit up. She didn't know everything.

Millie made no comment right off. She would have to remember not to be so open with her remarks about the shortcomings of the area. Her father, even before he became ill that last time and overly critical, had always told her that she was far too outspoken . . . for a woman. Something Woods had said rang a bell. "Bauxite mines? In Freeman?"

"Not far away."

"I recall now that Uncle Fred said something about mines and pointed out some huge piles of rock near the railroad."

Millie's wondering gaze swept the mountain ridges, their lower parts bathed now with splinters of the late afternoon sun making its descent behind them. The ridge road that they followed seemed to lead straight toward the low-lying range. She had to admit the scenery was new, spectacular. Several times she had glimpsed below them little tumbling streams rushing over rocky beds in the deep shade—and shivered to think what kind of slimy crawlers might be lurking in the underbrush. She darted a look at Woods's hands. Though they were apparently those of a working man, no grime marred the neatly cut fingernails. "Do you work in the mines?"

"You might say that," Woods replied, his generous mouth quirking at the corners and lifting his mustache. The motion of the wagon was gradually moving Millie's skirt up from where she had placed it to cover her legs. Her high-button shoes still rested on the footboard, but now the tops, hugging slim ankles, were in plain sight . . . and a stretch of silk-encased lower leg as well, he noted with appreciation.

"Exactly what is bauxite, and what's it used for?" Millie asked, wondering why Woods jerked his head forward at just that minute. His man-size nose and strong chin formed an arresting profile, she decided. She might have been too judgmental earlier when she had entertained the thought that Chairman Sanders resembled the outlaw on the wanted poster.

"It's an ore with a big aluminum content. After we mine the bauxite in open pits, we haul it to the plant at Elmwood where it's ground up and shipped by railroad to the big aluminum plant in Niagara Falls." He talked with authority.

"Then it's made into cookware?" Millie had used aluminum pots in the parsonage kitchen. She liked the way Woods made the complicated process sound simple. As a teacher, she knew that to do so was an art. Without his coat and tie and with his hat pushed to the back of his head, he looked far less formidable than when she had first seen him. She couldn't decide what there was about his blue eyes that fascinated her so. Maybe because they contrasted sharply with the black eyebrows and tanned face?

"It's used for other things, too, such as electrical conductors and small parts for machines." Were all schoolmarms as interested in everything as this one seemed to be? Somehow, he'd always figured that they were no fun to be around.

"I'd love to see a bauxite mine in operation someday. I've never been to a mine of any kind," Millie said after a brief time. "What job do you perform?"

"No particular one," he drawled, switching the reins from his right to his left hand.

Woods cut his eyes at his passenger, not surprised to find her studying his face. She seemed to think he had some answers written on it, judging from the many times he had caught her watching him with slightly narrowed eyes and a look of intensity. He shaved around his mustache every day, and trimmed it every Saturday night, so he knew that what his mirror showed was not what he thought of as a handsome face, that it was long and angular with that pesky cleft in the chin—so why did Millie keep sneaking looks at it?

· *Chapter Three* ·

Though it was an hour or so before dark, the sun was already behind the mountains by the time the wagon rolled into Freeman. Millie almost gasped her disappointment at its small size, but she didn't. Ever since her mother's death, her father had insisted that she keep her inner feelings secret.

Freeman, as both Woods and Uncle Fred had told Millie, sat at a crossroads. The couple traveling the sixteen miles from Elmwood since late in the morning came to Booth's Livery Stable first. While the wagon rumbled by out on the road, Woods nodded in a friendly way at a couple of men lounging in front of the rambling, tin-roofed livery stable with a large fenced area behind it. Millie took it all in, even a deserted mule-drawn hay rake off to the side with its wooden tongue half-hidden in dying weeds.

Woods nodded greetings at a family loading goods into a wagon in front of Steven's General Store down the road a few hundred yards. Surprised that the store was open on a Sunday, Millie felt their eyes assessing her covertly and wondered if they also held disapproval because the new teacher was a woman.

A big black dog bounded toward the wagon, barking and sizing up Millie with yellowish eyes before Woods called out, "Duke! You're being downright unfriendly. Get on back home." When two smaller dogs hurried to add their barks, he called them by name, too, and scolded them. All three trotted off.

Beyond the tree-covered lot directly across from the store, Millie saw a boxy white church with a squat bell tower over the front entrance. So that was where Uncle Fred came every first Sunday to hold services, she surmised.

Though the wide-eyed woman from Little Rock did not count, she guessed there must be a dozen homes spread out along the ridge road running right on through the hamlet. She wondered if there might not be more houses out of sight.

The bisecting road seemed to come from flat land behind the general store and the livery stable, then arch up between the two buildings to the ridge before crossing over and plunging down into a deep valley. Millie figured that the sharply disappearing road on her right led to the foothills in the near distance, then to the mountains farther away.

And that was Freeman, Millie concluded with a sigh. Two businesses, a church, and a dozen or so homes—plus a new, unpainted building sitting at the back of a lot on the other side of the church. Busy looking at the widely spaced houses with their separate garden plots, barns, and outhouses, Millie did not see the new building until the wagon veered off the rocky road. Two seesaws and three rope swings hanging from large oaks out front told her what the building was.

"How do you like our new school, Millie?" Woods wanted to look at her face to see what she thought, but he held back and gave his attention to stopping the team around at the back of the rectangular building. She had not allowed many of her thoughts to show through all day, now that he thought about it. Probably the schoolhouse looked pretty miserable to someone from the city. With pride he eyed the long building with its two metal stovepipes, cedar-shaked roof, and small belfry over the little front porch. One of the mules blew out a blubbery breath, its harness jangling for a moment. The wagon and its occupants sat still. He added quietly, "And your new home?"

"Home?" Millie echoed in disbelief. They had stopped near the back section, and her eyes darted to the door there before racing to question his. "I'm to live here at the school?"

"You didn't realize we had a teacherage on the back of the school?" he asked, meeting those brown challenges. What had she expected?

Teacherage? What a strange term. Millie tightened her lips to keep from blurting out her inane thoughts. Did mountain people keep chickens in a *chickerage?*

Not trusting herself to voice an answer to his question, Millie shook her head "no." Her hat wobbled, and she let it complete its fall, catching it in her lap and absently securing the pins in its crown. Unknown to her, her curls were clusters of warm red in the approaching twilight, and her eyes brown pools of disappointment. She turned away from Woods's intense scrutiny.

"Of course if the living quarters don't suit you, we can always call off the contract." In profile, without the hat and without the hairstyle affected by all the women Woods knew —a pouf of hair framing the face and fastened into a knot at the back of the head—the schoolteacher looked like a young girl. Woods's earlier thought that she might leave because she wasn't satisfied with the place had lost all of its appeal; though for the life of him, he couldn't figure out why. Millie Monroe was still not the one for the job he had had in mind from the beginning.

"Nonsense, Woods. It was a surprise, that's all. I'll manage nicely."

Millie was determined to make the best of her new situation. She looked around at the grove of trees behind and on the far side of the building, spotting the two privies marked BOYS and GIRLS sitting on opposite sides of the large grounds. The church sat on the adjoining lot but was much closer to the road. There was no house directly in front of the school, but she recalled there was one in front of the church and another a hundred or so yards down the way.

Even with others living nearby, Millie reflected, she had the sinking feeling of being surrounded by a wilderness, of being cut off from all that was familiar. Her pulse raced. Calling up the worn but apt aphorism, she conceded silently that when in Rome. . . . Aloud she said, "I suppose the first thing to do is get me moved into the . . . teacherage."

"Nope. The first thing to do is to get you out of the wagon in a better way," Woods replied with a laugh, admiring her obvious acceptance of the situation. He removed his hat and hung it on the hand brake before dropping to the ground.

"You've changed my name, Woods Sanders, and it appears that your school is going to make even greater changes," Millie quipped with false bravado when he came around to help her descend. "I hope all will be for the better."

Expecting Woods to offer his hand, Millie was surprised when he caught her at her waist and lifted her down from the wagon as though she didn't stand five feet eight inches tall and weigh one hundred sixteen pounds. For balance, she placed her hands on his shoulders. She felt his muscles ripple beneath the fabric of his shirt as he lowered her to stand facing him.

Whatever the heady scent was that emanated from Woods, it screamed masculinity and attacked secret parts of the inexperienced woman from Little Rock. The touch of his hands around her waist and his overpowering nearness sent unrecognized tinglings throughout Millie. Stunned at the debilitating attack on her senses, she let her hands fall like dead weights from his shoulders.

Millie hadn't realized she was short of breath until she murmured, "Thank you. Your way of stepping from a wagon is far better than mine."

Her eyes traveled no farther up than the cleft in his chin, but Millie could feel his gaze chasing all over her flushing face. Even after Woods dropped his hands and freed her, she felt that a magnetic field held them motionless. A mule stamped a foot against the ground, rattling its harness and breaking the spell. She stepped back, sending her hands behind her to examine her stiffening spine. She felt more than a little foolish from her dramatic reaction to what had been merely an act of courtesy. With an attempt to gloss the awkward silence, Millie said in what she hoped was a light tone, "I may never be the hopscotch queen again."

"Is your back giving you trouble, Millie?" When she moved away from him, Woods had turned to attack the trunk, but he now took a step back toward her. She had been as light as a girl when he lifted her down, and he had noticed how his hands had met around her tiny waist. That he had felt no confining corset or stays surprised him. His hands remembered the warmth of Millie's firm feminine flesh. And even after the day's tedious journey, she had smelled of jasmine. "That was a nasty fall you took when we stopped to eat."

"No, no. It was nothing. I'm just stiff from the ride. I'll be fine. I can even help you with those boxes of books." He had sounded as if he were truly concerned, she mused.

"That might be asking for trouble. You go on inside and light the lamp while I unload. It'll be dark soon." When Millie made no move, Woods asked, "Aren't you curious to see what it's like?"

Millie made her way to the door, opened it, and peered inside. Woods was right. "Millie" was the proper name for the person to live in the—her befuddled brain fumbled for the right word—teacherage. There was nothing elegant about it. The raw smell of new lumber, kerosene, and warm oilcloth tickled her nose. She saw two lamps sitting on a table near the stove over in a corner, but she didn't need to light one to examine her new home. The late afternoon light bathed the room with a soft glow—a nice touch, she decided, since the place needed all the help it could get.

Her face masking her inward trepidation, Millie examined the large room obviously built to serve as kitchen, dining room, and living room. An open door invited her to take a look into what must be the bedroom.

The sharp sound of the wooden heels of her button tops as Millie walked across the rough board floor seemed to echo, and she tried not to think of the worn but attractive carpets in the varied Methodist parsonages where she had grown up. When she stuck her face around the doorway, she saw a double bedstead of freshly painted, white iron spokes banded across their delicate tops with a sweetly curved arch of gleaming brass. A small, walnut chest of drawers, obviously having seen better days, sat beneath a window that gazed out on the large backyard and its bordering forest. Framed by two gathered feedsacks posing as curtains were the mountains on the horizon, barely visible in the purplish twilight. A loud noise behind her made her jump.

"What do you think?" asked Woods, his deep voice startling Millie that time almost as much as had the first loud sound, made when he set one of her boxes on the bare floor. When she made no reply, he went on, "Where do you want the trunk?"

"Here in the bedroom, across from the bed," Millie replied, fully aware that she had not answered his first question. She was certain that School Board Chairman Sanders did not want to know what his new teacher truly thought of her living quarters.

After Woods fetched her camelback trunk and placed it with a thunk and scrape where she indicated, Millie returned to the outer room. Being alone in the bedroom with a man made her fidgety. She didn't like the fact that this blatantly virile man sometimes made her feel intimidated.

"What do you think about the teacherage?" Woods asked again. *She has a way of concealing what goes on beneath that cropped hair,* he thought for the umpteenth time since meeting her that morning.

"I think it will serve quite well. All the essentials are here." Woods stood watching her with a puzzled look on his face. *Would he leave now? How far away did he live?* All at once Millie didn't care about being intimidated. "Could you show me how to operate the cookstove before you leave? It looks different from any I've used." She forced a smile, one that did little to light her face. It stopped short of reaching her eyes.

"Sure thing. Kerosene stoves can be tricky," Woods answered, wondering if Millie might be frightened about living in her new home in a strange place. He then discarded the idea as ridiculous. *Her very coming here under half-false pretenses showed that she was unafraid of anything.*

"What is this?" Millie indicated a wooden apple crate sit-

ting beside the black tin heater backed up to the wall dividing the classroom from the living quarters. She leaned over
to inspect its contents. "Has someone already done my
shopping for me?" On top sat several small baskets holding
eggs, potatoes, and onions. Curious, she removed them to
find containers of salt and pepper, a wedge of paper-
wrapped cheese, canned goods, a slab of bacon, a tin pail of
syrup, sacks of flour, sugar, and meal.

Coming to stand beside her, Woods replied, "The town-
folk said they'd probably drop off a few supplies for the new
teacher." When she gave him a quizzical brown look, he
added, "Just their way of saying 'welcome.' Freeman is
made up of a close little bunch of people. Not over forty in
all, counting dogs." His feeble attempt at humor failed. He
heard his chuckle lurch around the room all by itself before
it died.

"I'm overwhelmed," Millie managed. Only forty people?
Her father's congregations in and around Little Rock had
numbered far higher. She had figured there were dozens
more houses down the road passing in front of the school, or
down the crossroads. How could forty people—and their
dogs—call themselves a town? If she didn't need the job so
desperately—"Will they be sorry they've brought these
things when they learn the new teacher is a woman?"

"I don't imagine anyone except me gave the matter much
thought," Woods remarked absently, turning to the stove and
fiddling with the burners. "Anyway, what's done is done—
unless you want to tear up the contract and go back to Little
Rock."

Giving Woods her best schoolmarm stare and indignant
tone, Millie replied, "I wouldn't give you the satisfaction of
seeing me renege on a contract."

Woods grinned at her and returned to his maneuvering of
the burners. "I didn't much think you would."

Aware that Millie had come to stand behind him and
watch, Woods struck a match, adjusted the circular wick,
and soon had a steady, bluish flame. Out of the corner of his
eye he could see the rise and fall of her breasts as she leaned
to inspect the stove. Even over the biting scent of kerosene,
he caught a whiff of jasmine. "If you'll start unpacking and

get things ready for your first night here, I'll cook us something to eat."

"You can cook?" Millie's tone revealed her doubt. The cooking area was small, and his bulk dwarfed hers. She felt cornered. He had invited himself to stay for supper, and the notion pleased her, for some strange reason that she chose not to examine, but that he would prepare it. . . .

"Sure, I can cook," Woods answered with a low laugh, studying the face lifted to his. In the twilight her freckles had faded; her curls had deepened to a velvety auburn. The crazy wish to touch the silken ringlets made his fingers tingle. "I'll fetch some water from the well out back and get the coffeepot going while you put your bedroom in order."

Millie watched Woods remove a shiny dipper from its matching pail and loop its curved handle over a nail that he seemed familiar with. As if he might be at home, he lifted the water bucket from the counter and ambled outside, leaving her to stare after him in disbelief.

Upon arrival, Millie had seen the boxed water well beneath a neat shed out back. She had spent her earliest years in small towns and knew about wells and drawing water. Not until she heard the creak of the pulley letting the rope lower the bucket did her senses return. When had she ever felt so out of place?

Pulling herself together, Millie removed the fat chimneys from the two lamps sitting on the kitchen table. At least there was something in the place with which she felt comfortable, she mused while locating a box of matches nearby. Noting that the clear glass bases were filled with fuel, she adjusted the unburned wicks before striking a match against the roughened side of the box.

Millie breathed in the familiar, sharp odor of flaming sulfur and pine meeting an unused wick steeped in kerosene. The wicks seemed unusually white and virginal. *Virginal?* a part of her hooted. *Since when are wicks called virginal?* Millie mentally slapped down the wayward voice, going ahead to adjust first one orange flame and then the other to a level that produced no black smoke.

After returning the fragile chimneys to their niches, Millie took one lamp with her into the bedroom, not wanting

Woods to catch her still standing and gaping when he returned.

Millie's Methodist conscience—if she truly had one, which had often been a subject of debate between her father and her—nagged her about spending almost all day alone in the company of a man. An unmarried one at that. Never had she seen a man even pretend to be at home in a kitchen, and her curiosity at what Woods Sanders might concoct intrigued her.

While Millie found bedding in her trunk and made up the bed, she could hear Woods moving about in the next room. She was hanging up her few skirts and waists in the dressing alcove when a new sound joined the banging of cookware: He was whistling snatches of "The Arkansas Traveler" and tapping his foot along with the rhythm!

In the small mirror propped on top of the chest of drawers, Millie saw the reflection of a woman thoroughly confused. First, the man banging pans and stomping around in her kitchen had treated her like a criminal for being a woman; and now he was pampering her, she who had never received or expected more than a polite thank you from a man, even from her father for all the extra things she had done for him long before he became an invalid. Still unaccustomed to the shorn hair, she shook her head and fluffed at the short curls. She felt light all over.

"Supper's about ready," called Woods just as Millie put away the last item in the chest of drawers.

It was completely dark outside when Millie, after a trip to visit the outhouse and freshen up at the washstand near the well, came back into the large room where tempting smells wafted from the kitchen end. The lamplight spread out from the small table in a golden circle of invitation.

Woods set two heaped platters on the table before taking down cups and saucers from the overhead cabinet near the cookstove. "I hope you like bacon and eggs with pancakes."

"I love them," Millie confessed, sniffing appreciatively at the tantalizing smell of fresh-cooked bacon and gazing at the tall man with a flour sack dishcloth tucked into the top of his black breeches for an apron.

Millie did not add that she never had thought of this menu

for an evening meal—obviously called supper in Freeman. The events of the day had thrown her into a kind of shock. They had followed no logical pattern that she could determine. Up until she had met Woods earlier that day, her life had fallen into modulated steps, with a few highs and lows, but mostly lodged in between the two in a comfortable, unsurprising fashion. She wondered if an actress might not feel the way she felt when taking on a new role. It was downright scary.

When Woods moved to pull out her chair for her, Millie sat down and looked at the table. Everything was in order. Someone had furnished the teacherage—she was glad that she no longer stumbled over the word—with some odds and ends of silverware and dishes.

"I had no idea you're so talented, Woods," she said with a smile after serving herself and getting a fuller whiff of his mouth-watering offering. She saw that the bacon was crisp and brown, the way she preferred to eat it. A coziness permeated the small kitchen corner.

Woods raked the remaining food upon his own plate before looking at her. "I take all the compliments I can get," he drawled. She seems far more relaxed now, he thought, enjoying her smile, thinking again how it made her so damned beautiful. The way that she attacked the scrambled eggs and bacon told him more than her words how much she enjoyed his efforts. He never had liked to see a woman pick around at her food.

"It was lovely for the people of Freeman to stock the kitchen," Millie said after her hunger was so pleasantly appeased. She watched Woods sipping his coffee across from her. His blue eyes had twinkled roguishly when he earlier had moved the lamp to the side, mumbling something about wanting to enjoy the view. No ready comment came to her lips, but she mentally agreed that it was better to have nothing between them except the small tabletop while they shared supper. "And it seems the finest of welcomes for the board chairman to cook my first meal here. Freeman may be small, but I can tell it has nice people."

"Thanks," Woods replied, polishing off the last bit of

syrup-drenched pancake and wiping his mouth and mustache with his napkin.

Suddenly he had the urge to make Millie see the hamlet as he did, and he leaned toward her, his elbows resting upon the oilcloth and his hands clasped together loosely. "Freeman has the chance to become more than a wide place in the road if the right man can get elected to the House in next year's election. With the bauxite mines sprouting up around here, we're getting a few new people in the area with wages to spend. We'll have more clout in the legislature in a year or two." He watched her set her cup down and found himself admiring her tapering fingers and small wrists. Everything about Millie seemed so . . . so feminine.

Millie pursed her lips in recollection. "I remember having read about some re-districting being done since the preliminary results of last year's census. Are there many qualified men planning to run?"

"Two are talking about it, but neither is from close around here; and neither cares a hoot in hell—pardon my blunt language—about what the mining companies from the East are doing to our state. They're mainly concerned with needs in the heavier settled areas where they live."

Woods rose and poured more coffee for both before continuing. "Arkansas has some laws on the books requiring the mining companies to pay a severance tax based on tonnage, but so far no one has bothered to see that the law is carried out. We need a representative who'll stand up and holler for that law to be enforced, and then ask that part of the tax proceeds be returned to the area where the mines are located. And follow up on it."

The deep timbre of his voice fascinated Millie as much as the logic of his words. He was far more than a simple man from the hills. "You make it sound so sensible that I can't see why it hasn't already been done."

Millie sensed the same unleashed power in Woods that had invaded the parsonage that morning when he had entered and become so angry upon meeting her. The intensity of his eyes in the lamplight captivated her against her will, and she forced her gaze downward to his hands resting against the red-checked oilcloth covering the table. They were the lean, callused hands of a working man, as she had earlier noted. Without warning, Millie felt a curious urge to touch those capable-looking hands, to feel the texture of the dark hair covering his wrists and his arms before it disappeared into the turned-back cuffs of his white shirt.

Millie sensed that Woods was looking at her in a way that no man ever before had looked at her, but she couldn't fathom what made it different. Aware that the recent loss of her long hair had nothing to do with it, she felt dangerously light-headed.

While they drank their coffee in silence, Millie tried to view the man across from her objectively as a candidate for state office. Good—no, excellent carriage and general appearance. Intelligent eyes that seemed to see right inside a person. The deep, musical voice with undertones of hidden yet potent power. Its lusty volume would let it ring out in legislative debates and persuade others to follow his reasoning. She imagined his handshake would be firm, positive. And Woods Sanders had a vision to pursue that was supported by seemingly logical plans. A likely candidate. "Perhaps you're the perfect man to represent your district. Have you ever thought about running?"

Woods toyed with his coffee cup. "Not really. We need someone who can get things done, who can persuade the legislature to build a road between here and Elmwood that will be passable all year. Freeman missed out on the railroad, but if we had a topnotch road into Elmwood, we could get better use out of the one there. In the winter the teamsters have the devil of a time getting the ore to the rails." Her eyes seemed an even darker brown in the lamplight, and the interest he read therein spurred him on.

Forgetting that he was speaking with a woman, Woods continued. "I believe the future—the whole country's future —is tied up with the automobile and that all the little places like Freeman will die if they don't build roads good enough for the car to use year-round. I've seen one of the trucks coming on the market now, and I wouldn't be surprised if some day they don't take over the hauling, once decent roads get built. I guess you heard about the four autos that set the new speed record last year for travel between Pine Bluff and Little Rock. Forty-three miles in only four hours!"

The look on Millie's expressive face led him to add in a lighter vein, "I get all het up about this type of thing, don't I?" From where they rested on the table, he lifted his hands palm upward in mock self-defense and smiled. "I'll hush."

"You've sold me already, Woods, and I've never even thought about the issues before," Millie said, liking the way his resonant voice filled the room, liking the way he shared his ideas with her as though she were an equal. She also liked the way one heavy eyebrow angled upward in accent to his self-mockery. "I think you should declare your candidacy right away and run for representative next year." When Woods stared at her, blue eyes shadowing down deep with something akin to pain, she added with enthusiasm, "I do, Woods. I really do. Who else can present Freeman's problems so well as you?"

"I don't believe I'm the one to run," he replied. He drained his coffee cup, then said, "You're just being polite to say that."

Millie said, "I'm not being polite at all, merely stating a fact. You seem perfect for the job." Somehow, she hadn't expected such a great degree of modesty. Up until the past few moments, Woods Sanders had seemed almost too cocksure about everything. Was there something in his past that couldn't bear the public scrutiny a candidate has to endure? No, of course not. She was being absurd even to think such a thing. The man was what he seemed; she was sure of it.

Woods's face took on a closed look, and he slid his chair back, its legs making a jarring, scraping noise against the rough boards. "We'd better get started on these dishes. I put the kettle on before we sat down. It's getting late."

Again not believing her ears at Woods's offer to tackle "women's work," Millie joined him without argument in stacking the dishes, allowing him to find the dishpan and soap. When she insisted on washing, he didn't protest. He found a stack of clean flour sacks in one of the boxes and dried each item after she had doused it in the pan of hot rinse water. Neither seemed to find much talk necessary until the last skillet was washed and put away.

"Woods, I can never thank you enough for your helping me get settled in." Millie moved from the kitchen area over beside the sofa. An unaccustomed feeling of shyness overtook her . . . rather like the one she'd had when the two had stood in her bedroom earlier. What was there about being around Woods that seemed to make her overly aware that they were of the opposite sex? she wondered with exasperation. She told herself that she was overreacting because she was so far from all that was familiar. Being in a strange place was nibbling at her usual tranquility. "The supper was delicious."

"You probably could've done much better."

"As a matter of fact," Millie admitted with a resigned look on her face and a half laugh, "I was never Pulaski County's best cook and won't be tops in Lexington County either. I've cooked a lot, but I don't seem to have a knack."

"Maybe you didn't have a good teacher." Woods knew that he should be leaving and not keep standing there making small talk. Deep inside something reminded him that he should have left before dark, that there had been no real need to stay at all after he unloaded her belongings and showed her how to work the kerosene cookstove.

"Actually I had no teacher. My mother died from grippe when I was barely in my teens," Millie replied in a matter-of-fact tone. "Although I'd always helped her in the kitchen, I had never prepared a meal by myself. I had to jump in and learn on my own and try to take her place beside my father. A preacher needs a woman to help minister to a congregation, especially in a city. Going to school and coming home to take care of a parsonage didn't leave much time for experimenting." Woods's eyes were burning into hers as though what she was saying fascinated him. And all she was doing was babbling, Millie realized. He likely didn't give a fig about her girlhood.

"Will you be afraid to stay here alone?" Millie seemed terribly vulnerable to Woods, now that he had learned of her early years without her mother. Was that why she tried to appear so confident and all knowing—because she had tried to assume the role of a preacher's helpmeet when she should have been giggling with girls and flirting with boys? He noticed again that without her hat and the elaborate pompadour worn by most of the women he knew, Millie looked less like a grown woman and more like a schoolgirl, maybe the one she was telling about. He could almost envision thick red braids hanging down her back.

"Me, afraid?" Millie scoffed, pushing down her earlier feeling upon arrival of being out of her element. "Fiddlesticks! I've never been afraid to be alone. In fact, I like my company."

"Folks hereabout tend to mind their own business, so I don't figure anyone will try to bother you. Just in case, though, you should have in mind some way to protect yourself." Woods looked around the small room, his eyes lighting on the small hatchet beside the wood box near the heater. "Maybe you'd better keep the kindling hatchet near the door."

Touched at his concern, Millie laughed. Not even her father had appeared protective toward her, she mused. His attitude had suggested that since she was his daughter, she was therefore as capable as he. "Thanks for the advice, but I'll be fine. I've learned to be resourceful."

"I guess I'll be going on home then." Woods took a step toward the door before turning around to face her again.

"Where do you live, Woods?"

"Right behind the schoolhouse, as the crow flies. A hill or two gets in the way, though, and I have to go about six miles to get there. Widow Marks and her boy, Warden, live across the road from the church. If you need anything, they'll be there to help you. She lets out rooms and cooks extra for anybody stopping over, so she's used to people knocking on her door."

A compulsion to touch Woods overcame Millie, and she stuck out her hand to shake his. "Good night, and thank you again." Their hands met, and all kinds of havoc took over her entire body. She had been right about one thing—Woods Sanders did have a positive handshake. Her breath sputtered, and her heart hammered so loudly in her ears that she wondered if she would ever again hear anything but its persistent drumming.

Woods dropped his eyes to the small hand that his enveloped, expecting to see something out of the ordinary, something capable of producing such a dousing current of feeling inside. There was nothing extraordinary about the hand, except that it was dainty and perfectly formed, he thought with surprise as he pulled Millie toward him.

Woods lowered his head and pressed his lips to hers, sampling their honey with a reverence that surprised him and almost stole his breath. When Millie's soft mouth opened with tantalizing innocence, his tongue lightly traced the pattern of her full bottom lip. The earlier hints of jasmine became a warm fragrance teasing his nostrils and leading him to wonder if the scent came from her very pores. Deep inside, a rush of passion became infused with a feeling of awe at the way her warm breasts melded against his hard chest, and his arms tightened. He wanted to make the moment last.

Her heart beating wildly, Millie felt the silkiness of Woods's mustache against the sensitive skin above her top lip, savored the branding of her mouth by his, and almost gasped at the unexpected onslaught of his tongue spreading new fire on the inside of her bottom lip. She had been kissed before, but never like this. And never by a mountain man.

During their long engagement and infrequent times together, Luther Osgood had held Millie in his arms and planted moist kisses on her lips, but Luther's kisses had never sent slithering flames coursing through her veins or made her forget that she must maintain decorum at all costs. Thoughts of propriety held little rank in Millie's scrambled mind now. Along with her new name, the tall mountain man had gifted her with something else new: aroused passion.

Millie could feel the iron muscles in Woods's arms tighten as they pulled her closer, and the incongruous idea flashed to mind that their bodies fit together as perfectly as the halves of a severed, ripe peach. While her heart beat a rapid, deafening *ta-tum*, her untutored lips parted hungrily.

Why, Millie wondered with awe, had no one ever hinted to her that a man could taste and smell so marvelous . . . so uniquely masculine? Her arms searched upward and found a haven around his corded neck as his kiss deepened and called seductively to those rejoicing secret places that she had not known existed.

Frightened at her sudden sense of standing too close to the edge of a precipice—near to losing her tenuous balance and tumbling no telling where—Millie let her arms fall and stepped back from Woods's breathtaking embrace. Her racing pulse seemed to take on a slight humming sound. She couldn't decide if the worst thing to do would be to look at him and let him see the unsettling passions warring within, or to look away and let the moment die. The warmth and taste of his kiss lingered about her lips. Her heart still beat its alien rhythm.

"A better ending to this day than the beginning, wouldn't you say?" Woods asked in a husky tone even deeper than the one Millie had admired earlier. His heartbeat had been running a private race ever since he had taken Millie in his arms, and breath was hard to muster. When she continued to hide her eyes behind lowered lids, he noticed the pink moistness of her full lips and fought against tasting their sweetness again. Chiding himself that he had no right to take advantage of her as he had just done, Woods vowed not to do so again.

After all, Woods reminded himself, Millie was the new schoolteacher, and he was officially her employer. He knew that he had many shortcomings, but forcing himself on young women was not one of them. It was just that Millie Monroe was so damned beautiful, so desirable. "People will be coming by to meet you, and I'll drop by before school starts on Wednesday to see how you're settling in. Good night, Millie."

Through the open door, Millie called, "Good night, Woods," while she watched him walk away. Coming as it did over a sudden thickness in her throat and without sufficient breath, her voice did not sound at all like hers. She became aware for the first time of the chorus of unfamiliar sounds from the night callers out in the forest and felt a host of goose bumps tracing up her spine. Why? she wondered. The September night held only a trace of a chill.

Even after she could no longer hear Woods's wagon

bumping off into the darkness, Millie stood at the open door and stared into the night, unaware that an index finger traced the shape of her still-tingling lips. Her instincts had been right, she reflected. Millicent Monroe from Little Rock was, indeed, out of her element in the foothills of the Ouachita Mountains.

Part Two

Home to some may be but a place to others,
And therein lies a sadness.
Kind words may ease the schoolmarm's pain,
But how can she feel gladness
When she longs to see the mountain man again?

· *Chapter Four* ·

"Double damn!" Millie muttered as she sailed her cartwheel hat onto her bed. She was sick of fighting to pin it securely to her short hair. On her first morning in Freeman, the crowing of roosters had roused her at an ungodly hour and led her to wonder if each household might not have more than one of the noisy rascals.

Feeling more at peace with the world now that the sun was up and she had promised herself to accept her new situation with grace, Millie was on her way to the general store to make herself known. Woods had told her that Steven's General Store served also as the Freeman post office.

Millie wanted to appear presentable, despite her decision to leave off her hat. She smoothed at her navy skirt and fluffed up the muttoned sleeves of her blue flowered waist before stepping outside her apartment. No, she corrected herself, Woods had called her living quarters the teacherage. She must remember to defer to local speech and customs if she wanted to fit in—a lesson in which her father often had drilled her. And she must forget the disturbing kiss of last night from Board Chairman Woods Sanders.

After walking across the open yard in front of the schoolhouse, Millie eyed the neighboring church of freshly painted white boards. She could not resist the urge to see if the front door might be unlocked, as those in her father's charge had been for impromptu, private prayers. When the big brass knob turned in her hand and she went inside, she sniffed at the musty but clean smell of a building infrequently used. The feel of softness beneath her button tops surprised her, and she looked down at the wine-colored carpet in the vestibule.

With a hand holding open one of the double doors leading into the sanctuary, Millie saw the carpet stretching down the aisle between the straight-backed pews and covering the altar area. How lovely, she thought, noting the way the morning sunshine slanted through the small stained-glass windows and splayed pretty patterns of muted colors on the polished mahogany pews. What a shame that the Freeman congregation apparently could not afford a full-time minister and had to settle for services only on the first Sunday of each month. It was easy for Millie to imagine Uncle Fred behind the pulpit and Aunt Phoebe seated at the pump organ over to one side. The smell of aged books reached her nose, inviting her gaze to the stacks of hymnals sitting on a small table beside the organ.

On her way out of the vestibule, Millie noticed the empty vases atop the two tall wicker stands. Perhaps she could find some wildflowers to put there before first-Sunday preaching, she mused as she again recalled Aunt Phoebe's words.

Feeling comforted somehow, Millie continued on her way to the general store and let her thoughts run on. The large white house directly across from the church must belong to the Widow Marks, the woman whom Woods had told her to call on if she needed help.

Millie looked around cautiously for yesterday's welcoming committee of dogs as she walked on past four more houses, relieved when no animals rushed out at her. She glanced up and down the rocky road at the several widely spaced houses, noting the signs of children in some of the yards: a couple of red wagons, a tricycle, rope swings hanging from outstretched tree limbs. By then she was gaining a good view of the store up next to the crossroads.

The most handsome house, two-storied, painted a gleaming white and trimmed luxuriously with ornate gingerbread molding, sat back on the lot adjacent to the store and blinded Millie to details of all others. She surmised that it likely belonged to the owner of Freeman's single store.

Two artistically shaped oaks shading the sharply gabled store from the morning sun brought an admiring smile to Millie's face. A giant bucket of golden paint might have been splashed over the broad leaves, she thought, so mixed were the varying tones of gold and green. When Millie drew closer, she saw a well shed and a watering trough near the now empty hitching rails stretching underneath one of the huge trees.

"Pleased to meet you, ma'am," said Henry Stevens, the portly storeowner, when Millie went inside and introduced herself. He didn't completely hide his surprise when she told him who she was and what she was doing in Freeman, but he wasn't rude. "I'm a member of the school board, and we're right proud to begin our first school with a teacher fresh from our capital city."

"Miss, not ma'am," Millie corrected absently, still awed by the pleasant disorder of the large store and its unique mixture of smells. The distinct odors of tobacco, coffee beans, spices, yard goods, and leather harness were some she could identify, though all were well blended.

So Mr. Stevens had also been expecting a man, Millie mused while soaking up the comfortable atmosphere of Freeman's only store. At least Mr. Stevens had been kind enough to attempt to cover his surprise . . . and probable disappointment. Despite the apparent change in Woods's attitude before he left last night, she found it hard to forget entirely his initial reaction upon meeting her. She wondered if he was the only citizen to be so against having a woman teacher. And if so, why?

"Come over here and meet Miss Monroe, Annabelle," Henry called to the blond woman straightening bolts of material back in the store. He returned his attention to Millie. "Annabelle is my only living child, and I suspect she's going to be tickled right out of her button tops to find there's going to be another single woman in town," the soft-voiced storeowner confided to Millie. With a practiced hand, he shifted his pipe from one corner of his mouth to the other, taking a deep puff and letting the aromatic smoke drift out before adding, "I suspect she gets a mite lonesome at times, living with an old widower like me."

Millie liked Annabelle Stevens from the first moment that she looked into her wide blue eyes. Annabelle's smooth skin was the pale pink so perfect for her golden hair, Millie thought as she admired the way the stylish pompadour fluffed about the woman's pretty face before being caught up in a casual topknot at the crown. A lushness of figure made Millie aware of her own slight frame, and she wondered if someone wishing to be critical might not think that the smiling blonde was almost overweight. Annabelle's friendly smile and breathless way of speaking appealed to Millie, and the two found it easy to chat.

"All you have to do to get your mail is come to the window and ask for it," Annabelle explained with a wave of her hand toward the back of the store where Millie glimpsed a small barred window. "Handling the mail is my main job. How do you like Freeman so far? I saw Woods and you drive by late yesterday afternoon."

If one were to judge by the fine lines between the pale eyebrows and around the large eyes, Millie thought, then Annabelle Stevens was a few years older than she was.

"I'm sure that I'll find teaching here pleasant," Millie said to Annabelle after they had talked easily for several minutes. Ever since having heard Woods's enthusiastic talk about his home community, she had viewed the upcoming year in a totally new light. "I'm looking forward to meeting my pupils. I should have asked Woods yesterday how many I will have."

"Somewhere around twelve, from what I've heard Woods and Papa say when they're talking school business. Several too young to attend live here," Annabelle replied. "My nephews, the children of Lucas Milstead and Fern, my dead sister, will be attending. Papa and I are thrilled that they'll not have to go away to Hot Springs again this year for their schooling."

"Oh, yes," Millie said, recalling what Woods had told her when they drove past the Milstead farm. "Ransom and Steve. Woods told me about them."

"We're all indebted to Woods for tackling the old dream of having our very own school in Freeman. He has a way of accomplishing whatever he sets out to do."

I'll bet he does, Millie reflected.

When Millie made no comment, Annabelle leaned across the counter and smiled like a conspirator before asking in a low voice, "Is that the latest hairstyle in the city? On you it looks wonderful." Her admiring eyes assessed the short red curls.

"Thank you for the compliment," Millie replied. Pretending interest in brushing lint from her skirt, she said briskly, "A dedicated teacher has far more important things to do than waste time on her hair. I grew tired of having to bother with putting it up each day so I just whacked it off."

"Bully for you, Millie," Annabelle exclaimed with a laugh of open admiration. "I wish I had your courage." Then she said, "I hope you don't mind that I called you Millie— and I hope you'll call me Annabelle. I'm looking forward to having another single woman around as a friend. I've got a feeling we have a lot in common."

Not until she was reassuring Annabelle that first names would be pleasant and that they likely did have common interests did Millie notice the sadness in the pretty woman's intelligent blue eyes. She pulled out her shopping list then and let Annabelle show her around the well-stocked store as she filled the small order.

Henry Stevens busied himself with sweeping up near the front until a plump, dark-haired woman bustled in.

"Wouldn't you know I got sidetracked this morning and let my new neighbor get off before I could meet her?" the woman said in a loud, friendly voice, moving on back to where Millie and Annabelle stood, but not before having shot a gap-toothed smile at Henry and said something to him in a low tone. "Pleased to meet up with you, I'm sure. I'm Mabel Marks."

After Millie gave her name and politely murmured her own pleasure, Mabel went on, "Most folks call me Widow Marks. I live 'cross from you in the house with the 'Room and Board' sign in the front window. Did you see it when you left the church?"

Millie nodded, and Mabel took the floor again. "Since my husband passed through the pearly gates five years ago, it's just been my boy, Warden, and me in that big place, so I rent out the extra rooms. Warden's eighteen and already big as a full-growed man. He's always took to learnin' a sight better'n I ever did. My brother was like that, too, God rest his soul. There warn't enough money to send Warden to Elmwood to study last year, and he's already hankerin' to be back in school. He says he's gonna be a vet, and he reads every minute he can."

"How nice," Millie replied when the woman paused for breath and rewarded her with her open, gap-toothed smile.

"Warden's a handfull, but smart as a whip," Widow Marks said, fluffing at her gray-streaked pompadour and narrowing her black eyes at Millie's cap of red curls. "Can't say as I ever seen a woman with short hair before. Did you have a sickness? I knew a woman once who had typhoid fever and lost all her hair, but she ordered herself a wig out of the Sears and Roebuck catalog 'til it grew back to a decent length. She never let nobody see her without that there wig, not even her husband—or so I heard tell."

When both Millie and Annabelle remained silent but exchanged amused glances, Widow Marks went on with a good-natured laugh. "'Course I can't say as how not havin' all of your hair hurts your looks all that much, Miss Monroe. My mama—God rest her soul—allers said beauty is more than skin deep." The buxom widow preened a little and sent a secretive look toward Henry Stevens, who seemed engrossed in cleaning the glass of the candy counter sitting near the front door. "It's the inner soul that counts."

Millie nodded and, recalling Woods's remark that people from his community didn't stand on ceremony, asked the Widow Marks to call her by her first name.

"Millie was telling me earlier how much she appreciates all the nice things she found in the teacherage," Annabelle said, putting the last article from Millie's list in a large basket and sliding it across the counter.

"I figured when Woods didn't leave last night until after dark that he must've stayed to help get the new schoolmarm settled in," the older woman replied with a pursing of her mouth and a knowing look. Returning her attention to the newcomer and glancing down at the gold band on her own plump finger, she made it plain that she knew Millie wore no ring at all. "He's some fine man, our Woods. Don't you agree, Millie?" Mabel Marks cocked her head to one side and rested a hand on her generous hip, slanting little looks at

Annabelle as she waited for an answer from Millie. She obviously expected agreement.

A bit annoyed that the woman plainly wanted everyone to know that she knew exactly when Woods had left the teacherage last night, Millie agreed and made all the right answers. What was that bit about "our" Woods—had Mabel been including Annabelle in some private way?

After polite farewells to the two women and another to the storeowner still working at the candy counter, Millie departed with her purchases and the certain knowledge that before the Widow Marks left the store that morning, she would try to learn every word falling from the new teacher's lips. Every one of her father's congregations with which Millie had been acquainted had contained at least one kindhearted but big-mouthed woman like Widow Marks. Millie let out a sigh of resignation.

From underneath the shading oaks in front of the store, Millie looked beyond the crossroads at the only other place of business, Booth's Livery Stable. The two-wheeled hay rake still rested on its long wooden tongue out front, as if forgotten. She could see several horses and mules grazing in a sloping pasture behind the fenced lot.

The ringing sounds of iron repeatedly striking iron snapped Millie's attention to a blacksmith at work underneath the open shed attached to the side of the tall barnlike structure. She wondered if it would be improper for her to wave at the man if he looked her way. He never did glance up from his noisy hammering, though, and she turned down the road toward the schoolhouse.

A carrot-topped boy and girl playing with a wagon and a fluffy cat in one of the yards that she passed on her way back to the schoolhouse shyly returned Millie's wave, but not until after a brief, private consultation. A white dog with black spots dashed out from beneath a porch and barked. Millie tried to give a friendly whistle, aggravated that she failed as miserably as when she had tried repeatedly while a youngster. For some reason the dog wagged its tail, then trotted back to its resting place. As the child of a minister living in church-owned parsonages, Millie had never been allowed to have pets. She was ill at ease around animals, almost fearful.

A house with soaring gables calling for no special notice during Millie's stroll to the store earlier drew her attention on her way back to the schoolhouse. She could not have explained why, unless it was because it was the only house with a picket fence hemming it and a tree-filled yard from its neighbors. When she drew closer, she saw that it had a window shaped like a keyhole.

Millie noticed that both the fence and the house had once been painted white, but that now they bore a ghostly look of neglect. If the house had neat little plots of now dying flowers around its front porch or entry as all of the others did, the fence hugging close to the house hid them. All that Millie could see were the tops of bushy shrubs growing up several feet and almost hiding the front porch that curved out on one side of the front door.

Above the porch sat the window shaped like a keyhole, the small, oddly placed kind of window that often served to light a staircase, Millie realized. It wasn't a true two-story home, she reflected, but it had windows jutting out up high from what must be at least two rooms on a second floor.

A slight movement at one of the windows beneath the tall roof made Millie wonder if she might not be the subject of someone's secretive scrutiny. Was that what had drawn her attention to the deserted-looking house—that eerie feeling of being watched? Fighting down a little spate of goose bumps, she switched the basket of goods to her other hand and forced herself to look away from what she now thought of as the Keyhole House. She had a penchant for hanging private tags on objects and people.

The sight of the new schoolhouse set back in its grove of trees with the distant mountains and closer foothills as colorful backdrop seemed far more comforting to Millie than when she had first seen it. Up closer then, she wondered how the shiny black bell, suspended in its simple frame atop the roof of the front porch, might sound when set into motion by the rope reaching down to coil about a set of wooden pegs. When she thought about how much she had to get done before school began the day after tomorrow, her steps quickened.

Poring over the textbooks she had brought, as well as those already stacked in the classroom, Millie worked all afternoon to set up a general plan of study for her pupils, no matter what their ages. The sun was already behind the mountains before she realized that she was without enough light to continue. She looked at the new desks still sitting haphazardly in the back of the room, trying to visualize the pupils who would be filling them.

Teaching had always given her deep pleasure, Millie mused with typical honesty. She would make a place for herself in Freeman, she promised herself as she left the classroom. She would make everyone glad she had been the one to come—even Woods Sanders. And, if she had any luck at all, even herself.

Millie threw together a light meal and went to bed early, too tired to feel more than a little annoyed that a partial bath was all she could manage with the small foot tub provided. Not that she wished to fill a larger tub, she conceded when she realized that her hands and arms were tired from the unaccustomed drawing of water and lugging it inside. Her mind kept jumping from one topic to another as she lay chasing sleep.

Too often Woods intruded into Millie's thoughts, and just as often she cast him aside. Hadn't she already learned that she knew nothing about judging men accurately? And hadn't she vowed never to place her trust in another?

From the time Millie was eighteen, Luther Osgood, a young member of her father's congregation in Little Rock, had claimed her limited spare time and attention. His imposing presence had sent any other possible suitors to seek out other young women; thus Millie, overburdened as she was with the duties imposed by her father, never came to know any of the other young eligible men.

When Luther had proposed to Millie and asked to take her with him to Tennessee where he was earning his college degree, her father had refused his permission, telling the young couple that they must wait until Luther completed his planned studies in law school. The idea of going against the minister's wishes never occurred either to Millie or Luther. A college student herself at the time, Millie had believed, along with her father, that she had achieved what all young women needed and wanted—a young professional man who confessed his love for her and his desire to make her his wife.

Studying for her teacher's license and performing house-keeping chores in the parsonage kept Millie busy those first years of Luther's absence. Once she began teaching, she hardly noticed that Luther's letters from Vanderbilt were becoming briefer and farther apart. His visits home, he always assured her when he did come, were becoming fewer only because of the demands of his job and his studies in his final years of law school. His arrival after graduation with a bride was a cruel blow to the young woman who had waited for and believed in him.

She had survived, Millie conceded without rancor while lying in her new bed. There had been moments of brutal honesty in which she admitted that Luther might not truly have been her ideal man. Actually, Millie confessed right before she conquered sleep, she doubted there was such a person alive; besides, she had accepted her life as an unmarried schoolmarm. She promptly dreamed about a blue-eyed man with a cleft in his chin.

Still wearing her nightgown and her green silk wrapper, the elegant garment with a wide ruffle edging its neckline, overlapping front, and sleeves being one of the few luxuries in which she had indulged herself, Millie sat sleepily dawdling over a cup of under-brewed coffee the next morning when she heard hoofbeats outside. She usually rose at dawn when teaching, but despite the heralds from Freeman's roosters, she had pampered herself on this last free day.

A rap on the door of the teacherage intruded. Irritated that she had not been left alone to awaken at her leisure, Millie tightened the belt to her long wrapper and half stumbled to the door. She opened it only a few inches, for there was no screen door offering partial security.

"Good morning," said Woods, wearing a doubting smile

on his lean face as he removed his hat. "I hope I didn't wake you."

"Nobody can wake me before I'm ready," Millie replied, her hands flying to the neck of her wrapper to make sure no cleavage showed and freeing the door to swing open. The night's dream flashed to mind, causing her to view the blue-eyed caller with suspicion. "What do you want at this ungodly hour?"

"A smile would help." When she continued to glare at him, he added, "A cup of coffee would cure. May I come in?"

From the minute Millie opened the door, Woods had been struck with how pretty she looked in the green wrapper in spite of her attempt to look cross. She seemed unaware that her skin glowed in the morning light and that her brown eyes had a fresh-washed look. He had a sudden urge to kiss away the little girl pout on her pink lips and let his fingers ruffle even further those tumbled red curls.

"What are you doing here?" And what are you gawking at? Millie almost added. She wasn't at her best early in the mornings, and she made no pretense of being otherwise— one of the few idiosyncrasies in which she knowingly allowed herself to indulge. She had often joked that if there were a course offered through the Chautauqua Series called "How to Wake Up Instantly Alert," she would fail it. She couldn't work up enthusiasm for any caller before she had gotten ready for the day. Maybe if Woods had waited until she downed her second cup of coffee. . . .

"I came to make sure all is ready for school to begin tomorrow."

So he had come in his official capacity to make sure she had everything ready for tomorrow, Millie thought with her characteristic, early morning shortness. Double damn! As though she hadn't already taught for four years.

"Suit yourself," Millie huffed. She stood aside for him to enter. "You own the place." A spicy masculine fragrance came right in with him. Bay rum, but with something added, her sensitive nose told her. It dawned on her that she wore nothing beneath the wrapper except a thin nightgown, and a little ripple crawled up her spine in an insidious way.

"I gather you aren't at your best in the mornings," Woods said cheerfully, ignoring the unfriendly look she was sending him. He ambled over to the cookstove as though he belonged in the teacherage. "I have a sister like that. Maybe you'll feel better after you get dressed." He was pulling out a cup from the overhead cabinet and pouring himself coffee before Millie's morning brain could think up a reply. "Don't worry about me. I'll just make myself at home." With that announcement, Woods pulled out a chair and sat down with his back to her, apparently intent on drinking his coffee and gazing out the small window in the kitchen area.

At a loss for words, Millie spun around and dashed into her bedroom, closing the door against her unwelcome caller. Who was Woods Sanders to make himself "at home" in her place? she wondered with annoyance, aware that she was waking up fast. He had done exactly the same thing Sunday night. Did he think that because he and his board had hired her he could intrude upon her whenever he chose? she argued silently as she flung off wrapper and gown and donned a pair of her shortened drawers, then a full petticoat.

Or was it because she had kissed him back on the night before last? While Millie tucked her blouse inside her skirt with haste, the mental war went on. She would tell the imposing man that he needn't expect to drop in on her anytime it suited him, that even if she did work for his school board, he had no right to invade her privacy and—

No, Millie decided as she tied the laces of her everyday high-top shoes, she wouldn't mention the kiss. Anyway, she had almost forgotten about it, as she was sure he had. What was a single kiss to a man as cocksure of himself as Woods Sanders? Her hairbrush moved through her curls like a weapon while she mentally rehearsed the speech she would make.

"I enjoyed the coffee, Millie," Woods said when she marched from her bedroom with a look on her face as fiery as her hair. What would she do if he told her that the hem of her dark skirt was creased up on one side and revealing her ruffled white petticoat? Having grown up in a house with five sisters, he voted not to find out. "I lit the burner and let it perk a little longer. Want another cup now?"

Woods rose and stood looking down at Millie with an expression that baffled her and made her forget her intentions to give him a piece of her mind. Was it only the cleft in his chin that made him look so different from any other man she had ever seen? she wondered.

"I owe you an apology for barging in on you like this," Woods was saying when Millie focused on his words. "Sometimes we mountain folks forget our manners."

Wondering if Woods Sanders would remain an enigma to her, Millie found enough breath to say, "I'm not at my best so early in the morning." When she could breathe more normally, honesty made her add, "And I really did oversleep this morning. I'm usually up at the crack of dawn just so I can go through the motions of waking up at my leisure." The crazy thought ran through her mind that she might not have brushed her hair, so intently was he staring at it.

Millie sank upon one of the straight chairs and lifted the cup of coffee that Woods had poured for her. Gingerly she sipped the fragrant brew while he cocked his head and watched from where he sat across the table.

"There," he said after a silence falling as naturally as the sunshine streaming through the window. "Isn't that better?"

Not wanting to admit that the extra perking was needed, Millie made no reference to the improved taste. "Yes, I always feel better after a second cup of coffee." She may have forgotten all about the speech she had rehearsed, but not Sunday night's kiss. The way Woods's eyes—even bluer than she had recalled—kept lingering on her mouth made that impossible.

When Millie agreed after awhile that she was ready for the day, they went outside and entered the side door of the classroom. Once there in the large rectangular room, both went to work dusting and arranging the desks and stacking books onto shelves. He surprised her by letting her be in charge.

"I met Annabelle Stevens and her father yesterday at the store. And the Widow Marks also," Millie said after they had paused and were admiring the neat lines of desks. She noted how their polished oak surfaces contrasted against the new, unpainted plank floor and walls. Some were smaller than others, but all had room for two pupils to sit side by side. Their slanted writing tops had individual pencil and pen indentations at the top, plus little circular cutouts for ink pots. "Annabelle told me there might be twelve pupils."

"What did you think of Annabelle?" His face wore little expression, but his steady gaze revealed a decided interest in her answer.

"I liked her very much. She's one of the nicest, prettiest women I've ever met." Millie almost bit her tongue to keep from adding that Annabelle also had the saddest eyes. She wondered at the way the morning sunshine slanting through the windows seemed trapped within the blue depths of Woods's eyes and lent extra sparkle to them. Why was he sweeping her with those measuring looks? Her tongue wet her suddenly dry lips.

"Is there anything else I can help you with here in the classroom?" Woods asked. He tore his gaze from the tempting glimpse of Millie's little pink tongue outlining her lips and glanced around the room with obvious pleasure.

Woods no longer seemed interested in her opinion of Annabelle, Millie thought. And he had not even asked what she thought of the others she had met, Mabel Marks and Henry Stevens.

"No, I don't need help with anything else, thank you. I appreciate all you've done." She hated thinking that now he would be leaving.

It was then that Millie became aware of a kind of inner humming, a barely discernible rhythm that seemed in harmony with her heartbeat. When had it begun? Having heard Woods's occasional, deep-voiced comments and his boots clomping against the board floor all during the morning as he arranged desks and helped with the dusting in his unhurried way had made her feel that she was not the only one who was excited over the new school year.

Already Millie had noticed that Woods's blue denim shirt complemented his fascinating eyes and suntanned skin— and that his black chest curls showed in the vee of the unbuttoned section below the collar. Darker blue denim breeches replaced the elegant ones that were part of the black suit he had worn that first day. Millie had seen more than once how his breeches clung like a second skin to his lean hips and muscular thighs. Looking up at the tall man, she sensed, as she had upon first seeing him back in Uncle Fred's living room, that his lean, muscled body contained a powerful strength that he carefully controlled.

"We could take some bread and cheese and eat down by the Gooseneck River, if you'd like," Woods said, breaking the long silence.

"Where's the Gooseneck River?" His suggestion surprised Millie. Would leaving with him cause a scandal? But the thought of eating alone in her kitchen had no real appeal; and, after all, she reasoned, he should be just as concerned that the woman he had hired be of good reputation as she. She was being silly, letting that single kiss affect her thoughts. Outside of a few sidewise glances when he apparently believed she wasn't looking, Woods had not paid her any particular attention as they worked. Probably he kissed women all the time.

"The river's about a half mile down the road," Woods replied, already leaning to open the door. "It's the only running water in town." When Millie looked at him questioningly, he explained, "On pretty days, the women go there to do their laundry. They say it beats drawing water for their washtubs." At her understanding nod, he asked, "Why don't you bring yours along and get it done while we're there? It'll soon be too cold to wash in the river. You might as well learn how to live in Freeman, now that you're here. That's part of my job as chairman of the board, to get you settled in."

Millie hesitated. Was his suggestion as innocent as it sounded? Everything seemed different in Freeman.

When Woods invited her to go with him again, Millie replied, "If you think it's proper. After all, you have to answer for the schoolmarm and her actions."

"Good. I'll unsaddle Major and tether him out back."

"I'll join you outside after I gather up some food . . . and my laundry." She could hardly believe her own words. Who was this creature called Millie?

· *Chapter Five* ·

With their lunch in Aunt Phoebe's basket and her little pile of laundry in a pillowcase, Millie followed Woods as he led the way through the trees behind the schoolhouse, showing her the shady shortcut he knew.

An autumn breeze wafted the heady fragrances from the little clump of forest to their noses and serenaded them with a plaintive little melody from its play among the drying leaves. Soon they came upon a faint trail. Woods waited for Millie to catch up and walk beside him, taking the pillowcase from her when she did, despite her protests.

"Is that the river I hear?" Millie asked, tilting her head toward the gurgling sound joining the crackling of leaves underfoot. The path had become rockier and was making a fast descent. Sunlight pierced the deep, fragrant shade in those places where the trees had already shed numerous leaves. Those still hanging had that papery, translucent look she had often noticed came just before they took on their fall colors.

Woods merely grinned and took her arm. Before she had time to wonder at the tinglings from his touch, they rounded a bend and found the river at their feet.

"It's beautiful," Millie exclaimed, round-eyed with wonder. She loved the musical sounds that the clear water was making as it rushed along its rocky bed. About as wide as a road, the Gooseneck was shallow enough for her to see the rock-lined bottom, except in a few quiet pools of green hollowed out from the banks in its many curves. "I think I would have found a prettier name for it than the Gooseneck River." She looked up at Woods and smiled.

"Would that have made it any prettier?" The thought that

nothing could make Millie any prettier than she was at this moment, her smile lighting her face and eyes in that way he found fascinating, kept rattling around inside Woods's mind.

A breeze riffled Millie's curls then, turning them to dancing swirls of copper in the noon sunshine. Seeing her lifting her face to the sun, Woods knew why freckles sprinkled her pert nose and smooth cheeks. Most young women he knew would have worn a sunbonnet on such an outing, but was he not already learning that the new schoolmarm was unlike any other woman he had ever met?

Millie turned back to face Woods, her eyes serious. She seemed to be weighing him, and he wondered what her opinion was. What was it about her that fascinated him so, other than her beauty? he asked himself. Was it her sassiness, her unique air of independence? He shied away from what threatened to be serious contemplation.

"No, Woods," Millie replied thoughtfully after the lengthy silence, "a more apt name might not have made the river prettier. It's just that I like pretty words." Now he would think she was being schoolmarmish, she fretted. Her face heating up, she turned from his intense look and sat down on a large flat rock near the edge of the clean-smelling water. She reached into the basket and shared the cheese, crackers, and apples that the friendly people in Freeman had left in the teacherage.

They munched in companionable silence, each seemingly enjoying watching and listening to the racing water. Neither thought about how unusual it was that they had known each other such a short time but were eating their third meal together. When Woods finished his apple, he tossed the ragged core downstream, then picked up a small flat stone and skipped it across the surface of a nearby pool of green. Laughing at his dare to give it a try, Millie strove to imitate him, but her stone sank to the bottom with a gurgling plop.

"You're a regular smart aleck, Woods Sanders." He had just repeated his earlier performance and turned to Millie with the eager look of a little boy wanting an adult's approval for a trick performed well. How could she not reward him with a smile? She was glad that he hadn't worn his hat. The sun kicked up highlights in the glossy black hair, and

she was tempted to ask him if he had Indian blood. The cleft
drew her attention then, and she found herself wanting to ask
all about it. What she asked was, "Will you teach me how to
make a stone skip across the water?"

After showing Millie how to select a flat, round stone
from the wealth of rocks on the riverbank, Woods took her
hand. Both seemed intensely interested in studying the way
his engulfed hers. Clearing his throat and getting on with the
teaching, Woods fitted the stone between her thumb and
fingers just so before telling her in a soft growl, "Turn your
body sideways. Aim at the water's surface, and fling the
stone with its flat side down."

Millie was eager to forget the way Woods's touch and
nearness affected her. She did as he said. Success came, and
with the exuberance of a child, she gathered a score of flat
stones to throw, laughing at each achievement, frowning
prettily at the failures. She basked in Woods's teasing praise,
unable to remember when she had felt so young and carefree. Being Millie seemed a lot more fun than being Millicent, she reflected.

"Are you going to ignore your laundry?" Woods asked
after both seemed to tire of the sport. As though it were his
own, he turned the pillowcase upside down, dumped the
clothing and the bar of soap on the rocky bank.

"What do you think you're doing?" Millie shot back, not
liking that a man was seeing her clothing. Some of it was
her unmentionables! "I'll wash my own things, thank you!"
She felt a blush sweep up her neck. Woods might have
grown up with five sisters and live now only with his mother
and aunt, but she had no intentions of having a man see her
intimate undergarments. She had figured that he would leave
her to do her laundry alone when the time came, maybe take
a stroll.

"Have you ever washed anything in a stream before?"
Amusement underlined his words. Millie had not been that
flustered when she had fallen from the wagon—but, Woods
reflected, she had never realized all that she exposed then. A
tiny grin threw the black handlebar mustache off center.

"What could be so difficult about it?" Millie retorted. He

has that sanctimonious look some men get when they think they are dealing with a stupid woman, she thought.

Millie was about to utter an apology for her curt reply when a sudden vision of the temper fit that Woods had thrown upon first meeting her shot to mind and quelled her words. So they both had short fuses, she thought, but with brief flares quickly subdued.

Refusing to look at him, she knelt beside him and took the bar of soap and lathered her dishcloths. He was so close that the spicy, masculine smell of him reached her nostrils along with the less appealing scent of the naptha soap. In spite of her wishing it to not be so, the memory of the way Woods's lips had felt and tasted during their kiss surfaced and taunted her without mercy.

Still not looking at Woods, and wishing he would go sit somewhere else while she worked, Millie laid the soap on a big rock nearby and turned to rinse the dishcloths. One had floated out in midstream and, to her consternation, seemed hell-bent on riding down the river.

Millie muttered a "Double damn!" underneath her breath and started out to get it; but Woods, with an I-told-you-so look, put a restraining hand on her shoulder and hurried into the shallow water, heedless of boots and denims. He splashed back with the wayward dishcloth and rinsed it for her, wringing it into a neat little wad before depositing it inside the pillowcase.

As though she had planned to follow that method all along, an indignant Millie did the same with the others. She would have to be on the lookout, she reminded herself, or Woods Sanders would take over every aspect of her life. An annoying inner voice whispered, "Would that be so bad?"

Removing his boots and pouring out the water, Woods propped against a distant rock in the warm sun and, his eyes half-closed against the glare, chewed at a long blade of grass while Millie finished the remainder of her laundry.

Now that she had the hang of washing in the river, Millie made sure that no other item escaped with the swift current. Sometimes she thought she could feel Woods's gaze wandering over her body, but each time she tried to catch him at it, she failed.

"Now aren't you glad I told you about washing clothes in the river?" Woods drawled when Millie wrung out the last garment and stashed it in the now dripping pillowcase. Propped indolently upon one elbow, a blade of grass still caught between his teeth, he smiled across the rocks at the sight before him.

From where she had knelt beside the stream, Millie's skirt was wet from her knees down. She had rolled up the long sleeves of her waist before beginning her little chore, and her arms were now red from the cold water. When she began pulling down her sleeves, Woods sat up and yanked on his boots, almost dry now from their stint in the sunshine. He stood then and stretched his long, lithe body indolently, his eyes fixed on the pretty red-haired woman.

"I have to admit that doing my laundry here was more of a challenge than it would have been back at the teacherage, but it was more fun, too," Millie confessed, wondering what in the world was causing Woods to stare at her so. What other woman with apparently good sense would have thought of spending an afternoon doing her laundry beside a river with a man as handsome as Woods Sanders? she mused with an added sparkle in her eyes. Was the breeze from the river getting chillier? Something was bringing goose bumps.

"Let me carry that pillowcase back for you," Woods offered, stooping to take the wet laundry before she could reply. "Unless you want to stay and take a bath before we leave."

"A bath? Here?" Millie looked at the green pools so easily seen. Some were only a whit larger than the bathtubs she had used during her years in Little Rock. Her face flamed at the thought of bathing in the open, and again at the racier thought of Woods doing the same. Oh, my! Where had her old sensible self gone? If she hadn't known better, she would have suspected that she might have left it back in that trash can in Little Rock along with her long hair. "You like to tease, don't you?"

"So I've often been told," Woods admitted with a careless shrug and a sheepish grin. "But people really do bathe in the streams around here. We don't have many bathtubs—as you've probably already noticed." The blush on her face made him think of the pink winter roses that always bloomed next to the front porch of his home when all other flowers had died from the cold.

"We don't need to discuss such things," Millie managed to say. She fought down her earlier mental pictures of them without clothing. Whatever had gotten into her? Being around Woods Sanders was leading her to wonder if she knew herself at all.

"Why not discuss them? I'll bet you miss having 'such things' as a bathtub, coming from the city and all." His voice was matter-of-fact. They had turned toward the path leading through the woods to the schoolhouse.

What Woods had said made sense, Millie realized. Why was she acting so prudish? As he had pointed out, he was only doing his job to acquaint her with her new surroundings. With so few people living close together, no doubt social rules in Freeman and the surrounding community were less rigid than those in larger towns and cities.

Millie's thoughts moved on as they walked. Hadn't she herself often chafed at society's demand that men and women avoid each other's private company unless they were kin, married, or courting—or engaged in a questionable relationship? More than one male teacher at the girls' school in Little Rock had appealed to Millie as worthy of getting to know as a friend, but propriety had forbidden the chance to follow through.

When Millie viewed Woods as board chairman, almost a member of her profession, the matter of their relationship appeared less threatening. As she had no intentions for a repetition of that first night's searing kiss, she discarded the shameful possibility of a situation bordering on that of a questionable relationship. Now that she had buried her former longing to marry and have a family and had realized how much she enjoyed her life as an unmarried teacher, she could see no reason why Woods and she could not become friends.

"Woods," Millie said, "I confess that I do miss having a tub, and I'm thinking of asking Mr. Stevens to order me one." There. Now they could drop the ticklish subject.

She was not used to being around men much, and none at

all who said whatever came to mind around women, Millie
reflected. Maybe Woods's having grown up in a house full
of females had led him to view women in a different light
from the way most men did, though his reaction upon first
meeting her cast doubt on her optimistic conclusion. Likely
Woods never even thought about the image of her naked in
her bath when he talked of such things as her not having a
bathtub. She was being ridiculous to let the thought of either
one of them bathing in the river get her all flustered.

"You're likely the most unique man I've ever met,
Woods." The birds overhead twittered as Millie and Woods
strolled into the afternoon shade in the woods and left the
singing river behind.

"How's that?"

Millie kicked at a little pile of dead leaves and searched
for words. "You seem so . . . so relaxed."

"And why shouldn't I be?"

Woods's deep voice seemed intimate there in the forest,
Millie thought. Not loud at all. Maybe it was because he
belonged in such a setting. She could tell that he was studying her face, and she felt giddy, but she couldn't figure out
why. The westward sun did not penetrate into the closely
spaced trees, and the air had become more seasonal, so she
couldn't blame her light-headedness on the sun as she had
done earlier upon their arrival at the Gooseneck River.

"Almost all of the men that I've met just aren't easy with
themselves, that's all," Millie replied after giving his question some thought. Woods truly was the easiest man to talk
with that she had ever met, she reflected. She ran her fingers
through her curls and purposely slowed her stride to match
his. Her father had always complained that she didn't know
how to do anything at a moderate pace, even walk.

"Are you saying I'm not like most men?" His tone showed
a touch of displeasure.

"Yes, but I'm saying it in a complimentary way." Millie
looked up into his face then, wanting to make sure that
Woods understood that she had not meant to be critical. In
the deep shade, his eyes were veiled, though, and she gained
no hint of what he was thinking. Their footsteps were not
matched, even though she had slowed down. When she

thought about how much longer his legs were than hers, she realized why. "I believe that most men don't know how to enjoy the simple pleasures of life as you seem to . . . and that they're worse off for not knowing your secret."

Her words must not have sat well, Millie agonized, because Woods's gaze left her face, and he seemed more interested now in the path ahead than in his companion. Why had she blurted out what she was thinking? Her father often had warned her that no man likes to hear what a woman truly thinks.

"I'm sure I have no secrets anyone you've ever known would be interested in, Millie," Woods countered.

Through Woods's alerted mind flashed images of all kinds of debonair men such as he had seen in the cities, men he suspected must be the kind she had known and now made reference to. Millie had not needed to remind him of how different he was from them.

A band of uneasiness tightened around Woods's heart and made him think, as he had on the ride home after he had kissed her that first night, of what diverse backgrounds the two of them had and. . . . Woods felt his pulse skip at the thought of the promising dream surfacing while he was helping plan the building of Freeman's first schoolhouse, the dream dying instantly when he first had seen that the new teacher was a woman. What would be, would be, he thought with acceptance.

Millie searched for a way to explain better her meaning about Woods being special, but she came up with a zero. Maybe she was just being overly sensitive. Her father had criticized her for that, also. Maybe Woods had not taken offense at her words as she had feared.

They reached the place where they left the worn path to travel through the trees behind the schoolhouse then. Now that she, too, knew the way, Millie moved on ahead.

Playful gray squirrels chased around a tree up ahead, and Millie joined in Woods's amused chuckles at their antics, glad that he was not brooding. A mountain man would never be moody for long, she told herself with appreciation for the sound of his manly laughter in the beautiful patch of forest.

When they once again walked side by side, Woods asked,

"Would you like to hear one of Freeman's favorite tall tales?"

"Oh, yes."

Liking the way her face brightened with apparent interest, Woods began spinning an old yarn about a legendary mountain man called Tater. Tater, Woods told her, was forever complaining about the way a big coon always outsmarted him and his hunting cronies. Millie watched Woods throughout the telling of the yarn, glints of amusement in her sparkling brown eyes deepening at each new humorous revelation.

His words twanging and drawling in the rhythm and dialect of a natural-born storyteller from the Arkansas mountains, Woods continued as they neared the schoolhouse. "Well, one night the hounds treed that wily skoker in a big beech, and ole Tater, determined that on that night he'd win out for shore, shimmied right up to get him.

"After that coon and him done bit and scratched and fought eyeball to eyeball for a peart spell, he yelled down for the best shot in the party at the foot of the tree to blast up at'em. When they called up, they might hit him 'stead of the coon, ole Tater yelled back, 'Don't matter a'tall which'un you hits. By God, one of us needs some relief!'"

Shattering Millie's bursts of laughter and awe for Woods's gift as a teller of tall tales, an accusing voice rang out.

"So, there y'all are," called Widow Marks. "Anybody could've heard y'all laughin' for at least a quarter mile." She stood at the back of the schoolhouse with her hands on her broad hips. "I've been lookin' everywhere for you, Woods." Her sharp black eyes took in the dripping pillowcase of laundry and Millie's animated face.

"Now you've found us, Mabel, tell us what it is you're dying to tell," Woods said in a dry tone as they walked on to meet her. He set the laundry on the base of the well.

"Annabelle has been lookin' for you. We saw Major grazin' out back. I told her I'd give you the message 'cause she had to get back to the store." It was plain that she was dying to say more than she was saying.

"Fine, and thanks for letting me know, Mabel," Woods said. "I'll go right on over." Without another word or look at anybody, he left to check on his horse tethered at the far corner of the grounds.

"Well, I guess I'll get on home and start supper," the buxom widow said. "Come over to see me and set a spell when you get time, y'hear?" She fixed Millie with an arch look before disappearing around the schoolhouse.

Millie had finished hanging out her laundry on the clothesline stretching behind the teacherage by the time Woods came close, leading Major. She noticed that the big chestnut was spirited, a horse with no marks on its glossy coat other than gleaming white sox on both front legs. From the gentle way he handled the horse and talked to it, she could tell that Woods prized the handsome animal.

"Thanks for helping me so much today, Woods." It was one of those days that she wouldn't have known how to end, Millie realized, so maybe it was just as well that Annabelle had sent for him.

"Is there anything else I can do?" Woods asked. When she shook her head, the sight of the close-cropped red curls dancing pleasured him in the nicest kind of way. She seemed shy all of a sudden, and he wondered why she sent her gaze wandering off toward the mountains in the distance. "I enjoyed the day."

"So did I." Was she just imagining it, now that she was looking at Woods, or did he seem reluctant to leave? Millie choked down the desire to ask him why Annabelle Stevens seemed to have first call on his time, why she could send him a message and expect him to come immediately. Nothing Woods Sanders did was any of her business, she reminded herself sharply.

"Good luck tomorrow on your first day of teaching in Freeman." Woods doubled the ends of the reins in his hand and half turned toward the stirrup. "I'm glad we've become friends." He kicked at a tuft of weed with the toe of his boot, then cut his eyes toward Millie. "We kinda got off to a poor start, didn't we?"

"You're right. Likely Aunt Phoebe and Uncle Fred wouldn't believe that we've come to terms and become friends." She had taken to the notion of their being friends as soon as Woods stated it as fact.

"I'll check with you later to see if you're having problems. Take care."

"Thank you."

Millie watched Woods mount, admiring the way his muscles flexed in one liquid movement and the easy way he settled onto the gently complaining saddle, his broad shoulders straight but leaning forward a bit. She pretended to be going on inside the teacherage, but she slowed enough to watch him ride away on the frisky horse. In the slanting afternoon sunshine, she saw how Major's silky front legs, their white stockings reaching the knees, flashed and commanded attention.

A loneliness such as Millie never before had known washed over her when Woods disappeared around the corner of the church without a backward glance.

· *Chapter Six* ·

The teacherage looked strangely empty to Millie when she went on inside and exchanged her wet skirt and shoes for dry ones. It was while she was fastening the last button on her second shoe with her buttonhook that she heard voices outside, followed by a knock at her door.

"Miss Monroe?" a smiling woman asked when Millie opened the door. Snuggled up against either side of her caller, as if they might be supple vines clinging to a stalwart tree, were the red-haired boy and girl whom Millie had seen on her way back from the store. "I'm Lessie Booth, wife to Edgar, the owner of the livery stable." She held something balanced on one hand. "My kids saw you leaving the store yesterday, and they've been pestering me ever since to come calling." She looked down at her gift and lifted it toward Millie. "I hope you like apple pandowdy."

Millie accepted the cloth-covered pan being held out toward her, liking the wonderful smell of recently browned pie crust mixed up with the equally tantalizing smells of tart, cooked apples and cinnamon and sugar. She liked the warm looks washing over her from her first caller, too. Unless one counted Woods Sanders as her first caller, a part of Millie pointed out. Well, another part replied promptly, Woods did not count as a caller—the man was merely doing his job as chairman of the board to help her get settled in. Besides, they were friends. Even as the brief, unsettling exchange went on in her mind, Millie graciously accepted the woman's offering and gestured for the three Booths to come inside.

"I'm pleased to meet you and your children, Mrs. Booth. How lovely of you to come visit and bring one of my favorite desserts," Millie said with her widest smile. She ushered her callers to the sofa and then set the still-warm pie on the table near the cookstove.

"What are your names?" Millie asked the seemingly bashful youngsters after she perched on the side chair near the sofa. She noticed that both had their mother's even features and brown eyes. "I hope you'll be reporting to school tomorrow. I have lots of fun things planned for us to do."

"My boy's name is Noble." Lessie Booth ruffled his bright red hair with a fond hand, the action appearing to increase the blush on his freckled face. "He's been staying with kin close to Elmwood during the past two school years and going to school. I'm glad he won't have to be gone from home anymore. Noble is eight and this—"

The mother's words and her turn toward the little girl seated on the other side of her were interrupted.

"I can tell my own name, Mama," the child broke in with a pert smile that revealed telling spaces in her small front teeth. "I'm Francine Booth, and my papa's a blacksmith just as much as a liveryman. And I'm six years old, and I ain't never been to school." Her fat little legs, encased in black stockings and dangling below her blue calico skirt, swung rhythmically from where she perched on the edge of the sofa. When her speech was over, she seemed to become keenly interested in inspecting her neatly laced, high-top shoes.

"Oh, my," Millie replied. "I feel this might be my lucky day, to be meeting two of my pupils." She noticed the devilish sparkle in Francine's brown eyes as they darted upward and examined Millie's short hair. "If you want to, Francine, you can come closer for a better look at my hair. Likely nobody around here has seen many women with their hair cut so short."

Francine bounced up and rushed to Millie's side. Hesitating only a moment in apparent shyness, she sent fat little fingers to pat the red curls. "Your hair looks a sight purtier than my braids." She tossed one of her thick plaits over her shoulder with a practiced movement of her head. "It ain't as red as Noble's and mine, Miss Monroe, but it's kissing cousin close. Did you get your red hair from your papa, too?"

"Yes, Francine," Millie answered with an amused laugh. "My father was a redhead, too." From the corner of her eye, she could tell that Lessie was relaxing against the sofa. The earlier blush no longer stained Noble's freckled face.

"Everybody's excited about school starting here in our very own building," Lessie remarked after motioning for Francine to resume her place beside her on the sofa.

"So am I." Millie watched the little girl ignore her mother, then dart toward the bedroom and peep inside. How would she ever calm that one down in the classroom?

Talk moved between the two women, a bit hesitantly at first but with increasing ease. The children made no bones about listening to every word, but neither did they hide their interest in their new teacher and her living quarters. Before long, Noble joined his sister in her silent investigation of the teacherage. Millie tried to keep her mind on the chatty comments that Lessie was making about her neighbors in Freeman, but the children's darting movements and whisperings kept distracting her.

". . . and Annette, being sixteen, will be one of your high school pupils," Lessie finished.

"So you're saying that Annette Bordeaux lives in the

Keyhole House and will be coming to school tomorrow?" Millie asked, wishing she had been paying closer attention.

"Yes," Lessie replied. Her pleasant face screwed up in puzzlement. "Who told you the place was called the Keyhole House? Most everybody calls it the old Witherspoon place after the girl's grandpa."

Millie smiled and explained, "No one called it anything to me. I dubbed the house with that name when I noticed the unusual window on my way back from the store. The place seemed different from all the others—maybe because of the little window shaped like a keyhole—and I wondered at first if it might not be deserted." The memory of the movement behind the upstairs window rushed to mind.

"Well, it's not deserted, though it's just Annette and her mother rattling around in that big old place, now that their housekeeper died last year. The girl's as pretty as her mother was at sixteen, everybody says. I'm not old enough to be remembering anything about Selma Bordeaux except gossip, even if I'd growed up around here, which I didn't. I can't say as how I'm partial to such kinky black hair, myself, but I can't deny Annette Bordeaux is a pretty young woman."

"And, boy, does Warden Marks think Annette's pretty!" Francine added from where she and Noble were meddling with the burners on Millie's cookstove. "He acts like he don't care a'tall that her ma's a loony. Me and Noble seen them kissin'—"

"Hush up, Francine," Lessie scolded, a frown clouding her smooth forehead. She stood and called the children to her in a stern voice before turning back to her hostess. "It was nice to meet you, Millie. I'll expect you to be returning my call real soon, y'hear?"

At the door, Millie assured Lessie Booth that she would, indeed, visit her soon. She thanked the friendly woman and her two youngsters again for calling on her and bringing her the apple pandowdy, then watched the trio cross the school-yard and disappear beyond the church.

From what her visitors had told her, Millie reflected while closing her door and going back inside, she knew that the Booth home was the one this side of the Henry Stevens place—where Woods was likely at that very moment visiting with Henry's daughter, Annabelle . . . in the parlor, now that the sun was almost gone behind the hills in the distance.

Ignoring the unwelcome thought about Woods, Millie stooped over and tried to light the round wick of a cookstove burner. In spite of her knowing that she should never set much store in gossip told by children, she had to admit that Francine's remarks about Annette Bordeaux and her mother intrigued her. And the bit about Widow Marks's son, Warden, and Annette having been seen kissing stayed with her, too. The match burned out then and scorched her finger.

"Double damn!" she muttered as she stuck her finger in her mouth. She couldn't seem to get any of the kerosene burners to light. What had Francine and Noble done to her cookstove?

Wasn't it strange, Millie mused as she decided to eat cheese and apple pie for supper and give up on the burners, that Lessie had made no attempt to retract or explain Francine's remarks in any way? Why hadn't she asked more about the Keyhole House and its occupants? Now her curiosity was running rampant.

A sprinkling of rain came about midnight, but the first morning of school dawned crisp and clear.

Millie arose at an early hour, determined to conquer the temperamental cookstove. Her normally groggy morning brain didn't help matters, but she finally got one burner lit. Once she got the flame adjusted, she set the gray-enameled percolator over the smelly flame and hurried outside to the well to refill her water bucket.

The bracing morning air slapped an unsuspecting Millie in the face. She was wide awake by then. With a touch of homesickness, she recalled the warmth of her small apartment on the grounds of the girls' school back in Little Rock . . . and its conveniences. Had Board Chairman Sanders been there at the moment, she mused irritably, she would be delighted to tell him exactly what she thought about his teacherage.

While Freeman's new schoolmarm was hurriedly making her ablutions with cold water in her chilly bedroom, she promised herself that in the future she would remember to bring in an extra bucket of water before dark. She had not liked chasing around outside in the damp dawn air with nothing on but her green wrapper over her nightgown. If she ever got the hang of that fool cookstove, Millie reasoned when goose bumps popped up all over from the punishing cold washcloth and her nipples puckered painfully in protest, she might manage to heat some in her wash pan and have a more rewarding toilet.

During the past four years of teaching, Millie had learned that the first day of school was no more frightening to her pupils than to her. Recognizing that her nervousness was making the morning harder than usual to lean into and embrace, she took three deep breaths and ordered herself to calm down and chase away her negative thoughts.

Millie chose her frilliest white waist, one that she had made herself, with soft tatting around the high neck, the tiny front tucks, and the wide, fitted cuffs of the long sleeves. Her brown skirt, she decided after giving it a brisk dusting and brushing, gleamed like new above her best button tops, polished now to a brown mirrorlike finish.

Millie picked up her mother's cameo and fingered it lovingly before pinning it at the meeting point of the banded neck of her frilly waist. Attaching her father's pocket watch to her belt by its heavy gold chain and a cleverly concealed pin—his last congregation had presented them to him when he'd had to leave the pulpit because of his poor health, she recalled fondly—Millie sucked in a deep breath and warned her pulse to act right. She was ready to leave the teacherage and enter the side door of the schoolroom. Just before opening the door, she crossed her fingers for good luck.

Within a short time, Millie was greeting and meeting the few mothers who accompanied their children. She wondered if she would ever get them all straight, both pupils and mothers. Had she ever been so nervous? Grateful that she previously had met two of the nine pupils who showed up, she was able to greet Francine and Noble Booth with special cheer—until she recalled how they had messed up the burners of her cookstove. Before the thought had time to alter Millie's smile, the two redheads grinned up at her and charmed her all over again.

The secretive stares at her shorn hair turned out to be less debilitating than Millie had feared, though she found herself fighting hard not to acknowledge the questioning eyes from both adults and children and offer explanations. How lucky could she get? she wondered. Everyone seemed to be accepting her in spite of her different look.

Even as involved as Millie was in the classroom with righting the normally chaotic disorder of a first day of a new school year, she had no trouble recognizing Annette Bordeaux when the pretty girl came in the front door alone. Lessie's descriptive word "kinky" seemed too demeaning for such lovely hair, Millie decided right off. Half expecting that Widow Mark's son, Warden, would be accompanying Annette, Millie was disappointed that Warden was not present.

"Annette," Millie said after the last mother had left and the nine pupils sat at random in the desks lined up in front of her own, "perhaps Minnijean Blackstone and you should share the desk she's sitting in, seeing as how you two will be the only high school girls here."

Millie looked meaningfully at the row of four adult-size desks on one side of the long room, each designed to seat two. Ransom Milstead, the third of the older pupils present, almost filled one desk with his broad shoulders and thick body. Insofar as Millie could tell, Ransom had done little but stare at Annette Bordeaux.

"We won't be the only two girls in upper level," Minnijean replied, looking askance at the dark-eyed Annette, who sat alone across the aisle from her in one of the larger desks. "Gladys Hobbs will be coming to school. I'm still thirteen, but Gladys is already fourteen. I'd like to share my desk with her."

"We'll see," Millie hedged. So Minnijean and Annette weren't great friends, Millie thought. Or at least they weren't on that particular day. "Annette, you may move into one of the larger desks temporarily. Minnijean, do you know why Gladys Hobbs isn't here today?" She watched Annette move gracefully to the other desk as requested, then heard a discernible titter sweep the room.

"No, ma'am," Minnijean replied. She reddened and became involved in adjusting the blue ribbon that held her straight brown hair back from her round face.

"Does she live here in Freeman?" Millie suspected that Minnijean knew more than she was telling.

"No, Miss Monroe. She lives down in the holler," Minnijean answered.

"Hollow, not holler," Millie corrected smoothly, turning toward the other pupils. "Does anyone know anything about Gladys being absent, or when she'll be coming to school?"

When no one answered, Millie put her question aside and went on. There must be something unusual about Gladys's absence, she decided with an instinct sharpened during her four years in a classroom. "Isn't Warden Marks supposed to be here at school? Does anyone know why he isn't here?"

"Warden's mother said that he went before daybreak to help Mr. Cushing with his sick cow," Annette replied in a low musical voice. As if she was accustomed to attracting attention, the pretty sixteen-year-old seemed unaware that the younger students turned and stared at her while she spoke. "I guess he hasn't gotten back yet." She hesitated before Millie's steady gaze. "Warden's house is next to mine."

"Warden says he wants to be a cow doctor," Francine Booth announced with gravity from the small desk that she was sharing with another first-grader, Daisy Green. "He's always been hog crazy over animals, my mama says." Somebody sniggered behind a covered mouth. Francine toyed with her red braids, then asked doubtfully, "Can somebody really be a cow doctor?"

"Yes, Francine," Millie replied. She could tell that some would like to laugh at the little girl's bold question, and she shushed them by lifting her palm upward and frowning slightly. "A doctor who is trained to treat ailing animals is called a veterinarian. Some people shorten the name to 'vet.' Thank you, Francine, for giving us our very first vocabulary word." She turned and wrote it on the blackboard hanging on the wall behind her desk, aware of the storm of protesting whispers going on. "Copy it and the definition, then learn both. You'll find the word in our first spelling bee. We'll have one each Friday afternoon."

The business of assigning seats and passing out textbooks to those who had their money that day, then talking privately with each student about his previous school experience took up the rest of the morning.

Millie was delighted to find that her six younger pupils were of ages to learn and study together. The two little Green girls, Daisy and Charlene, were the exact ages of Francine and Noble Booth, six and eight. Junior, Minnijean's younger brother, was seven and had never attended school. Steve Milstead told her that he was nine.

Ransom Milstead was by far the oldest boy present, Millie reaffirmed after she announced the noon break. Those not going home to eat went out back to the toilets and the washstand beside the well. She had promised to join them in the play yard out front where all would sit on the grass and eat from their lunch pails and get better acquainted.

As Woods had told her that day when they had ridden past the Milstead farm on the road from Elmwood, Millie reflected while looking over her roll, Ransom, the older boy, would soon be sixteen, while Steve was nine. She recalled, too, that Woods had told her how the boys would be spending the weeks of school in Freeman with their grandfather, Henry Stevens, and their aunt.

Millie had seen upon first meeting the Milstead boys that both of them bore strong family resemblances to their Aunt Annabelle Stevens, who had come with them to the schoolhouse for a brief time that morning. The contemplative schoolmarm wondered if the boys' dead mother might not have been a beauty such as Annabelle was, for they had sparkling blue eyes and blond hair, though neither had their aunt's fair skin. She felt her inherent curiosity aroused as to what kind of person Fern Stevens Milstead had been.

That night, while Millie fought with the cranky kerosene cookstove and tried to prepare a hot meal, she looked back over the events of the opening day of Freeman's first school. All in all, she consoled herself as she adjusted the sputtering burner to an acceptably blue flame and removed a skillet from its nail on the wall, things had gone extremely well.

Without warning, the thought surfaced that Woods, as

board chairman, would have been pleased. It would be nice if she could be sharing her little successes with the deep-voiced mountain man, Millie's thoughts ran on pell-mell. Too, it would be nice if he could be there to work his magic on the burners of the recalcitrant cookstove. Then the grease got too hot in the iron skillet, and she had to concentrate on keeping the potato slices from cooking too fast.

The second and third days of school passed without disaster, too, and Millie found herself far more relaxed on Friday afternoon when all of the pupils had scampered from the schoolhouse. Both Warden Marks and Gladys Hobbs had shown up that day, and she assumed that she now had all of her pupils.

Millie found Warden a smooth-featured boy of eighteen. She admired his spunk in attending a school in which all of the pupils were younger than he, with the majority being under ten. She had found out in a hurry that the Widow Marks had been right about her only child: He was unusually bright and already as big as many grown men.

Though she had tried, Millie consoled herself as she changed into her oldest shoes in preparation for taking a stroll down the road, she had been unable to ascertain why Gladys Hobbs had not come to school on the first day. Neither could she figure out why the fourteen-year-old had such a haunted, vulnerable look. The girl was as pretty as Minnijean Blackstone, obviously her best friend, but not nearly so lovely as the exquisite Annette Bordeaux.

"Wait up, Millie!" called a voice when Millie had walked past two houses down the road toward the Gooseneck River.

"What a nice surprise," Millie said after turning around and halting. Coming toward her was the friendly daughter of the storekeeper and several dogs.

"Where are you going?" Annabelle asked with unabashed frankness. She turned around and scolded the dogs for following her, as if they might be children capable of understanding each word. They stopped, then trotted back up the road toward her father's store and the livery stable.

"I like to stretch out the kinks from being in the classroom by taking walks," Millie replied. She marked the feat that

Annabelle had accomplished, figuring that she would have
need of knowing how to order the hamlet's several dogs
about. She had no wish for anyone to know that she was
more than a little afraid of animals. "I was figuring that if I
walked on down this way, I'd see the other houses in Freeman and come to the Gooseneck River."

Annabelle laughed. "That you will, though it's likely a
half mile or more down to the bridge."

"Good. I usually walked a mile or more back in Little
Rock on the grounds of the girls' school where I taught."

"Nobody from around here ever walks for any reason
other than that he has to." Annabelle chuckled. "Millie
Monroe, you are probably the freshest drink of water that
Freeman has ever had. First your hair, and now your walking out by yourself because you like it."

"Maybe so, but what if Freeman isn't thirsting for any
kind of drink?" Millie quipped. Her brown eyes sparkled in
the late afternoon sunlight and revealed her unspoken thanks
to Annabelle for the left-handed compliment.

"Last year Papa and I went to Hot Springs with Ransom,
Steve, and their father to attend a Chautauqua concert. On
the program for the year, I saw that one of the lectures
would be on hygiene and exercise. Are you a devotee of
Teddy Roosevelt's program for physical fitness?"

Millie tried to conceal her surprise that anyone in Freeman
knew of the traveling groups offering adult education and
entertainment to communities throughout the nation, much
less attended any of the varied programs. Back in Little
Rock, Millie and her women friends seldom had missed any
of the Chautauqua Series.

"Hardly a devotee," Millie replied with a little laugh.
"Though I hated to see Roosevelt leave office a couple of
years back. I hope he really is planning to run again next
term under the banner of the new Progressive Party. I liked
him as president, didn't you?"

"Would it have mattered, one way or the other?" Annabelle rejoined without rancor. "Women aren't supposed to
have any thoughts about politics, or else we'd be allowed to
vote, wouldn't we?"

Millie studied the pretty face close to hers now, not surprised that an obviously sharp mind operated behind it. Even when she hadn't liked it when Woods had left her a few afternoons ago and hurried to answer Annabelle's summons, Millie had not pondered why Woods would like to be around the pretty blonde. Annabelle was innately feminine and beautifully alive, in spite of the noticeable sadness lurking within her blue eyes. For the first time, Millie wondered if that sadness had anything to do with Woods Sanders.

"Someday we women will be voting," Millie said. "There are too many movements underway for all of them to fall by the wayside. Look at the progress our own Catherine Cunningham made before she died three years ago. Her Political Equality League is off to a big start, and I'm a member. Are you?"

"I'm not a member, but I've read issues of Cunningham's *Woman's Chronicle*."

Feeling again as she had upon their first meeting that Annabelle was someone very special to know and that the two had a lot in common, Millie said, "If you were coming to visit me, I can always postpone my walk, or we can cut it short."

"Oh, no, I was on my way to see you, but I'll enjoy walking with you and acquainting you with the houses of our neighbors. It's so close to time for chores and supper that I doubt anybody will still be on their porches."

The two women began walking then, neither giving any thought to the contrasting figures they made there on the natural road of gravel and larger rocks: one with her blond pompadour and petite size, yet curved a shade generously, and the other with her unheard-of cropped red curls and her tall slenderness.

"Has anybody mentioned the box supper to you, Millie?"

"No."

"Papa had the schoolboard meeting at our house the other night, and they decided to have a box supper tomorrow night at the new school. I forgot to tell you about it when I came to the school with Ransom and Steve on Wednesday. The board members figure on raising a little money for library books and letting everybody meet the new teacher at the same time."

"How nice." Millie wondered if she was ready for being put on public display.

"I guess you've been to box suppers before."

"Yes, my father's churches nearly always had them on fifth Sundays as a kind of social for the members."

Already Millie was terrified at the thought of having to cook an acceptable meal. And what would she prepare, even if she had a decent stove? Maybe Woods would take pity on her since she had told him of her scarcity in culinary talent and buy her box. It would be fitting, she reassured herself, since he was unmarried and the chairman of the board and she was the new teacher. And they *were* friends, she reminded herself.

"We've got a whole coop of chickens behind the store, if you'd like to get one," Annabelle said. When Millie appeared not to have heard, she went on. "Nearly everybody from around here expects to find fried chicken in a supper box at a social."

"That's a grand idea for me to get a chicken and fry it. Thanks. You must have been reading my mind." Millie crossed her fingers and hoped that was untrue. She had no wish for her new friend to know that her thoughts had too often dwelled upon Woods Sanders since her arrival in Freeman on the past Sunday.

As they walked on, Annabelle told Millie a little about the people living in the houses on both sides of the road. Some of the houses were large and some were small. Each seemed to present its very own personality, Millie mused, as if it might be something alive. It pleased the new schoolmarm when she recognized the last names of some of her pupils. Then Millie, at Annabelle's request, gave accounts of recent happenings in Little Rock.

When a companionable spell of silence claimed the walkers, Millie reflected that Annabelle had been right about everybody being inside or out back of their homes. Recalling instances from those early years in her life when she had lived or visited in small towns, she figured that those outside probably were tending their chickens and livestock before caring for their own needs in readying for the autumn night.

Once Millie thought she heard the high-pitched squeals of

an ungreased pulley as if water was being drawn from a well, and she thought of the refreshing coldness, the sweet smell and taste of the water from her own well beside the teacherage. She suspected that the only reason the curious dogs, bounding out from time to time to greet the two chatting women and sniff at the hem of Millie's skirt, returned to their resting places without being told was that they knew Annabelle.

"I gather that most of the men in Freeman either farm or work in the bauxite mines," Millie said after putting together all that Annabelle had confided.

"Yes, but they raise cows and horses and pigs, too."

"And chickens," Millie added in a playful tone.

Annabelle laughed. "Yes. You'll get used to hearing those roosters every morning."

While they walked across the bridge arching over the Gooseneck River, Annabelle gestured toward the shadowed trees stretching behind the houses. "Nearly all the houses have lanes running behind them that reach to pastures and cultivated fields in the valley of the Gooseneck. Some men farm land down this road leading to Dierks but they choose to live here and ride back and forth on horseback."

Without the need for further talk then, the two women continued down the narrow gravel road, both watching and listening to the numerous birds twittering and darting from one tree to another, as if the creatures might be checking out places to roost during the approaching night. Millie thought about how she really should try to learn more of the names and calls of the birds in the area before they migrated. The only song she recognized was one floating on the cool air from an unseen mockingbird.

Though the houses were widely and unevenly spaced, some separated only by garden plots and some by narrow strips of forest as well as the small plowed areas, Millie got the feeling that she was looking at a friendly, closely knit community. There was something cozily inviting about the stone chimneys—stones like the ones piled along the edge of the road and obviously removed from its bed to make traveling easier, she noted—the wide, shadowed porches and their slatted swings, and the thick-branched trees protecting the front yards.

Millie saw a few dead leaves scattered on the front yards and glimpsed little piles of leaves off to the sides of a few houses, mute testimony to the pride of some housewives in the appearance of their homes. They obviously cared too much to allow their yards to remain cluttered until after all the leaves came tumbling and claimed each foot of the carefully scraped earth. Millie imagined that when enough leaves fell for the homeowners to burn them, the smoke would fill the air around Freeman with the autumn smell peculiarly its own—pleasingly tangy and more than a little poignant.

Not since she was a youngster visiting Aunt Phoebe and Uncle Fred in a small town west of Little Rock had Millie had such a close-up view of front yards scraped clean of all rocks, grass, and weeds and dotted with rock-edged beds of bushes and flowers. Not many blooms brightened the yards, but she saw some pale chrysanthemums edging one circular flowerbed that was centered with tall hollyhocks, their spikes of blossoms still a breathtaking blue, though true daylight had gone and the western sky was fast outlining the distant hills with a glorious wash of mauves and pinks. Millie thought about how beautiful the stately hollyhocks would look in the vestibule of the church and hoped that frost would not kill them before the first Sunday in October.

Then, not far away, a cow lowed. Closer by another answered, reminding Millie that milking time must be about over. She cocked her head and listened. How long since she had heard the discordant but soothing sound of a cowbell?

Now that twilight was a reality and the two women had turned back toward Freeman, Millie saw lamps glowing from within a house or two. Families were gathering for the evening meal and time of closeness. She could hear voices calling from somewhere out of view and being answered by soft, muffled sounds coming from within a house.

"What a peaceful place your town is," Millie said, breathing in the homey smell of woodsmoke curling from stovepipes jutting up from the rear sections of the houses, all of them set far back off the road. A breeze brought her a tantalizing whiff of hot bread and something being fried.

"Isn't it your town now, too, Millie?"

"Why, yes," Millie replied, realizing that she spoke with a lot of honesty threading through what she initially had felt was no more than a polite reply. "I suppose it *is* becoming mine, too."

When Millie and Annabelle came back to the low stone bridge over the swirling clear waters of the Gooseneck River, they paused. Lost in private thoughts, they gazed at the rushing stream in the gloaming. Then they walked on toward Freeman, leaving the sinking sun to complete its disappearing act behind the purple hills in the distance.

One minute with anticipation and the next with little pangs of uneasiness, each woman thought secretly about the social planned for the following night: Would, perhaps, a very special man bid the highest for the privilege of sharing her food and her company in the presence of the people of the community?

Part Three

"Immune to women," the mountain man said;
He'd ne'er be ruled by other than his head.

Oh, yes, the Jailer of the heart is diligent,
But Jailers, too, are oft beguiled.

The redhead vexes him, scorches him with a kiss.
She seems so different, this big-city miss.

He puzzles; he wavers; his body, it burns.
Is it to win her that he secretly yearns?

· *Chapter Seven* ·

"What'm-I-bid?" intoned the auctioneer from the little raised platform on which the teacher's desk sat in the schoolroom. "Gotta-basket-for-bid. What'm-I-bid?"

Though his usual roles were those of owner of the livery stable and blacksmith, Edgar Booth obviously was enjoying his Saturday night stint as auctioneer, Millie reflected from where she sat among those crowded into the schoolroom on Saturday night. Little Francine might have inherited her apparent love of being the center of attention as well as her red hair from Edgar. Likely the man had picked up the jargon and rhythm of a true auctioneer from having attended numerous sales of mules and horses in the area.

Someone had told Millie upon her arrival that the numerous straight chairs almost filling the room had been borrowed from the Sunday school rooms of the church next door. She moved her shoulders nervously against the back of hers. That Edgar had grabbed Millie's basket from those sitting on boards thrown across sawhorses and now was holding it up for all to see sent little shivers up and down her spine. What if no one bid for it? She agonized. Maybe the father of one of her pupils would buy it along with his wife's so that she would not be left alone.

Earlier Millie had entered through the side door after she had begun hearing friendly noises coming through the wall dividing the teacherage from the classroom. She had not wanted to be noticed right off, but people had swarmed around her anyway while she added her basket to the numerous collection of boxes and other baskets already in place. The warm attention had made her feel less like a newcomer.

Millie had been astounded by the festive atmosphere that

permeated the long, narrow room. Someone had hung glowing lanterns from well-spaced hooks in the ceiling. The soft
cadences of the liquid dialect of the mountain folk gathered
for an evening of pleasure touched the heart of the new
schoolmarm, reminding her of the welcome sounds of an old
friend's greeting after a long separation.

A mixture of scented soap and perfume overcame the
mundane smells of the kerosene fueling the lanterns and the
new unpainted lumber in the nicest kind of way, Millie decided from her first whiff. While returning the shy wave
from one of her first-graders across the room, she noticed
that the side windows had been propped open to let in the
warmly fragrant breezes. There were so many new faces and
names to hang onto that she felt she might be back in Little
Rock, floating out in the middle of the treacherous Arkansas
River on a runaway barge.

Immediately upon arriving Millie had glimpsed Woods's
tall figure over near the front door. Though she chided herself for being foolish, she had suspected that she could hear
his resonant voice over all others. He had been surrounded
by so many people that she doubted he knew of her arrival,
though his eyes did appear to flick in her direction for a
riveting second or two. She had seen Annabelle and her father, Henry Stevens, among those conversing with Woods.
Had the three come together?

Then Edgar's voice stepped up to a singsong nasal twang,
and Millie's brain lurched back to the moment. "What'm-I-
bid? A basket—ho! I've a basket—ho! Bid-'em-up, gents!
A basket with wildflowers on the handle—ho! What'm-I-
bid?"

"Fifty cents!" a deep bass voice called from somewhere in
the back.

Millie let out a silent breath of relief and kept her suddenly burning face toward the auctioneer. When had she enjoyed such excitement? All of the earlier bids had begun
with only a quarter. She would have known Woods's voice
anywhere. She uncrossed her fingers.

Ever since Millie's fried chicken had turned out looking
so pale and sickly late that afternoon, she had hoped against
hope that Woods would be the one to purchase her basket.

She had muttered mild obscenities at the cookstove and had even refilled the fuel tank with more kerosene, all to no avail. The flame had refused to cooperate. Her potato salad wasn't bad, even if she, herself, did say so, but the fried chicken was a disaster. The meat was done, but it had no visual appeal. Woods would remember about the troublesome cookstove and her confessions that she was no prize-winning cook and not be surprised or critical. After all, Millie reminded herself, hadn't the handsome man with the cleft in his chin said that they were friends?

"Seventy-five cents!" This, from a male unknown to Millie. She stiffened. She could hear tittering. Several people were spearing her with amused but friendly looks. Their looks hinted that the bid had not come from a well-meaning father of one of her pupils.

"One dollar!" Woods was not giving up, Millie realized gratefully. He truly was her friend.

While another round of bidding went on between Woods and the stranger, Millie fingered the little bunch of wild-flowers that she had pinned at the waistband of her brown skirt and let her thoughts run backward.

For a brief time that day, while she was contemplating what she should wear to the social, Millie had regretted having nothing special to wear. That afternoon she had walked in the forest behind the schoolhouse and gathered an armful of yellow crownbeard, which always reminded her of the earlier blooming wildflower called black-eyed Susan. She had found some fronds of fern near the Gooseneck River.

When Millie returned to the teacherage and filled a stone pitcher with her find, the idea had struck her to decorate her basket with a few of the yellow blossoms and some sprigs of the curly fern. To add a few flowers to the band of her skirt had seemed a nice touch.

Soon after her arrival, though, Millie had seen that none of the other women wore flowers and that several had sent little darting, sharp looks at her waistband—after having first given seemingly judgmental looks at her short hair. Maybe, Millie thought while awaiting the next move in the auction, it was just as well if everyone learned right off that their new schoolmarm was a tad different from most people.

So far, she realized with thanksgiving, everybody had seemed to accept her anyway.

"One dollar and fifty cents!"

At the outrageously high bid from the man with the alien-sounding voice—none of the earlier auctioned boxes had brought more than a dollar—Millie's heartbeat skipped around like crazy and snatched her thoughts back to the auction. Who was the man in the back with the clipped way of speaking? Millie was too embarrassed to lean over and ask Lessie Booth, who was sitting next to her and beaming at her clowning, auctioneer husband. Edgar was grinning at the frozen-faced Millie.

The man bidding against Woods must not be from around Freeman, Millie assumed as she tried to ignore her warm cheeks and the apparent mood of merriment from the high-spirited crowd. Surely he had no way of knowing that the basket was hers—but then everyone seemed to know, she realized with a start, else why all the attention being directed toward her? Maybe the man was eager to contribute to the fund for library books. Had not Woods mentioned that traveling salesmen sometimes stayed at the Widow Mark's house? Maybe the stranger was a salesman passing through.

"A-dollar-fifty. Got-a-dollar-fifty," intoned Edgar in the accustomed babble of auctioneers. "Who'll make it a quarter more? These wildflowers do look sweet, gentlemen."

Millie could hear much good-natured laughing, whispering, and shuffling of feet against the wooden floor while Edgar's comments rang out among the crowd. She estimated there must be at least forty people present—not counting the children or the dogs making occasional noises outside, she amended.

Would Woods abandon her to the mercy of some stranger? Millie agonized. She knew well that a dollar was a steep price to pay; more than that was outrageous, especially for fried chicken without the expected brown crust. Her hands, primly folded together across her lap, became damp.

"Two dollars!" came Woods's determined bid.

"Three dollars!" came the stranger's.

Millie reddened more and shrank on the inside while Edgar went through the final spiel of getting the bid settled.

Woods had given up. He had let her down. She vowed never to forgive him, even if he were to ask her, which was not likely. She swallowed at the gorge threatening to choke her. Her disappointment was of her own doing, some inner voice reminded her and helped her get a hold on herself. Why had she let herself expect Woods Sanders to buy her basket?

As the daughter of a Methodist minister, Millie knew the rules of such socials: She was expected to be gracious and eat with whomever it was who had paid such a ridiculously high price for her basket and pretend to be pleased. How would she explain to anybody but Woods about the god-awful chicken?

Millie suspected her usual air of self-control might be tee-tering. She had the awful feeling that Woods Sanders had not meant it when he said he wanted them to be friends. She should have realized it when he never came back to ask how things went on the first day of school. Probably he had been toying with her from the beginning, just to show he had power over her.

Well, Millie's punishing thoughts ran on, she had fallen right into Woods's hands that first night, kissing him back like some man-starved hussy. She could feel angry indignation washing over her, though she was unsure if it was directed toward Woods or toward herself.

Edgar went ahead with auctioning off the remaining baskets. Millie sat demurely throughout, her hands clasped tightly on her lap and her gaze fixed ahead. She blinked hard and forbade her lips to tighten when she heard Woods's voice boom from the back again. He was jumping in on the bidding for the final box. When she appraised the blue-ribboned white box being held aloft by the auctioneer, she knew for certain that it belonged to Annabelle Stevens and that the chicken inside it was browned to perfection.

Even as Millie heard Edgar let the prettily decorated box go for a dollar and a half to Woods, she wondered who the man was who, with a barely audible bid, had initiated the bidding for Annabelle's box. It had not been Woods. Whoever the first bidder was—and Millie was fairly sure from his accent that he was a local—he must have been too timid to pursue the matter further after Woods spoke up. Could it be that the beauteous Annabelle had more than one admirer in the crowd?

Millie could not deny that ever since the afternoon Annabelle had sent for Woods, she occasionally had entertained the idea of Annabelle and Woods as a couple, for both were so outstandingly attractive and easy to be around. And the way Woods had asked what Millie thought about Annabelle rose up as further reason for questioning. She had discarded the thought that their interest was truly serious when she realized that both had been of marrying age for a good while. Circumstances were not always what they seemed, Millie reminded herself, and maybe there was a reason the two were still courting. Still, it did seem strange that neither Annabelle nor Woods mentioned the other very much in conversations.

Gathering her whirling thoughts as the crowd rose and began milling about, Millie scolded herself for letting thoughts of Woods flood her mind all week. Now that it seemed plain there was something between the pretty blonde and him, she was even more embarrassed that she had kissed him back that night. True, she would have liked being friends with Woods, but that seemed out of the question now. Why, Millie agonized, Annabelle Stevens *was* her friend and she never would want to interfere in a woman friend's affairs of the heart.

"Miss Monroe," the stranger standing beside Edgar Booth said after the auctioneer brought Millie's basket over and introduced the two who would be sharing its contents. "I'm delighted to have such a lovely schoolmarm sharing my supper on my evening in Freeman. I'm not from here, you see."

"Thank you, Mr. Durham," Millie replied uncertainly. She was too aware that almost everyone was waiting for the two of them to do more than tiptoe through the amenities. Who was this Clive Durham and what was he doing at a box supper in Freeman on a Saturday night? She had noticed right away that the man's inordinately pink face was clean-shaven. He was not bad-looking in his handsome suit and high, starched collar, Millie decided, if one cared for the just scrubbed look and the sophisticated air of a man from a big city.

"Would you care to sit outside on the school porch?" Clive asked.

"Whatever pleases you, Mr. Durham, will be fine."

"The night seems warm enough, you see, and some of the others are already out there."

When Millie made no protest, Clive guided her through the noisy, milling group with a gentlemanly hand upon her elbow, her basket in his free hand. Millie almost flinched from Clive's touch; his hand felt soft, almost feminine and not at all like Wood's.

Millie was glad that Woods and Annabelle were not among the few chattering couples sitting on the edges of the low porch floor with their feet on the ground. She was going to have to get accustomed to the idea of their truly being a twosome.

After exchanging greetings and introductions all around, Millie and her supper partner sat as the others did. She watched Clive's gold-rimmed glasses reflect the light streaming through the opened front door and hide his eyes.

Were Clive Durham's eyes blue or gray? Millie wondered in a kind of panic. Usually she noticed people's eyes right off, for she held with the idea that they were the windows to the soul. About all she could recall about Mr. Durham's eyes was that they were pale, almost without any color, as if they had nothing to reveal from within. She realized that the round-faced Clive was staring at her, obviously waiting for her to remove the dish towel covering the meal in her basket. With no heart for the task, Millie obliged.

"Some of the kind folks have already informed me that you came here from Little Rock only this week, Miss Monroe," Clive Durham said while Millie took out plates and proceeded to fill them with her "blond" chicken and potato salad.

Deliberately Millie blotted out the image of the man with whom she originally had hoped to be sharing the meal. She could not permit further thoughts of Woods Sanders as being anyone but Annabelle's beau. Here was a city man who apparently thought highly of her. Something on the inside perked up at the thought that her basket was the only one bringing more than a dollar and a half.

Three dollars, Millie mused. Clive Durham had paid three dollars to be able to eat with her. Why, that was more than the price of the skirt and waist that she was wearing. The thought was heady to one who had been jilted by a lawyer only months earlier—a woman who had kissed a mountain man with newly awakened passion recently, a mountain man who had turned his back on her during the auction because he already had a woman.

In her sweetest tone, Millie replied, "That's right, Mr. Durham. This is my first Saturday night in Freeman." The man's words kept coming out clipped and a shade nasal. Was he from the East? Millie wondered.

Relieved that her supper partner was responding to a question from one of the other men out on the porch, Millie set out jars of water for each, then brought out two forks. The only bread she had packed was in the form of soggy biscuits she had baked over two hours ago—not actually baked, she corrected. Honesty made her admit that she had merely attempted to bake them. The oven designed to sit atop two of the burners of the vindictive cookstove had turned out to be a cruel joke. All that the excuse for an oven had done was turn the undersides of the biscuits to a ghastly brown bordering on burned, while setting a pale, slick glaze on the tops of the dough and ignoring the vital center parts.

Millie, in a moment of pure abandonment, longed to toss the biscuits to the dogs loitering out in the shadows with eyes fixed greedily on the diners there on the porch. The thought that one of them might come up and bite her after tasting her biscuits sobered her. The Woods she had believed him to be—wanted him to be—would have laughed with her over what had developed into a first-rate catastrophe, now that a stranger was sharing the sad contents of her basket. She almost giggled all by herself.

In spite of her vow not to pay any attention to Woods as a man, Millie glanced through the opened door and saw Annabelle and him sitting side by side in one of the big desks. They did make a handsome couple as they ate from the daintily decorated box, laughing and talking in between bites with those around them. Millie could not help but feel her heart lift a little when she saw her pretty friend appearing so happy.

In other desks turned to face the couple sat the two Milstead boys and a man whom Millie had not yet met. He must have arrived after the auction began. Was he, perhaps, Lucas Milstead, father of Annabelle's motherless nephews? All of them seemed to be sharing the food from Annabelle's huge box. Millie stared with jealousy at the richly browned piece of chicken that Woods was attacking with obvious relish.

"This looks like a real feast," Clive said after he ended his conversation with one of the men on the porch and returned his full attention to Millie and the plate she had served sparingly.

"Thank you. I hope you won't be too disappointed." Millie looked across at him in the dim light and thought: *You don't know much about food, Mr. Durham.* She was mustering up courage to attack her own smaller servings.

"Would I be too bold to ask what brings you to Freeman?" Millie asked after taking a bite of potato salad and finding that it was, as she had earlier decided, not bad.

"Not at all, my dear young lady. I came to Arkansas from Buffalo—an industrial city in New York State—three years ago as the regional manager for Southern Bauxite Mines. I have offices in Hot Springs and in Elmwood, but I stay in Elmwood most of the time.

"Since Freeman's mines are in my territory, you see, I travel here nearly every week to deliver the payrolls and check on our mines." Clive picked up a piece of chicken, turned it slowly in the half-light, and gingerly took a small bite before laying it back down on his plate. "Edgar Booth at the livery stable acts as local agent in my absence, but I often spend the night here at the Widow Marks's place so as to get to know the local people." When Millie continued to watch him with apparent interest, Clive went on in what she deemed an unctuous tone. "Such things as the manager showing up at community socials helps the company to show good faith, you see."

"I see." Millie almost bit her tongue for having fallen into

Clive's trap. She wondered if she might not have sounded like a parrot.

One of Millie's pet peeves was hearing men talk down to women, as if they had to simplify and offer some pat answer for the supposedly empty-headed women to hand back to them. She had the urge to tell Clive Durham that she knew Buffalo was not only an industrial city in New York but it was also a sizable port on the Buffalo River at the eastern end of Lake Erie, but she quelled it.

Millie had no wish for Clive Durham to think of her as rude or as a smart-aleck, not when he had honored her by bidding so generously for her supper basket and adding to the fund for books. If he wanted to search for an excuse to criticize her, her fried chicken and her biscuits would suffice; words would not be needed.

Millie tried to eat a few more bites of potato salad, all the while listening to Clive's polite conversation and making what were apparently acceptable comments. She had no wish to see his reaction to the unpalatable supper and thus kept her gaze averted as much as possible. The night air was warm for September, she noticed, and a fat moon was rising over the hills in the distance.

"From my first sight of you before the auction, when Woods told me who you were, I knew you were different, that you couldn't have come from around these parts," Clive said in a private voice after awhile. Though some had already gone back inside the classroom, two other couples were still on the porch with Millie and him.

"Oh?" Millie knew that that the man was offering a compliment, yet she was feeling a bit on the defensive from his words; though for the life of her, she could not figure out why. So Woods was the one telling Clive who she was back before the auction began, Millie mused with a trace of indignation. Had he, perhaps, encouraged Clive to bid for her basket?

Millie couldn't think about that nagging question right then because another cropped up. When Clive had leaned closer to make the intimate remark, had he tossed a piece of chicken out into the darkness? She was almost sure that she had seen him make such a movement—not that she blamed him.

Millie asked, "What made you so sure I didn't come from around here?"

"Your sporting haircut, for one thing, and your putting flowers on your basket and your skirt band, for another. I like seeing women glory in being themselves, you see." Clive nodded politely to the other two couples who had risen and were going back inside. "With your being educated and from Little Rock, you naturally would have more modern ideas than the people in Freeman, you see."

Millie chewed another bite of potato salad and swallowed it. She resented his words like the devil. Who was he to be criticizing Freeman's citizens? Why, if he knew even a fraction of what she had learned about how at least two of them thought about modern issues. . . .

There went that furtive arm movement again, Millie thought when the image of a bounding dog crossed her peripheral vision. And now there was no chicken left on Clive's plate. She almost giggled. So the man did know good food. Somehow, she liked him a little better.

In a nicer tone, Millie said, "Not many men feel as you do. Almost all that I've known seem to want to bottle up women and dispense them in carefully prescribed dosages." There she went again, she scolded inwardly, ignoring her father's warning that men did not care to hear what a woman truly thought.

"I know," Clive agreed in a tone bordering on the patronizing. "And more's the pity." As had been the case almost the entire time they had been sitting out on the porch, his glasses were little circles of reflected light below his pink, rounded forehead.

Two tail-wagging dogs inched near where Millie and Clive sat on the edge of the porch then, their eyes fixed on the man who she suspected had been throwing them food surreptitiously all evening.

"Look," Clive said, the surprise in his nasal voice sounding forced. "There are some dogs around here. Poor fellows must be hungry. I think I'll throw them my biscuits." Like a warmed-up baseball pitcher stepping to the mound before a batter with two strikes gone, he aimed the soggy missiles out into the darkness and watched the animals chase after them.

Millie tossed back her head then and let out her repressed laughter in hearty peals. When she could sober enough to speak, she said, "You're most kind to reward the dogs in such grand style. Let's hope they're grateful."

Clive Durham studied the beautiful laughing face lifted to his in the light coming through the opened door, apparently as newly charmed by Millie as were most people when they first watched her smile or heard her laugh. "Would you think it too bold of me if I invited you to go riding with me tomorrow afternoon in my new Model-T, Miss Monroe? I could show you one of our mines, if you like." As if struck by a streak of inspiration, he added in a rush, "I could ask Widow Marks to fix us a picnic lunch."

Millie did not know what to say. She searched in her basket for the candy she had bought at the general store for dessert while her mind danced with all the possibilities. During the summer while she was getting herself together, she had decided that her life was complete without a man in it. As a companion, either for a short or a long duration, the easterner had not impressed her as being singularly interesting or attractive. He was a zero.

For one thing, Millie reflected, she suspected that Clive's words about his respect for free-thinking women were hollow and that his condescending manner and speech were far more accurate revelations of what he truly thought. Maybe if his glasses had not hidden his eyes all evening, she would have a better feel for what went on inside the man. As it was, what else could she tell Clive other than that she would not be going out with him in his new car—even to see a bauxite mine, which was, indeed, something she had hoped to do in the near future?

Just then heavy footsteps sounded on the porch, and Millie heard Wood's familiar bass voice as she laid two peppermint sticks on Clive's empty plate.

"Millie," Woods said jovially, squatting in that casual way of men when they're planning on staying in a spot for a brief time, one knee up, the other down, his body weight balanced against the back of a booted heel. "I hope Clive has

been treating you kindly, as I advised him to." He looked
over at her bespectacled companion, who seemed to have a
hearty appetite for peppermint. "We're plain tickled to have
Millie teaching here, Clive, and we try to make sure she gets
special treatment." Woods glanced at Millie then and
winked.

Millie felt flustered and far too warm. Woods should not
be winking at her like that! What if somebody saw and suspected the two of them might be interested in each other?
She kept thinking about how he was Annabelle's beau. Her
earlier suspicion that Woods might have urged Clive to buy
her basket surfaced. Now she heard from his own lips that
Woods had asked the easterner to pay attention to her, and it
burned her up. She did not like anyone to meddle in her
affairs. Had they been alone, she would have told him so.

If Annabelle and some others from inside the schoolroom
had not come through the open door then, Millie might have
found some kind of comment to make to the amiably smiling
Woods. There was no doubt that the black-haired man had
her upset, she thought while listening to Annabelle's greeting and then her introduction to the man who had been sitting near Woods and her inside.

"I'm pleased to meet you, Mr. Milstead," Millie said, her
outward composure flawless. So this was the man who had
been married to Annabelle's older sister, Fern. She was
grateful for the years of helping her father minister to his
congregation, for she had mastered the art of dissembling.
"Your sons Ransom and Steve"—she smiled at the boys
standing on either side of their father—"are both bright. I'm
expecting good things from them this year."

"I hope you'll let me know if they don't keep up with
their studies," Lucas Milstead responded soberly.

Millie noticed that Lucas was not as tall as Woods, who
had risen when Annabelle and the others came out onto the
porch. Unlike the more slightly built Clive Durham, Lucas
looked as trim as Woods and nearly as broad-shouldered.
Lucas wore a mustache, but it was a small, squared-up affair, not at all like the huge handlebar job on Woods's face.
What was wrong with her, Millie scolded whatever was

passing for her brain at the moment, to be comparing other men to Woods Sanders?

"Why, Lucas," Annabelle said teasingly, her blue eyes smiling up at her brother-in-law. "Are you afraid I'm not going to be a good aunt and see that my nephews do what their teacher wants them to do while they're living with Papa and me?"

Lucas gave a one-shouldered shrug and, in a pained tone, he said, "Surely you knew that I never meant my remark as criticism of you, Annabelle."

"Of course she knew that," Woods hastened to say. He turned to Millie and Clive, both standing now. "I hope your supper was as good as the one Annabelle fixed."

"It was fine eating," Clive replied with a courteous little bow toward Millie. "Miss Monroe is a prime cook. Yessir, a prime cook."

When Clive bowed and leaned his head down in her direction, Millie saw in the light coming through the open door that his blond hair was so thin that skin showed through on top. She did not have to look up to see how thickly Woods's black hair grew. In fact, she had a hard time pushing down the memory of the way the crisp hair at the back of his neck had felt when she had kissed him and put her hands there. Had Clive's remark about her being a fine cook brought that dancing sparkle to Woods's blue eyes?

Annabelle and Lucas pulled Clive into conversation then, and Millie had time to collect her thoughts.

Millie had no idea why standing in the presence of Annabelle and Woods together was making her so miserable, but she figured it had to do with her embarrassment over not knowing about Annabelle and him and with her letting her temper get stirred earlier when he did not buy her basket, back before she saw what was taking place. She had been wrong about many things, she realized. As in Little Rock, a simple friendship between a woman and a man in Freeman was impossible.

But Woods had been wrong about something, too, Millie reminded herself as her unsettling thoughts skipped on. She looked upon his apparent request for Clive to buy her basket and treat her kindly as meddling in her life. The idea set her teeth on edge. She knew that sooner or later she would have to tell him what she thought and warn him not to do so again.

Maybe, Millie thought with the partial brain ruling her at the moment, one way to show Woods that she handled her own affairs was to accept Clive's invitation. No doubt when Woods saw that Clive and she had struck it off right away, it would show him that Millie Monroe could handle her own affairs and did not need his help.

A wheel in Millie's brain squeaked and threatened to slip a cog with that final thought, but she slammed it on forward so as not to have to admit how it had hurt to learn that there truly was something going on between Annabelle and Woods. Seeing them together—she had never seen Annabelle so animated and bubbly—was not creating a climate for true logic in Millie. Had she known how to discern the cause of her misery, she would have labeled it plain old-fashioned jealousy.

"Yes, I'm staying over at the Widow Marks's place until Monday," Clive was saying in answer to Woods's question when Millie wrenched her thoughts back to what was happening on the schoolhouse porch.

Millie brushed at the loose curls in front of her ear and said, looking up at Clive all the while, "Mr. Durham has kindly invited me to take a ride with him tomorrow afternoon to visit a bauxite mine, and I've accepted." She shifted her gaze to Woods then and iced it over, along with her voice. "Thank you for advising him to be kind to me, Mr. Sanders."

Woods cleared his throat in that deep-voiced way that Millie had noticed upon first meeting him and stuck his hands in the pockets of his dark breeches. She looked up at him and gave him a measuring look. Where had the mischievous lights in his eyes gone?

The evening disintegrated from that moment on, or so it seemed to Millie. Some other people joined those already on the porch, and talk became general and sometimes spirited in the groups that soon separated Millie from Woods, and then from Clive.

"Yes, Mrs. Blackstone, I remember you from when you came with your children on the first day of school," Millie told Minnijean's mother. The woman had sidled up to introduce her husband, Barton, and to remind the schoolmarm of their earlier meeting. "The first days indicate that the year is off to a good start. Your daughter and son are doing very well. I appreciate the apples you sent with them yesterday."

Unaware that her eau de cologne radiated from her perspiring body with an overpowering jolt to Millie's acute sense of smell, Mrs. Blackstone simpered and fingered the pearl earrings nesting on her fat earlobes before she replied, "Now, there ain't no call to be persnickety with us, even if my husband does happen to be the foreman at the biggest mine around here. Everybody from hereabouts calls him Barton and me Thelmer, and we'd like you to do likewise."

Millie thought that if the short, square-built man beside Thelma Blackstone was even listening to his wife as she tried to put on airs, his stolid face made no show of it. Too aware that Woods and Annabelle still stood side by side in the little cluster of people nearby and that she was going to have to get used to seeing them together, Millie replied, "Thank you, Thelma. I'll remember that, and I'll ask both of you to address me as Millie if you choose."

"We moved from the holler last year when we built a new house in town—the purty one down toward the Gooseneck with the stained glass in the front door; you prob'bly noticed it when you'n Annabelle was walkin' yesterday afternoon—and we was figurin' on givin' you an invite soon to eat with us. Folks sez I'm a plumb good cook." Thelma smoothed her black taffeta skirt down over her ample belly and hips, then flicked at a food crumb clinging to her generous bosom. Her husband, Barton, still stood as though alone in a world of his own, gazing out into the darkness of the play yard.

"I'm sure you are a wonderful cook, and I'll be looking forward to visiting all four of you. To be honest, Thelma, I'm no kind of cook at all," Millie replied as the Blackstones' two children came from inside.

Within seconds, the youngsters had swept their parents along with them out into the yard. Millie knew that she should not have resented Thelma letting her know about having seen Annabelle and her take their walk on Friday, but she did. Getting used to living in such a small place was going to take awhile longer than she had anticipated, Millie reasoned, but she reassured herself that she could do it.

Millie happened to be peering into the classroom—it was far better than meeting the frequent puzzling looks coming from Woods's piercing blue eyes—when Mabel Marks and Henry Stevens left by the side door. Both had spoken to Millie individually before the bidding began, but she could not remember having seen them since.

Had the widow and the widower shared their supper? Millie had not paid enough attention to whose boxes and baskets were whose to recognize the pairing off of the few single people attending. She smiled at the thought of a romance between the older couple, but not for long. She was too busy trying to recall if Mabel's son, Warden, and the pretty Annette Bordeaux had been present for the social.

The hour was growing late. Everyone obviously had enjoyed the first social event at Freeman's new school and wanted to talk about it before parting. By the time Woods and Lucas and his two boys walked with Annabelle out into the night, the full moon sat a goodly piece above the mountain peaks.

Millie sank onto her bed when she reached it. Clive had insisted on walking with her to the door of the teacherage and seeing her safely inside before going on across the road to Widow Mark's place. He had been extremely courteous and proper.

Millie's conscience pricked her. She felt guilty because she was not looking forward to going riding with Clive tomorrow in his new auto. Never had she thought it right for a woman to take advantage of a man in social matters. She herself had had few dealings with men socially, what with her having been engaged to the usually absent Luther Osgood for—Good Lord! Had it been for nearly eight years?

Well, Millie comforted herself after giving in to a satisfy-

ing yawn in the moonlight peeking through her bedroom
window, maybe the outing would prove pleasant. Had she
not expressed a desire earlier to see a bauxite mine?

Yes, a suddenly honest Millie admitted to the demanding
inner voice before she drifted off to sleep, but she had
wanted the blue-eyed mountain man to be her escort.

· *Chapter Eight* ·

"What in blazes—!" Millie muttered groggily, fighting
against leaving her blessed state. How long had she been
asleep? One eye slitted open. Yes, it was still Saturday
night. Through the loosely woven feedsacks serving as curtains at her window, moonlight bathed her bedroom with
silvery reflections. What was the scraping noise coming
from the classroom? That must have been what awakened
her.

Millie sat up and reached for her green wrapper. Two
more muffled sounds came from the classroom before she
managed to get the wrapper tied around her middle. A dog
must have gotten closed up in the building after the box
supper was over, she decided when her brain could function
on an acceptable level. Having no need of a lamp in the
bright moonlight, she walked barefooted into the kitchen and
grabbed her broom to swoosh the dog on its way.

Not trying to be quiet, Millie stepped down the three steps
leading from her own door, her key to the classroom in one
hand and her broom in the other. When she touched the
doorknob on the door into the schoolroom, it turned in her
hand.

Cautiously Millie pushed the door open and peered inside,
wondering at the silence. "Puppy? Come on out, puppy."

Her words returned to her with that singular hollowness signifying that no other ears but her own had heard.

Had the dog, perhaps, jumped out of a window carelessly left open by whichever school board member had been in charge of closing up the classroom after the social?

Millie, wary but unafraid, padded on bare feet to check the moonlit openings along the sides of the long room, not totally reassured when she found that the windows were closed. Then what in thunder was the noise that had awakened her? she wondered. The only sound in the room was the soft whisper of her gown and wrapper billowing out around her ankles.

Suddenly, through one of the widows facing the church on the next lot, she glimpsed a human shadow approaching the side door. Millie sucked in a startled breath and clutched at the broom handle. Somebody had been in the classroom earlier and was on his way back inside at that very moment!

Millie dashed across the floor of rough boards, almost crying out when a splinter of wood pierced her big toe and slowed her pace. Positioning herself behind the door and experiencing a searing indignation that anyone would dare sneak into *her* classroom, she raised her broom in readiness to strike as soon as the intruder entered.

The door opened back with an eerie squeak toward where Millie crouched against the wall. Not waiting for the door to be closed before she attacked, she stepped forward and brought the broom down across the culprit's shoulders and back, demanding at almost the same instant, "Get out of my classroom! What do you think you're doing?"

"Millie! Whoa, damnit!" Woods croaked, all bent over from the surprise and the pain of the broom striking him smartly across the shoulders. With a reflexive arm movement, he had grabbed the broom as soon as it landed on him and yanked on it, pulling its wielder up close and encircling her slender arm with an iron grip. By then, from only inches away, Millie was staring up at Woods in horror, her contorted face showing clearly in the moonlight.

Woods burst out with undisguised anger, "I'd like to ask what in hell you think you're doing out of bed in your nightclothes and taking on anybody who might be prowling about at midnight?"

Millie swallowed convulsively, then echoed, "Midnight? Is it midnight?" She had not been afraid until she brought the broom down across the intruder's shoulders. Suddenly she realized what a foolish thing she was attempting, and her heart threatened to jump into her mouth. Having seen that the man was Woods, she could not figure out why her heartbeat did not return to its normal rate. Where his hand still clutched her arm, pain was shooting out in all directions. And the splinter in her big toe smarted like the dickens.

"What are you doing in here?" Woods demanded.

Millie tried to free her arm and loosen her hold on the broom handle, but she failed. She had not realized how big and strong Woods actually was. She felt trapped there behind the door and all out of breath.

"I asked you first, Woods Sanders." Was that shaky voice truly hers? What had she stumbled into? She craned her neck and darted searching looks all around to make sure he was alone, not convinced that finding nobody else present was a blessing. She dug deeply for courage. "Let go of my arm!"

Woods realized then that he still held Millie's arm and that the broom straws were prickling against his neck. She was so close that he could see what looked like fear in her eyes. Surely she wasn't afraid now that she had seen who had invaded the classroom. Despite her spirited struggles to disengage her arm, he still held it with ease.

No longer closed properly, Millie's green wrapper had parted and slipped to the sides of her breasts. Woods couldn't tear his gaze from the expanse of her heaving bosom showing above the loose, scooped neck of her thin nightgown. Was Millie perhaps a little afraid, now that her plan to punish a supposed thief had failed and she was the one entrapped? Maybe, Woods thought wryly when he caught a whiff of jasmine and felt a stinging warmth in his groin, he should teach her a lesson.

Only the ragged sounds of their breathing broke the silence of the midnight hour. Neither seemed able to unlock their gazes.

Who, Woods reflected with secret amusement, but a

sharp-tongued schoolmarm would be foolish enough to be out in the middle of the night trying to attack a prowler with nothing but a broom—and half-dressed, at that?

Woods doubted in that instant that any other woman could so cleverly conceal as many of her womanly charms underneath regular clothing as Millie Monroe. He had seen her exposed from the bottom end when she had fallen from the wagon, and now he was seeing the top end. Each was a revelation, and he doubted that he could ever forget either—and he didn't want to. Images of what must lie in between taunted him and fed the surge of heat in his groin.

"What if I don't care to let you go?" Woods asked softly, with unquestionable insinuation. Though he would have thought it impossible had he been asked, her dark eyes widened even more as she continued to struggle. He reached with his free hand and removed the broom handle from her grasp as if it was no more than a toothpick and tossed it aside.

Whop! The sound of the broom hitting the floor reverberated in the silence. Millie jerked her head farther back. The loud noise contributed to the little quiver deep inside her, the one that Woods's curiously furred voice had set into motion. What did he mean about not letting her go?

Again trying to twist her arm free, Millie tried shrinking farther away from the big man towering over her. Could he truly be Woods? Suddenly she recalled how menacing he had looked and sounded that morning—only six days ago? she agonized—back in Uncle Fred's living room and how, for a moment, he had reminded her of the outlaw on the wanted poster. She swallowed at the lump swelling in her throat. What did she really know about the man? Each time she was around him she had learned how different he was from anyone she had ever known. The realization that the schoolhouse sat too far back on the huge lot for anyone to hear if she screamed for help struck her with frightening potency.

"Let go of my arm!" Millie felt the rough boards dig into her back and shoulders as she backed against the wall. She heard her uneven breathing but did not recognize it. Her hasty movements had plunged the splinter deeper into her toe. She gasped, whether from the pain in her toe or from the cruel grip on her arm or from fear, she was not sure. All she knew for certain was that she never before had been in such a disastrous situation. When Woods continued to scowl down at her and make each step that she did, perceptibly reducing the distance between them until she felt his clothing, then his body touching hers, Millie snarled and brought up her free hand to slap his face. "You mountain monster—"

Woods laughed low in his throat and deftly caught Millie's hand, freeing her other arm and bringing his large body against her far slighter one. Mountain monster, was he? Though his prisoner moved her head violently and opened her mouth as if to revile him further, he leaned down with lightning swiftness and fiercely captured her parted lips with his own.

A million stars seemed to be exploding behind his eyes, Woods reflected with awe as he kissed her. He forgot all about his plan to frighten Millie and make her see that never again should she, single-handedly and with nothing but a broom, try besting a big man who might be intent on doing evil.

All the besotted Woods could think about was the wonderful feel of Millie's slender, warm body squirming there in his arms, unfettered this time by the stiff fabric of regular clothing. He barely noticed that her fists beat against his shoulders in protest. Through the softness of her green silk wrapper—no longer serving as a covering except across her shoulders and back—Woods could feel against his shirted front the stimulating firmness of her breasts through her filmy nightgown. Too, he could feel her gently curving hips and thighs moving in restless protest against him.

Suddenly Millie's body stilled. Her arms turned from stiff weapons hammering at Woods's chest into tendrils of beguiling softness creeping up around his neck and shoulders. Woods's hands caressed her back hungrily, then slid down the green silk covering to trace the marvelous feminine dip at her waist and hips with a gentleness only a man's big hands and fingers can manage when presented with such an exquisite discovery. It pained him to think she might be thinking of nothing but escape when all he could think about was. . . .

There behind the side door in the schoolroom, with the loving fingers of moonlight brushstroking in silver all around them and creating a tiny intimate world of midnight shadows, Woods's kiss eased from one of planned reprimand for a feisty schoolmarm into one of hungry quest for the most exciting woman he had ever met. An unbidden bass purring back in his throat begged Millie, along with his sometimes pressing and sometimes lightly retreating warm lips, to reward him with what he had not known he desired above all else.

Without Woods's conscious knowledge, the faint scents of jasmine and feminine satiny skin, which seemed an intrinsic part of the fascinating woman in his arms, wrapped themselves around his scarred thirty-five-year-old heart and turned it into that of a far younger man, a man pulsating with an unrecognized joy and hope that he had thought lost to him forever. His senses ruled and kept the transformation secret.

This time while Woods kissed Millie, his tongue did more than trace the shape of her bottom lip; it boldly searched past her now answering lips, on past her teeth and ravaged the virgin depths of her sweet mouth, at first with savage passion, then with tantalizing, rhythmic forays into the velvety little cavern that tasted to him the way she smelled.

Pure woman! Woods exulted, rocked to the soles of his feet. When Millie's tongue took up the delicious dance and returned thrust for thrust, Woods felt his racing heartbeat thud painfully against his ribs. More woman than he had realized, Woods thought as the fire between his legs blazed.

Millie had blamed the initial rushing of her pulse on fear. As soon as Woods's mouth on hers buried without ceremony her planned tirade at him for treating her so roughly, she recognized that fear had nothing at all to do with what was sending rivulets of flame rushing throughout her veins. The fiery rhythm of her pulse became a lovely, persistent humming.

Caught up in something alien but irresistible, Millie breathed in the male essence of the tall man holding her against his hard body and breathed out abandonment. The evening's discovery that Woods apparently was Annabelle's beau sailed out the open door. Who could think of anything right then but the moment?

The brush of Woods's mustache against her skin was as titillating to Millie as it had been during their first kiss. She savored the enervating taste of his mouth devouring hers. Glorying in the feel of his heavily muscled arms enveloping her, she wondered if she would ever forget the heady effect those singularly male qualities were wreaking on her composure. She hoped against hope that what she was smelling, tasting, and feeling at the moment would ever remain with her and reward her with sustenance. Her dancing heartbeat seemed a celebration of her every sense.

Life, the befuddled schoolmarm from Little Rock thought, had far more to offer than she had been led to believe before meeting Woods Sanders and coming to the hamlet of Freeman. The mountain man was teaching her lessons that she had not known to seek—and in a most exhilarating way.

Her breathing gone haywire, Millie had the driving urge to clasp Woods closer, as close as the wall had felt when she had slammed into it earlier and found that she had backed herself into a place of no escape. There was nowhere else that she wanted to go now but forward against that virile body. Her arms seemed an embodiment of that desire as they curled up around Woods's broad shoulders more tightly and staked a silent claim on the thick neck bending lower to accommodate the wet, mind-boggling kiss.

Never in her wildest dreams, not even on the night of their first kiss when her innocence had been mightily diminished had Millie Monroe imagined that being held and kissed as Woods was holding and kissing her at the moment could create such wanton but wonderful emotions. What she had felt during that first kiss had been merely an introduction, she thought with awe. The capture of her mouth by his seemed a welcome kind of madness, while stirrings down deep inside her womanhood were burning and threatening to explode into liquid flames.

The touch of Woods's big hands and fingers as they fondled her silk-clad back and hips so tenderly stoked Millie's inner fires. She stood on tiptoe in order to satisfy the longing to soak up more of the blue-eyed mountain man. Whenever had she felt so feminine or so greatful for being just that? If her locked-away passion had heard a knocking at the door during that first kiss from Woods, it now was out of the closet for good.

Alarmed by the new torrents flooding her and threatening to sweep her into a vast, tempting unknown, Millie, with a gigantic inner struggle, called back her sensibility. What was wrong with her, allowing herself to get lost in this man's arms—this man on whom Annabelle Stevens had first claim?

Tears welled up from Millie's naive, overflowing heart as she forced her unwilling arms to desert their newfound home around the mountain man's neck. Whether her tears came from her sudden realization that she had kissed her friend's beau or from her startling discovery that a possibly fathomless well of passion dwelled within and had sought to overwhelm her, Millie did not know. All she knew for certain was that she was miserable.

Woods felt Millie's withdrawal. His better self convinced his other self to free her. What had caused him to take advantage of the beautiful redhead as he had done on that first night? True, she was temptation in its most desirable form, but he should not have grabbed her and kissed her when she so plainly had tried to stop him.

Besides, Woods reminded himself when a throbbing part of him down low did not wish to embrace his somewhat noble declaration, he had been immune to the charms of women for a number of years now—except for casual physical pleasures now and then when he was in Hot Springs or other cities, of course. None of those encounters rated a ranking with what was tempting him at the moment. In fact, nothing had. Suddenly he felt a flash of nameless fear, as of something unknown, but threatening just the same.

Stepping back only enough to look down into Millie's upturned face, Woods drank in her beauty. The moonlight showed him her love-swollen lips, and he thought he might die from lack of breath if she did not look at him. Time stretched between them, marked only by irregular breathing and unspoken thoughts and the plaintive barks of two foxes from a faraway foothill. With wonder Woods noted that Millie's eyelashes were smudges of silken soot fanning down against her creamy skin. What was she thinking? Because his hands could not seem to stay away from her, he let his fingers touch her tousled red curls and then trace down her soft pretty cheeks.

"Millie," Woods said, breaking the silence with husky protest, "are these tears?" His fingers had not lied. Now he could see the teardrops beading her thick eyelashes like tiny crystalline balls displayed against a backdrop of black velvet. One tear was tracking a lonely path down beside her straight little nose. "Have I hurt you? All I meant to do was kiss you and maybe scare you a little bit so that you'd not dash out of your quarters again just because you heard a noise."

Millie wished that Woods would remove the finger tipping up her chin so that she could remain hidden behind her eyelids. She did not want him looking into her eyes. What if he could read therein what she was thinking, what his kiss and the feel of his body against hers had stirred up inside her? She ached and burned all over.

"Say something, Millie."

Millie, swallowing at the lump in her throat, asked as sharply as she could manage, "What are you doing sneaking around the schoolhouse at this ungodly hour?" She looked up at Woods then and was glad he was not suggesting that they leave yet. She doubted that she could walk since her knees were still wobbly. Though it was absurd, she wished that she had touched the cleft in his chin before she had come to her senses. The indentation drew her gaze; in the moonlight it was an intriguing shadow.

"I was returning the borrowed chairs to the church next door." Taking in a deep breath, Woods wondered when his pulse might settle back to normal. The ache in his groin plagued him like the devil. Obviously the kiss had not unseated Millie's usual calm, he reflected with a welcome levelheadedness. Come to think of it, he doubted that she allowed anything to ruffle her.

"What a stupid time to be returning chairs!" She wanted to talk about anything except what was going on inside.

"There's nothing stupid about it but that I made too much

noise and waked you. I thought it was smart to get it done before I went home, so I left Major tied in front of the store and walked—"

"Of course," Millie broke in. She needed no further reminder that Woods had escorted Annabelle home after the social and that they were a twosome. "I wouldn't have figured you to be leaving the Stevens place this early." When he cocked his head as if her words made no sense, she added, "What with the night being so pretty and all."

"Nobody over there put up any fight," Woods replied with a note of mocking laughter in his dark voice.

Millie wisely said nothing. A taste of salt—or was it gall?—seeped into one side her mouth. She wiped at a remaining tear hugging a corner of her lips. "I guess I made a fool out of myself by rushing over here with my broom." *And an even greater fool when you melted in his arms like a hussy,* a telling inner voice reminded her. Colossal fool, she corrected the voice with cold candor. It's the second time. The douse of icy honesty was slowing her heartbeat and smothering the delicious inner humming.

"Not a fool, Millie. You could never be called that." He realized that they still stood within inches of each other, but he hated the idea of moving away from her. "I think I should lock up now—that's what I was coming back to do when you attacked—and see you safely inside." When she made no comment, he asked with a slow smile, a note of secret longing in his voice deepening it, "Do you have a better idea?"

"Certainly not," Millie retorted, embarrassed at his apparent reference to their impassioned kiss. The moonlight seemed to be adding mystery to his resonant voice and his incredibly blue eyes. She lifted her chin and looked away from his delving gaze.

"What were you crying about?" Woods asked. Maybe she had been as moved by their kiss as he, after all. The surprising little spark of hope kindled such a few minutes ago still lingered, in spite of his attempt to extinguish it and pretend that it didn't even have a name.

Ignoring his question—how could she give him an answer when she did not have one even for herself?—Millie

took a step toward the open door. The splinter, forgotten
until then, stuck even deeper into her big toe, and she grimaced. "Ouch!"

"What's wrong?"

"It's my big toe. I stuck a splinter in it when I was rushing
across the room to get behind the door."

"Is that why you were crying?"

"Yes." Millie welcomed his offering her an excuse for the
tears. She would have died rather than have him know what
really brought them. Crying never had been her style, and
she was still aghast that she had done so. It bothered her,
too, that she had not recognized the woman clinging mind-
lessly to Woods and returning his kiss with such abandon.

Woods scoffed at himself for imagining that Millie's tears
had spilled over as a result of their scorching kiss. "Let me
see if I can get that skoker out of your toe. Come over to the
door so I can see."

Millie hobbled along, grateful to Woods for offering his
arm. Once in the doorway she obediently lifted her bare foot
when Woods squatted down and motioned for her to rest it
on his knee. Her gown and robe flowed against his body, the
whispering sibilant sounds much like those made when he
had grabbed her and kissed her. Though both reacted on the
inside to that new touching of hands, foot, knee, and clothing, neither displayed any outward sign. The moonlight was
bright, but it was not bright enough for either of them to
grasp the sliver of wood and remove it.

"Millie, I'll have to have better light to get it out."

"I can light my lamp and get it out myself. You really
should be going now. It's late."

"My mama's not likely to be waiting up for me. Don't
forget that I've been a grown man for a long time."

Woods was standing beside her then, and Millie looked up
at him drolly. His deep voice had been heavy with irony.
Why did he have to be so damned likable . . . and handsome?
She smiled. "I could have figured that one out for myself."

"Guess you could, at that." He could not take his eyes off
her beautiful face, not that he wanted to, Woods realized.
With the moonlight brushing across her daintily featured
oval face like that and turning her curls into silvery auburn,

he could not think of a more beautiful sight in the whole United States than Millie Monroe. And he had done a fair amount of traveling in his time.

Woods no longer pretended that he had kissed Millie to scare her or show her anything. Hell! He had kissed her because he wanted to. Now he was torn between wanting to apologize for forcing her into kissing him against her will and wanting to let her know that the kiss had meant far more to him than a casual encounter.

Instead he chose to joke about it. Long ago Woods had found that laughing about things—anything—helped cover up a mountain of seriousness that could lead to despair if allowed to hog the limelight and grow. "I'm pretty good at scaring women and kissing them, wouldn't you say?"

Millie stared up at Woods, not believing his audacity in putting their soul-searing kiss away as something casual, something to be joked about. She was not so naive as to have missed the unmistakable signs that he, too, had become caught up in whatever had come over them.

Maybe Woods, not bound by the confines of Little Rock's society as she had been for most of her life, did not view their kiss as an act of disloyalty to Annabelle, Millie mused while they stood gazing at each other. And maybe, also unlike her, he was accustomed to dealing with passion as an ordinary part of life. For sure he was different. Like a mountain man, suggested the part of her that liked to hang tags on people and things.

Riveting Millie's attention then was her memory of the kiss. Would she ever be able to forget it as the most thrilling experience of her life? Even as her mind strove frantically for a better way to handle the situation, Millie admitted defeat and lowered her gaze. She had already learned that she did not know herself anymore since coming to Freeman. Why not follow Woods's lead? She was back to uncharted territory, and, as when she first saw the teacherage, she tried out the old line: When in Rome. . . .

Able to look at Woods again, who had stood as still as she during their moment of silence there in the moonlight, Millie said in a voice as teasing as his had been, "I think you've shown that you're well-schooled in those fields, yes."

"You rate pretty good in kissing yourself—and you're a demon with a broom." Woods prided himself that he could talk about their searing moments of passion with such a light tone. He wondered if he might not be falling a little in love with Millie, so much did he admire her tactfulness in helping him ease over what could have been an insurmountable barrier between them over the remaining months of the school year.

Woods turned with Millie toward the teacherage. The thought of falling in love again scared the hell out of him, and he trampled it with vigor. As he had decided that day when she fell out of the wagon and had come up laughing, he thought again that Millie Monroe was one of a kind—in or out of his arms. If he was half as smart as he figured he was and if he liked his present life as much as he thought he did, he would be wise to keep Millie out of his arms in the future. Maybe they truly could be friends. He could not deny that he liked talking with her and being around her. And he liked looking at her, too.

Woods broke the silence then. "Just think how much better you're going to be at kissing when you reach thirty-five, like me." Soon he was holding open the door to the teacherage, and she went in before him, hobbling to protect the injured toe.

"You're incorrigible," Millie said over her shoulder.

"What in hell does that mean?"

"Impossible."

"Nice word. Incorrigible. I'll hang on to it."

While Millie readjusted her wrapper and smoothed her tangled hair, Woods found matches and lit the lamp sitting on the table. Shortly he had removed the splinter and, after dousing the wound with stinging kerosene over her horrified protests and yelps of pain, tied a strip of clean flour sack around her big toe. Instead of leaving, Woods sat down at the table on the chair next to Millie.

"Tonight's social was quite a success, wasn't it?" Millie asked, thinking about the box supper and the little pile of money that Aaron Booth had collected for the library fund.

"Yep." Woods paused. "Especially for Clive Durham . . . and maybe for you."

"Whatever do you mean?" Millie's earlier anger at him for shoving the pompous Clive Durham on her returned. She found that it was a far more welcome emotion than the one with which she had been battling earlier. "I don't like people interfering in my life, and you had no right to decide who was going to eat with me."

"Whoa, there! I didn't sic old Clive on you; he was the one doing all the questioning when he came in and saw you sitting down front. You must have heard me bidding. I wasn't the one deciding who bought your box. Maybe I didn't have enough money to go up against a big company man like Clive." Woods heard the sharpness of his final words and shrugged. So what the hell if Millie learned that he had no use for Clive Durham?

Millie puzzled. "But you were waiting to bid on Annabelle's box and just upping the price to make Clive pay too much, weren't you?" She was not sure that she believed Woods when he said he had not urged Clive to buy her box. He was joking, she thought, making light of his relationship with Annabelle and the whole evening.

"What difference does it make now?" Woods went on, interrupting her thoughts. "A city woman like you probably deserves to meet somebody other than the hill folk from around here. Clive and you might have a lot in common."

"You're wrong there."

"But you said you're going riding with him tomorrow in his auto. That's a sure sign of a man sparking a woman, isn't it?"

"Sparking?"

"You know," Woods explained, turning a hand up in midair in emphasis. "Courting. We say 'sparking' for 'courting.' You *are* unmarried and—"

"And I am not expecting to change that status."

"Do you mean to tell me you're not interested in being sparked by a man and getting married some day?"

"I most certainly am not interested in men . . . that way. I have a good life and have no need of a husband."

Woods stared at her blankly in the circle of lamplight. One hand fingered his mustache. Millie was the most beautiful, desirable woman he had ever met. His lips pursed. Her brown eyes had appeared to be glossed over with some kind of hidden emotion ever since their encounter in the schoolroom. "You're the damnedest woman I ever met."

Because Woods seemed to be staring at her hair, Millie's hands went to her cap of curls and her fingers traced through the short strands of red. She could feel his blue eyes following each movement and dropped her hands to her lap. "I guess you're saying that because I cut my hair."

Woods threw back his head and laughed as if at a huge joke. "That's the least of it." He leaned closer, his heavy eyebrows no longer arching upward in amusement. "Why, Millie, you're too beautiful and too much of a woman to live the rest of your life by yourself. You need to find yourself a man and have those five children you said you wanted."

"There you go," Millie accused, "thinking you know more about what I need than I do myself. I don't need a man to think for me, thank you, Woods Sanders. Maybe Annabelle likes—"

"Annabelle has no place in this conversation," Woods was quick to say in a firm tone. When her face flushed and she seemed about to protest, he added in a softer way, "I don't mean to be meddling in your life, now or before. I guess your harebrained thoughts about marriage surprised me."

"They are not harebrained," Millie declared with a lift of her chin. "I didn't reach my conclusions without a lot of thinking." She thought briefly of the past months when thoughts of her future had filled her brain and knew that she spoke what she believed was gospel truth.

"I can believe that."

Millie watched Woods's mouth turn into a smile suggesting indulgence for one demented, and she moved restlessly on her chair. She chided herself for having fallen again into the comfortable trap of telling him exactly what was on her mind, as if they might truly share the friendship he had offered that day beside the river. Had she not already learned earlier that night that his life was entwined in some way with Annabelle's? There was little hope that she could be good friends with both of them, not in the way she would have liked and certainly not in the way she had believed possible that day down beside the Gooseneck.

And, Millie went on doggedly, had Woods not told her that his grabbing her and kissing her breathless had merely been his way of scaring her into staying in the teacherage where she belonged? She guessed that might be the reason he could have kissed her senseless and not feel he was betraying Annabelle. The crux of the matter seemed to be that she did not understand Woods Sanders a great deal better than she understood herself. "I hardly think this is a suitable topic for the board chairman and the teacher to be discussing so late at night. You really should be going now."

"I don't want to be accused again of interfering, Millie, but I doubt Clive Durham is the type of man you might enjoy knowing."

"What difference does that make? I'm merely taking a ride with him. And you know now that I'm not looking for a man to marry."

"It seems to me," Woods said after a thoughtful silence, "that, considering the way the world operates, every woman ought to be looking for the *right* man and—"

"Woods Sanders," Millie interrupted angrily, "you might not know everything. I'm disappointed in you." *But mostly in myself.* Of course Woods would think that her declarations were false, she reflected, especially after the way she had fallen all over him out there in the classroom only a short while ago. Her face felt too hot. He was trying to make her look like an empty-headed fool . . . and she did not need any help. With a sigh for all that had gone wrong that evening, Millie rose haughtily, but was humbled by the pain shooting up from her big toe. She had to discard the notion of marching to the door and holding it open for him. "I'm ready for you to leave."

"I guess I have overstayed my welcome. Good night." Woods was furious that Millie had refused to let him finish his last statement: ". . . and every man ought to be looking for the *right* woman." It might be no more than a general statement that he had heard somewhere—and it no longer applied to him since he had found the right woman and lost her—but it seemed to fit in at the time. There was no call for her to be so snippy and butt in. Did she think *she* knew everything?

Without further ado, Woods stalked across the room and left after a mighty slamming of the door. Great balls of fire! When Millie Monroe got a crazy notion in her head, it seemed to be there for good, he thought as he heard her turn the key in the lock with what sounded like more force than necessary. How had she come up with the ridiculous idea that she didn't need a man? And she had dared label *him* with that fancy word, "incorrigible!"

Well, Woods mused irritably all the way to where Major waited at the hitching rail in front of Henry Stevens's store, it was a damned good thing that he had become immune to women. That was a fool notion back there when he had wondered briefly if he might not be falling a little in love with Millie. Their kiss must have shaken him up even more than he realized, but he was back in control now.

Right off Woods made up his mind that he was not going to give the beautiful woman from Little Rock another thought. She was different; let her stay that way. He glanced overhead, angered anew because the man in the moon seemed to have a smirk on his face.

Before he remembered that he was wearing his best boots, the frustrated Woods kicked at a big rock in his path with a gleaming leather toe. Maybe it was a good thing that he had not more than two dollars with him and had had to drop out of the bidding for Millie's supper basket. Millie Monroe and Clive Durham probably deserved each other.

· *Chapter Nine* ·

"This is a deplorable situation, Miss Monroe," Clive Durham said in his nasal fashion the next afternoon. "I had no idea that a recent rain had made the creek so deep across the road here, you see." He looked at the muddy water swirling around the fenders of his new but stalled Model-T. "I should have returned to Freeman by the road that we came on—er, the road on which we came, that is."

"How far are we from Freeman?" Millie asked, ignoring Clive's annoying practice of upgrading his perfectly acceptable grammar for her benefit. Had she not told him at least three times that she was a teacher only when she was in the classroom? Once she had tried to joke with him by asking if she had a sign pasted on her forehead reading, "Schoolmarm." Up until then she had hoped that she was wrong in assuming the polite but dully serious easterner had no sense of humor. His blank stare at the time had killed all hope.

Not without effort, Millie concealed her dismay at having to prolong the outing with Clive. She leaned from underneath the roof of the car and looked up through the trees, judging it was nearly mid-afternoon.

"It's my guess," Clive said peevishly after letting out a sigh, "that Freeman must be four or five miles away."

"Maybe someone lives nearby who can help us," Millie offered. Clive appeared so upset that she was almost tempted to reach over and pat his hands and say, as she would to one of her pupils, "There. There. Everything will be all right." Instead, she clutched her hat to her bosom, relieved that she had caught it when the car jolted to an abrupt silence in the rock-bedded stream and sent the wide-brimmed hat tumbling from its precarious perch on her short hair. She had had to catch it or hold on to it during the afternoon's windy ride to the bauxite mine and again on the way back.

Other than the mild, sunny weather, Millie reflected, nothing had gone right, and there seemed little chance of a reversal. The vistas of the colorful valleys and foothills emerging into mountains in the distance had been breathtaking, but now her view centered on the singing creek guarded by legions of trees wearing fall colors. She saw that Clive's pink face was deepening into an even more unbecoming red as he surveyed his pride and joy with visible anguish. Clearly he was in love with the shiny black machine.

Tearing his pained gaze from the dampness now staining the floorboard of his Model-T, Clive pushed his gold-

rimmed glasses up on his nose and peered around the heavily
forested area. "I believe that Woods Sander's place is on up
this creek. We must have passed the road leading into it back
a mile or so. Not that any of these trails through the hills and
hollows can truly be called roads, you see."

"Isn't there someone else you can ask for help—maybe
someone closer by?"

Millie veered from the idea of meeting up with Woods that
day. Not only was she still disturbed over last night's soul-
wracking kiss and the mountain man's abrupt departure, but
also she had a new reason for being upset with him.

Within the past hour Millie had learned that the Southern
Bauxite Mine, Sanders #1, the mine Clive had shown her
and had described as the biggest and richest in the area, sat
on land belonging to none other than Woods Sanders. Obviously Woods held some kind of interest in the mine being
operated by the company from Buffalo. When she had questioned Woods on the way from Elmwood that day—and she
recalled that she had used the utmost tact—why had he not
told her that his position at the mine was that of overseer and
that the mine sat on his property? Self-righteously Millie
reminded herself how much she despised deception. With
the shortsightedness she was wont to call up at any moment,
she ignored the way she had signed her contract, deliberately
leading people to believe Ezekial M. Monroe was a man.

Clive let out a woeful sigh and smoothed at the thin
strands of blond hair on the top of his head. "The only thing
for us to do is follow the creek through the woods to the
Sanders place. I can't imagine why anyone—even these
hillbillies—like being so far back in the hills." He leaned
over and looked at the water. "The mud has cleared now,
and we can see where to step when we get out." Turning
back to his perturbed companion, he said, "If you'll permit
me, Miss Monroe, I'll carry you to the bank so that you'll
not get wet. It wouldn't be safe for me to leave you here
alone, you see."

"Botheration, Mr. Durham," Millie muttered. Would she
be able to hear "you see" one more time without screaming?
She deplored the notion of being held in the man's arms for
any reason; actually, her thoughts ran on, Clive was not

much larger than she was, and she doubted his ability to
carry her through the swift creek with its bed of head-size
rocks.

For a moment Millie considered staying in the car until
Clive returned with help, but the vivid memory of having
seen a wildcat back down the road a way killed the thought
aborning. "I can manage quite well on my own, thank you.
The water doesn't look more than three feet deep." Not having missed the way Clive had sneaked looks at her ankles
during the afternoon's ride when he thought she wasn't
looking, she added, "That is, if you'll turn your back so I
can lift my skirt while I wade."

They got the matter settled, and Clive, his round face still
flushed, left the car first and waited on the bank with his
back toward Millie. She gathered up her skirt and petticoat
and splashed after him, almost crying out when the icy water
swirled around her feet and legs. Her bandaged big toe set
up an instant protest when the water soaked into her shoe,
but she merely grimaced and set out with Clive through the
forest of hardwoods mixed with a few cedars.

"Why, the place is charming," Millie exclaimed when
they rounded a huge bend in the creek and sighted what
Clive told her was the Sanders place. It sat upon a rise some
twenty feet above the racing water. Directly across from the
house, a steep mountain ridge reared straight up in tree-
covered splendor. A rash of excited barking from some dogs
penned up a goodly distance behind the house announced the
arrival of visitors. "The house seems to be a natural part of
its surroundings, with its logs and shaked roof and stone
chimneys."

Then Millie saw two women sitting on the wide porch
running the entire width of the large house. Stretching down
the middle of the house, and measuring some ten feet in
width, was an open hallway, the peculiar Southern structural
device called a dogtrot and used to connect two parts of a
house. Farther back underneath the numerous trees sat a
barn and several other outbuildings, all made of weathered
gray logs.

Millie figured that the clearing visible down the ridge

must be a garden, for a split-rail fence zigzagged around it. Big oaks, elms, and cottonwoods nearly hid the house until Clive and she were almost directly in front of it. Off to one side of the porch, a child's swing hung from a low limb of an oak. Now that they were approaching a rock-edged path curving upward from the creek, Millie sensed a warm ambience bathing the peaceful scene.

"Why anyone with so much bauxite on his land chooses to stay buried in this godforsaken place amazes me," Clive remarked under his breath with what sounded like a sneer to Millie. While she was gazing around with appreciation, he had paused beside her on the creek's bank of rocks. "Some folks—and this goes for all these hillbillies in the Ouachita Mountains with mines—don't know what to do with good fortune when it slaps them in the face, you see. Why, if I had control of this land. . . ."

"You'd do what, Mr. Durham?" Millie asked when his voice got lost in the song of the clear water rushing over its rocky bed. For one of the few times since she had met Clive the night before, she could see his eyes clearly through his lenses. They were a pale almost colorless gray. For a moment she had suspected that a flash of something was lending them fire; but even as she looked, it faded and led her to wonder if she had imagined it. They seemed cold and veiled now.

"Never mind," he said. "We've been spotted."

"What a lovely surprise to have company this Sunday afternoon, even if a rising creek is the reason," Glovina Ridgely said when the rather bedraggled couple appeared at the porch of the Sanders' home and explained their tacky situation. After inviting Millie and Clive to be seated on wide, comfortable rockers there on the porch and offering them coffee, she turned to the gray-haired woman sitting in a large porch swing. "Agatha, you'll recall that Woods was telling us about the new schoolmarm in Freeman, and now we're getting to meet his Miss Monroe. Mr. Durham has been to call on us several times before."

Millie saw then that a large dog lay underneath the swing,

its pointed ears and black eyes alert now that attention had become directed to Agatha Sanders.

"Easy, Shep," Agatha said lowly. "Friends." She smiled and kept her face and fixed blue eyes turned toward the newcomers. "Yes," she replied in a voice both rich and warm, "I recall your voice and your visits, Mr. Durham. I might not be able to see in the way most folks see, Miss Monroe, but I can tell that you're every bit as pretty and nice as my Woods told us."

"You're both very kind," Millie said as she shifted the foot with the aching toe to a more comfortable position. Though Glovina had swept her cropped hair with a curious look, she had made no comment, for which Millie was grateful. She was relieved that the reclining dog seemed content to drop its head back on its front paws and watch from underneath the porch swing. It occurred to her that the animal must serve the blind woman as eyes.

"I have a pot of coffee on the stove," Glovina said, rising and moving down the open hallway. "I'll bring some for all of us while we wait for Woods. I know he'll be happy to help you out."

Meeting Woods's mother and her widowed sister, whom he had told Millie about that first day, might have been more pleasurable under different circumstances, Millie mused while Glovina fetched coffee for the four of them, but she could not remember when she had felt such physical discomfort. Not only was her toe throbbing, but also her feet hurt from the mile-long walk in wet shoes, and she suspected blisters had popped up on her heels. The sight of two rosebushes growing on either side of the porch steps reminded her that brambles from undergrowth had snatched at her skirt and torn it while Clive and she had walked through the forest along the creek bank.

Where was Woods? Millie wondered while talk flowed easily on the porch. Obviously his aged, blind mother and his middle-aged aunt weren't going to be able to help Clive get his car out of the creek and cranked up again for the trip back to Freeman.

The four of them had not finished their coffee before two huge hound dogs, white with liver-colored spots, bounded from upstream and leapt toward the porch with deep baying barks. Millie held up her coffee cup for safety and shrank against the cowhide forming the back and seat of the rocker when the dogs, after pausing and fixing Clive with yellow-eyed looks, selected her to sniff and rear up on. From his resting spot beneath where Agatha sat in the swing, Shep, though wide awake, appeared oblivious to the newcomers.

"Nice doggies," Millie managed shakily when both Glovina's and Agatha's soft-voiced reprimands went begging.

"Jake! Maud!" Woods yelled from where he was clambering up the bank from upstream. Emitting a shrill whistle, he cradled the rifle he carried and clapped his hands together smartly. "Get to the backyard where you belong."

When the hounds raced down the open hallway as commanded and disappeared, Woods kept moving toward the porch, his eyes and face showing his puzzlement at finding Millie and Clive sitting on the front porch of his home and drinking coffee with his mother and his aunt.

Both Glovina and Agatha began filling Woods in on their unexpected guests as soon as he came within earshot. Slipping in quiet greetings to Millie and Clive and laying down his rifle and game sack on the porch, he took off his old hat and flopped down on the edge of the porch, then leaned back against a smooth log pillar. He was careful to keep clear of the leggy rosebushes growing beside the steps. Throughout Glovina's and his mother's little recital, Woods watched the frozen-faced Millie at every opportunity. Then Glovina hurried away to bring him a cup of coffee, and it was Clive's turn. Woods forced his attention to the mining company's regional manager and what he was relating.

"Sure thing," Woods told Clive when the clipped voice stilled. "I'll hitch up my mules and pull the car out of the creek. I won't be much help if the motor doesn't crank right off. I don't know much about cars."

"I appreciate your kindness," Clive said. "I planned to get Miss Monroe back to Freeman before dark, you see." He glanced at Millie sitting in the rocker beside his and frowned, as if he might be wondering why she was acting stiff and edgy now that Woods had appeared. "Why a man who owns as much land as you do—and with the richest mine on it—doesn't buy himself a car is quite beyond my reasoning."

"I'm not surprised to hear you say that, Clive," Woods rejoined with asperity. "You always have seemed to think property and money are the same thing."

Millie nervously fingered the Irish lace edging the cuffs of her long-sleeved waist, then rechecked the clasp on the cameo at her neck, thinking that some kind of unpleasant tension lay between the two men and that it had nothing to do with cars or mules. Clive was looking smug.

After handing her nephew his cup of coffee and fixing him with a scolding look, Glovina took over the talk then. Woods winked at Glovina and sat back. His fondness for her showing on his face, he thought of how his aunt was usually careful to include everyone in her conversations and make all join in—and, though Woods forgave her the small short-coming, Glovina sometimes put in more than her portion and just as often shared tidbits that should have been kept private.

Woods let the talk wash over him; he was having a good time just looking at Millie and wondering what she was thinking about his family and their home on the low ridge above Iron Creek.

It was plain to Woods after he tried unsuccessfully a time or two to get in a friendly remark to Millie that she was still swelled up over whatever had gotten her crossways with the world last night. Her comments to everyone else came out nice and normal but when she had to address him, she sounded to him as if she had a mouth full of briars. Had her toe gotten infected, maybe, and was it paining her and making her irritable?

As for himself, Woods thought wryly upon remembering last night's bizarre happenings, he had awakened with a sore shoulder from the thwack of Millie's broom handle. He gave up trying to talk with her or anybody else and concentrated on his coffee. Was he imagining it, or had Millie begun spending more time looking at Clive, all dressed up in his suit and neck scarf like a dandy, and returning his smiles and flirty looks?

Steering clear of the rosebushes, Woods stepped down

from the porch and stretched, then repositioned his hat on his head at a rakish angle. Maybe Millie had already changed her mind about not wanting a man to spark her. He doubted that anything the woman from Little Rock could do would surprise him any longer.

"I'll be on with the team by way of the road if you two want to start on back to where the car is," Woods said. "It's a sight closer through the woods, the way you came. The sun will dip behind the hills before long."

Millie deigned to look fully at Woods then. If he was willing to let bygones be bygones, then so could she. "If you're going around the road in the wagon, perhaps we could ride with you."

"I was planning to ride Caesar, one of the mules. Taking the wagon would be slower because it's piled high with firewood from the week's cutting, and it would take a spell to unload. The walk through the woods wasn't so bad, was it?"

Unconsciously Millie glanced down at her foot with the sore toe as she lied, "No, it was all right."

Woods saw the look, though, and guessed what her problem likely was. "I could saddle Major if you'd rather ride. I've even got an old sidesaddle in the barn that I won in a poker game." He laughed before he made the next remark. "I can't picture you riding Caesar or Cleopatra, even on a sidesaddle."

"Walking beside the creek will do fine, thank you." Easily remembering the hugeness of the two mules, Millie blushed at the ridiculous picture Woods had suggested and watched him disappear around the corner of the porch in the direction of the barn, his tall lean body moving easily. In spite of her earlier jumbled thoughts, she found herself thinking how she liked being around a man with a sense of humor.

Now that Woods was gone, Millie wished she had not allowed her indignation over his not having told her anything about the bauxite mine belonging to him and his family to lead her into being standoffish with him. It was none of her business what the chairman of the school board did or what he owned or whom he chose to squire about to social events.

Millie locked away her thoughts then and made her heartfelt speeches of thanks and farewells to Agatha and Glovina. When they pressed her, she agreed to return for another visit soon.

"Wait up, there!" Woods called when Millie and Clive started down the path to the creek. "I've got the sidesaddle on Major, and Clive can ride Cleopatra. Come on. We need to get started."

"I'm not much of a horseman," Clive said, eyeing the big mules standing at the corner of the house beside Woods, their harness and back bands serving as the only covering on their backs. "I prefer to walk, thank you." He turned to Millie. "Which do you prefer, Miss Monroe? I noticed how you were limping by the time we got here. If you prefer—"

"Yes," Millie replied, her throbbing toe and smarting heels urging her onward. "I think I'll ride the horse, Mr. Durham." During her youth, she had ridden horses while visiting friends in and around Little Rock. Millie was unsure that such limited experience qualified her as an equestrienne, but she called up to Woods, "I believe I'll ride Major."

Leaving Clive to walk on back beside the creek, Millie retraced her steps, half limping up the steep incline to where Woods and the animals waited. She was glad that Glovina and Agatha were still on the porch while Woods helped her get settled onto the worn sidesaddle. Neither Woods nor Millie dared look at the other during the necessarily close encounter. With a false cheeriness, Millie waved farewell again to the women and let Major follow behind Woods and the mules.

For a goodly spell, the strange procession traveled without sounds other than those of the squeaks of leather, the jangling of harness and chains, and the steady rhythm of hooves upon the narrow, rocky path through the forest. Every so often, Woods turned his head and checked to see if Millie and Major were still following the fast-stepping mules.

Woods had suspected from the beginning, when Millie had settled herself gingerly upon the broad saddle and tried to get her rather narrow skirt adjusted to cover most of her legs, that she was more than a little afraid of riding. Figuring that her toe must really be aching for her to accept his offer to ride Major, he at first had decided that she was getting no more than she was due. Streaking around in the schoolhouse at midnight with her nightclothes on like that, he reflected, she probably deserved more than a splinter in her toe. Each time he had looked back, though, the way her eyes seemed stretched open so wide in her unnaturally pale face, as if they had forgotten how to blink, nagged at him.

When they turned onto a wider road and there was room for the three animals to travel side by side, Woods looked back at Millie and asked, "Why don't you ride up beside me now? We'll be at the creek soon. Give Major some slack and lean forward a little."

Millie nodded her understanding, surprised when the handsome horse with the white front stockings responded to her loosening of the reins and her small forward movement.

"You're not doing bad, Millie," Woods said after the horse adjusted its pace to that of the mules. "Relax and enjoy the ride. Is your toe still aching?"

"How do you know it's bothering me?"

"I heard what Clive said about your limping, and I remember that was a mighty big splinter I took out of it."

Millie digested both his words and his tone. How could Woods sound so nice and concerned about her welfare when she had been cross with him last night and again this afternoon on the porch? She had questions of her own: "What about your neck and shoulders today? Did I hurt you with the broom?"

Woods chuckled. "I'm a little banged up and stiff in one shoulder, but it's nothing serious." He tipped back his old black hat so as to see her better. Damned if she didn't seem to get prettier each time he was around her. The sun already had ducked behind the hills, and soft shade bathed everything with shadow. He admired the way her short curls seemed like a silken patch of deep red against the backdrop of hardwood trees wearing their autumn shades of yellows, reds, and browns.

"I'm not sure I ever apologized for last night's . . . mishap," Millie said. "I'm terribly sorry."

"No need to apologize. We both learned a lot last night, didn't we?"

Millie darted a look Woods's way. From his sideways,

slouched perch upon the broad back of the mule, one long leg hanging down, the other hooked at the knee across the animal's huge padded collar and resting there, she assumed that Woods had spent many hours riding as he was doing.

Millie eyed the collar around the mule's neck, noticing, as she had during their ride in the wagon on their way to Freeman, that little rings on short curved horns of metal atop it held the twin leather lines connected to both bridles. The lengthy lines from the harness of both Caesar and Cleopatra lay looped several times over Woods's forearm. Easily he held the leather ends bunched up in one hand.

Dangling by one of its large end rings from those same horns on top of the collar was a tapering piece of wood looking to be about the size of a baseball bat. The contraption rattled with each step the mule took. Millie wondered if it might not be what she had heard called a whiffletree, used to equalize the load being pulled by animals. She remembered having seen one of the wooden devices hooked behind each mule during the wagon ride from Elmwood. Something about seeing the muscular, handsome man so easily in control of the powerful animals pleased her and made her feel secure.

Millie's thoughts zipped back to Woods's statement. Was he referring to their unsettling kiss as something both had learned? She sent him an inquiring gaze, exasperated when the cleft in his chin seemed as fascinating as ever. She could not detect an outward sign of teasing, but her instinct told her that his remark held a double meaning. A warmth crept up and claimed her face. Never could he know how much she had learned—about kissing.

"Yes," she admitted, "I suppose we did learn a lot."

"In spite of our little, uh, misunderstanding, Millie, I realize that Freeman is lucky to have you in the classroom. We have a lot to get done this year—me as board chairman and you as teacher—and I want to be your friend. Maybe I was wrong to put down your beliefs last night, and I'm sorry that I got you riled." Was she really as surprised at his apology as she looked? Woods wondered.

"Thank you." She wasn't sure that he had offered a true apology, but—She *had* been overwrought and maybe sounding as if she were censuring all men. "I like it when people respect others' beliefs, even if they might not understand or agree."

Woods decided he wouldn't touch that statement with a ten-foot pole. He had gained ground, and he intended to keep it. "Have you enjoyed riding with Clive this afternoon and seeing more of our mountains?"

"The mountains are spectacular, but I suspect they're especially so at this time of year." Millie doubted that total honesty was called for. There was no need to make disparaging remarks about her escort of the afternoon. No matter what silly reason had moved her to accept Clive's invitation, she had made the choice.

Woods couldn't figure out why Millie had gotten stiff with him again unless it had something to do with Clive Durham. Hellfire! he reflected against his better judgment, maybe Clive wasn't as bad a sort as he had been figuring ever since the man arrived three years ago. Woods found his mind stumbling on the thought that maybe women liked the easterner. He sneaked a glance at Millie, finding the thought even more distasteful as he saw again how beautiful she was.

They traveled up the last hill that stood between them and the Iron Creek crossing where Clive's car was foundered. Woods pursed his lips then shifted his hat around before getting it set right. "Like I said, Millie, we've got a job to do together, and I'd like to think we're friends."

"So would I." She tried to bring up the subject of Annabelle, maybe sneak in some casual remark to let him know that she now was aware of their being a couple, but it stuck in her throat. Anyway, her idea of friendship and his were different. Talk would not erase that difference.

"We just got off to a bad start last Sunday."

"You were so loud and arrogant . . . and suspicious."

He squinted assessing blue eyes her way. "Yep, I expect I seemed that way, and I'm sorry. Guess I had too much on my mind to think about what you must have been going through. We'll make it as friends now, though."

Millie nodded her agreement, more relieved than she cared to admit that they were once more on pleasant terms.

She liked that Woods was seeing beyond their unsettling personal relationship and emphasizing the importance of having a productive school year. Millie did not have to pretend that teaching filled her with satisfaction; it did.

"I truly enjoyed meeting your mother and your aunt." A glance over at his thoughtful face told her that she had pleased him. "Your home seems perfect for the mountains. I can see why you obviously love living here."

"It's nice of you to say so. I could tell that Mama and Aunt Glovina took a liking to you from the way they made you promise to come see us again." Against his better judgment he asked, "Did you mean it when you told them you'd like to come back?"

"Yes, I did." Millie did not add that another visit to the Sanders home, as tempting as the prospect might be, seemed highly improbable—unless Annabelle might invite her to come along some time when she was visiting.

The stalled car sitting in the middle of Iron Creek came into view then. Before they reached it, Clive appeared from downstream and looked up the road toward them.

Millie dismounted, with Woods's solicitous assistance, and perched on a fallen log while the men set about getting the car out of the water and onto the road on the far side of the creek. She admired the way Woods hitched the team to the front axle of the car and called orders to the mules. When he called out "Caesar, come up, boy!," then "Cleopatra, gee!," she remembered how he had talked to the mules on their trip from Elmwood, as if they might be humans . . . and old friends.

Though she craned her neck, Millie could not see what Clive was doing up in front of the car after it sat on the dry road across the creek, but from the intermittent noises she assumed he was trying to crank the engine. The motor coughed a few times, then burst into clattering sounds that set the mules into frenzied snorts and lunges before Woods calmed them. The two men conferred briefly before Clive waved toward Millie and stepped into his car. Woods, not bothering to ride, sloshed across the creek, leading the still-jittery mules and speaking softly to them.

"Millie, Clive says he'd better stay in the car and get the

motor revved up good," Woods said. He hitched the mules
to a sapling over on the side of the road, near where Major
was straining against his tether and eyeing the now-backfir-
ing automobile with distrust. "I told him I'd get you across
the creek."

"Good. We'll be back in Freeman before dark." Millie
stood and started toward Major.

"No need to try riding. Major has been around so few cars
that he'd likely balk on you."

Before Millie could guess his intention, Woods had
scooped her up in his arms and was striding into the shallow
creek with long-limbed ease. She threw a glance at the car
facing ahead toward Freeman, but Clive was obviously engrossed in adjusting the speed of the engine, his back to the
creek and to them.

"I could have ridden Major if you had led him." Millie's
mind and senses reeled from the feel of Wood's strong arms
holding her so close to his broad chest. Surprising her, the
earthy scents of man and mules and virgin forest assailed her
nostrils and tugged at something secret and primitive within
her nature. The pattern of her pulse disintegrated into an
uneven series of jerks. Though she knew it was not true, she
felt as if the tall mountain man was hugging her in an intimate embrace instead of merely transporting her across the
stream.

Looking down into Millie's face, Woods asked in a soft
voice that sounded even more resonant to Millie than when
heard at a distance, "This is a lot more fun, though, isn't it?"
Her parted lips and startled eyes supplied all the answer he
needed. "Put your arms around my neck." When she shook
her head in refusal, he added, "If you don't, you could fall if
I stumble."

Millie complied, blushing when her movements brought
her body even closer to his. Not for a minute did she expect
Woods to stumble. Against her will, she drank in the blue-
ness of his eyes so near, surprised to see that dark flecks
swam therein and led her to want to get lost in their tantalizing depths.

In spite of her attempts to keep herself aloof and remember it was Annabelle's beau who was carrying her, Mil-

lie felt like a cosseted little girl, so securely did Woods hold
her and maneuver a path across the rock-filled creek bed.
Against her relaxing body, the movements of his breathing
felt far too good to the part of her protesting that she should
not be enjoying the moment so intensely. After all, Woods
was doing no more than making a friendly gesture.

"Thank you," Millie said in a breathy little voice. He had
reached the other side of the creek and seemed to have no
plans to set her down.

"My pleasure." What would she do if he planted a light
kiss at the turned-up corner of her sassy mouth? Woods
wondered with an amused smile. It felt so good, holding her
in his arms. And the closeup view of her velvety brown eyes
was feeding his soul. Clive was so intent on listening to his
clacking machine that he seemed unaware that anyone else
was around—not that Clive's presence bothered Woods in
the least.

Millie sucked in a deep breath and, with the greatest of
efforts, summoned a commanding tone. "Put me down now,
please." She dropped her gaze, though she could feel his
eyes still brushing over her face and settling upon her mouth
in a most disconcerting manner.

"Take care of that toe when you get home," Woods said
after lowering Millie without haste. He held her arm until
she gained her footing. Her cool demand had not dampened
his ardor, but he knew that if he had not put her down as she
demanded, he would have kissed her pretty mouth and likely
not been able to stop. At least, he consoled himself, now
that he had set her down, they could remain friends. He
cleared his throat and smiled down at her, sensing that the
smile was lopsided and giving a clue to his inner thoughts.
"You probably need to douse it again in kerosene."

Clive leaned from the driver's seat and saw them then. He
called over the racing engine. "Will you escort Miss Monroe
around to the rider's side? I daren't leave my auto."

"Have a nice ride back home," Woods told Millie as he
walked with her to the other side of the car.

"I will," Millie said, wondering if the little cloud of foul-
smelling fumes from gasoline might not be robbing her of

voice. She had not felt right since Woods set her down. "Thank you for letting me ride Major."

Before he leaned to open the car door and get her seated, Woods winked at Millie and jerked his head knowingly toward the oblivious Clive over in the driver's seat. The noise of the engine kept his words private. "Old Clive is a fool to be paying more attention to his automobile than to you."

Clive started the car forward soon with a jerk, and Millie did not bother to answer Woods or wave good-bye. She was strangely spent. Deciding that for the wind to blow her curls was better than fighting to keep on her hat, she gripped it tightly on her lap. At least it was something to hold on to.

On the entire bumpy drive into Freeman, Millie stared straight ahead and replied to Clive's feeble attempts at conversation in monosyllables whenever possible. Her toe throbbed in unison with the motor of the Model-T. Her blistered heels burned inside her wet shoes. Her heart labored with questions and answers having no seeming relationship. Whenever had she spent a more unsettling afternoon?

Part Four

What about this city schoolmarm?
Has she left more than tresses behind?
She may find it more than trying
When she learns that she has a revamped mind.

· Chapter Ten ·

A steady rain crept into the hamlet of Freeman on Monday and, to Millie, seemed a harbinger of cooler days and nights. Straight-falling raindrops peppered the shaked roof of the schoolhouse with a low, monotonous song and turned the heretofore bright days into gray, forbidding ones with a decided tang to the air.

Activities within the schoolroom stepped up as Millie moved from learning group to learning group and dug into the business of becoming better acquainted with her pupils and getting on with the business of teaching. As she had suspected when she first met the carrot-topped Booth children on the day before school began, both Francine and Noble were bright—and Francine was far too full of herself to be contained easily. Noble teamed up with the younger Milstead boy, Steve, and led their teacher to suspect that trouble brewed behind their deceptively docile miens.

Minnijean Blackstone's friend, Gladys Hobbs, was absent on Monday and Tuesday and volunteered no excuse when she appeared on Wednesday after the rain stopped. Millie made a mental note to find out where her family lived and make a call, even if she had to consider renting a buggy from Booth's Livery.

Getting to know more about the beautiful Annette Bordeaux and her only friend, Warden Marks, intrigued Millie. In many ways, they belied their tender ages of sixteen and eighteen. Though it was plain at recesses and noon breaks that the two were smitten by first love, they buckled down to their schoolwork and wasted little time exchanging soulful looks and smiles, even during recitations. They seemed unaware of the other nine pupils in the large classroom.

By Wednesday, when the rain ceased, Millie had decided she would survive her wounded toe and heels. She never acknowledged what nipped at her heart, though she suspected that Woods Sanders had made some kind of indelible impression on her other than to stir up passion that she had not known she possessed. Her entire world was new and strange, and her reactions to everything puzzled her. New surroundings were inviting new attitudes, too.

Millie thought of how she had left her best friend and confidante, fellow teacher Louise Nipper, behind in Little Rock and how it was only natural that she would be open to new relationships. Why, she reflected during her probing interior monologues, just look at the way Annabelle Stevens and she had hit it off right from the start. She wished she felt better about admitting that she liked being around the blue-eyed mountain man. With little effort she sidestepped thinking about Annabelle and Woods at the same time.

Even when she tried, Millie could not forget the unexplained little humming inside her pulse that had begun on the day Woods had come by and helped her get the classroom in order. The picnic by the Gooseneck River and their satisfying conversations all that day had whetted her appetite for more of that kind of camaraderie with the mountain man. She wanted to hear more of his yarns and more of his deep laughter, learn more about his thoughts on how legislators could help bring prosperity to the people in the Ouachita Mountains, learn more about . . . Woods, the man.

Doggedly the virgin schoolmarm faced up to having discovered that she might be infatuated with Woods, no matter that he was Annabelle's beau. She vowed to keep her feelings about him buried forever—and crossed her fingers to make sure.

It pleased Millie to categorize Woods as a friend, she acknowledged while busying herself in the evenings with grading papers and preparing lessons for her pupils. For one thing, it allowed her to look forward to seeing him again without feeling guilty. As he had wisely pointed out during their ride to Clive's foundered car, the two of them had much to accomplish during the school year. Also, the practical side of her insisted, she needed him to do something about her pesky cookstove.

"Millie, are you home?" came Annabelle's friendly voice outside the teacherage that Wednesday afternoon after school. "I brought you a loaf of bread."

"Come in, Annabelle, and stay awhile. Thanks for the bread." Millie smiled at the pretty blonde at her door and ushered her inside, finding it not nearly so awkward to talk with her as she had feared. When Annabelle handed her the loaf, Millie leaned her face close to it and sniffed hungrily, as happy as a child upon smelling and feeling the warmth through the paper wrapping. "Freshly baked bread is one of my weaknesses."

"I didn't know when you bake yours, so—"

A trill of low laughter burst from Millie. "I don't bake yeast bread, don't even know how to make it."

"What do you do for bread? I gathered from our talks that you kept house for your father a good while."

"I did, but somehow people kept us supplied with bread or else I made do with biscuits or something else. There always seemed to be more important things to do than making yeast bread."

"Millie, you amaze me. Every time I'm around you, I find out more and more what a unique individual you are." Annabelle sent her friend a warm smile. "And I like you for it."

Millie's face flushed, but she did not know how much of the rush of heat came from Annabelle's kind words and how much came from her twinges of guilt from having kissed Annabelle's beau—and loving the hell out of it.

"I'm glad," Millie said as she placed the loaf on the table. She was glad that she had gotten all the facts sorted out in her mind about Annabelle and Woods and herself, she mused. Maybe this afternoon would be a good time to ask Annabelle how she felt about Millie and Woods being friends and point out how both shared a common interest—the school. "If I can manage to get a burner lit on Monster, I'll brew us some coffee, and we'll have bread and butter with it."

"Monster?" Annabelle laughed, the tinkling sound welcome in the starkly furnished teacherage. "May I ask why you call your cookstove such a horrible name? Don't tell me you're actually talking aloud to inanimate objects."

Millie joined Annabelle's laughter then and knelt to hold a match to the recalcitrant wick. Not until a blue flame sputtered promisingly and she set the coffeepot over it did she turn back to her caller. "Sometimes I do mutter 'Monster' out loud because the name fits. The dratted stove terrifies me by never doing what a stove is supposed to do. It probably will blew up on me someday, just to show it's the boss."

"I heard Papa and Woods talking about choosing kerosene because the supplying of wood or coal for other kinds of cookstoves was more costly and troublesome." Annabelle eyed the tin heater backed up against the wall dividing the teacherage from the classroom. "When it gets cold enough for you to stoke the heater with wood, perhaps you can put a pot or pan on its surface and ignore Monster occasionally."

"That's a good idea. So far, though, I've not needed heat badly enough to fire up the heater. I just throw on a shawl or get into bed. I admit this infernal cookstove is a headache."

"You'll have to ask Woods to see about it the next time he's in town. He usually comes over on weekends. He's good with all kinds of things like that."

"Yes, I had planned on laying my problems on the shoulders of the school board chairman." Did Annabelle's remark indicate that Woods had not been to Freeman during the week?

"So you noticed those broad shoulders, huh?" Annabelle teased, her blue eyes squinting with mischief and losing a tad of their normal sadness.

Perplexed that Annabelle exhibited no sign of jealousy, had in fact turned Millie's casual reference into one with overtones of sensuality, Millie sent her fingers riffling through her short curls. The fact that her cheeks were not warming up reassured her that she was mastering her inner feelings about Woods—whatever they were. "I may be unmarried and not interested in changing that status, but I'm not blind. The man *is* big and strong, as you well know."

"Are you happy being single?"

"Yes. Are you?" Millie asked, uncomfortable about the

direction of the conversation. Surely now Annabelle would confess whatever plans Woods and she had made.

Annabelle shifted about on the sofa. "I like my life better than when I was married."

"You were married? To whom, pray tell?" Millie knew that she should not have let her shock show, or blurted out probing questions, but it was all over before she could call up self-control. Her father had always scolded her for being overly curious about people, saying that he had learned more about others than he wanted to know merely by being a good listener. Thank goodness, Millie reflected, that she had stopped herself before asking anything about Woods.

Annabelle's fingers fidgeted with her dark skirt, and her pale face took on a rosier hue. "If I didn't feel you and I are destined to become best friends, I wouldn't even have said as much as I did. Most folks know about my wild fling—"

Millie sat up straighter. Pretty Annabelle, the soft pink and white blonde, had done something wild? Millie's old bugaboo—her inordinately active curiosity recognized and scorned by her father—reared its head higher, but she poked it down. "I'm not much for repeating what people exchange in confidence, but don't tell me about it if you'd rather not." *Tell me about Woods and you.*

"Someday soon I will," Annabelle replied. "Woods is always telling me that it's good to have friends to talk with. I've counted him as that kind of friend for a long time, and now I feel I can count you as one as well."

"You can," Millie assured her. Her heart danced in celebration. "I had wondered if maybe the two of you might not be more than friends, or maybe planning to be. You're both so easy to talk with and—"

Annabelle smiled and shook her head. "No, you're way off in left field with that thought. You might have thought there was something going on between us because he bought my supper box, but—well, it was not what it might have appeared to be. There never has been anything between Woods and me, never can be. He and I both know that. I just plain like the man. Don't you?"

In a flash Millie answered, "Yes. I like him very much." She could not recall having felt such enormous relief in her life. Now she would not have to feel guilty for liking the mountain man and wanting to get to know him better.

Soon other topics were fleshing out their conversation as they sat in the teacherage, each welcoming the chance to sound out their ideas on the other.

Millie found her visitor interested in the general activities in the classroom. Annabelle pleased the schoolmarm part of Millie by not inquiring into private happenings between pupils and teacher. By the time the tempting smell of fully brewed coffee blended with that of the warm yeasty bread and wafted over to the sofa, the two women had made a sizable addition to the bridge of mutual affection so apparent to them at their first meeting.

"During the lull in the rain Monday, Widow Marks walked over and visited with me a few minutes in the schoolyard after school let out," Millie said. They had moved to the table where both had taken a few bites of the crusty bread slices smeared with butter, then followed up with sips of the fragrant hot coffee. "She was kind enough to give me this pound of butter we're using. Warden seems as fine as his mother says in every other sentence."

"Mabel is a good woman and mother, despite her meddlesome, nosy ways. I'm glad to hear that Warden isn't letting either his mother or himself down. He'll likely make a fine veterinarian. Even when he finds occasional work at the mines, he finds time to doctor animals." Annabelle lifted an eyebrow and looked serious as she asked, "What about my nephews? Are they settling into the new school year?"

Millie was glad that she could reply truthfully in the affirmative. She added a few anecdotes involving Ransom and Steve that she felt sure would set Annabelle's mind at ease about the progress of the sons of her dead sister and Lucas Milstead.

"Your sister, Fern, would be proud of her boys," Millie said. "She must have been a lovely person."

"She was." Annabelle's gaze shifted to the window.

"What a pity she died so young."

"I doubt she would think so. She had become bitter. I don't think Fern was born to find happiness in Freeman. She started out breaking the hearts of others—and ended up breaking her own."

"I'm sorry."

"I guess Mabel wanted to hear all about your ride with Clive Durham on Sunday afternoon," Annabelle said, switching the talk back to the Widow Marks.

Millie laughed good-naturedly. So Annabelle, too, had a passle of curiosity. "I suspected that's what she wanted so I started right off telling her how gentlemanly Clive was and how impressed I was with the mine we visited and how lovely the mountains were. She corrected me, saying these are foothills around Freeman, not mountains.

"Mabel told me how she recalls from her school days in Elmwood that anything rising straight up from a level surface to a height of at least a thousand feet is a true mountain. I told her that she was, indeed, correct. Right away she said that since I'm the teacher, I can call them mountains if I want to."

"My," Annabelle said with a laugh, "you must have impressed Mabel to gain such a concession. By the way, which mine did Clive show you? What did you think about it?"

"He took me to the Sanders Number one. I'm glad I got to see a mine, but I was disappointed. I had expected it to be more than a giant, open pit with only a few shallow shafts sunk back into the mountain. It reminded me of a deep gravel pit."

Annabelle smiled and nodded knowingly as she leaned nearer from across the table. "Did you enjoy being with Clive Durham?"

Millie pursed her lips. "No." She fixed her gaze on her coffee cup. "There's nothing wrong with the man, but I don't find him...exciting." Funny, she mused, the word "exciting" held an entirely different meaning since she had met Woods.

Annabelle did not press the matter and soon stood to go, saying at the doorway, "You really should come check on your mail every day or so, else I'll have to send somebody here with it as I do for Selma Bordeaux."

"I've been so busy since I arrived that I've not given mail

a thought. Let me grab a shawl, and I'll walk back with you now."

When the two women passed in front of the Bordeaux home—the Keyhole House to Millie—she asked, "Why doesn't Mrs. Bordeaux come to the store and pick up her mail? Is she ill?"

A tiny frown marred Annabelle's pretty forehead. "Not ill, but a recluse. Annette does all her shopping and usually picks up the mail. Selma Bordeaux is a strange woman. Nobody wants to do anything to upset her, so nobody bothers her."

Millie glanced over at the huge house with the picket fence up close around it, wondering if the fence served to shut people out or shut people in. Several of the town's dogs trotted toward the two women on the road. To Millie's relief none were barking or eyeing her as a stranger. "What do you mean by 'strange'?"

"She has more or less locked herself away from the world. She never goes outside her own yard."

"Does she receive visitors?" Millie asked, seized by a sudden yen to call upon Selma Bordeaux and her lovely daughter, Annette, and meet the mysterious woman.

"Sometimes she does; sometimes she doesn't. The only one who goes to see her is Mabel Marks, who, as you know, lives next door." When Millie looked puzzled, she went on. "Selma and Mabel were childhood friends."

"Perhaps I'll meet Mrs. Bordeaux at church when Uncle Fred drives over from Elmwood on first Sundays."

"She doesn't go to church or anywhere. Sometimes I've seen her walking at dusk inside her yard. You might hear her playing her violin. Selma is some ten years older than I am, so I barely knew her. After trouble with her father when she was in her teens, she stayed away at a private school in Memphis. She didn't return here until after she brought the bodies of her father and husband to be buried. She was pregnant with Annette and has been here ever since."

"What happened to her husband? Was he from around here?"

"I've heard she met Mr. Bordeaux at the school of music in Cincinnati where they both taught. Some have wondered

if there might not have been some kind of confrontation between the two men."

"Poor woman," Millie said. "She must have suffered
much grief."

"True, but do come along. Lucas is coming for the boys
this evening and will be eating with us. I want to get supper
started," Annabelle said with obvious impatience when Millie's steps slowed considerably.

Once more matching her steps to the faster pace of her
companion, Millie glanced sharply at Annabelle, surprised
to see a secretive smile on her face. What in heaven's name
could be so special about cooking a meal for her brother-in-
law?

Millie dismissed her first impression that Annabelle's
smile had anything at all to do with Lucas Milstead. After
all, with his having been married to Annabelle's sister and
being the father of her adored nephews, the man was likely a
brother to her. And, judging from her pleased smiles when
Millie had praised the perfect loaf of bread, Annabelle
seemed the kind to set much store on her culinary skills.

All the way back to the teacherage, Millie puzzled over
Selma Bordeaux and her reported withdrawal from the people of the hamlet. Was it a mental illness—she hadn't forgotten little Francine's derogatory word "loony"—or was it
something else that prompted the woman to lock herself
away from what seemed to Millie to be warm, friendly people?

Millie's single letter was from Louise Nipper, her friend
from Owen Academy for Girls, the school where Millie had
taught for the past four years. She promptly forgot all about
her curiosity over the Keyhole House and its two occupants
when she reached the teacherage and read the newsy account
of happenings in Little Rock. A wave of homesickness
washed over her.

"Why didn't you tell me last Saturday night that the stove
was acting up?" Woods demanded the following Friday afternoon while he fiddled with the handles on Millie's cookstove. When he first arrived, he had asked about her toe and

seemed relieved that no further problems with it had developed.

"I don't know," Millie replied from where she sat at the kitchen table watching Woods. *Because you had kissed me senseless, you fool.* His blue denim shirt seemed freshly laundered, if one could judge from the crisp lines of the collar open at the neck and allowing black chest curls to show.

With her elbows propped on the table and her chin resting against the heels of her fists, Millie was thinking of how happy it made her to know Woods was not linked romantically with Annabelle. If there *was* another woman in his life, she was not sure she wanted to know about it. "Can you fix the cookstove?"

"I could if I had some pliers. Do you have a pair?"

"What would I be doing with a pair of pliers?"

"You don't have to get testy."

"I'm not being testy." Millie smiled at him to prove it. "I've never had any use for pliers, that's all."

From where he still squatted before the kerosene stove, Woods slid Millie an exasperated glance. Too well he recalled that she had as good as told him that she had no use for men either. How could she make such preposterous statements and still look so damned beautiful and desirable? Why, Millie Monroe was made for some man to adore and cherish. "I'll go across the road and borrow a pair from Mabel and Warden. That way, I can fix the burners before I go home. You can get your gear together."

"Why are you leaving so soon?" Millie asked, not comprehending anything beyond the thought that he was not going to stay at the teacherage long. "You just got here. We've not had any time to talk."

"Can this mean that you've missed seeing the pesky chairman of the school board?" Woods sent a questioning look her way and stood up.

Millie shook her head slowly and pursed her lips as if in deep thought. "No," she conceded, "but I've missed having a friend to talk with about what's going on in the classroom."

Woods smiled then, his blue eyes crinkling in that way she

had thought about over and over. Before she knew it, Millie was telling him about Annabelle's nice visit and about receiving the letter from her friend in Little Rock and how reading the letter had made her wish for someone with whom to talk over the happenings in school.

From where he had stood leaning against the wall with his arms folded, Woods bowed in half-mocking fashion, then twanged in comical dialect. "Ah'm honored, ma'am, jes' plain honored to be missed, in any old way yo' heart comes up with. Tell me which young'uns is actin' up an' ah'll give'em the old razzle-dazzle, an' if that don't work, ah'll switch'em good with a hickory stick."

Millie giggled. "What is the 'old razzle-dazzle'?"

Woods stroked his mustache and squinted his eyes, as if considering whether or not to share his vast knowledge. "When I think you're old enough, I'll tell you."

"Twenty-six seems old enough to know almost anything." She returned his friendly grin, liking the way his teeth flashed so whitely beneath his mustache.

"Not razzle-dazzle." Considerably cheered that Millie was in high spirits and apparently had missed him and wanted to share accounts of her week's activities with him, Woods went on. "I usually don't get into town except on weekends when I come to pick up the mail and buy whatever Mama and Glovina need at the store. If you ever need me for something that Henry Stevens can't take care of, though, you can send a message up to Booth's Livery."

When she cocked her head in question, he sat down on the chair next to hers and explained, "The work crews living near Freeman leave from Booth's Livery every morning about daylight on a company wagon. Before dark, the wagon returns those not drawing night watch at the mine."

"I recall Clive saying something about Edgar Booth being a local agent of some kind and that he himself didn't have to come over every weekend."

"That's right." Woods squelched the desire to ask her if Clive might be coming to call on her that weekend. "When Clive isn't planning to bring the payroll on Saturday morning, he sends it to Edgar on the Friday run of the passenger carriage coming over twice a week from Elmwood. Edgar locks it up in his safe overnight, then parcels out the money to the workers on Saturday according to the time charts turned in by the foreman, Barton Blackstone. Edgar also supplies the wagons and teams for hauling ore."

"Running a mine sounds complicated."

Woods shrugged a shoulder. "If you deal with workers and a product, I guess it's bound to be complicated at times."

"One day I heard this awful, thundering noise during recess, and the children told me it was the wagons hauling ore from the hills and heading toward Elmwood." It was so good to be talking with Woods and hearing his deep-voiced comments, Millie realized. He knew so much about her new surroundings, and she knew so little.

Woods breathed in the jasmine-y fragrance of her and eyed her shining curls. "I've already been by the store. If I go on and get the pliers and fix the stove, can you be ready to go by the time I get through?"

"Go? Go where?"

"Go home with me."

Oh, the words slid into Millie's ears and on down to some secret spot as if they might be warm honey soaking into a hot, split biscuit. She swallowed and fingered a strand of hair curling across the top of her ear. "Why are you inviting me to go h—go to your house?"

"Mama and Aunt Glovina threatened to make me sleep outside with the dogs if I came back without you." When she continued to fidget with her hair and hide her eyes behind her long eyelashes, Woods felt his original doubt rear up again. "Unless Clive is coming to call on you this weekend, that is."

Millie liked it that Woods seemed to be aware that she had a life of her own. "I have no plans for the weekend."

"Then you'll go?" Woods levered his tall body up from the chair. "I'll take Major on over to the livery and rent Edgar's horse and little two-wheeled buggy. He told me when I stopped earlier that it was available."

Her face brightening at each word, Millie smiled at the thought of a touch of adventure in the company of the handsome, blue-eyed Woods. "Is it a shay, as in Irving's poem, 'The One-Hoss Shay'?"

Woods looked down at his boots, hitched up his denim breeches over his slim hips, and walked over to the door, his steps loud on the bare, plank floor. In a curiously flat tone, he said, "I don't know about your poem, but I'll fetch the buggy and the pliers and be back."

"That was very nice of your mother and your aunt to invite me to spend the weekend," Millie said after Woods and she had traveled in the bouncy little buggy down the ridge at the crossroads and left Freeman behind. In her fancy, it was indeed a "one-hoss shay," and she eyed the simple lines of the two-wheeled vehicle with appreciation. There was something about being around Woods that stepped up life's space, she thought with a sigh of unadulterated happiness.

"They both liked you a lot, and you did promise to come back and stay longer."

Woods wondered if he had made a grievous error to have allowed the two women in his life to play at matchmaking one more time. Oh, he reflected, he had not let on that he had known what they were up to when his mother and his aunt had insisted on his bringing Millie back with him from Freeman, but he had not forgotten their similar attempts over the years to find him a woman to be his wife and bear his children. What they did not know was that he was immune to women.

Millie, her eyes moving leisurely, drank in the picturesque landscape. The approaching twilight cast purple shadows on the mountains up ahead, the degrees of color varying with the distance and height of the peaks. The sun, already hidden from view, was painting a dazzling display of reds and oranges on a distant bank of clouds. If rain was to visit again, as the clouds hinted, she hoped it would not reach the nearby mountains before Woods returned her to the teacherage on Sunday afternoon. She couldn't remember when she had looked forward to anything as much as spending two nights and days with Woods . . . and his family, she added hastily.

Millie mused that when she had traveled the same road with Clive in his Model-T last Sunday, the warm feeling of contentment and oneness with her surroundings had not enveloped her with an unexplained happiness in the way that they were doing now. Did it have to do with the mode of transportation?

Readily Millie confessed a preference for the steady clip-clops of the horse's prancing, shod feet upon the rocky road over the whir and roar of the motor machine. And, she reflected, the livery horse was fine looking, though not as beautiful as Woods's saddle horse, Major. The little valley they were passing through seemed removed from Freeman and the mountain ridges and peaks up ahead. She realized then what a hollow really was. Only an occasional path branched off from the main road with its deep twin ruts in the dirt and gravel, an obvious result of the ore wagons traveling over them regularly.

Or, Millie wondered, did her enhanced mood of the moment have to do with the company? Her thoughts kept turning, right along with the twin wheels of the chaise. How well she knew that the sight of the tall, lean mountain man dressed in light blue denim shirt and darker blue denim breeches pleasured her eyes far more than did that of the smaller but finer dressed easterner. She called up her earlier suspicion that she might be infatuated with Woods Sanders and, with a secretive smile, admitted there was no longer any doubt.

Perhaps it was folly to try to understand what had her feeling so good and so vibrant, Millie reasoned as she sniffed at the crisp autumn air and realized that she was smiling at the hazy horizon for no apparent reason. She feared that if she worried with the reason for her elation too long, it might disappear as quickly as it had come, rather like the doodlebugs glimpsed during childhood play in the sand.

Millie recalled the incidences clearly. Chanting "Doodle-bug, doodlebug, fly away home," she and her playmates would squat down and stir lightly with twigs into the apexes of the small but exquisitely formed conical indentations in the sand. Though the young Millicent never quite gave up on the hope that one day a doodlebug might actually fly away, all that the disturbed insects would do was surface for a brief moment, then scuttle back deeper into the earth and refuse to budge again. No, she would not seek out the real reason for her joy.

They had left Freeman behind for no more than thirty minutes when, across a field up ahead, Millie saw some cows ambling toward a small barn and house almost hidden by a host of trees.

"Who lives there?" Millie asked, welcoming an excuse to turn and look at Woods fully. In profile, with his manly nose and chin, he was as handsome as in frontal view—though she barely could distinguish the fascinating cleft from that angle.

Woods, lost in thought about how alive it made him feel to be in Millie's company and how such a thing made no sense at all to a man who had been immune to women for years, startled. "Oh," he said when her question dug into his addled brain, "that's where James Hobbs and his family live. You have Gladys and Artis on your roll, don't you?"

"I have Gladys only, and she doesn't come every day. I was planning to talk with you about the board's policy about absenteeism. Is Mrs. Hobbs alive and well?"

"Yes, but James and his bunch stay mighty close to home."

"I'm planning on renting a horse and buggy from Edgar and driving out for a visit. I'm glad to learn where they live."

Woods tipped his hat back from his face. "James and his wife, Mary Lee, have a sickly baby. Things haven't gone too good for them over the past couple of years. Some of us on the board talked about maybe trying to furnish books for their kids and buy them some shoes. When I talked with James about it, he stiffened his neck and said he could manage."

"It must be hard for them. Does he work in the mines?"

"He says he's needed about the place too much to be gone daily. Mary Lee takes in washing from the folks in Freeman, like Annabelle and her daddy and others that can afford to pay for such." Holding the reins loosely in one hand, he turned and faced the beautiful woman whose short red curls were ruffling and fluffing up prettily from the play of soft twilight breezes. "You're truly concerned about Gladys and her attendance, aren't you? Are all teachers like you?"

"Insofar as I know," Millie replied, liking the visual bath her face was receiving from his searching blue gaze and wondering if the inward glow she was feeling might not be showing. She often had thought of a purple twilight as a magical time; never had it seemed more so. "I know that I want to lead the students to know as much as I do and then have them go out and find out all those countless things about which I have no knowledge. Learning, as you already know, is a lifelong adventure that begs to be shared."

"What about those who get left behind for various reasons?"

"Then it's up to them to run and catch up and demand what's theirs. Teachers are always eager to help them." Millie smiled at the seriousness on his handsome face. Had he, too, become caught up in the plight of the Hobbs children?

Millie's heart took on a heaviness as the horse trotted on down the road and the Hobbs place disappeared from view. She suspected that now she knew why the fourteen-year-old Gladys was not attending school regularly. And what about the little boy—Artis, wasn't it?—who Woods had assumed was also in school? Yes, Millie decided as she deliberately relegated the problem to a holding place until after the weekend, she would look into the matter of the Hobbs children. And soon.

Rewarding himself with another direct look at his passenger, Woods broke the silence by clearing his throat and saying, "If the weather's good next Sunday, the laymen of the church will have a hayride. I was wondering if maybe you'd like to go with me. Most everybody will be there."

"I'd love to go." What was a hayride? Not that it mattered, Millie realized. She was so infatuated with this man that she likely would go anywhere he asked her to go.

Woods saw her perplexed look. "Hayrides are good ways to add to our Fund for Building Maintenance, since people usually donate a few coins. Have you ever been on a hayride?"

"No. I don't know what a hayride is, actually."

The two of them really did have different backgrounds, Woods reflected as he glanced down at the reins in his hand, then watched a rabbit scamper into the bushes up ahead. Though Millie had told him once that she had lived in places smaller than Little Rock when she was very young, he recalled that those she had named were larger even than Elmwood, which was at least four times as big as Freeman.

Eager to explain, Woods continued. "Edgar Booth furnishes a couple of teams and wagons from his livery. He removes the wagon planks on the sides and the back, then piles the bed with hay two or three feet high—thick enough to make a good cushion—and everybody climbs on for a ride out to the brush arbor clearing beside Crooked Creek."

Millie, feeling less of a greenhorn, announced happily, "I know what a brush arbor is. I remember attending summer revivals under them when I was a child."

Pleased upon noting that Millie's face and eyes revealed her interest and approval, Woods went on. "We sing and tell yarns on the ride out, then roast sausages and marshmallows over a bonfire when we get there—and drink apple cider."

"It sounds like a wonderful treat. How many couples usually go along?" She tried not to notice how heady was the thought that Woods and she would be a couple, but she failed.

"Hayrides are for everybody, not just couples, though they are mighty popular with the young sparking ones. If a wife or husband happens to be unable to go along, the other does. All the children go, too." He slid a teasing grin her way in the sweet twilight. "And the dogs wouldn't miss it for the world."

"I'll be looking forward to going," Millie assured him, wondering if Woods had figured out she was afraid of dogs. Her earlier thought that Freeman might be a fine place to live echoed in her heart and mind and became next door neighbor to a fact.

"Good night, Woods, and thank you again for inviting me to visit in your home," Millie said in a low voice when he accompanied her down the dogtrot and opened the door into the bedroom designated earlier as hers. The lamp he carried in one hand encircled them with its golden glow and shut out all that was beyond its reach. Was he going to go inside and set the lamp down for her, or should she reach out and take it? "As you heard me tell your mother and Glovina before they went to their bedroom, the supper was pure heaven. You're talented both in catching and frying catfish."

"Thanks. I liked the way you didn't hold back on seconds," Woods replied, also keeping his voice quiet in deference to the two women who already had retired. "And it's a good thing, too, if you meant it when you said you'd like to do some climbing and exploring tomorrow. You'll need a lot of strength for that." He let his gaze drift downward, as if he might be weighing her mentally.

"Yes, I meant it." Millie put her hand on the door facing and leaned back against it, feeling the slightest rush of light-headedness when he took a step closer. The day had been long, and a Friday at that. She must be overly tired, she reflected when her knees felt shaky. "I'm looking forward to tomorrow. I'm glad I brought my comfortable walking shoes, and I hope no rain falls until at least Sunday."

"I looked awhile ago, and the clouds still seem banked far in the west. Aunt Glovina says she'll fix us a huge sack lunch to take along, just in case we don't make it back 'til dark. If it showers, we can duck inside a cave until it lets up. I know every one of them for miles around."

"Your aunt and your mother have been a lot of fun to talk with. They make me feel so at home." She noticed that Woods seemed far more interested in using his sense of sight than that of hearing. "Of course the same goes for you, too."

Millie noticed the way the night sounds from the surrounding forest served as a choral background for their soft voices there on the dogtrot. She heard the slow bass calls of bullfrogs from the singing creek below the ridge and marked the way the deep sounds kept butting in and jangling the rhythm from the forest, creating a pleasing syncopation. Some insects had discovered the blaze of the glass-based lamp and were circling it, occasionally bumping into the thin glass chimney with tiny plinking sounds. She was so accustomed to smelling the kerosene fueling her own lamps that the odor emanating from the burning wick seemed homey. "Do you truly think it's all right if I take up Glovina's suggestion to wear one of the grandsons' clothing left here from a visit?"

"Sure. Why not?" He grinned. Millie never failed to surprise him. Here stood a beautiful, soft-eyed woman who had dared cut off her hair in an age of big, puffy pompadours and now was fretting about dressing properly in a remote hill area. "There's nobody to see you in breeches except them and me, and we're all your friends."

"Of course. I hadn't thought about it like that." Millie turned away then, feeling that inner humming, which his nearness seemed to bring, become more pronounced, like a minute vibration. He was standing within reaching distance, and he was looking at her in a way that felt as intimate as a touch. At first she had thought it was the heat from the flame behind the nearby lamp chimney that was warming her cheeks, but now she knew better. "I'll take the lamp and go on inside." The transfer of the lamp from his hand to hers did not take long, but the necessary touching of hands sparked her pulse into a more rapid pace. "Good night."

Millie turned away quickly, but his low voice recaptured her. She paused just inside the bedroom, breathless all of a sudden.

"I'll come tap on your door before daybreak so you'll have time to wake up. I remember how grumpy you were that morning I called on you at the teacherage so early."

Millie allowed herself to turn around and look up at the mountain man again then, relieved that his tone had been teasing and that a smile was jauntily lifting his black mustache at both ends. Even so, she was determined to keep Woods at bay, and, with both hands, she gripped the lamp more firmly and held it between them.

Having become better acquainted that evening with whoever the new Millie of Freeman was, she returned his wide smile with one equally as mischievous. "Don't you dare, Woods Sanders! You'll just have to put up with me being grumpy for a little while. Now, good night."

"Good night."

· *Chapter Eleven* ·

An unseen bird made a whirring noise, a seeming inquiry of the couple picking their way across the rocky crest of a lofty ridge in the Ouachita Mountains. All that Saturday morning the sun had played quick games of hide-and-seek behind hordes of gray clouds floating overhead. Here one moment for the hikers' pleasure was an angled shaft of sunlight warming the gray slabs of stone and dark soil, only to be replaced in the next with imperceptible movement by a blanket of shadow without beginning or end.

"Are you about ready to stop and have a bite to eat?" Woods asked when he paused and looked down at the tall red-haired woman walking along beside him.

Soon after the sun rose above the clear peaks in the east, they had begun their day of exploring some of his favorite foothills. It was close to noon now, and Woods still had not gotten used to seeing Millie in his nephew's outgrown clothing. How could she look so uncommonly female in such common garb?

No matter that Millie's every curve was well covered, Woods could see them in tantalizing detail as he never before had seen them in her ankle-length skirts and high-necked, long-sleeved waists. Though he had glimpsed other, far more revealing parts of her body through misfortune—hers, he acknowledged, not his—the Millie he was seeing today seemed totally new.

Even the way she walked appeared different, he mused while his thoughts raced back over the happenings of the morning. Never before had he realized that her hips swayed so seductively when she walked or that the feminine manner in which she swung her arms and set down her feet were delightfully her own. He wondered if the word "graceful" might not have been invented with Millie Monroe in mind.

"I'm not ready to stop and eat. Not yet," Millie replied as she, too, paused. Squinting up at the overcast sky, she said, "I thought you were going to show me a real cave before we stopped. The ones we've seen were no more than big holes full of cobwebs and debris. Or do you think it's finally going to rain on us and ruin our day?"

Chuckling softly to himself, Woods combed back his black hair with his fingers where the pesky breeze that lived on the crest of the ridge had been playing. He had not missed the way it also was teasing Millie's red curls into shining disarray.

"Millie, you're not going to get me to sound like a fool again and predict weather. No, ma'am! If you had believed me a couple of hours back when I thought we should turn around because it was going to rain, we'd likely be back at the house already. We're closer to caves than we are to home now, so we may as well keep moving ahead."

Woods looked out over the valley below them, then on to the cloud-shrouded mountain peaks in the distance. He suspected that rain was already falling in the northwest, but he saw no reason to reveal his thoughts to the high-spirited Millie. Maybe the clouds would empty themselves before they reached the ridge on which they were hiking. He switched his gaze back to a far more inviting sight and said gruffly, "I don't want to wear you out before we rest again, though. You're not used to climbing."

Full of herself, Millie grinned and stuck out her tongue at him when he kept watching her. She credited her exuberance to the abundance of oxygen from the trees marching up the ridge right up to its stone-encrusted summit, trees into whose colorful tops she could peek if she looked straight down. Feeling that something had gone wrong since their last stop, she glanced down at her middle.

At Woods's suggestion, when it had become too warm for her to wear his nephew's denim jacket, Millie had tied its empty sleeves together around her waist in front and allowed the jacket to flap loosely across her hips and buttocks. As she had suspected, the fabric had become loosened. She knotted the sleeves tighter, taking her time to answer. One of the nicest aspects of the outing, she conceded, was that time seemed to have lost its former hold on her. Silences hadn't begged to be filled.

Something about the relaxed style of living in Freeman pleased Millie in a way she didn't understand, and she wondered if it might not have a lot to do with the way that people in the community appeared to stand on less ceremony than those she had known in Little Rock. Why, she reflected, for her to be spending so much time alone in the company of a bachelor as she had been doing with Woods Sanders over the past two weeks would have been cause for scandal. In a burst of self-knowledge, she realized that she felt free for the first time in her life, free as the mountain breeze that bothered her not at all by mussing her short hair.

Millie replied, "I'm not too tired. It's warm, and a little rain won't kill us if it does come. In fact I doubt I've ever felt so exhilarated. How high up do you think we are?" She took in a deep breath and gazed with admiration at a scrubby oak up ahead, all gnarled and twisted from its bouts with punishing winds.

"Close to eight or nine hundred feet, I reckon." During the morning of necessarily close proximity as they sometimes walked and sometimes scrambled up steep pathways, Woods had discovered that Millie's eyes were more than the dark brown he had first thought. They held numerous shades of brown and gold and near black. Each time he looked into them, he spied another new combination of shading. Now, with the sun peeking almost straight down through the edge of a racing cloud, her brown eyes seemed filled with golden mystery.

"I love peeping over the edge of this ridge and seeing the Gooseneck River curving around down below like a length of wet silvery fabric. Knowing that it goes on to flow near the schoolhouse makes me feel I'm not completely in another world." Millie peered in the direction from which they had come, her hands serving as shields from the sunlight. "We've not been able to see your house and Iron Creek for a long while."

"No. When we waded across Iron Creek"—he grinned

when Millie shivered and made a face at the memory of their icy crossing earlier in water reaching her knees—"and climbed up Prayer Mountain, we changed directions so as to reach this ridge—which I named Promise Ridge when I was a boy because nobody seemed to call it anything but 'that long ridge beside the Gooseneck.'"

"I like that name." So Woods had pretended on the day they had picnicked beside the river that her expressed dislike of the name of the Gooseneck had made no sense, had he? she mused. Her eyes sparkled with new happiness. She must not be the only one who liked pretty words. "How far does Promise Ridge run?"

"A couple of miles or so. It's the closest one you can see from your bedroom window."

Millie's curiosity about everything she saw continued to amaze and delight Woods. Ever since they had waded across the creek, she seemed to have reverted to a carefree girl. She laughed at the least thing and seemed to welcome his teasing, even invite it by teasing back. She jumped to catch at overhanging leaves, exclaiming at their shape or color or texture and soaking up his offerings as to the names of trees and plants unfamiliar to her. At times she seemed to be bursting with talk, though he confessed that she listened with the same intensity showing on her pretty face as when she was doing the talking.

They walked on then in the leisurely pace they had enjoyed all morning. Though Millie was tall for a woman, she was four or five inches shorter than Woods. Her legs were long, though, and she was accustomed to walking. At first she had a little trouble matching her stride to his. When she mastered it, she took a measure of silly pride in the little feat.

The ease with which she could move about in the boys' breeches found in her bedroom at the Sanders home had amazed Millie all morning. Did her unaccustomed clothing, perhaps, contribute to her unexplained sense of freedom, of being someone new? Made of navy denim like Woods's breeches, her borrowed ones fit in the hips and thighs almost as tightly as his.

Before serving breakfast that morning soon after dawn,

Glovina privately had reassured the doubtful Millie that she did not appear indecent or unladylike in the masculine attire. Woods had made no comment about how she looked all morning, and, strangely, she took that as a compliment: They were friends on an outing, not a man and a woman.

"Did the extra pair of socks I brought along take care of your wet feet after we crossed the creek?" Woods asked after a spell of comfortable silence.

"Yes." Millie looked down at her walking shoes sticking out from below the legs of the still alien-looking denim breeches. In a tone more rueful than critical, she said, "I think it would have been better to wade with my shoes on. Those rocks nearly killed me. That's the only bad thing about the entire day, knowing that we have to cross that cold creek again."

"I offered to carry you across, remember?"

"Yes, but that wouldn't have been fair." Or wise, she thought.

They walked on. Soon they found their heretofore acceptably smooth passageway on the crest of Promise Ridge turning into a challenge. Rearing up before them was a jumble of huge slabs of gray limestone lying along a section of the crest, sometimes half-hidden underneath soil and a few bushes and trees, and sometimes veering upward at sharp, unadorned angles. The great pile of weathered slabs up ahead, angling in places as high as twelve feet, triggered Millie's imagination: Had a giant tossed them there centuries ago, much as some mortal might fling a set of dominoes carelessly from a box onto a tabletop and forget them?

Woods held out his hand to Millie at the most perilous places, and gratefully she took it. After several minutes of careful maneuvering, and much laughter at her greenhorn mannerisms and questions, they reached a point that Woods told her was more than halfway across the jutting stones. Nodding her agreement when he suggested they take a breather, she settled happily upon a lichen-splotched ledge across from him.

Millie let out a little cry of delight when she realized that she was seeing their surroundings from the highest vantage point of the morning. While the breeze evolved into a full-fledged wind with a cold, wet breath and tore at her curls, she drank in the sight of the numerous mountain peaks, ridges, and valleys so easily seen from their perch.

Patches of green dotting the panoramic view told the wide-eyed woman from the city that pine trees, and perhaps cedar as well, were interspersed among the hardwoods with their autumn foliage aglow. Because Woods had already told Millie that corn was the chief crop grown in the valleys, she assumed that the clearings seen here and there were cornfields lying fallow since recent harvests. The constantly moving play of light and shadow on the vistas below and in the distance, a result of the numerous clouds rushing in front of the sun, fascinated Millie almost as much as her loftly perspective.

"Woods," Millie said, turning to him for the first time since having become newly entranced with the scenery. "I keep seeing little spirals of smoke. Are they from homes?"

Woods tore his gaze from her rapt face and sent it in the direction of her own. "Yes, almost all of them are." He narrowed his eyes and pointed, liking the way she obediently tipped her head closer and let her gaze follow where he indicated. "Do you see the trace of smoke over at the base of that mountain with the bald top?" When she nodded, he added, "That's likely coming from Lavelle Landeen's still."

Millie turned incredulous brown eyes up at him. "A whiskey still? How horrible! I thought whiskey stills were only in Tennessee and Kentucky." She felt her mouth drawing up into a prim little grimace. "Who is this terrible man, Lavelle Landeen, who is so openly breaking the law? Why doesn't somebody arrest him?"

Woods laughed and reached over with the twig he was holding and brushed it teasingly across her pursed lips. She looked like an indignant girl ready to march forth and reform the world. "Don't be such a prude, Millie. It doesn't go well with your haircut and your boys' clothing."

"I don't care. The man must be an ignorant hillbilly—"

"Hold up, there!" Woods interrupted angrily. "You're talking about a friend of mine and one you don't know anything about. If he's an ignorant hillbilly, then so am I."

"Oh, no," Millie exclaimed, aghast that she had allowed a

shallow part of her former self, of which she was ashamed, to rock the new relationship between Woods and her. From the hardness in his blue eyes and the set of his black eyebrows, she sensed that the same kind of anger that had charged him up the day she had first met him in Uncle Fred's living room was stirring. "I had no right. I don't think of the people from around here as ignorant hillbillies, honestly I don't. I don't know what got into me. Please forgive me for mouthing off that way." Without her willing it to, her hand reached out and touched his forearm. "I do so want us to remain friends."

Woods felt the touch of Millie's hand on his arm before her apology sank into his self-torturing thoughts and redirected his thinking. He had learned during his thirty-five years that his flares of temper were usually ignited in an instant and just as quickly gone, especially when he put his mind to the task. He searched deep into Millie's obviously troubled eyes and saw only innocence and pleading.

"You're forgiven, Millie." He realized then that she was trembling. In a much softer voice, he went on. "You'd better untie your jacket and put it on. The wind's getting cold."

Millie welcomed both Woods's acceptance of her apology and his observation about the change in the temperature. She had not known that she was shivering until he pointed it out, and then she couldn't seem to stop. Within minutes she had donned the denim jacket and removed the knitted cap from its pocket and pulled it down over her ears.

By the time Woods had untied his own jacket from around his middle and slid his long arms inside the sleeves, Millie was ready to continue their trek atop Promise Ridge in search of what Woods had called his favorite cave.

"What do you think?" Woods asked. His hand gestured toward the high-ceilinged cave in which they stood. It sat immediately below the crest of Promise Ridge. Raindrops had found them only minutes away from the shelter, and, laughing and holding hands, they had raced to reach the cave before getting drenched.

"I like it." Millie eyed the smooth stone surfaces forming the cave, judging its length to be at least thirty feet and its width in the center some ten feet larger. It was obviously uninhabited and too large and dimly lighted for details such as old cobwebs and gnawed bones and other debris to claim the stage. "It's almost like a tapering tunnel."

Figuring that Woods had stepped outside to relieve himself, she brushed away the raindrops on her face and, after removing her damp cap, walked toward the much smaller opening facing away from the Gooseneck River. Without having to stoop over, she could stand in the elongated opening and gain a view similar to the one she had enjoyed earlier when they had rested on the rocky ledges.

One hand holding on to the rock side, and mindful of the steady drizzle falling just beyond the opening, Millie poked her head out a fraction and looked around. No longer was the sun playing games with the clouds. The day had become dark, forbidding, and decidedly chilly.

Steps on the smooth stone floor behind her told Millie that she was no longer alone. She asked, "Is Freeman visible when it's not cloudy and raining?"

"Yes, you can see Freeman clearly on sunny days. It's no more than a couple of miles away, as the crow flies. You can see this cave from the schoolhouse if you know where to look."

Millie smiled. It might be fun to look for the cave when she returned to the teacherage. She recalled having admired the long, tree-dotted ridge through her bedroom window.

Woods went on in a remembering voice. "I used to play here when I was a kid and imagine I could hitch a ride on an eagle and zoom right on over to Stevens's store." While he talked, Woods removed the knapsack strapped to his back, then went over to a small pool of water near the main entrance. "How many caves have you seen with their own running water?"

Millie turned, jerking off her cap. Eager to get inside out of the bone-chilling rain, she had not noticed the small stream of water flowing from a crevice in the stone wall near the entry. She concluded that the sounds of the gusting wind and the brisk rainfall had prevented her from hearing the musical notes of the water falling several inches into a miniature holding pool.

Walking over to kneel beside Woods and take in the new marvel, she replied in a mocking tone, "You know I've never seen a cave before this very morning." She watched him rinse his hands in the collected water resting in a circular indentation in the limestone before it spilled over and trickled down the slanting floor and on down the side of the ridge. "You don't have to brag to impress me, mountain man. I'm impressed enough on my own."

"I'm glad, though I like talking about my home territory." Mountain man? She had called him that—no, it was "mountain monster"—that night in the classroom when he had grabbed her. Hardly the same. He leaned then to form a cup with his hands below the stream of water and drank deeply, cutting his eyes up at her afterward for approval. When hers crinkled at the corners and her lips parted enough to show her pretty teeth in the way he had hoped for, he went on. "I would've hated for the day to be a total loss because of the dratted rain." Rising and drying his hands on his handkerchief, he asked, "Would you care to get ready for a bite to eat, courtesy of Aunt Glovina?"

When Woods turned to where his knapsack lay, Millie stepped outside and found a nearby clump of bushes for privacy in relieving herself. By the time she returned, a shade damper from the stepped-up rainfall, and washed her hands in the natural washbasin, she was feeling almost comfortable about being in the darkened cave.

A narrow ledge up as high as her head caught Millie's wandering gaze. Something large and bulky lay there, apparently covered with a tarpaulin. Goose bumps threatened to march down her spine. Shivering, she forced herself to look closer at her surroundings.

For the first time Millie noticed that the remains of a campfire lay over on the other side of the cave and that the stone ceiling up above the charred wood bore smudges of black. Now that she was more aware of the nuances of the interior of the cave, she realized that an odor of old smoke blended with those suggesting an incongruous mixture of mustiness and autumn dampness . . . and something primeval. Enhancing her sudden mood of apprehension, the light creeping inside the cave through its two openings dimmed perceptibly. She heard the rainfall pick up its speed.

Millie sat cross-legged on the dirt floor near Woods. "Has somebody been living here? What's that on the ledge?"

Completing his task of laying out the simple meal, Woods looked at Millie closely. Was she afraid? Strange. She had not seemed afraid that night when she thought she was defending her classroom. "Nobody lives here. When I was a boy wandering the hills, I often came here as we've done today to get out of bad weather. Then when I was older, I spent nights here with friends after some of our coon hunts —one of them was the moonshiner, Lavelle Landeen."

Woods watched Millie's eyes hide behind her dark lashes and her mouth take on a vulnerable look. She must still be distressed at having blurted out her thoughts about his friend, Lavelle Landeen, he reflected. Had she, perhaps, been wounded so painfully in the past that she guarded against revealing her inner feelings and thoughts?

Glancing up at the ledge, he explained, "The packet holds candles, matches, and the rug—well, it came from the first bear I killed. I brought my nephews up here last year after a coon hunt, and we left our unneeded supplies wrapped in the tarp. Sometimes other hunters might need a warm, dry spot and come by here. Several of the larger caves hold such things left behind by climbers and hunters."

Millie accepted his matter-of-fact explanation in the manner in which he offered it: facts about a kind of life that she had known nothing about before coming to Freeman. Her earlier thought that Woods was not unlike those pioneering mountain men of the West came to mind.

Also Millie accepted a biscuit stuffed with skillet-fried ham, both left over from the solid breakfast that Glovina had prepared. Happily she munched right along with the mountain man sitting tailor fashion beside her. A wedge from a round of Glovina's cheese had a pungency signifying careful aging when Woods sliced it off with his pocket knife. He speared it and held it out. When Millie bit into the golden cheese, she sighed in near ecstasy at the smooth, tangy taste.

"How does your apple taste?" Woods asked, smiling upon

seeing her polish its red skin against the arm of her jacket before sinking her teeth into its crispness.

"Like ambrosia." *He has such a nice smile*, she thought.

"It came from my trees." *She's so natural*, Woods thought, *so easy to be with. And so beautiful*!

"I don't recall seeing an orchard."

"It's over near the garden. What with our soil being so rocky around here, we have to hunt patches here and there that are easily cleared of the bigger stones."

"I'm amazed at how self-sufficient you and your family are and more than a little impressed."

"This is the greatest place in the world to live."

"Have you tried living anywhere else?"

"Briefly." He finished his apple and tossed the core out the opening into the heavy rainfall, explaining, "Some animal will be glad to find a little tidbit when the rain clears."

"Where did you live when you left the mountains? What did you do?" Millie leaned forward to hear his answer better.

"I went to Hot Springs and worked at a livery stable, but it was a long time ago when I was still wet behind the ears." Grinning, he sent a thumbs-up mocking gesture toward himself. "I became the top hand at teaching the society ladies how to ride."

"My, you must have charmed a score of them, at least."

"Yep," he replied facetiously. "They were falling all over themselves to take in a mountaineer with manners not half so elegant as those of the fine-blooded mounts they were learning to ride."

Millie laughed at the ridiculous self-painted portrait. "Come now. You don't have any scars showing. When you win the race for representative and show up in Little Rock—"

"I told you I won't be running."

"You should reconsider it, Woods. You've already told me some of the things you feel should be done for the area. It sounded like a good platform to me. I saw at the box supper how people seem to hang around you and listen." Almost as an afterthought, she added, "And everybody who talks with me seems determined to tell what a fine man you are."

Woods avoided her gaze. "Folks have a way of being nice

about one of their own, I reckon. I didn't say I wasn't going to work to get a good man elected." He smoothed at his mustache and fixed his gaze on the rain outside the cave. "We've been holding community gatherings around the district over the past year. In fact, there's a meeting next Saturday night in the schoolroom for people to talk about the issues at stake. I aim to be there."

"I'm glad you're keeping your hand in, even if you won't consider being a candidate—which makes no sense to me." Millie shivered and wondered what Woods's piercing gaze had to do with her sudden chill. A cloud seemed to have floated across his blue eyes. "It must be getting colder."

Woods rose and went to the darker side of the cave where she had seen the blackened remains of a fire. "I can build us a fire. The rain ought to let up in a little while."

During the next hour as they sat before the crackling fire and got warm enough to shed their wet jackets and spread them on nearby rocks for drying, Millie and Woods talked on and on. She told him more about the happenings in the classroom and what she hoped to accomplish throughout the school year. He told her more about the operation of the bauxite mine and the needs of some of the workmen. There was a give-and-take to their conversation that fell as naturally and effortlessly as the raindrops pattering outside the cozy cave.

"You're sleepy," Woods accused after Millie smothered a third yawn in a matter of minutes.

"Probably so. We did get up with your roosters. I notice you're looking sleepy-eyed, too."

Before she could figure out what he was up to, Woods had risen and taken down the tarp-wrapped bundle from the ledge. "Here," he said as he rolled out a bearskin with a flourish and laid it on the rocky floor near the softly burning fire. "You can rest on my pride and joy—or at least it was back when I was fifteen."

Millie praised the softness of the dark brown fur and the supple skin on the backside, even as she demurred and said she was not all that sleepy. She realized then that the earlier whiff of something wild there in the cave might have come from the bearskin and that it attracted some elemental part of her nature far more than it repelled her fastidious nose. She shivered. Where was the old Millicent, the woman she had known? Never would she have—

"Humor me and stretch out on the rug," Woods was saying when Millie jerked her thoughts back to the moment. With only the spread-out bearskin between them, he was kneeling and looking across at her soberly.

Millie felt that mysterious bit of humming start up inside. "I—I really shouldn't. The rain will let up soon, and we can start back." Her eyes overruled her brain and met his questing gaze. In the reflection from the slow-burning campfire, she could see her image mirrored in the black pupils of his blue eyes. The absurd thought that she might have already lost herself within those fascinating depths surfaced and brought a skip to her pulse. She must be more fatigued than she had realized, she consoled herself.

"Frankly, Millie, we'll have to wait a couple of hours more for the Gooseneck to run off some of this rainwater, even if the rain slows. I looked down at it when I went out to scout some tree limbs to burn, and it's muddy and dangerous."

Millie's face showed her uncertainty. Her stomach tightened at the thought of being stranded for a long while with the handsome mountain man whose two kisses over the past two weeks had shaken her so thoroughly. She had come to terms with the discovery that she was experiencing an infatuation for Woods—maybe not too different from those of the girls she had taught when they first began receiving attention from boys—but she needed more time to think things through.

"What if the river doesn't go down enough to cross it?" she asked. "Won't your mother and Glovina worry?"

"Likely the river will be fordable before dark. Mama and Glovina know what happens when it rains in the mountains and how the streams rise and fall. They know, too, that I'm at home in a dozen or more caves around here. We have water here and plenty of extra food along. They'll not be overly concerned." When she made no reply and her mouth pursed up in obvious concern, he asked, "Don't you believe I can take care of you? Are you afraid?"

Millie lay down on the bearskin then. His explanation sounded plausible. She had nothing to fear—except herself. Always she had been in charge of herself. She might be a bit confused about not knowing herself as well since arriving in Freeman, she reflected uneasily, but she still ruled, didn't she? "I'm not worried if you're not." She yawned again behind her hand, this time not even trying to disguise it. "After all, you're a mountain man. You can chase away all varmints."

Watching Millie turn on her side and cradle her pretty head against her arm, Woods chuckled. "That's right. I'm a regular Kit Carson, and don't you forget it."

· *Chapter Twelve* ·

Kit Carson? Frontiersman, trapper—a man dead at least thirty years, if he remembered tales from childhood correctly, Woods mused after Millie's eyes closed. He already had learned over the past two weeks that the schoolmarm from Little Rock had her own way of looking at things, and he admitted that being around her was entertaining, exciting . . . and puzzling.

Upon seeing Millie's soft, regular breathing patterns as she lay curled on her side on his bearskin rug, Woods figured the beautiful redhead was sleeping soundly. The sight of one slender hand lying near her face, with palm open and fingers nestling in the brown fur of his rug, touched him in a singular way. A weary child might sleep with such complete surrender in unfamiliar surroundings, but he doubted that many women so recently transported into a new world would have. Wonder why she had called him a mountain man? For some reason the term pleased him, as if it might be a term of endearment.

Not for Woods to tolerate was the despised word that Millie had used when referring to his friend from childhood, Lavelle Landeen: hillbilly. From all the stories that he had heard told about the explorers and trappers of the mountains in the Old West, he reckoned that the title "mountain man" was a bit of a compliment.

After dashing outside and checking the still-dripping clouds almost directly overhead, Woods brought in another armload of fallen tree limbs and fed the small campfire as quietly as possible. He was grateful that the small opening at the back of the cave allowed the wind freedom to whisk through at intervals and clear away any accumulated smoke. All in all, he had learned over the years, the cave served well as shelter.

Feeling a bit tired himself, Woods used his jacket as a pillow and stretched out beside the bearskin rug where Millie lay sleeping. He forced himself to turn his back to her, for the temptation to continue gazing upon her face and admiring her loveliness loomed too large. There was something about watching the beautiful woman sleep that touched at the vast well of tenderness abiding within him.

Then thoughts of what might happen if the rain continued and they couldn't ford the Gooseneck before dark plagued Woods. He had no fear that the two of them would not be safe and comfortable in the cave, even if they had to stay all night. What Woods feared was his growing fascination with Millie. The matter was downright spooky.

Why, if anyone had asked, Woods's thoughts ran on, he would have sworn that he had been immune to women for at least the past ten years. Those moments of careless spilling of passion into the willing bodies of nameless, faceless women when nature demanded did not count. No, he referred only to women who would deserve more attention. His decision that he had no need for a lasting relationship with a woman had come after much thought, in spite of what his mother, aunt, and five sisters kept telling him.

Woods allowed the past to parade openly in his mind for the first time in years. Though a few pretty faces had held him enthralled briefly during his stints as a young riding instructor in Hot Springs, never had a woman invaded his heart and soul as had the one who charmed him before he was twenty. One reason was that Woods guarded against such a disaster, for he had no wish to go through agony a second time. No, sirree, he had reassured himself. Once bitten, he had stayed clear.

Bitten was only part of it, Woods mused. Charmed him good, turned him inside out, then cast him aside like a used-up mess of coffee grounds before he was twenty—his thoughts tore at him in spite of his wishing they wouldn't. Fern Stevens.

Blonder and more beautiful than her younger sister Annabelle, more beautiful than any other young woman in the area, Fern Stevens had wreaked havoc with the hearts of many men in the Freeman community—as well as those of some in Hot Springs where she and Annabelle had attended a girls' academy. Through the years Woods had concluded that Fern had seemed driven to seek more than a single share of life's bounty and that she had not cared what pain she might cause others in her search.

Woods closed his eyes in bittersweet memory. What ecstasy the amply curved Fern and he had shared during those summers when she was home from school and both were leaving childhood behind and reaching out toward adulthood with exploring hands and hungry bodies! How long since he had allowed himself consciously to think her name in connection with his own? It had been several years, way back before Fern had died six years ago while giving premature birth to her third child by the man she had chosen to marry, Lucas Milstead.

Now thoughts of a tall, slender woman with short red curls, a forceful yet charmingly feminine voice, and velvety brown eyes were jostling long-locked-away, hazily recalled memories of the petite Fern's blond loveliness, soft lilting speech, and pale blue eyes. Woods shifted his position and let out a sigh. He would have to step up his guard. He was not about to let another woman march in and whistle the tune for him to dance.

Besides, Woods reassured himself, Millie Monroe had shown no interest in sharing anything with him but friendship. He grinned and made an addition: or maybe an occa-

sional argument. Even if he wanted to find instances of her
flirting with him—and he was certain that he did not—he
would come up with a zero. Having kissed her twice, he had
learned that though she seemed unaware of the fact, she was
brimming with passion. But Millie was no flirt. Was that one
of the things that had attracted him to her?

He hadn't liked it one bit when Millie had announced that
she had no need of a man in her life, but afterward he realized that she was independent enough to believe it. An alien
thought loomed, startling him: If he could say that he had no
need of an emotional relationship with a woman, why
couldn't she say the same about a man? Maybe she, too,
guarded a secret but dead love.

The recollection of how his angry kicking at rocks that
night after leaving the teacherage had rewarded him with a
ghastly permanent scar on the toe of one of his new boots
wiped away Woods's musing smile. The sassy redhead did
have a way of getting him riled. And he had the permanently
marred boot as testimony.

Living with memories when the need arose, Woods decided before he fell asleep on the ground beside the bearskin, was likely a sight easier than opening up his heart
again—even if Millie showed interest in his doing so, which
she did not.

Protective arms tightened around Millie in the nicest kind
of way. She felt all woman-y and desirable and cherished.
Deciding she must be dreaming, she murmured and snuggled nearer to the warmth of the solid body holding her
close. The air was decidedly damp and cold, but she could
feel a furry warmth underneath her body. She shifted her
head until a warm mouth eased atop her own and stilled all
movement for a breath-stealing moment.

What a dream, Millie thought groggily. The man was
kissing her in the same way that Woods had kissed her. And
she was responding in the same way, too, letting her lips
answer those hot, demanding ones working such welcome
wet magic. Her arms slid upward, freeing the last portion of
the loose shirt from the waistband of the borrowed breeches
she wore. The sensuous movement threw her breasts in con-

tact with the hard planes of a man's broad chest—likely that of a mountain man, her half-sleeping mind whispered. She wriggled her shoulders and let those ample signs of womanhood spill freely against the manly chest. Her breath wobbled from pure ecstasy. Dreams were for pleasure, weren't they?

Woods opened his eyes. What was going on? The campfire had burned down to a few glowing coals. A gentle rain still fell outside. Neither observation surprised him.

But awakening to find himself lying on the bearskin rug with an aroused, compliant Millie in his arms, kissing him with wild hunger, shocked the daylights out of him. How had the two of them become locked in such a passionate embrace?

His mind blurred by what was happening, Woods recalled that he had fallen asleep at least a foot away from the bearskin. Had Millie awakened and decided to tease him? Maybe he had been wrong in deciding she was not a flirt. A small part of him—it was a tiny part, really too small to heed—tried telling him to pull away and question her surprising actions.

Never one to examine a blessing too closely, or listen to weak inner voices, Woods shut his eyes again and let nature direct his movements. More than once he had recalled how warmly Millie kissed, but now he believed she must have been holding something back at those previous times. Her mouth was honey warmed up in a blaze of sweet spring sunshine, and he couldn't seem to get enough of the taste of her. He wasn't surprised to smell the fragrance of jasmine; it was undoubtedly a mysterious part of her soft skin. Already his blood was heating up something fierce, as was the telltale spot in his groin.

When his hand trailed down Millie's back and began a new upward path underneath her loose shirt, Woods half expected her to open her eyes and slap him, or at least protest in some way. Instead her arms clung even closer around his neck, and her tongue darted to meet his where it played at the inner sides of her lips. His breathing and heartbeat stepped up noticeably, as did hers. His questing hand discovered what it sought, and Woods's senses reeled from the feel of her firm breast beneath his exploring fingers. In no time at all, his thumb had teased her nipple into a tight nub. Her hips and legs moved restlessly as his fingers caressed first one warm, satiny breast and then the other. On the inside he felt as if a storm of fire might be going to eat him up.

Millie squirmed lanquidly. What was happening to her? If this was a dream, she was going to explode any minute and never live out the last scene. She had no wish to open her eyes. Waking had always been a chore. The mind-boggling kiss might end if she let herself awaken. Worse, whatever was turning her swelling breasts into heated mounds of ecstasy might disappear forever.

Never in her twenty-six years had Millie Monroe experienced anything like the enveloping waves of liquid warmth floating her body and her senses into another world . . . and not alone. That seemed the best part. She felt like singing out. She was no longer alone. A man—no, a mountain man —was sharing her overpowering dream, forming a vital part of the euphoria transporting her. Strange, but there was that tenuous humming sensation inside her body again, the one that often livened when she was around Woods. Was it what was calling to her?

"Millie." Woods lifted his mouth from hers, seeing then that her eyelashes formed twin semicircles of lustrous black silk against her pale skin. Could it be that she was truly asleep, that she was unaware that their bodies were entwined in intimacy? Had he started all of this wondrous passion without either's conscious knowledge? His thoughts did a double step: Or had she?

In the near darkness of the cave, Woods could detect no movement behind Millie's closed eyelids, though her arms loosened their hold around his neck at his husky call. His earlier thoughts held no meaning, not when he was drinking in the sight of her lying in his arms. Her hair, her face, the texture of her skin, the tiny flaring of her nostrils as she breathed—these were real and served as a feast to a man starving for such nourishment. Her lips, branded wetly with his kisses, curved up sweetly . . . for his eyes alone, he realized with a feeling bordering on reverence.

With gentleness Woods unfastened the buttons of Millie's

shirt and opened it. At the sight of her slender rib cage and surprisingly full breasts covered only with the thin white fabric of her camisole, he tried swallowing the sudden lump filling his throat. His storming pulse took on a faster pace while his gaze swept over Millie's face and body again. She was more beautiful and desirable than he had imagined.

"Hey, Millie. Are you asleep?" His voice came out furred and deep while his eyes studied her blissful face. Her eyes remained closed.

One of Millie's arms slipped down from around Woods's neck then. Her soft hand and fingers leisurely explored his manly cheek, then his mustache, his lips, and, last, his chin. In the manner of one rewarded at last with the choicest of prizes, she sighed when her forefinger traced the shape of the cleft on his chin. Her finger lingered there for a moment, almost as if it might be bestowing a kiss. Her mountain man was the right one, she exulted. She welcomed the additional heat fueling her runaway pulse at the discovery that she was not dreaming.

Millie's eyelids fluttered open. Incongruous thoughts seized her. Why not pretend no world outside the one inside the cave existed? And why not imagine that only one man and woman peopled her tiny world? A secretive smile brought an additional glow to her face.

Seeing that Millie was awake and smiling, and moved unbearably by the caresses of her hand upon his face, Woods slid her camisole aside and gave in to his desire to lave her exposed neck and breasts with kisses.

"Sweetness," he murmured while his hungry mouth and tongue suckled at will upon the warm silken flesh and turned it into hot wet femininity. As he kissed and fondled her throbbing breasts, her hands came and rested in his hair with a sure touch. Her fingers dipped into the thick growth and gently determined the entire shape of his skull. Woods felt her caresses affecting him in a stabbing, arousing way that added honeyed fuel to the fire building in the pit of his belly.

Before Woods permitted his gaze to wash down fully over Millie's naked neck and breasts, he leaned and softly kissed each of her wondering eyes shut again. He let his lips linger on each closed eyelid, savoring the feel of her silken eyelashes beneath them. He tasted the essence of her sweetness and, after breathing in the barest hint of jasmine, wondered if he might not know now what femininity in its rarest, most delicious form smelled like, tasted like, and looked like. When his thoughts so plainly dwelt upon the magic of the moment, he reassured himself, he doubted that he could be blamed for thinking of nothing but the delectable woman in his arms.

"You're the most beautiful woman I've ever seen, Millie." He thought it only fair that she know. He spoke softly from a distance of a bare inch above her closed eyes. "Sweet girl, is this right for us?"

Millie opened her eyes and smiled up at him. Sweet girl? Before she had met Woods and he had nicknamed her Millie, she never had been called anything but her given name. Now he had added an endearment. Her voice grainy with deep feeling, she replied, "As right as the rain falling outside."

Partially closing her eyes, Millie shivered from the sound of his bass whisper. His velvety words and his tangy breath fanning so intimately across her face commanded her being. Like a gentle summer breeze caressing a newly opened rose and bending the bud to its will for a brief space of time, she thought.

"Kiss me again," she whispered. "I loved the way you were kissing me when I woke up." A thickness in her throat disguised her voice and gave rise to her earlier suspicion that she did not recognize the Millie on Promise Ridge.

Woods lifted his face. The time had come for a lasting decision. "If I kiss you like that again, there won't be any turning back." The ache in his groin flared in protest.

"I think I might die if we turned back now." She moved restlessly against the bearskin rug, her eyes fixed on his. Whatever part of her was new might die in its infancy, Millie thought, for it had been born such a short time ago. It was all that mattered now, though. She suspected that the new woman she had become first emerged when she had met the handsome mountain man who now was gazing down at her with—with what? If only she could fathom what was going on within those blue eyes.

"What about tomorrow, sweet girl, and the—"

Quickly she interrupted. "Tomorrow doesn't count. Only this moment is real." She thought only of easing the demanding ache to get lost further in Woods's embrace. He played a leading role in her imagined little world of the moment. She held out her arms. "Teach me, mountain man. I'm new."

No longer did Woods think of holding back. He was besotted with the need to take all that Millie offered and teach her about the ways of man and woman making love. Woods removed his shirt, aware that she watched with wide eyes, even as she slipped out of hers. With feverish haste they shed their remaining clothing, flinging garments right and left until at last they lay in resplendent nakedness on the bearskin. Woods's hoarse cry of longing filled the small space between them before he gathered Millie's nakedness close to his own.

Millie almost lost her breath and secretly admitted to a stinging wash of fear when she felt the hard length of Woods's body next to hers. He brought both hands to frame her face. He studied its oval shape, adorable nose, and full mouth, smiling his approval. Still without haste his gentle yet insistent mouth captured hers then and stilled her fear. Eagerly she kissed him back, welcoming the brand of his mustache on the skin around her upper lip and that of his furred chest on her crushed breasts. She felt giddy from all that was happening.

While her tongue dueled with his, Millie sensed that whatever was heating up her mouth and streaking periodically down to the virginal core of her womanhood was merely a prelude to what was yet to come. A gnawing, persistent craving replaced that earlier frisson of fear, a craving to learn all that the mountain man could teach her about the wonders of making love. She never again would find the right man and the right time, the new Millie told herself. There was only this once. She planned to remember it for the rest of her life, and she wanted the memory to be perfect.

There in the cave with its pungent, primeval scents blending with the somewhat domestic smells of wood smoke and the falling rain, Woods at first taught a sometimes breathless

Millie with fierce kisses, kisses that seemed to reach into the depths of her soul and disturb the rhythm of her heartbeat. She learned the inside of his mouth and came to welcome the roughness of his searching tongue in her own. Also he taught her with kisses rained upon her entire body, from the tip of her chin to the slight dimples of her knees.

When she demurred at Woods's claim to the inside of her thighs, he growled low in his throat and whispered, "Who's doing the teaching, sweet girl?"

Millie lay back and let him have his way after that, though she learned a few lessons from imitation and gave her own hands license to rove over the smooth rippling muscles of his chest and his back. The raw maleness of his tall, lean body awed her. Her hands delighted in the flatness of his stomach and his buttocks. She savored the proof of his latent strength and power beneath the lightest brush of her fingertips and doubted that she had ever felt softer or more feminine. When her shortness of breath made her feel foolish, she noticed that Woods suffered from the same ailment.

He showed her how a man's mouth and his hands, though work-roughened, can transport a woman's body into a heated mass of quivering desire, how a man's strength and tenderness is revealed in little ways—such as when he worked murderous wet magic upon her breasts and left her gasping, then lightly circled her navel with a teasing forefinger to allow her to catch her breath and once again lie still.

When Millie felt certain that Woods had turned her body into a roaring furnace of heat that could never be doused, one of his hands nudged her legs apart with telling persistence. She arched her head back and cried out when the caresses of his fingers on her sensitive flesh brought an unexpected charge of ecstasy that pierced her keenly.

"Let it out, beautiful girl. I like to know when I'm pleasuring you."

Millie judged that her thoughts must be as wanton as her body, for she wished that she knew how to pleasure Woods in some reciprocal way. Blindly she reached for the swollen part of him that had nudged hotly between her legs earlier and almost drove her into a frenzy. She cupped her hands around his manhood gently, surprised that it was warm and pulsating and seemed to be growing in her hands. At his sudden stiffening and his hoarse growl of joy, she laughed victoriously low in her throat and kissed his neck and the cleft in his chin, before recapturing his willing mouth.

Woods smiled appreciatively at Millie's open delight in making love and at her eagerness to share her passion. When her soft hands had closed around his shaft, he had known that he could no longer hold back. He pressed her against the bearskin rug then and matched up their wildly throbbing parts. Both trembled anew with joyful anticipation. Kissing her and murmuring against her mouth, he joined his body with hers.

Unprepared for the sharp, cutting pain, Millie stiffened and pushed against him in agony.

"Only this one stab of pain, sweet girl," he consoled in a ragged voice only a space away from her lips. And with those words of consolation, he captured her mouth again and sent his hot shaft home. When she quieted, his kiss softened, and he lay still, pulsating deep within her enfolding womanhood.

Millie felt more than the pain and the fiery throbbing of their joining. The old humming sensation had stepped up and was one with all the wondrous new feelings rushing over her. She felt shock at the penetration of her body; she had not expected to feel such excruciating pain any more than she had expected to feel that her body no longer belonged to her as it once had. The abandoned manner in which the mountain man began moving then within the burning depths of her womanhood, half withdrawing and then returning to that molten center, gave rise to her earlier thought that she was not her old self in any of the ways that counted and that nothing but the exquisite moment mattered.

She longed for a fleeting second to know why she felt that more than a fusing of bodies was taking place. From some primitive seed of knowledge lodged deep within, Millie cast aside all rational thought. As though she knew what to do from some secretive command, she opened herself freely to the man governing her every cell with his tantalizing movements. With abandonment, she matched her motions to his and learned the ancient rhythm of love.

Much as the chasing clouds had stepped in front of the sun and regulated the light and shadow on the mountains and in the valleys all that morning, Millie suspected that something as primeval was guiding her upwardly scaling senses. A being as powerful as the sun awaited her somewhere beyond the concealing clouds of her flesh, and she could hardly wait to spiral up to that zenith. Like a sudden flash of sunlight from behind a racing dark cloud, her spirit, blissfully joined with Woods's, burst free. The inner humming evolved into a heavenly shout. She sensed that they were soaring toward eternity for a brief moment and that never again would she be the same.

Their bodies still one, but no longer straining, the lovers spiraled down from that brief space of spiritual unity. The real world awaited.

His entire body trembling and drained from the mind-boggling climax to their lovemaking, Woods sank against Millie before finding the strength to separate their bodies. His gasps for air gradually subsided, as did hers, and he rolled away from her, spent as never before. He kept one arm across her slender middle. She was some woman, this sweet girl of his, he reflected. He did not realize how possessive his thoughts were sounding.

"Millie," he said after a spell of intimate silence, "I think you're no longer new to making love."

Millie smiled and lifted his head gently with both hands. She wanted to look into his face. "You're some fine teacher, mountain man."

Woods laughed low in his throat and gathered her close again, pleased that she was laughing softly, too. He had not known what to expect when their towering passion had spent itself, especially since he had learned what he had suspected all along about her being a virgin. He kissed her, with both their mouths open in laughter, and their teeth bumped, the action setting off another ripple of laughter, louder this time but still deliciously warm and private.

"The only thing I know to say is you're some fine pupil. I'm glad I pleasured you," Woods said before a tender silence claimed them, a silence threaded with gushes of unrecognizable thoughts begging to be collected into words.

"Does a man know how making love makes a woman feel?"

Never having given the matter any thought and never having had a woman talk with him about such, Woods gazed at her wonderingly and, still lying on his side, formed a resting place for his head by angling his arm and opening his hand. Would the beautiful redhead always surprise him with her unorthodox thoughts? The idea intrigued him. "No more than a woman can tell the same about a man, I guess. Why? How did it make you feel?"

Gazing outside the cave, her lips gently pursed, Millie replied musingly, "As if I might have been someone else, as if something within soared away."

"I hope it's not gone forever." He wanted to think about the thoughts whorling, wanted to think about the aftereffects of what had taken place between the new schoolmarm and him and what he should do about them, wanted to. . . . It was no use. All he could think about was that he wanted to make love to Millie again, right then.

With a glowing look on her face, Millie sat up and fluffed at her short curls. Aware that he watched with unconcealed interest, she reached for her camisole and pulled it over her bare breasts. On her way to the baby waterfall, thoughts of her feelings for Woods intruded with each step and reminded her that there really was a cosmos outside the cave and that she would have to deal with it and its inhabitants and their codes of conduct.

While cleansing herself Millie questioned what she might feel for Woods. What she formerly had relegated to an infatuation loomed now as something brand new, something far more threatening to someone who had no plans to form another emotional attachment to a man. For want of a better title—or maybe one not so close to the bone—she decided that it was a physical attraction that had kept the handsome mountain man uppermost in her thoughts since their first meeting, two weeks ago tomorrow. It stunned her to think that she had known him such a brief time.

Woods apparently had no deeper feelings toward her than a physical attraction, Millie's thoughts ran on, else he would have told her that he loved her during their tender lovemak-

ing, or at least afterward. Since she was not looking for
love, she did not want to think about love, not when it had
not been mouthed by Woods or even hinted at.

Besides, Millie reflected with what she believed was candor, she had been in love once and it had gone sour. In a
way she was grateful that such a powerful thing as this physical attraction she felt for Woods never had attacked her before. At the moment it seemed a lot scarier than the love she
once had known. She would have to be on guard so as not to
let a physical attraction take over her being.

Sobered more than she cared to be by her thoughts, Millie
returned to where Woods still lay naked on the bearskin rug,
watching her every movement with an unfathomable gaze.
As she looked at him, it came to her that it was not only his
face and head that made the mountain man handsome. She
thought of how his physique was fine enough to serve as a
sculptor's model, what with his heavily muscled chest,
shoulders, and arms and thick, corded neck. His flat belly,
narrow hips, and thickly muscled legs drew her gaze before
she turned and found her drawers. She had stepped into them
before Woods spoke.

"I wish you wouldn't get dressed," Woods said. He had
watched with growing disappointment as she kept covering
her winsome body with garments. The sight of her shortened
drawers tempted him to comment on them, but only fleetingly. Something about the look on her face was different.
With renewed appreciation for her slender, long-limbed
body, he noticed that her graceful movements reminded him
of a dancer that he had seen on his visit to the ballet in St.
Louis.

Millie was pulling on her breeches by then, aware that a
pair of blue eyes took in her every movement. "Making love
with you was right . . . for me, that is. But I want to get
dressed now." She did not dare look at him, for fear she
might give in and return to his arms. Escape was the only
answer, or so it seemed. If she could call up her customary
dissembling, she might manage to get through the next few
hours. Actually, she realized, she would settle for only one
hour at a time. Fifteen minutes wouldn't be bad.

"It was right for me, too. Come over here and let me change your mind."

"No."

"Why not?"

Considering every answer possible to one whose body cried out for things denied by its controlling brain and one whose reasoning process seemed to have trickled from the cave along with the little fall of water, Millie replied breathily, "I don't think it's wise for us to become too involved."

Woods sat up, tucking his legs tailor fashion, and crossed his arms. No words formed. He grunted.

"I'm not a woman of loose morals," Millie explained in a trembling voice. How could he sit there as if nothing unusual had happened? It would take awhile before she could sit so still. Maybe he did not feel quite the same overwhelming attraction to her that she felt to him; maybe their lovemaking had not meant so much to him as it had to her. Chiding herself for calling up those wonderful moments of passion and almost letting them rearrange her plans, she tucked her shirt inside her form-fitting breeches and forgot what she meant to do next. Oh, yes, she remembered when she looked around and saw her shoes and stockings, she needed to put something on her legs and feet.

Millie truly wanted Woods to understand her reasoning and said, "I gave in to impulse and I'm not sorry, but I'm fully awake now." When he grunted again, a grumpy sound this time, she went on, her voice sounding less positive now. "I'm assuming that you aren't any more interested in marrying than I am. I told you the other night that I have no plans to become involved emotionally with a man." Purposefully she made her mind go blank.

"Who said I was planning on asking you to marry me?" Woods retorted, stung by her seemingly know-it-all air.

"Well," Millie replied with a dash of vinegar flavoring her words, "I wasn't planning on accepting if you had." He didn't have to sound so arrogant about it! She reminded herself that she could not let emotion get in the way, not now when she had figured out a way to live with her compelling physical attraction to the handsome mountain man: Never again would she allow her desire for him to have such a ruling hand.

Woods snatched up his clothing and put it on. Hellfire! Millie Monroe had the wildest notions of any woman he had ever seen. Of any woman he had ever heard of, he corrected angrily. He must have been out of his mind to think even for a brief second that time in the teacherage that he might be falling in love with her. A man would have to be hunting for trouble to entertain such a crazy thought, he reassured himself as he tried understanding any woman who turned down a proposal before she received it. And not just any proposal, but *his,* Woods Sanders's, the man immune to women.

With a biting edge to his words, Woods said, "I never meant that you might have loose morals. What I don't see is why you're taking such an attitude toward making love again." Where did she get her absurd ideas?

Millie cocked her head and looked at him in the half-light in the cave. Even the way Woods held his shoulders, the left a fraction lower, seemed unique and a vital part of the forceful statement that the man made simply by existing. He was truly the most handsome, virile man she had ever been around. In her naïveté, she promised herself that never again would his mere presence affect her as it had done ever since she first met him, now that she knew what drew her to him. Physical attractions took awhile to wear off; she had heard that somewhere or maybe read it, she reminded herself when just looking at Woods was making her want to go hug him and lay her head against his solid chest and. . . .

"I won't make love again," she said, "but I like you and like being around you—more than any man I've ever known. We probably got carried away by a fleeting physical attraction this afternoon, but I truly want us to be friends and do things together like going on the hayride next Sunday."

Paying little attention to anything but her refusal to return to his arms, he said, "I want us to be friends, too. But can't we be friends and still—"

"No. I've read that such relationships never work."

"What you read could be wrong!" Woods's lifelong respect and awe for the printed word became distorted and tawdry. He could not figure out what had him so damned mad and confused. Was it only because she had told him "no"? He had no wish to think further on the matter. His mind and body were in turmoil enough as it was. Besides, Millie seemed to be doing enough thinking for the both of them—not that any of hers made a lick of sense.

"I doubt it." Millie could not help but think how Woods's deep voice reverberated in the cave, a little like a roar from an angry lion might have sounded if threatened by something it suspected might be dangerous.

"You don't know everything!"

"Neither do you," Millie replied sweetly.

With only her self-designed logic behind her reasoning, Millie felt mysteriously fulfilled and more in charge of her life than she had since her arrival in Freeman. She was ready to get on with the next chapter.

Her gaze darting to the darkening outside, Millie asked the silent, still-faced Woods, "Don't you believe it stopped raining quite some time ago? Chances are we can start back to your house now."

· *Chapter Thirteen* ·

Long before Millie and Woods returned to the Sanders home that Saturday at dusk, she was wondering how well her plan for allowing her attraction to him wear off was working. She found that she could not avoid viewing the mountain man in a new light, one far headier than the earlier one. Maybe, she mused, she should just treasure the memory of their passionate lovemaking and count it as the most enthralling experience of her life. Though it made no sense, she thought of the way the bugs had circled around the lamp chimney on the preceding night when Woods had escorted her to her bedroom.

Millie suspected that Woods was not quite his usual cheerful self during the remainder of her visit, but, in general, he seemed to have accepted her decision about there not being a repeat of their lovemaking. At least he never again made reference to it after they left the cave and made their way across the swollen Gooseneck River. Millie had no wish to bring up the subject.

During the next week, Millie threw herself into the demanding activities of teaching, reveling in challenges and victories alike.

Holding a fragrant bowl of small golden cubes seasoned with butter and brown sugar, Annabelle dropped by for a brief visit on Monday afternoon.

"Though I appreciate any and all food, I have to ask what you brought me," Millie said after Annabelle set the dish on the kitchen table in the teacherage and explained that she did not have time to sit and visit. Wonderful spicy smells wafted to her nose.

"Baked cushaw. Have you never eaten it?"

"I've never even heard of it. What is it?" She leaned closer to the bowl and sniffed. "It smells delicious!"

"Do you recall seeing a large green-striped, melonlike vegetable in some of the gardens we passed when we went walking?"

"I thought maybe they were giant gourds too big to grow on a vine." With her fingers Millie plucked one of the small amber-colored squares and plopped it in her mouth, chewing cautiously, then appreciatively. "Um-m! Cushaw tastes as good as it smells." Aware that Annabelle was sending her a rather shocked look for her uncouth manner of sampling food, Millie grinned. "My grandmother used to say it's all right to bend rules of etiquette if you know better." After reaching for another sample, she added impishly, "And I know better."

Annabelle smiled, her apparent admiration for Millie's devil-may-care attitude and exuberance over something so simple as tasting a new food lighting up her pretty face and eyes in the nicest kind of way. "Are you going to the hayride Sunday night?"

"Yes, and I was wondering if I should bring something for the supper." Millie fingered another sample of cushaw before following her caller to the door. She wondered if Annabelle knew that Woods had invited her, but decided against bringing up his name.

With a look suggesting that she suspected Millie was a lousy cook, with or without a cookstove like the Monster, Annabelle said, as if struck by sudden inspiration, "How about taking some marshmallows to roast? We have some at the store."

Mabel Marks invited Millie over for a cup of tea the next afternoon and sent her tall, red-haired guest home with a hunk of smoke-cured ham and a huge wedge of golden pound cake. Lessie Booth came on Wednesday afternoon and brought the new schoolmarm a loaf of bread, explaining that it was her baking day and, with Millie in mind, she had baked more than usual.

Millie welcomed the friendly gestures with more than her usual warmth. That all three women mentioned the political meeting planned for Saturday night in the classroom, then the preaching and the hayride coming up on Sunday created a keener anticipation in Millie. She was finding that she truly enjoyed having such kind, thoughtful neighbors. Though she gave the matter no conscious thought, her evening meals became far more pleasant affairs.

Dressed in her second-best twill skirt, form-fitting jacket, and a cloche-type hat, Millie hurried to Booth's Livery Stable after school on Thursday. Ever so politely she ignored Edgar's attempts to learn where she was going on her professed "little pleasure ride." She also ignored the stares sent her way from the few men hanging around the blacksmith shop.

Within a short time the determined schoolmarm had rented the small buggy—to her, she mused, it would always be a one-hoss shay. She suffered a pang of doubt when the liveryman handed her up into the buggy, for the horse at first pretended it didn't understand her nervous pulls on the reins. Edgar Booth seemed concerned and suggested that perhaps she had bitten off more than she could chew.

Recalling Woods's handling of the horse on the ride to and from his house on the preceding weekend, Millie made a clacking sound from the corner of her mouth and called, "Come up there, boy! Make tracks." Her straight little nose elevated and her mouth set firmly, she was soon wheeling toward the farm that Woods had told her belonged to James and Mary Lee Hobbs, the parents of her often-absent pupil, Gladys.

The short journey proved pleasant, what with the autumn breeze caressing Millie's face and teasing colorful leaves from the limbs of oaks, sweet gums, and cottonwoods to drift down and join those already lying on the ground. With pleasure she recalled her ride over that same patch of road last Friday with the handsome Woods Sanders. Before she knew it, she was feeling warm and fluttery inside.

After Millie's tedious conversation with the shy, overly proud James and Mary Lee Hobbs, they promised that their seven-year-old son would accompany his sister to school on the following day.

"Though Gladys is a good pupil," Millie explained in her best professional tone, "she's not the one to be teaching her younger brother. Arkansas now has a law that requires youngsters to be in school."

Then, her face softened with compassion, Millie held and rocked the Hobbses' sickly infant while she listened to Mary Lee's story of hardship. Not until her husband left to take care of the livestock had the sad-faced woman been so forthright.

"Gladys don't allers miss school 'cause I need her to help with the baby or the washin' I take in, like her pa said. With her bein' fourteen and all," Mary Lee Hobbs said with noticeable embarrassment, "she done outgrowed her clothes. She's got nothin' to wear 'cept my old hand-me-downs. Sometimes I can't spare my good shoes for her to wear all day, 'specially now that colder weather is here." She sneaked a glance toward the back door, obviously fearful that her stiff-necked husband might reappear shortly. "James don't take kindly to charity, so I can't take nothin' from neighbors' offerin's, like Annabelle Stevens and her pa. James says he ain't wantin' nobody walkin' up and tellin' his young'uns that they know who used to wear what they's wearin'."

Nodding with understanding, Millie considered what she had learned during the hour's visit. The light outside was fading, and she would have to leave soon. "What about used clothing from an unnamed source—perhaps from the members of a church in another area?"

Mary Lee's thin gray face lit up while the red-haired schoolmarm told a little about her life as the daughter of a minister. She then explained about the huge traveling garments project in the big Methodist church in little Rock where her father once had served. "I'll write one of my friends and ask her to send a batch of good secondhand clothing. There was always a nice range of sizes, for the congregation is large. They can be sent by train to Reverend Tate in Elmwood, and he can send the goods to Freeman to be put in the church. I'll handle it from there. No one will have to know except us."

Before Millie left, Mary Lee and Gladys had promised that, though Millie had declared it unnecessary, they would take on the job of cleaning the church after the monthly services there. Millie slept better that night than she had all week.

After school let out on Friday, Millie went to the store to pick up the marshmallows and other items and to mail the request for a traveling garments packet to a friend from the church in Little Rock.

"If you'll wait until I close up the postal window, I'll walk home with you and beg a cup of tea," Annabelle said after filling Millie's order and placing it in her shopping basket. "I didn't get my visit out the other day. Or do you have other plans?"

"I've no plans, Annabelle. I'd love to fix tea."

Stepping outside and waiting on the porch bench, Millie pulled her thoughts together. She confessed she was a bit uneasy about the direction her conversation with Annabelle might take while they enjoyed a cup of tea. During her brief visit on Monday, Annabelle had shown no more than friendly interest in the happenings throughout the weekend.

But Annabelle was wise, Millie mused, and she seemed to have insight about people.

Millie scolded herself for her farfetched worries. Since she had no intentions of confiding in Annabelle, no one would ever know about the tempestuous lovemaking in the cave on Promise Ridge. Woods Sanders not only was her friend, but also he was a gentleman. Certainly he had been reared as one, Millie reflected. She recalled how gracious his mother and his aunt had seemed while serving as hostesses during the past weekend.

Though Millie could not remember noticing any books, the small wind-up gramophone and its considerable collection of cylindrical records had impressed her. On that Saturday night, after supper and after Woods and she had tidied themselves from their day's outing, all had sat in the living room and listened to music pouring from the concert horn. The wax recording of John Phillip Sousa's stirring "Semper Fidelis" lacked the fullness of sound accompanying the performance of his touring band when, a few years back, Millie had attended a concert in Little Rock, but it had been more than satisfying. Satisfying, too, were the warm, contemplative looks that Woods kept sending her way. There had been times when Millie had felt the music wrapped around Woods and her in an intimate way and drew them from their separate chairs.

The style of living adopted by the Sanders family might appear simple, almost rustic to some, Millie thought, but they obviously kept abreast of the rest of the world outside Lexington County and knew all that was necessary about reaching out to a newcomer and making her feel welcome.

Before leaving with Woods the past Sunday afternoon, Millie had readily agreed to the invitations from both Agatha and Glovina for another visit. She still did not understand why Woods had seemed downright indifferent in the midst of the women's enthusiastic plans for her return. Had he not said that he also wanted the two of them to become better friends?

From where she sat on the bench waiting for Annabelle, Millie deliberately refused to let her gaze wander toward the ridge rearing up behind the church and schoolhouse down the road. Her joy was too precious to examine minutely. She recalled how when Woods left on Sunday afternoon, after having driven her in the buggy back to the teacherage, she had looked out her bedroom window. Easily spotted, since she knew how to recognize it, was the cave where she had so willingly made love with the mountain man. When her heart raced at memories of their glorious lovemaking and shown her that she had lost none of her desire for Woods, she had promptly yanked the curtains closed. She had yet to reopen them.

A commotion over at Booth's Livery Stable, on the other side of the crossroads in front of Stevens's General Store, caught Millie's attention. Several men were rushing from inside the huge barn. Shocked, she realized they were following two others who were fighting.

"What's going on over at the livery?" Annabelle asked when she joined Millie on the porch of her father's store and found the redhead staring across the way.

"There seems to be a fight going on."

Annabelle sighed and readjusted a hairpin in the coiled topknot crowning her full pompadour. "Lots of times on Fridays the workers stay on and play poker or shoot dice after the wagon brings them in from the mines. Somebody brings along a jug, and one thing leads to another."

Never having seen a fistfight between grown men, Millie kept watching the milling group. "Why don't the others stop the fight? It seems cruel for the men to be pounding each other like wild animals." She shivered, glad that she had worn her heavy cloak. The air had a definite fall bite.

"Some men are like that. Maybe they think they're following in the footsteps of the Great John L. Sullivan."

Millie grinned. "If they knew that the Great John L. is now involved in delivering temperance speeches across the country—sometimes on the Chautauqua circuit—they might not be so eager to beat up on each other."

"You're right. More likely they're fighting because it's Friday, and tomorrow is payday. Papa says that often the workers get all het up knowing that they'll have money in their pockets soon, especially the single men."

"I recall now that Clive Durham mentioned he sometimes

drives over on Saturday to bring the payroll." She craned her neck to see the circle of men better after she picked up her basket of goods and walked with Annabelle down the steps of the porch onto the hard-packed yard. The huge oaks towering over the front of the store were almost bare now, and their footsteps made crackling sounds on the dead leaves.

"Yes, he often does, but the payroll came in on the commuter carriage today. I saw the driver take the money bag inside to store in Edgar's safe."

"I believe the fight must be over," Millie said with obvious relief. "The crowd seems to be breaking up."

Annabelle pulled her shawl closer against the chill of a rising wind and turned again to take in what was happening on the other side of the crossroads. "About as I figured." Her usually sweet voice filled with disgust and disapproval. "That new man who appeared in Freeman one morning back in the summer looking for work was fighting with that hothead, Lavelle Landeen. I never did know the new man's name, even before he moved out of Mabel's house to a place of his own somewhere in the hills. He sometimes buys supplies from the store."

The name Lavelle Landeen rang a bell in Millie's mind: Woods's friend who made corn whiskey. Something else piqued her curiosity to a greater degree, though, as she gazed across at the two men brushing off their clothing. "Isn't that odd? For a minute there, I thought one of the men was Woods."

Annabelle let out a little laugh. "You wouldn't if you saw him up close. The only thing he has in common with Woods is a huge black mustache—and a lot of height. The man seems as rough as a cob, to quote Papa."

Millie turned then and walked with her friend toward the teacherage down the road. With far less fear than during her first week in Freeman, she eyed the several dogs lying on the side of the road up ahead. "Isn't that dangerous to store the mining company's payroll in the livery? Since it seems common knowledge when the payroll is being kept there overnight, I would think someone might try to rob it."

"Somebody did try that right after the mines started up operations two or three years ago. Edgar and the sheriff from

Elmwood tracked the man down, though, and nobody has tried it since. The thief ended up in jail for a long spell. Edgar hires a nightwatchman now."

Millie exercised her new bravery with the village's dogs when they loped up to sniff at her basket and lick her hands. Within a short time, they had obeyed her kind but firm orders and trotted off.

"You're becoming a real Freemanite," Annabelle said with a huge smile of approval. "The next thing you know, you'll be calling all the dogs by name."

"What about this Lavelle Landeen?" Millie asked after a spell of casual talk about the idiosyncrasies of the town's numerous family pets. "Woods told me they're friends."

The pretty blonde was still telling anecdotes about Woods's friend from childhood when the two women entered the teacherage. Annabelle laughed when Millie, fiddling with the Monster and setting the tea kettle on, confessed how she had almost lost face with Woods by calling the moonshiner a hillbilly who deserved to be locked up.

"Actually no one from around here much cares what the hill folk do as long as they don't cause trouble," Annabelle confided. "I expect everyone in town who wants whiskey buys it from Lavelle or others with stills. To tell the gospel truth, I doubt if any of the revenue men from Hot Springs or Little Rock would be interested in poking around in the hills close to Freeman for the few arrests they could make. From what I've heard, those living in the hills, man or woman, know how to handle a rifle and keep hair triggers."

"Do you ever visit with the people living in the mountains?"

"My sister, Fern, and I used to ride horses over to the Sanders place in the summers." Millie noticed again the sadness riding far back in her new friend's blue eyes as she told about her childhood. "We had great fun riding with Woods and going fishing with him and his family."

Then Annabelle accepted the cup of tea that Millie poured for her and stirred a spoonful of sugar in the steaming brew. "Before I was in my teens, our mama died, and Woods's papa died not long after. One of Woods's sisters was still unmarried and at home then. All of them live farther into the mountains with their own families now. My mother grew up with Agatha Sanders's younger sister, Glovina, over near Mt. Ida."

"Then Woods and you have been friends since childhood."

Annabelle dropped her gaze. "Yes. He and I go back a long way." She sighed and looked fully at Millie again. "You're really taken with Woods, aren't you?"

"No," Millie denied, hoping her face would not redden. She wished that she could shake the feeling that Annabelle knew of her physical attraction to Woods. Somehow it loomed as such a vital part of her that she found it hard to believe it did not show. "He asked me to go to the hayride with him, but we're just friends."

"Good." After taking time to sip her tea, Annabelle went on. "I say that because it doesn't look like Woods is ever going to fall for another woman, and I'd hate to see you hurt."

"Don't worry about my getting hurt, and don't stop your story now, for heaven's sake," Millie said with a shallow laugh and a patter of disruptive heartbeats.

"Woods and Fern, my sister who was two years older than I, were crazy for each other from their early teens. Everybody thought for sure that they would marry." Annabelle grimaced as if with inward pain. "Including me.

"Fern and I attended an academy in Hot Springs, and I never cared for any of the boys calling on me there. My heart has belonged to one man in Freeman ever since I was fourteen. I thought he cared for no one but me. I was crushed when Fern stole him from me to get back at Woods.

"Woods had a plan for his future, and he wasn't willing for Fern to smash it by insisting on marriage before he could provide for her in the way he wanted to. When they quarreled and she threatened to find her another man who was willing to marry her and build her a home, he didn't take her seriously."

Millie leaned across the table, her expression thoughtful. "Are you saying that the man your sister married to spite Woods is Lucas Milstead?"

"Yes," Annabelle replied in a lifeless voice. "The three of

them were older and had more privileges than I did. I was unware that Fern began flirting with Lucas after Woods and she quarreled, or that he was fool enough to fall for her. Usually the four of us did things together, but—" Her blue eyes filled with tears. "I loved Fern—everybody loved her —but she never thought of anybody except herself. She was so beautiful and full of laughter—until after Lucas built her a house and she gave birth to Ransom nine months after their marriage."

"Why did that affect her so? Did something go wrong?"

"She confided to me later during one of her many fits of depression that she had wanted the gossip from around here to be true, that she had wanted the child to be Woods's. From the start, the boy plainly belonged to Lucas."

"How tragic!" Millie's heart labored. Woods and Fern must have made love not long before her marriage to Lucas. Fleetingly she tried to imagine how he must have felt about losing his sweetheart to another. She herself had suffered when Luther had jilted her, though the two of them had not been nearly as involved as Woods and Fern apparently were.

"Fern never forgave herself for walking away from Woods. She never gave up her passion for him. About that time Glovina became a widow and moved in with Agatha and Woods. Agatha had been losing her sight even before her husband died, and by then she was blind. With all five girls grown and gone, Woods had been left with a big responsibility."

Millie, her heart and mind drinking in all that Annabelle was relating, made a little sound of compassion.

Annabelle went on. "Right after Fern married Lucas, Woods left his mother in Glovina's care and worked in Hot Springs for a few years. To my knowledge, Woods never again sparked anybody, not from around here anyway. He seemed all out of patience with marriageable women when he returned to live at home again."

"He seems terribly fond of you, Annabelle."

"Yes, but he has never looked upon me as anyone but Fern's little sister and his friend. Friendship he can handle. He seems to have a mortal fear of giving away his heart again." Annabelle finished her tea then.

Millie cocked her head in thought. Many details were falling into place. Almost quelling her rising curiosity and discarding her notion to ask more, she plunged ahead. "You told me once that you had been married. Was it to someone from Freeman, or would you still rather not talk about it?"

The blond head shook in denial. "No, I want to tell you about it. I acted a fool and ran off with a flirty salesman calling on Papa at the store. I couldn't stand the thought of people laughing at me because my sister had stolen my beau and married him before I was old enough."

Annabelle smiled with self-mockery and continued. "Wasn't that an absurd reason to marry? It didn't take me long to realize what a mistake I had made. Papa helped me file for divorce after the first three months, and I came back here to live with him and work in the store. By then I had grown up enough to make amends with Fern. When her boys were born, I adored helping her with them. They seem as dear to me as if I had given them life."

"What about Lucas? Was he happy with Fern?"

"It hurts to say this, but I think he was at first. After she became so bitter about being caught in what she called the 'trap of being a rural wife and mother,' I suspect there wasn't much happiness in their home. She often gave in to fits of depression and sometimes refused to get out of bed."

As Annabelle talked, Millie was recalling other incidences that now held new meaning. "You still care for Lucas, don't you? Isn't that why you were so happy about rushing home to cook supper one afternoon after a visit with me—because Lucas was coming that night for supper before taking the boys home for the weekend?"

"Yes."

Millie's brain was whirling now. "And I remember how when I looked inside the classroom that night at the box supper, Lucas was hanging on to your every word. And later, out on the porch, he couldn't take his eyes off you. It seems plain that he cares for you, too."

"He tells me that he does, every time we're together." Annabelle's fair skin turned pink, and she toyed with the spoon lying on her saucer. "He's been asking me to marry him for the past four years."

"It's beginning to make sense to me now," Millie said, her words tumbling out. "That was Lucas who started the bidding on your supper box, but he gave up and let Woods get it. Then all of you—the boys, too—sat and ate together. I recall now how you left with Woods and them. And later, Woods showed up here at the schoolhouse and said something about how he wasn't being missed over at your place. Why haven't Lucas and you gotten back together, now that Fern has been dead for so long?"

"I can't stand the thought of all the talk it would cause. I think I've already given everybody enough to laugh about." When Millie scoffed at the idea, Annabelle added, "You don't know how people in a small place talk about every little thing, Millie. Sometimes it can be dreadful."

"So what? People can't let themselves avoid achieving something worthwhile simply because others might like to wag their tongues. If they want to talk, give them something good to talk about. Surely nobody can accuse you of doing anything wrong by marrying your childhood sweetheart and making a home for him and his children—especially when the boys are your nephews."

"You don't mean that."

"Of course I do. Don't let false pride rob you of a second chance. If you truly love Lucas and want to be his wife, I think you should accept his proposal."

Annabelle fidgeted on her chair. "I value your opinion because I like you so much. Also you have a more objective viewpoint, being new in Freeman. Maybe I am letting false pride rule. Tell me, do you think it would appear that I was trying to take my sister's place, the one who was always more beautiful and more popular?"

"Not at all. You have your own place in the man's heart, and that's all that matters. I believe that love is too precious and rare for people to ignore it when it comes along. I say to hell with those who don't think it's proper just because Lucas was married to your sister years ago."

Annabelle threw back her head and laughed. In the light of the approaching dusk, her pompadour glowed like silken threads of pale gold. "Millie, you're putting all kinds of ideas into my foolish head."

"And I hope those sad lights in your eyes will disappear when you make up your mind to grab this chance at happiness and tell Lucas you'll marry him." In her earnestness, Millie leaned closer.

"If I do," Annabelle said in a perkier voice than Millie had ever heard from her new friend, "will you promise to be my attendant?"

"Oh, yes! I promise."

Annabelle left soon afterward, but not before assuring Millie that when Lucas came for his sons that night, she was going to talk with him about his proposal . . . and maybe give him a positive answer.

Sunday, the first in October, dawned clear and cold, a fact noted by Millie with keen appreciation: The hayride for that night was a certainty.

Millie dashed about stoking her wood heater and getting ready for a visit from Uncle Fred and Aunt Phoebe. If what folks had told her last night at the political meeting in the classroom was right, the preacher and his wife would arrive awhile before services began at mid-morning. With little rainfall during the past week to make the road muddy, she assumed that they would be able to make good time in his light buggy.

As she was giving a last brushing to her curls, already growing in the past three weeks to a length that brushed against the edge on the high neck of her blouse, Millie heard a loud clattering noise coming from out in the schoolyard. A knock on her door followed soon after the noise subsided.

"Miss Monroe, I hope you'll be happy to see all of us," Clive Durham said to the dazed young woman opening her door. His hat in his hand, the sandy-haired man turned toward the couple with him.

Millie smiled and welcomed Aunt Phoebe and Uncle Fred, remembering to include the bespectacled Clive in her invitation for her callers to come inside the teacherage. Thrilled to see the couple who had always been dear to her, she listened as they explained how the kindly Mr. Durham had invited them to ride over for church services in his Model-T.

"Yes, Millie," Uncle Fred said after an agitated Millie had given his wife and him a tour of the teacherage and the classroom, "you're lucky to have this job in Freeman. The setup here seems just right for you."

"Bad beginnings don't always mean bad endings," Aunt Phoebe added with a mischievous smile. "I could tell that Forrest appeared pretty wild in your eyes that day when you left with him. I figured you'd have him purring before the day was half over. He's really a fine man, isn't he?"

Woods was not Forrest to her anymore, Millie thought while the gray-haired woman prattled on about Woods to the plainly bored Clive Durham, and he was no pussycat. A lion, maybe, she reflected when the memory of Woods's loud denunciation of her remarks back in the cave surfaced.

Then Millie was remembering how impressive were Woods's deep-voiced comments last night to the group meeting in the classroom in the interests of better government. Though few other women had attended the meeting in the classroom, Freeman's new schoolmarm had taken her place among the forty or fifty men from the area without qualms. She had been delighted when a starry-eyed Annabelle arrived with Lucas Milstead.

Millie had tried not to be offended when Woods made no attempt to visit with her in the teacherage, either before or after the political meeting. He did come over and talk with her privately for a few moments, but it was plain to see that he was a vital part of the group of voters. He was allowed precious little free time from general discussions on the issues that were brought up. She saw Woods involved in several whispered consultations with serious-faced men, too.

It was after midnight before Millie had fallen asleep, for she truly had expected Woods to come by before going home. Never in a million years, she had promised herself upon awakening that morning with blurred eyes and brain, would she put herself through such agony again. She had no claims on the man . . . and didn't want any. Staying up late and grading papers with one ear cocked toward the door had been downright stupid. Never again would she act like a turkey.

". . . and I can tell you're settling in, just as Mr. Durham assured us on the drive over," Uncle Fred was saying when Millie stopped her remembering of last night's events.

Aunt Phoebe announced that it was nearly time for them to get to the church next door.

"I can't believe you're not going to wear a hat, Millicent," Aunt Phoebe said. She only recently had stopped herself from puzzling over the young woman's shearing of her beautiful red hair. Already that very morning she had displayed shock and bafflement upon being told that Millicent was using a nickname, but now at the latest startling announcement in the bedroom where they stood before the mirror to make last-minute adjustments to their hair, the gray-haired woman revealed near horror. "Whatever has come over you? I always thought you were so sensible."

"Well," Millie replied with a sweet smile, "there's no rule, like in some churches, that I have to wear a hat, is there?" She saw no reason in attempting to explain how hard it was to pin a hat to her short hair. Besides, she felt plain ornery and wondered if her few hours of sleep the night before might not be causing it.

The four rushed about then. When they reached the vestibule of the church, Clive noticed the flowers first and learned that Millie had placed them there the evening before. Then Aunt Phoebe and Uncle Fred—both apparently determined to ignore Millicent's new attitude toward hats and nicknames—praised the magnificent appearance of the stately blue hollyhocks that Millie had persuaded their owner to let her arrange in the vases sitting on the tall stands. Then, after exchanging looks of reassurance with her husband that their Millicent still had some of her marbles in her pocket, Aunt Phoebe bustled into the back room of the church alongside Uncle Fred. She always served as accompanist for his congregations and wanted to look over hymn selections for the day.

Even if she had not been feeling ornery, Millie knew that she would have preferred a different arrangement, but she had no choice but to sit beside the attentive Clive Durham on the second pew in the simply but effectively appointed sanctuary. The only signs of luxury were the stained-glass windows and the thick wine-colored carpet.

Millie was glad when Thelma and Barton Blackstone and their children, Minniejean and Junior, slid into the pew with Clive and her, even though the sickly sweet smell of Thelma's overly perfumed body added to Millie's miserable state. She watched a fly lurch in midair before buzzing lazily around Thelma, then make a beeline toward one of the stained-glass windows on the side. If she was a betting woman, like those wagering on the horses at the Oaklawn racetrack in Hot Springs, Millie thought idly, she would bet a quarter with ten-to-one odds that the fly would not be back.

Millie sat up straighter when she heard Woods's resonant voice coming from the back of the church not long after the pews had begun filling up. She no longer felt cantankerous. The light coming through the stained glass suddenly took on new beauty. She visualized how other churchgoers likely were smiling and speaking to the black-haired mountain man.

Telling herself that she was doing so to see if Agatha and Glovina accompanied Woods, Millie turned and looked toward the back. When she saw the two women, she nodded and smiled upon catching their eyes. How weird, she thought, that Woods's handsome, angular face seemed to stand out so much clearer than any other's, as if it might be etched from a finer substance.

Millie realized that she had noticed the same thing last night at the political meeting. That Woods was now staring at her with a stony expression bothered her, and she turned back around, shifting her gaze to the stained-glass window up behind the pulpit. Why had Woods's mouth squinched up as if he had been eating sour grapes? She figured she knew what had her heart racing around in circles as dizzying as those performed by the fly before its escape. Then a nagging doubt that Woods would show up that night and go with her on the hayride brought a tiny knot to her stomach.

Under Aunt Phoebe's ministrations, the pump organ wheezed out a hymn in recognizable rhythm when Uncle Fred announced the number for the congregation to sing prior to his sermon. Millie could hear Woods's vibrant bass ringing out from the back and noted that his deep mellow bass was one of the truest singing voices she had ever heard. "Amazing Grace" had always been one of her favorites.

Millie guessed it was the physical attraction tempting her to turn around and watch the mountain man sing. Apparently it had not lessened . . . yet. She was not sure what made her forget to sing the second verse from the hymnal Clive was holding out politely for her to share. Maybe it was because Clive's timid tenor, coming as it was right next to her ear, was as breathy as the melody being pumped into life by Aunt Phoebe's feet working the foot bellows.

After the sermon and the final hymn, Uncle Fred hurried down the aisle and stood at the open doorway to bid a personal good-bye to each attendee. Because they were sitting close to the back, Woods, his mother, and his aunt were among the first to drive away in their buggy. Millie, with Clive's unwelcome assistance, helped Aunt Phoebe get the hymnals and organ music put away before leaving the sanctuary. Almost sighing aloud when she reached the vestibule and learned that Woods and his family had gone, Millie puzzled over why the blue of the hollyhocks in the tall vases seemed a far paler hue than she recalled.

Clive's obvious belief that he belonged with Millie, the preacher, and his wife set Millie's teeth on edge and made her doubt that she had lost her earlier feeling of orneriness.

When Lessie Booth hung back behind the other departing churchgoers and announced that Edgar and she wanted the reverend and his party to eat the noon meal with them, Clive happily went along to the Booths home. No matter that Millie tried to walk alongside Aunt Phoebe, or Lessie, or her children, Francine and Noble, the bespectacled easterner managed somehow to appear by her side.

· *Chapter Fourteen* ·

A pounding on the door of the teacherage startled Millie awake late that Sunday afternoon. She dragged herself from where she had lain catnapping ever since her visitors from Elmwood had departed in Clive's Model-T an hour earlier.

"Woods!" She hoped he did not notice how high-pitched her voice sounded. "Come on in."

Woods peered around the room as he walked in, his boots making a fierce sound against the wooden floor. "Has your company gone?"

"Yes." His bulky jacket was unbuttoned, and she noticed that he was wearing a white shirt, but without a scarf at the neck as he had at church that morning, and neatly ironed denims. "I'm glad you came before it's time for the hayride." She did not add that she had fretted that he might not show up and that when she had carried her marshmallows over to Mabel's, the collection place for the evening's meal, she had been vague about whether or not she would be attending the hayride with an escort.

"You needed to see a friend, huh?" His eyes twinkled in that teasing way she had recalled all week. Within seconds Woods was shedding his flannel-lined denim jacket and hanging it on a coat hook near the front door.

"Always." Millie moved over toward the cookstove. Ever since he had worked on it, the Monster had been on fairly good behavior. "Would you like me to make coffee?"

"We'll both be better off if I do it." His smile brought an answering one to her lips. They did not move for a while, though neither was aware that they might have been mistaken for statues staring into each other's eyes.

Then Woods got the percolator going while Millie mar-

veled at the way he could charm the Monster—and her—
without seeming to try. The burner had sprung into a circle
of blue flame at the first flare of his match and begun sputtering evenly. And she had felt a rushing of her blood upon
seeing him, as if she, too, might have been waiting to be
spurred to life by the handsome man.

Soon Woods joined Millie on the sofa. One deep-voiced
question from him about how the week of school had gone,
and Millie was off with ready answers. She loved the way he
leaned back against the sofa and watched her while she
talked, his eyes so electric and penetrating that she sometimes felt their blue might be branding her face. Woods guf-
fawed at some of her accounts of antics played by the
younger pupils, then grew serious when she recounted her
visit to the Hobbs home.

"Ever since the compulsory school attendance law was
passed two years ago," Millie said, "we teachers have been
urged to spread the word to unknowing families that they no
longer have the right to decide if their children should go to
school or not. I'm glad the Hobbs youngsters and their parents will be looking at coming to school regularly in a new
light now."

Sniffing at the increasingly fragrant smells wafting from
the cookstove, Woods fetched coffee for Millie and insisted
that she remain seated on the sofa. She marveled at the way
he seemed to like waiting on her, but quickly reminded herself that she had seen him treat his mother and his aunt with
similar courtesy. It occurred to her that for a man to be so
comfortable with doing such deeds usually associated with
women must mean that he was inordinately comfortable with
his masculinity and did not have to go around proving it by
being gruff and demanding.

Woods brought over the empty wooden box that had held
Millie's first batch of staples and turned it upside down.

"Whatever do you think you're doing, Woods Sanders?
You're scarring up my clean floor." She felt her cheeks flush
for fear she might be sounding too fussy, but she *had* spent a
good portion of Saturday afternoon scrubbing the boards
with a brush.

Woods rolled his eyes and let out a deep sigh. "Women!

There's no pleasing them." Smiling and sending his black eyebrows upward in silent question, he returned to the kitchen area.

"See how your drying cloth turns the box into a regular serving table?" he asked when at last he settled back onto the sofa beside her, his own cup and saucer in his hand. With mock pride he admired his handiwork, obviously wanting her praise.

"You have a lot of hidden talent."

Woods cut a sidewise look toward her. "So do you."

Millie cleared her throat, annoyed at herself for uttering such a blatant remark and offering him a chance to reply with a double meaning. Quickly she returned to her concern about the Hobbs children, Gladys and her little brother.

"I'm glad that the Hobbs youngsters and their parents see now that their coming to school regularly is important."

Woods nodded and smiled at her musingly. "You don't want one pupil straying off where you can't get to him, do you?"

"You're trying to aggravate me, but you're right." It seemed terribly satisfying, hearing his voice so close beside her.

"What if I told you I know of a person who never went to school and would like to learn all those things that you're dying to teach?"

"Why, I would want to know who it is and invite him—or her—to let me help. As board chairman, you should have already told me about this matter."

"You really mean that, don't you?"

"Indeed I do. I wouldn't have said it if I hadn't meant it." The cleft in his chin should not be intriguing her and inviting her to touch it, but it was.

Woods set down his cup and saucer on the makeshift table. He turned to look at her fully then, his face solemn and meditative. "Yes, I've learned that about you."

"Tell me how to get in touch with this person. I admire him—or her—already for wanting to catch up on his education. Who is it?"

Apparently unaware of her question, Woods went on in a thoughtful manner. "It'll be better if I talk with him first—

it's a man, by the way—and ask him to drop by the classroom about dark tomorrow. Would that be convenient?"

After Millie agreed, Woods stood and helped her get things tidied up before leaving for Booth's Livery where the wagons would start out shortly before dark. Both seemed set on preventing their bodies from touching accidentally. She dashed into her bedroom and returned wearing her long coat, not surprised to see that he had slipped on his jacket.

"It was good that you came early enough for us to visit," Millie told him as he held the door open for her and she went down the steps. Oh, it was. It truly was. The entire week would go better, now that he had come by and let her see that their friendship was intact. The physical attraction seemed as powerful as ever, but she figured it might be going to take longer than she first had thought for it to lessen. And it was fun feeling so alive in his presence.

"Thank you for inviting me in." Things had gone better than he had hoped, Woods reflected. In the fading light, he glanced down at his boots as they walked along, angered at himself all over again upon seeing the ugly scar on the toe of one. "I'm glad old Clive had the sofa corner all warmed up."

"That's not a very nice way to talk . . . especially to a friend," Millie huffed. She had planned on telling Woods how Clive happened to be sitting with her in church, if he asked. Not now, though, even if he asked. Not when he was teasing her and maybe hinting that Clive was courting—no, sparking her.

"I figured friends could say about anything to each other, and it would be all right."

"Common courtesy still prevails." Her chin shot up.

Woods smiled at the fascinating view of her profile tilted at an upward angle, her short curls ruffling in the slight breeze, and her full lips forming a kissable pout. "Give me another chance on the hayride. I'll be so courteous you won't even recognize me."

Millie gave him a tentative smile. They exchanged searching looks, silently asking for and then receiving apologies and acceptances for their near tiff, and quickened their steps in the brisk autumn twilight.

A jumble of happy sounds met Millie and Woods when

they neared the crossroads. Already people, laughing and talking, were finding places on the two wagons waiting in front of Booth's Livery. And never had Millie seen so many of the hamlet's dogs in one group, milling and letting out barks and whines of pleasure.

Amid a flurry of shouts and greetings from both people and dogs, Millie and Woods joined the revelers. Millie sent private little waves to Annabelle, sitting at the front of the first wagon being driven by Lucas Milstead, and to Lessie who claimed a similar position on the second wagon manned by Edgar. When everyone insisted that the vacant spot between the exuberant Francine and Noble Booth at the end of the second wagon seemed tailor-made for the newly arrived couple, Woods lifted Millie easily and set her down on the cushion of clean, fragrant hay, then jumped up to land beside her.

Almost rubbing backs with Millie and Woods were Annette and Warden who sat close together, facing the front after welcoming the newcomers. With their legs and feet dangling from the back of the wagon, Millie and Woods exchanged huge smiles for no particular reason that either chose to identify.

By the time the wagons with their loads of hay and people sticking out untidily from all sides clattered across the bridge over the Gooseneck River, Millie decided that she had heard more laughter and nonsense than she could remember having heard in her life. Some passengers sat cross-legged in the center of the wagon bed, almost buried to their waists in the fat pile of hay and so close as to rub elbows and backsides with whoever sat near.

In carefree voices, the adults teased each other and the children; the children, with their own brand of humor and their higher-pitched voices, returned as good as they received, or so they liked to believe.

"Hey, Woods! Do you need any help takin' care of our purty new schoolmarm back there?" some man called from up near the front, his voice carrying over the noisy wheels grinding against the rocky road.

When good-natured titters followed, Woods called back teasingly, "Nope! And if I did, I'd have to take applications." He watched Millie the whole time and winked at her, thinking that her face seemed even more beautiful in the twilight, all flustered and rosy as it was.

Approving hoots and bursts of laughter followed, turning Millie's initial blush into a hotter one. Somehow Woods's appreciative smile and wink made the teasing fun.

Millie loved the way her pupils seemed to separate the Millie on the hayride from the Miss Monroe of the classroom and include her in their chatter. She looped her arm through Francine's, surprised that the child leaned her red head against Millie's shoulder. Obviously content to be a separate part of the teams and the wagons full of highspirited people, the dogs provided their own entertainment by barking and playing chase.

"Look at that!" Millie exclaimed, ignoring rules of etiquette against pointing and gesturing to the horizon. "Have you ever seen anything so beautiful?"

"Not very often," Woods replied, thinking that the rising moon to which she referred could not compare to the beauty of the redheaded woman sitting so closely beside him that he could feel her hip nudging his in the hay. What would she do, he wondered, if he held her hand underneath the hay, where nobody could see?

Those sitting close enough to have heard her comment followed the direction of Millie's hand and gaze and added their praise for the sight. As if on cue, those on the wagon ahead began singing an old melody about moon magic. Right away the revelers on the second wagon took up the sweet tune, linking arms and swaying in time to the song. Woods lost no time in taking the opportunity to pull Millie's arm through his, pleased when she seemed more than willing.

The cheese-colored moon, only three-quarters full, was rising higher at each romantic verse. The grandeur of the moon peeking over the faraway mountains held Millie's rapt gaze for a moment or two and, while swaying along with Woods and little Francine to the song's rhythm, she thought about how its benevolent light added to the beauty of the evening. And wasn't that strange? she wondered, since she had not known that further enhancement was possible. Overhead the stars were beginning to twinkle.

Woods gazed at the beautiful woman sitting beside him with an expression far more rapturous than the one Millie was sending the moon and the sky. When the singing and swaying ended, he slipped his hand underneath the hay and found hers. When her eyes met his wonderingly, he smiled and reached with the forefinger of his free hand to trace the shape of her straight little nose.

"Are you warm enough?" Woods asked right next to Millie's ear. Her nose felt like cold satin. All mixed up with the smells of the autumn night and the fresh hay, the delightful fragrance of jasmine reached his nose.

"Yes," Millie replied, goose bumps racing down from her ear at the sound of his voice so near. With her hip next to his, no matter that she wore a heavy coat, she was far from cold.

"Are you having a good time?" He knew it made no sense, but he was feeling a tad jealous that those around them kept talking to Millie and stealing her attention away. That she so obviously was liked and accepted pleased him, but. . . .

"Oh, yes," Millie replied. Did Woods have any idea how the touch of his hand on hers underneath the hay was affecting her? Had she truly been cold, she would not have been after his big hand claimed hers. When his forefinger had briefly caressed the top of her nose, she had felt a surge of tingling warmth where his skin touched hers.

"Isn't this a better wagon ride than your first?" he asked, determined to capture her attention for himself alone.

"You know it is," Millie replied with a half giggle. In a flash all that had taken place the first day of their meeting came to mind, and she gazed up at his handsome face in the moonlight, liking the effects of the shadows as they etched mystery around his eyes. Had her compelling attraction to Woods begun that first day?

Soon they were at the brush arbor being greeted boisterously by those living nearby and coming ahead to build the huge bonfire and set up makeshift serving tables. Millie saw the brush arbor in the shadows. Now that time for summer revivals was past, it was no more than upended logs stuck in the ground and holding aloft the slender saplings forming a network for a canopy of short leafy branches. She noted that a few remnants of the most recent covering still clung to the cross poles, only dead brush now with leaves either gone or dead and soon to be whisked away by the seasonal rains and winds.

While the talk surrounded her, yet left her mind free for the moment, Millie remembered that when she was a child, she had attended a revival with her parents, one held in a similar brush arbor in a rural Arkansas community. She recalled how warm and safe she had felt underneath the roof of multiple layers of tree branches thick with green leaves when a sudden summer rain had threatened, but failed, to disperse the crowd listening spellbound to the fiery sermon from the traveling revivalist.

Millie saw the rows of weathered logs—split in two, with the flat side up and supported by log wedges—and recalled that they were the kind she remembered sitting on. Her gaze rested solemnly for a moment on the pulpit, also crudely made of logs, and she found herself wishing that she might still be in Freeman next summer when it was time once more for revivals to be held under the brush arbor. Her childhood memories reminded her that brush arbors also served rural communities as ideal places for all-day singings and family reunions, both always accompanied by scrumptious dinners on the ground.

Putting aside her musings then, Millie accepted a cup of warm apple cider from Mabel Marks, who apparently had come early and helped set out the food delivered beforehand to her house. After Mabel assured Millie that she needed no help, the new schoolmarm visited with the women she had not already talked with on the wagon. She was surprised and pleased that she remembered nearly all of the names and that talk was as spontaneous as though she had lived in Freeman all of her life instead of only three weeks.

From the corner of her eye Millie saw Woods and some other men down near the creek cutting long limbs from some willow trees and peeling back the bark, preparatory to threading them with fat chunks of smoke-cured ham, sausage, winter squash, and apples. She knew she was not imagining that he was the most handsome of them all; he truly was, even in the uncertain light dancing down to the creek and into the surrounding trees from the huge bonfire in the center of the clearing.

"What fun to have the men do the cooking," Annabelle whispered to Millie when the two stood back from the fire and watched as Woods and Lucas, along with the other men and some of the children, held heavily loaded willow limbs over the red coals raked out to the edges of the blazing fire. With a fond smile she directed Millie's attention to Henry Stevens across from them. "Look. Even Papa is having to make do for himself—though I saw Mabel loading up the stick for him."

Sniffing at the tantalizing smells of wood smoke and roasting food, Millie agreed with Annabelle that it was nice to see the men having such fun preparing supper over coals and joshing with each other. She saw no reason to confide that each time she had eaten with Woods, he had done the cooking. Her mountain man was unlike any other man; he had nothing to prove. He was simply himself and that was sufficient. Her use of the possessive title went unnoticed.

"This is wonderful eating," Millie told Woods after he presented her with her very own stick of hot roasted food. She nibbled daintily at first, then plowed into the tasty tidbits with relish as noticeable as that of Woods and the people sitting or standing near them.

"Wonderful company, too," was his reply, which was almost muffled during his hearty attack on his own ham and sausage.

The apple cider flowed along with the hum of conversation around the bonfire. Likely tired from the three-mile trek, the dogs seemed to have known they were expected to rest near the wagons until their owners tossed them leftovers. Talk became less frenzied, took on a more normal tone after Henry Stevens passed around his hat and gained a goodly donation for the Fund for Building Maintenance. Everybody seemed to know that it was time to leave.

Millie became aware that a kind of hush fell upon the group after the final marshmallow had fallen from a bent

willow limb into the fire and burst into flame. The eyes of
the toddlers and those of the older children, she noticed,
took on that glazed look signifying that the sandman was
already at work. Everyone seemed to have full bellies, judging by the satisfied looks on their faces. Private pockets of
conversation no longer seemed bursting to be released to
waiting ears.

Throughout the evening, Millie and Woods had not been
apart for long periods of time, and she had delighted in
hearing him talk to others as well as to her. She suspected
she could feel his gaze on her when they were not together,
but she never actually found him looking her way. Once he
caught her watching him across the bonfire and sent her a
quick wink that heated her face far more than the flames
from the dying fire were doing.

With less energy but with as much enthusiasm, everyone
began loading back onto the two wagons after dousing the
last ember of the bonfire. The wind had risen and its nippy
breath bore a hint of frost when the teams of mules pulled
the wagons back out on the road. Almost overhead now, the
moon shone down with brilliant golden splendor, now that it
was no longer newborn.

"Who's trying to go to sleep on us?" Woods called when
no songs or jokes rose above the sound of the wagon bumping along on the gravel. This time he had grabbed Millie's
hand as soon as they settled back down in their places at the
end of the wagon. The way hers felt in his, soft and feminine and trusting, made him feel good all over.

Millie turned along with Woods to hear the good-natured
denials being called out, admiring the way his voice sounded
so manly. Without meaning to notice, she saw right behind
them that Annette was leaning her head on Warden's
shoulder as his arms hugged her close. Sweet, she thought.
First love was sweet. An inner voice tried to ask why only
first love was sweet, but Millie did not hear it.

"All right," Woods called, turning his head so as to be
heard better, "here we go with rounds. That's the only way
to keep everybody awake."

"Oh, no!" groaned some voices with mock despair. "Not
you and your rounds again."

While Millie watched with wide eyes, Woods began singing, joined almost immediately by those on both wagons:

"Oh! Ninety-nine coondogs bayin' at the tree,
Ninety-nine dogs at the tree.
If one of those coondogs left to . . . rest,
There'd be ninety-eight coondogs bayin' at the tree."

"Oh! Ninety-eight coondogs bayin' . . .

Before the second round ended, Millie was singing along with as much enthusiam as the youngsters sitting on either side of Woods and her. She leaned her head closer to Wood's, seeking to harmonize her alto with his resonant bass. When he squeezed her hand tighter underneath the hay and rested his head against hers, she then heard their voices blending in the way she had hoped and felt goose bumps popping up from her marvelous sense of oneness with the mountain man. The joyful sounds of all on the hayride rang out in the night, bouncing off the trees bordering the road and drowning out the noises of night callers—or else scaring them into their hiding places.

When Millie first heard the pause before "rest" in the regional ditty and realized that everyone was mentally supplying the rhyming word and having a good time grinning about it, she had been rather shocked. But not for long.

These warmhearted people from the Ouachita Mountains, Millie reasoned, lived too close to nature not to accept every part of it as normal and natural and incorporate it into their speech and actions—the good, the bad, the funny, and the sad. The warm pressure of the mountain man's hand on hers under the fragrant hay, plus that of his head and hip touching hers as they sang their private duet, made everything perfect.

Before the last "coondog" had ended its "bayin' at the tree," the wagons were stopping at houses to let passengers descend and go in search of their beds. Another round had replaced the earlier one by the time the wagons halted near the schoolhouse.

Watching her close neighbors leave the wagons and returning their good nights, Millie disengaged the arms of the sleeping Francine from her own and lay her down in the sweet-smelling hay. She noted that Woods was doing the same for Noble before he slid to the ground. Probably Edgar would stop the wagon and take his youngsters inside to their beds when he reached their home up the road.

"I'll be on to the livery to help you and Lucas get the teams rubbed down," Woods called to Edgar as he reached up and set Millie down. "I'll see the schoolmarm to her door first."

"No big hurry," Edgar called from the front of the wagon where he held the reins of the mules. After making sure everyone departing at that point stood clear of the wheels, he ordered them to move onward.

"I don't know when I've had such a marvelous outing," Millie said to Woods when they reached the door to the teacherage. The moonlight was hauntingly beautiful, she thought, purposefully keeping her gaze from that of the handsome man holding her hand. His chin with its manly cleft was a nice enought spot on which to look. "Thank you for inviting me."

"My pleasure," Woods replied huskily. He knew that people were still out on the road, some in little clusters as they bade each other private good nights in the bright moonlight, and likely were curious as hell as to what Millie and he might be doing beside the teacherage. He had no wish to cause more talk about Millie than the two of them appearing together tonight was going to create. Why, everybody knew he was not a marrying man, and some might even have suspected that he had become immune to women. Even so, he felt the temptation to pull her into his arms and kiss her tugging at his common sense.

"Good night." Millie freed her hand, struck by an absurd sense of loss. She did not deny that she would like Woods to hug her good night, maybe give her a light kiss on the cheek, but she was too determined to master the physical attraction she felt for him to allow the wish more than fleeting life. Feeling strengthened by that resolve, she looked at Woods then and moved onto the first doorstep of the teacherage. Suddenly she was giggling.

"What's come over you?" Woods asked, feeling himself drawn into her merriment and smiling, though he did not know the cause.

"I've just noticed that you've got hay stuck in your hair."

His gaze wandered from her face to her hair then, and he said, "So do you. Does this make us hayseeds?"

"Well, if it doesn't," she remarked with a little laugh, "it must make us kissing cousins of hayseeds." Millie winced on the inside. She should never have mentioned kissing, even in that teasing sense.

Woods was no more pleased at Millie's choice of words than she was. Kissing was too much on his mind anyway, and the moonlight was too damned bright for him to take a chance on giving the people out in the road anything new to talk about. And Edgar and Lucas were waiting. "Do you want me to get the trash out of your hair for you?"

Solemn-faced, Millie leaned her head over to let him remove the straw from her curls. It took longer than she had expected, and the light touches seemed to reach farther than her hair. Then just as methodically she reached out and plucked the several pieces from his black hair. There really was no need to be in a big rush, she told herself.

Just those light touches served to appease, at least partially, their hunger to do more than exchange verbal good nights.

"I'd better be going now," Woods said, turning away from temptation even as he spoke.

Millie hurried into the teacherage, all kinds of feelings stirring around inside and begging to be examined. Was it possible, she mused when she allowed one question to surface, to be falling in love with someone she had met only three weeks ago?

· *Chapter Fifteen* ·

Darkness had come unusually early, Millie thought the next evening as she moved the lamp onto the dresser in her bedroom. When her adult pupil showed up in the classroom soon, what would he think about Freeman's new schoolmarm? Maybe it would be someone who had been on the hayride, or maybe someone from outside Freeman whom Woods or Annabelle had already told her about. Should she cross her fingers that it not be the infamous moonshiner, Lavelle Landeen? A mischievous smile lifted the corners of her full mouth and added extra sparkle to her brown eyes.

Rarely had Millie paid a great deal of attention to her face and figure. Her father had told her often that vanity was a curse. Leaning over close to the mirror, she opened her eyes wider and peered at her oval face in contemplation.

Now that autumn was here and the sun during her afternoon walks slanted at such kindly angles, the sprinkling of freckles across her nose and cheeks was fading away. Her red curls lay in shining clusters, dipping here and there upon her smooth forehead and temples, now that they had grown a half inch. Was her haircut responsible for what appeared to be a softer look about her face than when she had last examined it? Though she could not put her finger on it, there seemed a distinctive difference in her appearance since she had come to Freeman.

Lifting a few tiny curls from where they nestled below her temples, Millie tried lodging them behind her ears, only to find that the red strands had minds of their own. She let them be.

Unbidden, Woods's husky declaration that she was beautiful rushed to Millie's mind and burdened her heart with

224

longing. Suddenly she was aware of her entire body. The pungent smell of the gently sputtering flame of her kerosene lamp assailed her nostrils, and the calls of locusts from nearby trees suddenly seemed plaintive and pervasive in the small bedroom.

Millie's face heated up, and she dropped her gaze from the mirror. Oh, she agonized, in spite of her willing that it not be true, fragmented memories of those moments in Wood's arms at the cave kept surfacing and haunting her in ways that she did not understand. Could she have been wrong in her beliefs that the intensity of her attraction to the handsome mountain man would lessen in time? Millie demanded silently of that woman staring back at her from the mirror.

Last night on the hayride, Millie confessed, she had been as enthralled by Woods as ever, maybe even more so now that she was letting herself recall the wonderful event. Never had it been the old Millicent's way to doubt her decisions outright, once she had made them, except for the time last spring when she had resigned her job at the school in Little Rock. That did not count, she argued; matters of the heart had been dictating to her then. Physical attractions had to do with the body.

Then what in thunder was wrong with the new Millie, she questioned inwardly, to be plagued by self-doubt? In spite of her unexpected dwelling upon what took place in the cave and her continuing fears that she might not ever dispel her desire to get lost in Woods's arms again, she did not regret the actual surrendering of herself to him. A part of her kept reiterating that she had belonged in his arms on that rainy afternoon. Another part stepped in and asked: *Can it be that you're falling in love with Woods Sanders?*

Millie snatched up the lamp and took it back into the living room, having to slow down when the flame leaned and flickered in protest from her careless sloshing of its fuel in the glass base of the lamp. Perhaps in time, she consoled herself after setting the lamp on the kitchen table, she would be able to look back on the way Woods affected her and laugh at what was no doubt a weakness plaguing most women at one time or another in their lives. She guessed she should count herself lucky that no such physical attraction for a man had struck her before. In the meantime while her body settled down, the structured part of her brain consoled her, she could continue enjoying being friends with Woods.

Had she not learned to live with the fact that she had disappointed her father by not having been born a boy? Millie mused. She knew the Reverend Monroe had been a good and wise man and that, in his way, he had loved her. Mind over matter; all things take place in their own good time—so Millie's father had told her repeatedly when she would become impatient about waiting for things to happen. Such maxims had worked before; they would again. She reached for her shawl, left the teacherage, and went into the classroom.

"Good evening, Miss Monroe," came a voice from the side door into the classroom.

"Woods," Millie exclaimed in delighted surprise. "Did you come with your friend?" She pushed aside the tablet on which she had been making lesson plans for the rest of the week.

"Not exactly. I'm the one who never went to school, Millie." Woods stood right in front of her desk then, his eyes probing hers.

"You must be teasing." Wasn't he? She was speechless, and it had nothing to do with his dark good looks.

"I'm not." Was Millie condemning him, she whom he had felt from the start was so different from him—so educated? Woods had prepared himself for almost anything, except the sudden galloping of his pulse.

Millie detected the raw sincerity in Woods's eyes and voice. She mustered up a weak smile of understanding and gestured toward the desk that she earlier had dragged near her own. How was it that the handsome black-haired man seemed to dominate any room in which he existed? Words would not come until after he fitted his lanky frame into the desk indicated. "Please tell me all about it, Woods."

"I don't want to take unfair advantage of our friendship by coming here tonight and asking for your help." When her lips parted and she seemed to be searching vainly for words, he continued. "I don't want to be treated like the chairman of the school board, either."

Millie was glad that she had not risen when Woods had come into the classroom. She felt boneless now. Her heart overflowed with feelings too complex for perusal; her mind spun with questions too personal to ask. How could the man who expressed himself so well and who obviously held the respect of the community for his ideas be unschooled? For crying out loud! He was chairman of the school board, wasn't he? People at the political meeting only two nights ago had been asking him to run for the legislature. Could a man be functionally illiterate and yet mask it from others who were not?

Millie reminded herself that the questions crowding her mind had no place in the classroom. What she must do is summon up all of her professional skills and her utmost tact. She must put aside personal interest. Had she not bragged recently to herself about her acquired talent for hiding her true feelings and thoughts?

With a calm demeanor, Millie began asking Woods exactly how much reading and writing he could do, the very questions she had planned on asking whoever appeared that night. She shoved a slate toward him, placing the chalk on its sleek surface with a little "clack!" so as to avoid touching Woods's fingers. She could dissemble just so far, she reflected as her heart threatened to go haywire.

"See?" Woods asked after making numbers and the letters of the alphabet while Millie was trying to make sense of her earlier concocted lesson plans. There was some quality about Millie's quiet questions and comments that had soothed his quaking heart and lessened his earlier doubts about asking a woman teacher to help him pursue his dream to become literate, truly literate. He had been right, he exulted. Millie Monroe was one of a kind. "I know the numbers and letters, and I know some of the easy, common words.

"Mama lost her sight completely before she got me past the simple lessons. After my pa died and my last sister left home—none of the girls cared to learn up as high as eighth grade like Mama had done—there wasn't anybody left to take care of Mama but me.

"Being nothing but a boy, I thought I was lucky not to have to be working over lessons. Mama got lost there for a while trying to adjust to her changed world and she slacked off about making me do schoolwork. It was easy to get out of it anyway. I was a big youngster, and I took on a man's work about the farm, with occasional help from neighbors and my sisters' husbands."

Millie digested all that Woods revealed to her, both by words and by inference. In a way, she reasoned compassionately, his blighted boyhood resembled her shortened girlhood, in that an untimely death in the family had shoved innocence aside and replaced it with the duties and responsibilities of adulthood.

The smelly kerosene burned low in the lantern hanging near the front of the classroom that Monday night. By the time the firewood had turned into a few glowing coals inside the iron heater in the corner, Woods had made inroads into conquering vowels and phonetic pronunciations of the words in the primer resting on Millie's desk. His innate intelligence, plus his living and speaking daily with the literate Agatha and Glovina, had provided Woods with far more knowledge than he had realized, Millie happily pointed out. It was easy to see how his being forced to manage the sums required in money management, both for his blind mother and himself, had strengthened his childhood facility with numbers.

Both teacher and pupil stood at almost the same instant.

"I want you to practice what you've learned tonight before you come back for the next lesson," Millie said. They went out the same side door where, some three weeks ago, she recalled with a wrench, she had whacked him with a broom and ended up in his arms in the moonlight. "I'll be available for more lessons any night after supper."

"I'll appreciate this forever, Millie." Woods closed the door after them, moving aside for her to turn the key in its lock. He had not forgotten her announcement after their lovemaking back in the cave that she had no interest in having an emotional attachment to a man, which he had taken to mean that she had no interest in him as a man. If friendship was what she wanted, then that was what she would have.

"You're welcome. I'm only sorry you didn't tell me earlier that you needed tutoring. What are friends for?" She was opening the door into the teacherage by then, and she turned back to face him. The glow from the lamp burning low in the room behind her reflected from his eyes as he looked up at her. No doubt it was gratitude that was softening his blue eyes and bringing the gentle smile to those lips that she had once innocently labeled sensuous. How well she knew now that they not only looked that way . . . Millie licked her suddenly dry lips and steered her thoughts back to the moment. "I hope you'll be back tomorrow night."

"I will, unless the weather gets bad." So far, Woods mused with wonder, she had not looked at him once with either disapproval or disappointment. In fact, though it made not a lick of sense, she seemed to be regarding him with a new kind of respect. What kind of woman was Millie Monroe? Would he ever know all of the different sides to her? "Good night."

Forrest "Woods" Sanders rode home that night with a heart full of hope. He scolded himself for having lost his temper that day in Elmwood upon seeing that Freeman's new teacher was a woman.

How could he have known that Millicent Monroe was totally unlike any other woman and that he would be able to swallow his ticklish pride and ask her to teach him? Woods reasoned. Now that his first night of lessons had gone so well, he doubted that a man, as he had assumed the teacher would be, could have put him at ease so quickly.

Jumping Jehosaphat! Woods thought. What kind of man would hang a name like Ezekial Millicent Monroe on a pretty baby girl—as he was sure she had been?

Ever since he had made love to Millie a little over a week ago, Woods had agonized over the way things had turned out afterward. He had not meant to give the matter another thought. Memories kept popping up, though, when he least expected them.

After that first class with Millie, Woods gave his horse its head on the familiar road home and thought about how no woman had ever set him on fire as the beautiful redhead had done and then quenched the blaze so gloriously.

Wasn't it odd, almost spooky, how none of her passion showed from underneath her unspectacular clothing and her polite manners? The memory of seeing the red garters when Millie fell from the wagon that day rose up. The saucy garters might have been a clue, Woods reckoned, but how was he supposed to tell? He had been immune to women for a long while.

Woods suspected that Millie's cool announcement after their lovemaking about not wanting him for anything more than a friend from that moment on was still nibbling at his masculine pride. From what he could remember—and the saints above knew as well as he that he had been half out of his head with wanting her—she had enjoyed making love almost as much as he had. Even though he was not interested in gaining a wife, he might really have proposed to her afterward, just to make things right, what with her being the teacher and him being the board chairman and all. And she was damned fine company.

But, no sirree, that hardheaded woman had set him down good by telling him—he remembered as he half slouched in the saddle how she had seemed as cool as a cucumber stored deep in a well—that she would not have said "yes" even if he *had* asked her to marry him. Woods spat off to the side of his horse. He did not like admitting that he had brooded over that little how-do-you-do for the rest of her visit, even after he finally had reminded himself how she was educated ... and likely too different from him for him to dwell upon the thought of the two having any kind of permanent relationship. Somewhere from a nearby hill an owl hooted.

By the time the handsome horse with the front white stockings loped up to the barn on the Sanders farm, Woods had given much thought to the relationship between Millie Monroe and himself. Not once did he allow himself to ponder what had triggered his decision to go ahead with his original plan of asking the new schoolteacher to teach him to read and write in an acceptable manner—and erase that difference he felt separated him from Millie. Woods Sanders's brain had been in charge of him so long that he would not have believed his heart still held one firm hand on the reins.

Woods did confess how it had taken him nearly all week to swallow the bitter dosage of the beautiful redhead's rejection of him as a man and go ahead and take her to the hayride. And he had the cord of firewood all split and stacked to prove it, he mused wryly. Now that he was being honest with himself, or as honest as he allowed at the moment, he wasn't so damned sure that he ever would get the taste of it out of his mouth. After rubbing down Major and putting fresh hay in the stall, the tall black-haired man spat again. Not that it helped matters.

Rain came that week, and colder days. Disappointments came to Woods, the pupil, but not nearly so often as the surges of happiness at his progress.

On his daily visits to the bauxite mine on his land to check with foreman Barton Blackstone, Woods carried along the books Millie had loaned him. No longer did he hang around longer than necessary in performing his normally undemanding job of overseer at the excavated area. Barton Blackstone was capable and needed little assistance in keeping the crews working. The piles of bauxite-filled ore to be hauled by wagons to Elmwood were growing satisfactorily.

If Major wondered that week what had turned his master into a talking machine as they traveled the short distance between the mine and the barn, he seldom acted as if anything out of the ordinary was taking place. The hills, rocks, and trees served as extra listeners, along with darting squirrels, skunks, and birds. Woods was sounding out new and longer words without faltering by the end of the first week of meeting with Millie in the classroom at night.

By the end of the second week of Woods's night classes, he was reading with considerable ease from the mid-level readers and history books. His inherent talent with numbers soon led him into elementary algebra.

Major sometimes flicked an ear and turned a wary head sideways when his master became carried away with a particular passage of some dead stateman's speech and repeated it again and again in his deep rolling voice. The hardwood trees, fast shedding their leaves, became spectators, at times nodding and whispering what Woods felt must be approval. More than once he wondered if the exciting episode in his life that had begun when he met Millie Monroe might not be one set into motion by a greater being than he.

"Millie, you're a great teacher," Woods said when he entered the classroom one Friday night and found her, as usual, waiting for him at her desk, her papers and books spread out before her. He felt taller than his six feet three inches. "I never knew anyone could teach me so much in just two weeks."

"Take the credit yourself. You're smart and highly motivated, and that's the secret of any successful student."

Millie watched the handsome man go over to the stove and dump the large load of firewood he had begun bringing in upon his arrival. Seeing him feed a couple of sticks of wood into the black stove while softly whistling reminded her of that first night in the teacherage when he had stayed and showed her how to use the Monster and cooked supper for her. Who, she reflected, would have believed that the two of them could have become such close friends since then?

Millie no longer pretended that the nights when Woods came for tutoring were anything but fleeting hours of contentment mixed with excitement. He had missed only two nights of lessons, both due to previous commitments on his part to attend political meetings in neighboring towns. She was dying to talk with him about his future plans, but she wanted to make sure that the time was right. There was no doubt in her mind now that his earlier comments to her about not being a fit candidate for representative were based on his lack of schooling.

"Has anyone spoken to you about your frequent visits here at night?" Millie asked after Woods had removed his jacket and taken his seat in the desk pulled up beside her own. He always wore a white starched shirt buttoned only high enough to cover most of the black hair covering his chest. Often, as now, she caught herself staring at the manly view and remembering. . . . "I've been getting questions from the

Widow Marks and some of the other women. I guess since we went on the hayride together, we set a lot of tongues wagging."

"Are they bothering you?" He frowned and stroked his mustache with a testing forefinger. "I told Henry Stevens what we're doing, and he seemed mighty glad. He said that he would try to steer talk in the right direction by mentioning some special studies being done for the school board."

"No one is giving me trouble, but I wonder if it's wise for people not to know why your horse is tethered out back almost every night." Millie looked down at the piece of chalk in her hand. The intensity of his gaze was making her feel naked. Strange how the little inward humming sound still started up each night when the mountain man arrived.

"Why, Millie, are you afraid they'll think I'm sparking you?" He winked at her while laughing low in his throat.

"No." Millie lifted her chin and wished that she could banish the flush taking over her cheeks. His soft laughter seemed designed for her ears alone. She had already learned that Woods had a wicked wink, one that always made her think about kissing. "That's preposterous! You said you don't want the news spread that you're just now catching up on your schooling. I understand, and I've not told even Annabelle, though I wish that you'd let her in on our secret."

Woods nodded thoughtfully, thinking how pretty her hair always looked in the light spilling from the lantern overhead. Millie was right. He did feel a mite clumsy about the matter, but what kind of backing could he get as a candidate for the legislature if everyone found out that he was learning to read and write decently for the first time at the age of thirty-five? More and more he was thinking he might throw his hat in the ring before the end of the year.

"Millie," Woods asked, "why would it be preposterous for me to be sparking you, what with you being a beauty and unmarried?" His eyes roved over her face and her short curls, coming to rest upon her full lips. Soft lips, he thought with an unexpected rush of longing to feel them beneath his own. She was soft and silky all over. The unbidden thought sparked fire in his groin. "Everybody knows I'm an old bachelor not planning on marrying, so.... Let'em talk. I figure nobody would believe me if I told them you don't want to get married either. You *do* hold some strange ideas on the topic, you know."

"You may be right. If you don't mind the gossip, then I won't either." Millie brushed back the curls nestling upon her forehead, bothered as she was by his penetrating gaze. She was disappointed not to have made any progress in her determination to look upon him as no more than a friend. She had not yet conquered those times of awareness of Woods as a man during their study sessions. But she would. "What made you decide to pursue your education? Did you have that in mind when you spearheaded the drive for a school in Freeman?" At his puzzled, almost shy look, she went on. "Oh, yes, I've heard from more than one person that you were the main supporter of the plan to get the school built here."

"I figured it was time I got on with my life," Woods replied after a moment, his deep drawl sounding unusually thoughtful to the perceptive Millie. "If a man isn't moving forward a little bit all of the time, he's likely missing out on life. As for me, I'd been still too long. It seems to me that a person needs to know where he's going, or he might as well not be going anywhere. I decided that I had me a place to go and that I'd not be making the trip if I didn't get some learning."

Her smile soft with admiration, Millie replied, "You already had much learning before you came here. I'm amazed that you've acquired such a good vocabulary and such a wide range of knowledge, all without knowing how to read except for the simplest of words. You might have been classed as a functional illiterate, but you know now that you can't say you were uneducated."

"Maybe. Maybe not." He shrugged his broad shoulders and shifted his boots against the rough board floor. Would he ever watch Millie's smile light up her face and not feel that the world had become a better place, at least for that space of time? "All I know is that I got tired of learning everything by listening to people and studying their faces and actions.

"A few years ago, I got this yearning to read what was being written about everything, to see for myself and not depend on listening to everybody else. 'Course I'm not giving up on listening, or on studying people either, because I can tell I've picked up a lot that way." Dropping his gaze then to keep Millie from reading further into his suddenly bared soul, he rearranged his feet and smoothed his hair with a restless hand. Was he going to regret having been so honest with her?

Millie leaned against the back of her chair. Even after having been with Woods almost every night during the past two weeks, she still found the cleft in his chin arresting. "Was that about the time that the bauxite mines were opened around Freeman?" She watched a surprised look shine deep within his eyes. "Was it when you saw the possibilities for your beloved Ouachita Mountains and her people that you got this urge—so that maybe you could run for office one day?"

"How did you put that all together, schoolmarm?" Woods could not get over how much it pleased him that Millie had figured out exactly what had taken place in his mind. He fought down the urge to place his hand over hers where it lay at rest upon her desk. Just thinking about how its small softness would fit into his big hand as it had done the night of the hayride brought a fullness to his throat. In the past two weeks, he had mastered more than words and numbers. He had learned how to control his frequent impulses to touch the beautiful redhead.

"Maybe I'm learning as much from you as you are from me." Millie forgot to dissemble, and instantly she wished her words had not slipped out.

"Well, now, since you brought up the subject—"

A clattering sound from out front interrupted the talk in the classroom and saved them. Both realized, after it was too late to turn back, how their conversation was twisting suddenly into a bittersweet reminder of their lovemaking back in the cave, back when he had been the one doing the teaching.

Millie and Woods paused and stared at each other. The small space between his desk and hers seemed fraught with unspoken questions. Not until they heard a knock on the door did they unlock their wide-eyed gazes with what may have been relief. Wryly Millie gave a fleeting thought to the old folktale that Woods had told her, about the coon hunter yelling down to his friends from where he was fighting with the coon in the tree that it didn't "matter a'tall which one of us gets hit. Shoot up in here anyway. One of us needs some relief!"

"I hope I'm not intruding," Clive Durham said when Millie answered his knock and ushered him inside. "I was a bit surprised upon seeing a light coming from the classroom." His derby in his hand and a slim white box wedged between an arm and his ribs, he shifted his eyes from Millie's solemn face for the first time. Harrumphing and following her across the room, he asked, "Well, Forrest Sanders, what brings you to the classroom on a Friday night?"

A mocking smile kicked up the ends of Woods's handlebar mustache. "Maybe it's the same thing that brings you." He stole a glance at Millie, wondering why she appeared so flustered. His eyes narrowed in contemplation. Perhaps she had not also announced to Clive that she had no use for a man in her life. What was going on here . . . and at church that morning? The man was wearing a suit and neck scarf and had a crepe paper rose tucked into a lapel . . . as though he might be sparking. And what in hell was that little box he held?

Clive glared at the bigger, casually dressed man who was blatantly sizing him up, then laid his hat on Millie's desk, as if staking a claim to some imaginary territory. "I stopped by the livery on my way over here. Edgar told me that Henry Stevens had told him there might be some kind of meeting going on about selecting library books with the funds from the box supper." His glasses flashing in the light from the overhead lantern, he turned back to Millie. His clean-shaven face took on a new shade of pink. "I brought you a little something, Miss Monroe."

Millie looked at the white box that the bespectacled easterner was holding out. A red ribbon crisscrossed its shiny surface and ended up in a perky bow in the center. *Oh, my!* Clive was taking far too much for granted from her having been nice to him two Sundays ago when he had driven Uncle Fred and Aunt Phoebe here for church services. One of her hands fidgeted with the cameo pinned at the neckline of her flowered waist before she reached out and took the gift.

Figuring that Woods's unreadable smile was proof of his amusement at what was going on, Millie felt unreasoning anger take over. Double damn! Just because he had so arrogantly informed her back in the cave that he had no intention of asking her to marry him, did he have to assume that no other man might entertain the idea? The humiliation of having had Luther Osgood jilt her merged with an unexplained need to show the watchful mountain man that another unmarried man might be finding her desirable.

"Thank you, Mr. Durham," Millie heard herself saying in sugary tones. She slid off the red ribbon, lifted the lid, and eyed the contents of the box with secretive revulsion. Since childhood, after overindulging in candy, Millie had been allergic to chocolate. Now the aroma of chocolate was overwhelming her. Little waves of nausea wafted up from her knotting stomach. "Please, won't you two have some candy?" She held out the box first to the pink-faced Clive; when he declined politely, she offered it to Woods who also was standing near her desk by then.

"Don't mind if I do." Woods leaned over and peered at the single layer of chocolates lined up in individual paper cups, taking his time to make his selection. Chewing with obvious relish, he said, "By damn! You have good taste in chocolate candy, Clive. I'm glad you brought us something to eat. I believe I'll have some more." With feigned innocence, he asked, "Are you sure neither of you wants any?"

Before Millie could do more than drop her jaw in disbelief at the strange scenario taking place—it was plain that Clive was as shocked as she that Woods was acting as if the candy was community property—he plucked another little mound of candy from the brown paper cups and plopped it into his mouth. The sweet smell of the chocolate in the warm schoolroom was wreaking havoc with Millie's stomach.

"Miss Monroe," Clive asked after a moment of awkward silence broken only by Woods's chewing of a chocolate-coated nut, "are you ill?" She had lowered the box of candy to her desk and was replacing the lid with shaking fingers.

Woods noticed then that Millie's face was taking on a

pale, sickly hue and that her fingers were moving restlessly against her throat. Swallowing his mouthful of candy, he asked, "What's wrong? Do you need to go to your quarters?"

"Yes," Millie replied in a strangled voice. "I believe I'm going to have to tell you gentlemen good night." She did not bother to get her shawl before hurrying outside.

"I hope you'll feel better soon," Clive called after her. "I'll be spending the night at Widow Marks's place, and I'll call on you tomorrow. Reverend Tate sent you a big box from some church in Little Rock."

Why, a spent Millie commiserated with herself long after her stomach no longer roiled and she had crept into her bed, had she not simply told Clive about her allergy and never accepted the box of candy? Now she was going to be stuck with at least one more visit from the easterner—and some more teasing from Woods.

Part Five

What's without and what's within
Are quite at odds, barely kin.
Friendship may be the name of the
game,
But hearts keep searching just the same.
Through his dreams he finds her striding;
In her thoughts he's forever hiding.

· *Chapter Sixteen* ·

Millie heard Clive Durham's car engine crank up Saturday morning from where it sat in front of Widow Mark's place. Idly she wondered if he might not be on his way to visit some of the company mines. Or had Woods, when she had left the two men alone last night in the classroom, said something to speed the dull man back to Elmwood?

Woods had seemed in a cantankerous mood when she had dashed from the schoolroom. She recalled how she had earlier sensed that the two men had little liking for each other and that it had nothing to do with her. Not pleased with the drift of her thoughts, involving Woods as they did, she busied herself with her household tasks.

Leaving his car motor idling, Clive stopped by the teacherage Saturday afternoon to leave the box sent by Reverend Tate. As Millie had suspected when Clive had mentioned the box last night, it bore the return address of her friend from the church in Little Rock, the one carrying out the traveling garments program. Good, she thought. Both the Hobbs children would now have decent clothing to wear to school.

Millie almost giggled at Clive's obvious agitation after he set down the box. His chief concern seemed to be the welfare of his Model-T if the road back to Elmwood became too muddy.

"A cloud in the west is building, and I'm heading back to Elmwood. I was sorry about your becoming ill last night," Clive said in his clipped manner, his round head cocked in the direction of the clacking motor outside. "I'm glad that you're well today." His glasses hid his pale eyes. "Weather permitting, I planned to come back next weekend, but Forrest Sanders informed me last night that you're going to be busy."

Millie felt her temper flare. Woods had turned into what she considered a boor last night when Clive arrived, and she had not forgiven him. Besides, it was not for Woods to be telling anybody of her plans, even if he knew. Had she not asked him once before to let her run her own life? And, she recalled, Clive Durham had been a subject of that conversation. Woods was assuming privileges he did not have! Or— and the idea delighted her fancy—was he perhaps a little jealous, as some devious part of her had halfway hoped? Still, the thought of spending any more time with Clive held no appeal.

Her foolish feminine pride urging her on, in spite of her wishing it would go away, she hedged, "I might be busy, Mr. Durham, but there's nothing definite planned. It would be a waste of your time to drive over just to see."

"Oh, no," Clive assured her, one hand smoothing at his thinning blond hair and a smile creasing his round face. "I can bring over the payroll to the livery and make it be an official business trip, you see."

"I might not be free," Millie offered lamely, alarmed now that she had allowed Clive an opening. Her aggravation at Woods for saying anything at all about her to the easterner still flavored her thinking, though, and she did not speak her true thoughts.

"I'll come by and check with you if I come over, Miss Monroe. How will that be?"

Millie realized that she had boxed herself into a corner, and all because of the vexing effect Woods Sanders had on her. Figuring that she had little choice then, she said, "That will be fine, Mr. Durham. I wouldn't want you expecting to find me available, though." In spite of the sudden fullness in her throat at the thought of the chocolate, she added with as much sincerity as she could muster, "And thank you for the candy."

By Sunday afternoon Millie had caught up on all her chores. From time to time she wondered how last night's political meeting over near Murfreesboro had gone; Woods had told her earlier in the week that he planned to attend. Not that she truly cared what the bossy mountain man did, she reminded herself. After all, he was nothing to her but a friend . . . and a pupil.

Restless and feeling cooped up by the rain still drizzling outside, she wrote a letter to Louise Nipper, her friend at the girls' school in Little Rock. Afterward she pulled on her water-repellant cape and walked up the road toward Steven's store. If the store was open, she would post her letter. If not, she mused, she would stop by the Stevens home and visit a while with Annabelle and her father.

Already Millie had decided that tomorrow would be a better time to deliver the box of clothing to the Hobbs home, for it was likely that the father would be at home on a Sunday and perhaps make a scene about accepting the used garments for his children. She had no wish to create new problems.

Millie stopped by the classroom, a hazy plan in mind for getting rid of the chocolate candy. She couldn't abide the thought of smelling it any longer. Tempted to hold her nose at the aroma of chocolate emanating from the box even through its lid, she decided to take it to Annabelle. She suspected that Ransom and Steve would love helping their aunt demolish the contents of the beribboned box. She couldn't abide the thought of keeping it around until she called on the Hobbses.

While Millie was passing in front of the Keyhole House, she saw Lucas Milstead and his two sons riding handsome horses into the yard of the Stevens place up ahead. She returned their friendly waves, then sighed, slowing her pace. She had no wish to intrude upon Annabelle and her beloved. The letter could be posted tomorrow on a regular business day.

A movement from one of the second-floor windows in the Keyhole House caught Millie's eye. Why not? She asked silently when the notion struck her to call on her pupil, Annette Bordeaux, and her mother. She had been wanting to meet Selma Witherspoon Bordeaux ever since Annabelle had told her about the reclusive woman. Plus she had already visited in the homes of several of her pupils, Millie's reasoning ran on, and Annette deserved equal courtesy, didn't she?

Millie made her way through the gate of the picket fence surrounding the big house, taking in the air of neglect that seemed to hover about the place. The small window midway up the house still intrigued her with its keyhole shape. She had detected no further movement behind the curtains of the windows on the second floor. From up close, the tall bushes concealing the encircling porch seemed as formidable as from the road some fifty yards out front.

As she climbed the front steps to the porch, Millie noted that drapes covered all the tall windows. From within she could hear the sound of violin music.

After what seemed an interminably long time, someone answered Millie's knock on the door and opened it a crack.

"Miss Monroe," Annette Bordeaux exclaimed. The sixteen-year-old's pretty face brightened at first, then seemed to fade, along with her voice. "Er...uh, have you come... calling?"

Millie didn't miss Annette's furtive look over her shoulder or the nervous note in her voice. Neither did she miss that the violin music still drifted from somewhere within the strangely darkened house. Clouds from yesterday's storm and today's intermittent showers still floated overhead, but the afternoon sun was peeking through frequently.

"Yes, Annette," Millie replied with a brilliant smile. "I'm here to visit with you and meet your mother. I hope I've not come at an inconvenient time." She had learned from her years as the daughter of a minister that sometimes one must push one's way into the homes of some people when visits seemed important. She deemed her visit today important. Her curiosity had been building ever since she had first noted the Keyhole House several weeks ago and then questioned Annabelle about its inhabitants. "May I come in?"

After a brief hesitation, Annette nodded her pretty head and moved aside. The music died. Millie followed her into a gloomy, musty-smelling foyer, then on into a large room where there was barely enough light to find one's way.

"Let me take your cloak, Miss Monroe." Then, the garment in her hands, she said, "Please be seated. I'll go put on the kettle for tea . . . and see if Mother is feeling up to receiving callers this afternoon."

Her footsteps making almost no sound upon the smooth carpet, Annette disappeared. Millie groped her way over to what appeared to be an elegant sofa and sat down, the box of candy still in her hand. Her eyes were adjusting to the dimness by then, and she jumped up and placed the box on the farthest table, eager to rid herself of the permeating scent of chocolate. Seated again, she guessed that she likely was in one of the most elegantly furnished rooms that she had ever visited.

Mid-Victorian style dominated everywhere, even down to the fashionable clutter of objets d'art claiming almost all available space on the marble-topped tables and the marble mantel topping an ornately faced fireplace. Millie itched to light at least one of the fat-based lamps of painted porcelain with matching chimneys that centered two of the numerous tables. The beauty of one with a fringed Tiffany shade sitting on a round corner table almost took her breath away.

Closer by, Millie saw a stereopticon and a huge tray of double-imaged slides lying on the tea table in front of the brocaded sofa where she sat. Why would anyone shut out the light behind heavy drapes when there was so much obvious beauty to enjoy, both inside the high-ceilinged room and outside in the foothills of the Ouachita Mountains?

Millie was admiring the huge cabbage roses decorating the carpet when she heard footsteps whispering on its short-piled surface and turned. Annette and a woman about her size were coming into the room.

"Miss Monroe," Selma Bordeaux said in a low, cultured voice after Annette made the introduction, "how good of you to stop by on this Sunday afternoon. We seldom have callers."

Freeman's new schoolmarm began visiting in a cordial way with the apparently shy woman after Annette excused herself and left to prepare a tea tray. Her hostess sat on one of the side chairs to Millie's left, soon responding readily to Millie's easy manner and casual talk about her life in Little Rock.

Even in the poor light, Millie could tell as they talked that the woman was beautiful and that the reports that her daughter and she favored each other were true. If only Mrs. Bordeaux would light a lamp, she agonized. Perhaps Annette would perform the little task when she returned with refreshments.

But she didn't. Annette set the tea tray on the oval table in front of the sofa, then presided over it with practiced ease, pouring first for Millie, then for her mother.

"Perhaps you'd like a piece of the candy you brought us, Miss Monroe?" Annette asked after Millie had shown her the little box on the table and explained that she wanted to give the remainder of its contents to Annette and her mother.

Before Annette could lift the lid, Millie hastened to say, "No, thank you. As I told you, I'm not fond of chocolate. Besides, I'm enjoying the lemon tea cakes you made." As if to prove her point, she took another bite of the tart cookie. She was relieved that the lid remained closed.

"Annette tells me she's enjoying your class," Selma Bordeaux said. "I was thrilled to learn that I'd not have to send her away again this year to Memphis for her schooling. I understand that Woods Sanders has done a commendable job getting the schoolhouse built. He must be a fine man."

"Yes, so everyone says." Millie had no wish to talk about the mountain man. She noted again that Selma's dark hair, as curly as Annette's and worn in the same loose style, covered almost the entire right side of her face. Why didn't they light a lamp? "You're welcome to visit us at school anytime you'd care to."

"Thank you, but I never go out."

"Didn't I hear a violin when I arrived? I've always loved the violin."

"You did," Annette volunteered. She smiled across at her mother with obvious pride. "Mother has a music room upstairs. She's full of talent."

"Would you play for me sometime? I miss not being able to attend musicales and such," Millie asked. When the woman hesitated, Millie added with sudden inspiration, "Perhaps you would play for my pupils some Friday afternoon when we have special programs instead of our usual spelling bee?"

"Oh, I couldn't do that." Selma leaned forward and set down her fragile cup and saucer on the silver tea tray with a noticeably trembling hand. "Annette can play almost as well as I. Perhaps she can oblige."

"We could play one of our duets," the girl said, her tone betraying her obvious plea that Selma agree.

Selma changed the subject adroitly. Millie listened in amazement as the woman chatted about music and musicians, concerts, and operas she had attended in the past. Way back in the past, Millie realized as she recognized names of a few people either dead or no longer active in musical circles.

"This has been a most pleasant afternoon, Miss Monroe," Selma said after Millie rose and announced that she must go. The tone of her voice spoke almost as clearly as her words. "I have seen from my music room how you have become such a part of our little town, and I admire you for leaving behind what must have been a very different kind of life to come here and teach. I will give your invitation to play for your pupils more thought. I hope you'll come back soon."

Annette looked from her mother to her teacher, a puzzled yet pleased look on her pretty face. "Please say you will, Miss Monroe. I can't recall Mother having such a good time visiting in a long while . . . or me, either."

The three moved toward the foyer then, their talk still cheerful in the unnaturally darkened house. Millie kept sneaking covert glances at Selma, but trying to hide her action for fear of being thought rude. Was the woman deliberately keeping the right side of her face averted?

When Selma hung back and only Annette accompanied her to the door, Millie had to abandon her attempts to see the woman's face more clearly. She knew for certain that she would accept the charming woman's invitation to return soon.

Annabelle Stevens might have believed that she, and apparently others in Freeman, was right in assuming that Selma Bordeaux chose to be a recluse, Millie reflected as

she left the Keyhole House and walked toward the teacherage. Somehow, though, she had gotten the distinct impression that the woman had truly enjoyed having a caller.

"Come over for a cup of coffee," the Widow Marks called
across the road to Millie after school on Tuesday.

From the edge of the schoolyard where she had been
watching her pupils scatter, Millie replied, "I will after I
mail a letter and check my mail."

"Warden will be glad to do that for you." Mabel Marks
turned to her tall son, who was watching Annette go through
the gate leading to her house next door. "Won't you, son?"

"Sure, Ma." A friendly smile upon his face, Warden met
Millie in the road, took her letter, then turned toward Stevens's General Store. "Wait up, Annette," he called. "Walk
with me to the store."

Millie and Mabel exchanged knowing looks when the
curly-haired Annette threw down her books and joined Warden.

"Annette and Warden make a good-looking couple, don't
they?" Mabel asked after ushering Millie inside her living
room and fetching cups of coffee for each.

"Yes, they do." Millie had been in Mable's house before,
but this was the first time the gossipy widow had not insisted
that they visit in her cozy kitchen. She glanced around the
plainly furnished living room, not surprised that it contrasted
sharply with the one in the Keyhole House. A nice extra in
the Widow Marks's home was the heavenly smell of recently
baked bread wafting in from the kitchen. "I'm sure they'll
miss each other when Warden goes off to college."

Looking troubled, Mabel brushed absently at her gray-
streaked pompadour with plump, work-worn fingers. "I
hope he can get a scholarship or some kind of aid. He wants
to be a vet in the worst kind of way, and he has so little
money saved. I ain't much help, what with so few comin' to
Freeman and needin' room and board. I guess I could put a
mortgage on my place, like—" Her mouth clamped shut for
a moment. "Some folks borrow from a bank for things their

families need in the worst way, but bein' a widow, I've no way to pay back a loan."

"I doubt you'll have to take such a drastic step, Mabel. Warden stands a good chance to receive a scholarship. He'll make a fine veterinarian, and he'll do well practicing in Lexington County. You know better than I that your son is bright and a very dependable young man."

"He is smart, and he does appear to have settled in a mite," Mabel conceded after a sip of coffee. "Do you know anybody over at that Oklahoma college where he'll have to go to study about doctoring animals, somebody who might offer him a job?"

"I believe so. I've written a friend of mine in Little Rock and asked her to check on the whereabouts of a man we both knew when we were in training. I'll write the University of Oklahoma before next spring and ask for a catalog, too."

"Do you think Warden stands much of a chance gettin' through with all his studies if he gets married beforehand? He says it'll take him at least six years to finish up."

"Marriage at eighteen?" Millie could not hide the disapproval in her voice. "Maybe for a girl, but not for a boy." Mabel's round face took on a serious look. "Why? Are Warden and Annette talking of getting married before he goes off to school?"

"They're both afraid that if they don't marry before he leaves, they might not ever get back together."

Millie asked, "What makes them think that? Does Mrs. Bordeaux or you disapprove of their marrying . . . someday?"

Mabel began talking then, and Millie had to listen closely not to miss anything.

"Selma Witherspoon, as she was before her marriage to Pierre Bordeaux, and I have been best friends since her pa moved his housekeeper and her to Freeman when we was kids. Purty soon Selma was ridin' her fancy horse over to my folks place—they was Turners and pore as the dirt on their farm. She played with me and my older brother, Willis, just like she was one of us.

"When it came time for us to go to school, her pa sent her off to a fancy place in Memphis. Most winters my brother and I stayed in Elmwood at a cousin's house and went to school. We still had the summertimes for visitin', though, and Selma and I were together lots. It seems sorta strange, but Selma liked comin' to our place better than she liked havin' me come to that fancy big house of hers. Mr. Witherspoon was gone a lot, him havin' a big horse farm and all and doin' lots of tradin' across the country."

Mabel paused long enough to refill their coffee cups before continuing her story. Millie's mind was whirling with all kinds of questions, but she was not ready to ask them.

"Things went fine, 'til one summer when Selma and I were about fifteen, Willis got to eyein' Selma—like, you know, like a young man eyes a purty girl. At first I never thought much about it, what with her bein' so purty and all; but by the next summer when both of us turned sixteen, it was plain as the warts on a frog that the two of them was havin' a hard time keepin' their hands off each other." Mabel stopped as abruptly as she had begun, her forehead wrinkling and her mouth turning down at the corners.

"I take it the romance ended about that time."

"You're right. Ended overnight. Old man Witherspoon must have seen Willis makin' eyes at Selma. Before you could say 'scat,' he took Selma back to Memphis in the dark of the night." Mabel's voice kept getting thicker. "I married not long afterward and moved away for a spell. I reckon when you visited Selma Sunday you seen the scar on her cheek."

Millie replied, "No, I never saw her face clearly." Was Mabel going to tell how Selma's face became scarred? She did not wish to appear nosy, but . . .

"She won't believe me when I tell her it's not all that bad. She keeps hidin' from folks anyway."

"Did Selma have a happy marriage to Annette's father? When did she come back here?" Surely such questions went beyond being nosy, Millie consoled herself.

"Yeah, she loved Pierre Bordeaux a lot. Both of 'em was music teachers up in Cincinnati. Her pa and Pierre met a couple of months after their elopement. Old man Witherspoon had some kinda spell while they was all walking beside the river and fell in. Pierre dived in after him and the current swept them away."

Millie sighed at the tragedy unfolding.

"My husband, God rest his soul, owned this lot next to Witherspoon, and we came back to Freeman and built this house the year Warden was born. Nine years passed before I saw Selma after she left in the night, and that was when she came back here to bury both her pa and her husband out in the cemetery by the churchyard. She stayed on with the housekeeper and had Annette. They been here ever since. Since Florence, the housekeeper, died last year, that house is about to go to pot."

"How awful for so many people! What happened to Willis Turner, your brother?"

"He ran off and left the country on a ship without as much as a fare-thee-well to nobody. We heard from him only onct after he became a sailor. After he never came home or wrote again in all these twenty-five years, I have to figure him for dead. I hear tell there's lots of storms at sea and lots of scrapes in ports clear 'round the world."

Millie agreed, her heart saddened at Mabel's story. She asked after a moment, "What does all of this have to do with Warden and Annette?"

"Why, don't you see?" Mable seemed shocked that Millie had to have the matter explained. "Selma has told enough about her fallin' for my brother and him disappearin' that Annette thinks if Warden leaves, he won't come back. Sometimes I suspect Warden ain't nearly so interested in marryin' next year as Annette is, but I can't say for sure." She arched an eyebrow and added, "You know how hot young blood runs."

"Oh, my. This is a complicated situation, isn't it?"

"And it's gonna get worse, for I'm gonna have to stand up to Selma on this matter purty soon. She and I ain't never had a big fallin' out before, but I can feel one brewin'. I already told her that she ain't playin' fair, tellin' about Willis as if he might have been some knight in shinin' armor. I loved him, but chances are mighty slim that the two of them ever would have married even if her pa had approved. They didn't seem right for each other, not to me, and I knew both of them better than anybody else did." Mabel pursed her lips together and folded her arms across her ample bosom. "Just because Selma suffered from her first love don't mean Annette and Warden have to."

When Millie made no reply, Mabel turned and asked, "Will you talk to Annette and Warden for me, Millie? Maybe with you bein' a teacher you'll know some right things to say."

Millie welcomed the sound of a door slamming out back. Warden must be coming into the house. She had heard more than she could take in for one day, and she doubted that she knew enough about such matters to counsel the troubled Widow Marks or the young couple in love. She stood up.

"Mabel, don't fret. Next year is a long time off. They might not even be caring for each other by then. I'll give this matter some thought before I try talking with either Annette or Warden." Her father had refused Luther Osgood's request to marry her and take her along with him to law school— and it seemed to have been a wise decision. What reasons had he given?

"I hope you're right, but I wish you would talk to them in a general way. They both respect you a lot." Glancing over her shoulder, as though making sure her son was not within earshot, Mabel added in a half whisper, "If you want to discuss it with Woods when he comes sparkin' tonight, I don't mind. I know he ain't no blabbermouth either."

Pink-faced, but with the nicely wrapped loaf of bread Mabel had given her in her hands, Millie marched across the road to her own place. She was too upset over Mabel's insinuation about Woods's frequent night visits to note that three dogs trailed right along beside her as if they belonged there. Would she ever become accustomed to the way everybody in the small town thought he knew all about everyone else's business?

"When did the stove quit working?" Woods asked. He was squatting before the kerosene cookstove in the teacherage and peering into its mechanism.

"Tonight when I tried to cook supper." Standing near where he worked, Millie leaned back against the wall, still annoyed with herself for not having been in the classroom upon his arrival a short while ago. Dealing with his over-powering presence in such close quarters was more taxing than in the larger, more impersonal schoolroom, she was learning. A desk stood between them there, and subject matter was factual, not personal. "It made me run late with everything. That Monster will be the death of me."

"I doubt that," Woods replied with amusement riding his voice. He removed the burners and examined them. "I suppose you checked the fuel tank."

Millie gasped and then moaned, burying her face in her hands for a moment. "Double damn!" When he cocked his head toward her and sent her an amused look, she went on feebly. "I must be losing my mind. I never once thought about seeing if I needed to add kerosene." *And you never once thought about your earlier anger at Woods, either.*

Woods soon had the fuel tank refilled and a burner lighted while Millie, feeling like several kinds of a fool, stood by and watched.

"Would you like for me to make some coffee before we get started on lessons?" Woods asked. "We can give the burner a good testing that way, and you obviously didn't have anything hot for supper."

Millie agreed and moved to sit at the table. When he had the pot brewing, he pulled out a chair with a noisy scraping sound and sat across from her.

"Maybe you've had lots on your mind that caused you to forget about putting kerosene in the tank," Woods said. His gaze brushed across Millie's solemn face. She had seemed withdrawn ever since he had knocked at her door and found her still inside the teacherage.

At first, before Millie had assured him that she was well, Woods had feared that whatever had caused her illness on Friday night might have returned. On those previous occasions when the cantankerous cookstove had stymied her, she hadn't seemed so distraught. "Are the youngsters nailing you to the wall this week? Want to tell me about it? Lessons took up all of our time last night."

Millie was busy wondering why she was no longer angry at Woods over what he had told Clive Durham about her

being busy on the coming weekend. She propped her elbows
on the oilcloth-covered table, then rested her chin atop her
clasped hands and drank in the sight of his familiar face,
cleft in the chin and all. Already she had thought about how
his presence and his deep voice filled the room in the usual
manner, right along with the comforting heat radiating from
the little black heater.

Was she making any progress in mastering her physical
attraction to Woods? Millie wondered even as the answer
"no" loomed. Never before had she claimed a close friendship with a man and she knew that she gloried in the one
between Woods and her. He was so easy to talk with and he
seemed to like listening to her give her views on matters.
Common interests linked them closer each time they were
together, she mused, and she loved being with him—and
not just because his presence set her pulse humming.

"Things are going well with the pupils," Millie told him.
Briefly she filled Woods in on her delivering of the box of
used clothing to Mary Lee Hobbs on the preceding afternoon. "The baby seemed not so fretful, and thank goodness
James was not in the house when I got there. I was worried
that he might not give his permission. But today," she added
with a wide smile, "Gladys beamed in her practically new
shoes and pretty dress. Little Artis sported a jacket that
might have been bought for another first-grader recently, it's
so right for him on these cold days."

Woods smiled during the telling of her thoughts, getting
lost in the lilt of her voice and the sparkle in her eyes.
"Sounds to me like you're getting a lot done here in Freeman
besides teaching the youngsters. So far you've not told anything that hasn't gone well."

"I suppose that what troubles me comes from a visit after
school today with Mabel Marks."

Woods chuckled. In the circle of light coming from the
kerosene lamp sitting on the table, her big eyes seemed
brown pools of concern in her pretty face. "You know by
now that the Widow Marks loves embroidering the truth at
times, don't you? She doesn't mean any harm; that's just
Mabel's way."

Millie then spilled out all that Mabel had revealed. He

asked few questions throughout, but his expressive face showed his interest in what she was telling. When the coffee finished perking and he poured each of them a cup, he sat back down at the table and listened to a brief account of her visit to the Keyhole House.

"So you're finding that living in a small place has both rewards and punishments, huh?" Woods asked after Millie quieted and sipped her coffee. "You find out folks' tender spots, but you also get your own exposed. Both can weigh down a person's heart."

"I wish I knew how to advise Annette and Warden. They don't act like hotheaded fools, not here at school, at least. He can have a wonderful future being a veterinarian, but he doesn't need a wife to be concerned about during his first few years." With a shock Millie realized that she was parroting her father's words about Luther and her some eight years ago.

"Tell them they're too young to make the decision."

"Neither will listen to that old song, not if Mabel is right and Selma has scared them into wondering if they can have a future together, once they get separated."

"I've not seen Selma Witherspoon in years. I recall that to me, a youngster, she was mighty pretty that summer Willis Turner was hanging around her all of the time. I've heard Mama say that Selma suffered a lot back when she was about Annette's age, a sight more than anybody should have to suffer over first love," Woods said thoughtfully.

"How much should one suffer over first love?"

"Hard to say, but maybe enough to grow up, yet not enough to leave festering that won't heal."

Millie slid a secretive look at the handsome black-haired man sitting beside her at her table. Was he judging from his own experience with Fern Stevens? According to Annabelle, his own wounds had never healed and had kept him wary of involvement with any other woman. Maybe he was unaware that his heart still belonged to Fern.

"Are you speaking from experience?" Millie asked, almost afraid to look at him, yet too eager to watch his face while he responded to lower her gaze.

"Yep," Woods replied. "I was hog-crazy over a girl when

I was about Warden's age, and I thought I'd die if I didn't get to marry her." He smiled mischievously then, his eyes crinkling at the corners. "But you see that I never married her, or anybody else, and that I'm still alive and kicking."

"Maybe you're the one to counsel the young lovers."

"What about you? I can't believe that Miss Millicent Monroe of Little Rock didn't have her own bout with first love. Turnabout seems fair play. Tell me about it."

Millie felt her face heating up. Could she admit out loud that her first love—her only love, Luther Osgood—had kept her living on promises nearly eight years and then jilted her only a few months before they were to have been wed? She cleared her throat and lowered her eyelashes.

"I thought I was in love once, too." *It was nothing compared to the wild attraction I have to you, yet I had known Luther for years.* After clearing her throat at the riveting thought, Millie went on in a musing tone. "If I had been allowed to marry Luther Osgood when he asked me to, back before I was twenty, it would have been the worst mistake possible . . . for both of us. He married someone else when he finished law school." She looked over at Woods, struck by the thought that if she had married Luther, she never would have come to Freeman, never would have met. . . . "It's frightening, isn't it, what a force first love seems to be in the lives of young people?"

"Maybe it's not always doomed to die when they grow up. My folks always said they fell in love when they were too young to marry but that they waited and were glad they did."

Millie pondered his remarks, then shook her head in puzzlement and rose. "I'll have to hope that the right words will form when the time comes for me to counsel Annette and Warden. I'm ready to go get started on tonight's recitations if you are."

On Friday evening when Woods was getting ready to leave the schoolroom, he asked, "Has anyone mentioned the hoedown they're having here Saturday night?"

"I heard talk about a hoedown but not where it was to be held." Millie gestured at the large classroom. "There's to be a hoedown here?"

"Yes. The schoolboard decided that inviting the musicians from the hills to come into Freeman during the winter might offer some good entertainment. In the past they sometimes played at Booth's livery barn, but unless the weather was mild or there was a caller for square dancing, folks got pretty uncomfortable." He wrenched his gaze from her lifted face and assessed the long room. "There's not enough room for more than one square here if many people show up, but dancing can wait until the big Harvest Party over at the livery next month. At least everybody can have a good time listening to the music."

Millie had heard of mountain hoedowns all of her life, and her blood quickened. "It sounds like fun."

"Then you'll be here?"

"I wouldn't miss it. I've never been to a hoedown."

"I'm glad. You wouldn't like staying on your side of that wall with all the noise over here."

Silence strung out between them as Woods lowered the wick in the lantern and followed Millie out the door.

She fumbled with the doorknob at the teacherage, terribly aware that he was so close that she could hear him breathing and that the fog of his breath on the cold air almost touched her. It seemed that only the two of them were awake in the stillness of the night.

Remembering her role as teacher, she said, "Keep up the reading, Woods." *Ask me to wait and walk over to the hoedown with you tomorrow night.* Going on the hayride with him had been such fun. He was standing beside the first step looking up at her, but she avoided looking him in the face for fear he might read her mind.

"I will." *Would you say "yes" if I ask you to let me walk you over to the hoedown, or has talk about my being here so much made you leery?*

Woods jammed his hands into the pockets of his jacket to keep them from reaching out and touching Millie. He wondered if he had enough breath left to get out the words, even if he mustered up the courage. He did not want her thinking that he was trying to spark her, not when she had made it plain that she was not interested in him as a man. But she seemed to have enjoyed going on the hayride with him. She was so close that he could smell jasmine in the crisp night air. Paying attention to her teaching had been harder than usual all evening.

"Good night." Millie opened the door and stepped inside the teacherage then.

"Wait a second, Millie." Woods cleared his throat. He was glad that three doorsteps separated them, for he had a powerful urge to kiss her breathless. "What would you think about me coming by tomorrow night and walking with you to the hoedown?"

"Why, I'd think that was the gesture of a true friend. I'll be expecting you." She hoped that Woods could not hear the little skips in her breathing. Gathering up all of her courage, she turned and looked down at him fully in the face. "Good night."

After she closed the door, Millie leaned back against it weakly and let out a tremulous breath. She barely knew herself anymore, and it was frightening. There for a second she had come close to throwing her arms around Woods's neck and kissing him again and again.

· *Chapter Seventeen* ·

Millie Monroe smiled—and not just on the outside—the moment she stepped into the classroom alongside Woods Sanders that Saturday night in late October. Her eyes lifted to his; they were bathing her face with unfathomable looks that came close to drowning her. A keen-edged pleasure pierced her heart, adding a precious new note to the private humming coursing through her veins ever since he had come to escort her to the hoedown.

Oh, Millie exulted when Woods kept returning his gaze to her face no matter who came to speak with them, the world of Freeman, Arkansas was sweet, and she felt wonderfully attuned with it. At times she suspected that she might be the center of the universe. She, who had missed few of the major musical presentations in Little Rock over the past ten years, sensed that she never would forget her introduction to a hoedown in the Ouachita Mountains.

Ever since dusk, Freeman's new schoolmarm had been hearing noises coming from the classroom, and she had awaited Wood's arrival with stomach-knotting anticipation. She had not known how much of the excitement she was feeling was created by the thought that Woods was coming to escort her and how much was caused by the noises coming through the wall separating her living quarters from the schoolroom. All she knew was that in the few weeks since she left Little Rock, she had tasted more of life than she had dreamed was available and that her appetite became more keenly whetted each day.

With a part of her mind, Millie registered the large numbers of people gathered in the classroom, even managed to nod and smile at the familiar faces of her pupils and their parents. If anyone thought it odd that she should enter with the school board chairman he gave no indication. She suspected that a fair-haired young woman might be sending flirty looks toward Woods, but he seemed unaware. As on the night of the box supper, the air in the large room seemed laced with the mixed fragrances of perfume, bay rum, and a healthy dollop of anticipation.

Unlike the night of the box supper, Millie glimpsed no curious stares at her short red curls. The notion that she might already be accepted as a member of the community pleased her and added to her vast feeling of contentment. Seeing the musicians up at the front of the large room piqued her interest and stole her rapturous attention away from the handsome black-haired man beside her.

Now Millie could see the men who apparently had been tuning their instruments over the past half hour in readiness for the evening's performance. A tall skinny man with a sand-colored mustache was cradling a violin beneath his chin and touching each string softly, experimentally with his bow. With awe Millie realized that the instrument was hand-made, though its golden wood was highly polished and shone in the light from the overhead lanterns.

"Do you like all of this?" Woods asked.

"I love it!" came Millie's reply.

Another man, older and heavier, sat with his violin resting on his lap, rubbing what Millie figured was a chunk of rosin over the gut strings. Nearby a lanky young man was looping the straps of a guitar around his neck and slanting the instrument across his unspectacular chest—unspectacular, she judged, when compared to that of the mountain man standing beside her. She watched and listened as the musician gently raked an oval-shaped pick across the metal strings, stirring up a haunting minor chord before he smothered it by resting his broad palm on the six strings quivering above the sound hole.

Someone had pushed Millie's desk into the corner opposite the big black heater, she noted, and she saw brown jugs and a washboard sitting where her textbooks usually sat. Before she could ask Woods if drinking was going to take place in the schoolroom, two men idled over and claimed the jugs. To her surprise and bafflement, they puckered up and blew short blasts of breath into them with obvious ease, sending out rhythmic bass notes to mingle with the discordant whines and squeaks coming from the other instruments.

The rich sounds of excited voices and laughter filling the large room served as a perfect counterpoint, Millie decided. And she was not overlooking that secretive rhythm humming inside her ever since Woods had appeared at the teacherage.

Admitting secretly that she hoped Woods was alone, Millie had asked when she answered his knock on her door only minutes ago, "Aren't your mother and aunt with you?"

"No, they said they didn't feel up to making the trip in the night air."

"That's too bad," Millie had remarked with halfhearted sincerity. On the inside she had exulted that she was to have the handsome man all to herself.

Millie saw that over near the heater a bushy-haired man, who looked slightly familiar, sat fiddling with the tuning pegs on a banjo. From time to time, he plucked its metal strings with his pick-encased fingers, bending his head and sending an ear close to the plinking sounds.

"Millie, I'd like you to meet my friend, Lavelle Landeen," Woods said after he led her over to the man with the banjo resting upon his knees.

"My pleasure, ma'am." Lavelle smiled up at the couple. His dark eyes crinkled and spilled over with good humor when they darted toward Woods's hand hovering near Millie's elbow. "I hear tell you been visitin' up in my part of the hills. How'd you like it?"

Charmed in spite of her remembering then that Lavelle had been one of the men fighting that afternoon out in front of the livery—and that he was also a moonshiner—Millie returned his infectious smile. How could she not? It reminded her of a field of sunshine. "I like everything about Freeman, Mr. Landeen." From the corner of her eye, she saw Woods's smile widen underneath his black mustache.

"Now how can I take you 'long on a coon hunt if'n you're gonna call me anything 'cept Lavelle?"

Millie struggled for words. Coon hunt? She looked up at Woods, counting on him to rescue her.

"Lavelle is holding his annual Ladies' Night Coon Hunt pretty soon, and no doubt you're invited," Woods explained, his eyes glinting devilishly down at her.

Was it her imagination, Millie wondered, or was the cleft in Woods's chin appearing deeper than she remembered from having touched it that afternoon in the cave on Promise Ridge? Perhaps it was a trick of shadowing played by the kerosene lanterns spaced across the ceiling at intervals.

"I appreciate the invitation, Mr.—uh, Lavelle," Millie said, pulling her attention back to the bushy-haired man. He was not dressed very well, but his faded overalls were clean, as was his shirt of homespun. Several other men wore almost identical garb, she realized. "I can't accept because I know nothing about hunting—coons or anything else."

"Not to worry, purty schoolmarm," Lavelle responded with another engaging smile. "Woods there will l'arn you. I been knowin' him since he weren't more than a tadpole, and he ain't good for a lot. But I'm thinkin' he'd be fine at teaching a teacher when it comes to gettin' around in our mountains." Undaunted that he was alone in his amusement at his feeble play on words, Lavelle laughed and slapped his thigh. His two listeners stared at him with tight expressions until he sobered and went on. "You might find out you like huntin' as much as Annabelle Stevens does."

Both Millie and Woods had tensed at Lavelle's unfortunate choice of words, then relaxed when they realized that no one but the two of them could know about the "teaching" that had gone on that afternoon in the cave. Lavelle's last statement stuck with Millie, and she almost gasped in surprise. Did the ladylike blonde truly go along on the Ladies' Night Coon Hunts? Only moments earlier she had glimpsed Annabelle coming into the classroom with Lucas and his two sons.

Millie was relieved when another musician, holding a fat-backed mandolin by its slender neck, joined them. She might have become a new person since arriving in Freeman, she admitted silently, but she doubted that she was ready yet to add coon hunting to her list of accomplishments.

Woods introduced Millie to the other musicians before he led her back to sit beside him in one of the large double desks against the wall. Each had spoken politely to her, then warmly, almost intimately to Woods. It pleased her beyond reason to see that Woods rated as highly with all of the band members as he did with those gathered to hear the music. Even after they were seated and the musicians became engaged in quiet conference, apparently about the sequence of numbers to play, new people continued to sidle over to Woods and greet him . . . and be introduced to his redheaded companion.

Millie stiffened when she saw a pretty young woman sitting on the other side of the room lean and catch Wood's eye. She tried not to notice the woman's flirtatious look being sent his way, but she failed. Sending a nervous hand to smooth at the curls on her forehead, Millie wondered how many other unmarried women might be casting secretive looks at her handsome escort. She had not forgotten the side-long looks given him earlier by the dishwater blonde. Did the comely young women live in the foothills near Woods's home and—?

"Are you having a good time?" Woods asked when they found themselves able to exchange a few private words.

"Oh, yes," Millie answered, relieved to have her thoughts interrupted. Why, she scolded herself, for a minute there she had been fuming as if she might be jealous. Spotting the Widow Marks in the back of the room, Millie returned her smile and wave with an affection that she would not have believed possible only a few weeks ago. It warmed her heart to see that the youthful lovers, Annette and Warden, sat beside his mother. For a second, she wondered if Selma Bordeaux ever attended any of the local festivities. Perhaps she would mention the hoedown to Selma and. . . . Her full attention skipping back to the man in the snowy white shirt sitting beside her, she said, "I've always loved music."

"Do you play or sing?"

"Not really. A kind church member gave me piano lessons for a while, but we never had a piano. Anyway, I never had time to practice. I seldom missed any kind of musical program back in Little Rock, though."

Woods looked away from her lips, aggravated that their pinkness seemed to be drawing his gaze against his will. "This hoedown won't be like anything you've heard before."

"I know. That's why I've been so excited all day. I love new experiences." When he looked amusedly startled and one eyebrow angled upward a degree, Millie blushed and rushed on with an explanation. "I mean like the hayride, and the hoedown." Woods was sending a look at her that made her feel woozy. Surely he didn't believe that she was referring to—Quickly she prattled on. "I've always heard about the wonderful music made by hillfolk, and at last I'm going to hear some. I hope they'll play 'The Arkansas Traveler.'"

Wondering if Woods even recalled that he had whistled the melody that first night in the teacherage, Millie allowed her gaze to meet his head-on. His hip almost touched her own on the bench of the double desk. Something about the way he was watching her was playing havoc with her pulse. If she had not known better, she might have suspected that his fingers had brush stroked across her face ever so gently. "Thank you for asking me to come with you, Woods."

"As you have said before," he murmured with a touch of

irony designed for himself alone, "what are friends for?" Why did she have to be so beautiful that he could hardly keep his eyes off her? Her striped waist of olive green on natural background seemed to him the perfect complement to her darker green skirt and matching bolero. He doubted that any other color combination would have set off her lovely red curls so well. The narrow ruffle around her high neckband formed a soft frame for her face.

"Do you play a musical instrument, Woods?" She already knew that he had a fine bass voice.

Woods never gave an answer, for the band struck up their first number then. A rousing rendition of "Turkey in the Straw," it brought a laughing gray-haired man to his feet in the small cleared space in front of the band. The crowd, hands clapping along in rhythm, seemed to be urging the dancer onward. He shuffled his feet in their worn high tops with easy syncopation, his body leaning forward while his hands slapped a smart rhythm against the sides of his striped overalls.

Smiling and clapping along with Woods and everyone else, Millie never before had seen such dancing as the hill folk did that night. During each number there was at least one person up before the hand-slapping crowd, seemingly oblivious to everything but the driving music. Sometimes there were several dancers, but Millie noticed that never did they attempt to dance together. Each pursued his own private patterns.

Are you having a good time? Woods's eyes seemed to ask Millie over and over.

I love it! Millie's own answered each time.

The crowd seemed especially pleased when an elderly woman, with wide gaps in her teeth, sashayed around the little open space near the band, lifting up her full calico skirt to mid-calf with both hands and revealing a red petticoat. Millie thought of how the smile on the woman's wrinkled face and the uncannily true tapping of her feet against the rough board floor showed clearly that the music was feeding her soul.

Then Millie sat back and listened with amazement as the lanky young guitar player stood and sang in a clear tenor a plaintive ballad about the infamous Jesse James. Cheers and calls for another song from the blushing young man brought about a charming rendition of "Bonny Barbara Allan" that left the woman from Little Rock awed and teary-eyed. Never had she dreamed that the old English ballad existed anywhere other than in the staid anthologies serving as textbooks.

With new respect Millie looked around at the mountain musicians and their audience; somehow they seemed to be an extension of the solid force of the Ouachita Mountains, living proof that time and civilization never stood still, that, in spite of little formal schooling, the hill folk held a private, vital link with the universe and all of its inhabitants. An awesome feeling of humility washed over Millie for having been allowed to become a part of the community—no, welcomed into its midst was more like it, she amended. And all because of the mountain man sitting beside her, because he had held a dream of bringing a school to his home area and had worked to make it come true.

Lavelle Landeen laid down his banjo and spoke up then, announcing that it was time for the band to take a rest. People stood, stretched, and gathered to talk in happy-faced groups. Some, mostly men and young people, scattered outside for a breath of fresh air. Millie could hear the pulley screaking at the well behind the schoolhouse and was glad that the bucket and dipper used during school still sat on the washbench out there.

Annabelle and Millie found themselves a private spot on the front porch after they declined invitations from Woods and Lucas to go with them to the well for water.

"Isn't this fun?" Millie asked, all smiles from everything that was happening, but especially from the wink that Woods had given her before leaving with Lucas. Almost every person present had come over and spoken to her and made her feel welcome. She felt that she might be glowing on the inside, right along with the lanterns and the scrap of moon overhead.

"Yes. I'm glad to see that Woods escorted you tonight," Annabelle whispered. Her pale eyes took in Millie's flushed cheeks and lovely smile. And she had not missed the wink from Woods, either. "If I didn't know better, I might think there was something going on between you two."

Millie fluffed at her curls and stared out into the night where some dogs and youngsters, several of them her pupils, were chasing each other in the moonlight, ably dodging the numerous wagons, mules, and horses picketed out near the road. "But you do know better. I told you that we're merely friends." Eager to change the subject, she whispered back, "Anything new between Lucas and you? Every time I look at you two, he's smiling like crazy."

Annabelle beamed, despite the near darkness of the porch. "Yes. We'll marry the day after Christmas."

Millie muffled a squeal of delight for her friend and hugged her. "That's wonderful, Annabelle."

"Do you remember that you promised to be my attendant?"

"Yes, and you can count on me. I'm happy for you two."

"Lucas wanted us to announce our engagement tonight, but I want to wait until the Harvest Festival next month when there'll be a much larger crowd—and the wedding will be only a month away. Lucas is going to ask Woods tonight if he'll be his best man."

Millie became caught up for a brief spell in the stimulating talk about Annabelle's plans for her wedding gown, to be made of ecru satin. No matter that Millie demurred, Annabelle insisted that she was going to ask Mabel Marks to sew a dress for her attendant.

"It'll be my gift to you. I have some samples at the store and can get the material here within a week," Annabelle went on in a low voice. "I believe a rich apricot silk will go perfectly with your hair and coloring, don't you? Both of us will have scooped necklines and show off our shoulders and bosoms." When Millie laughed at the daring thought, the pretty blonde whispered, "Won't everyone be surprised?"

Millie agreed, thinking what fun it was to be a part of something so exciting as the wedding of a good friend. Then she asked, "That character, Lavelle Landeen, said something about me going along on a Ladies' Night Coon Hunt. When I said I wasn't interested, he said I might get to like it as much as you do. Was he joking?"

"No. I've gone along for the past two years with Lucas and I had a marvelous time. They always pick a moonlit night before it turns too cold. Hearing the dogs baying across a hill and then dashing off to find what they've treed —it's quite thrilling, especially if the right man is beside you."

They were speaking privately, but Annabelle leaned closer so as not to be heard by anyone else. "I hope that if Woods asks you to go, you will. I'm going with Lucas, and there'll be other women along, too. The men cook up a big stew for us and treat us special, no doubt trying to make up for the many times a lot of them take off and hunt nights on end and desert their womenfolk. You might not know that a mountain man's coonhounds are something mighty special to him."

Millie shook her head in bafflement. She recalled having heard and seen the pen of hounds out behind the Sanders house, as well as the two huge ones that had come bounding toward her that first afternoon when she was sitting on the front porch with Agatha, Glovina, and Clive Durham. How long would she have to live in the foothills of the Ouachita Mountains to take in all of the customs so new to her?

With her children, Minnijean and Junior, accompanying her with what seemed reluctance, Thelma Blackstone left a group of chatting women and joined Millie and Annabelle then. After a brief exchange, Thelma said, "We got to be goin' on home now. Junior here done got a earache from playin' outside this afternoon without a cap. I need to put some warm mineral oil in it and get him to bed."

After consoling the little boy and wishing him good health on the morrow, Millie said, "I suppose Minnijean must leave now, too." She had noted the girl's dejected air and figured she was disappointed at having to leave at intermission.

"Yeah," Thelma replied with a sigh. "Barton don't hardly ever have to work night duty, bein' as how he's foreman of the mine, but one of the fellers got sick and it was too late for Barton to get anybody else. He ain't never cared much for hoedowns anyway. I was surprised he had such a good time on the hayride the other night." She gave her daughter a sympathetic look. "I know it ain't far to our house and likely others will be walkin' home at the same time, but you never know when some of these hill folk tappin' them jugs out back might decide she's a heap older'n thirteen an' start makin' eyes at her right there in the schoolroom. It don't seem fittin' for her to be on her own."

"Will you let her stay if she sits with Woods and me? We can walk her home afterward." She had read Minnijean's pleading look correctly, Millie thought when the girl's eyes took on a new sparkle and she sent her teacher a warm smile.

"Why, Millie, I never would've thought of that. I'll be beholden." After whispering a brief word to the now smiling Minnijean, Thelma wrapped her scarf around the protesting Junior's head and left with him in tow.

The crowd started back inside then, for the night was getting chillier, and there was time for more music.

After intermission the fiddle players seemed determined on stealing the show, Millie decided. She had trouble viewing the instrument as a fiddle until she watched the acrobatics of the "fiddlers" during the foot-stomping version of "The Arkansas Traveler." No fragile violin could have survived the shenanigans that the instruments were enduring, she told herself as number followed number in which the players held their instruments for brief periods on top of their heads, behind their backs, even stood close enough once to pull their bows across the other's fiddle. *Fiddle* fit the bill.

Too soon, Millie reflected, the musicians were playing a goodnight song to the ladies. Taking his time, Woods shepherded Millie and Minnijean through the milling, chattering crowd. Millie was pleased that when Woods had come to escort her back inside and learned that Minnijean was joining them, he had made all the right remarks and put the girl at ease.

The threesome made their way across the dimly lit schoolyard, accompanied by two or three dogs at a discreet distance. Without effort they carried on a spirited conversation about several of the numbers played and sung. Minnijean seemed as interested in Millie's joyful impressions of her first hoedown as Woods.

After watching Minnijean open the front door and walk inside her home, Millie and Woods strolled back toward the road. Millie liked the way he took her arm and tucked it in his as if it truly belonged there. Woods liked the way she made no protest when he put her arm in his, then covered her hand with his free one.

Millie asked, "Does anybody in Freeman lock his door?"

"Probably nobody except you—and you should, living alone and all."

Ignoring what she guessed was an implication that she was a woman and therefore helpless, Millie said, "I guess there's not much crime here, as there is in Little Rock."

"Not any that I've heard of in a long while."

With Woods's hand on hers, Millie barely noticed the icy fingers of wind clutching at them. Watching his black hair rippling ever so slightly, she recalled that Woods had left his hat in her living room, as if he meant to come back inside and visit. Even through the serge of her silk-lined bolero, she thought, the warmth of his arm penetrated to her bare skin.

Suddenly Millie remembered the day on Promise Ridge when Woods and she had walked together and she had matched her stride to his. There was no need to look at Woods directly as they walked toward the teacherage, for her peripheral vision reassured her, even in the pale light, that he was holding his broad shoulders, encased now in his dark jacket, in that fine, straight manner of his. She took a singular kind of pleasure in the way her long skirt rustled every once in a while against the legs of his breeches.

To Millie, the rhythmic crunch of their footsteps on the gravel road sounded good and right in the nippy night air. And the pattering feet of the entourage of dogs padding along after them seemed a natural part of Freeman, she mused. It seemed ages ago, not a matter of weeks, that she had been leery of them and their natural nosiness.

As they neared the teacherage, Millie saw Warden escorting Annette across the road toward the Keyhole House. "Annabelle and Mabel have made me curious about Selma Bordeaux and her love affair with Mabel's brother, Willis."

"It was a long while back, probably twenty-five years."

Millie leaned to look up in his face, and her curls brushed against his sleeve. She loved the way it made her feel, their being so close and talking so comfortably. "If Willis were to be alive and come back, do you suppose Selma and he might pick up where they left off twenty-five years ago?"

Woods let out a kind of laughing "humph." She was full of surprises, this redheaded beauty who had set him back with her bold declaration that she had no use for men in her life. The dent that she had put in his ego smarted even more when he recalled how she had filled him with such unreasoning desire that afternoon in the cave . . . and too many times since, now that he was thinking about it. "That doesn't sound at all like what I'd expect from you, Millie Monroe. I hadn't figured you'd be thinking about romance, like most women seem to do."

Stung by Woods's deriding tone and wondering what was nipping at his earlier good humor, Millie retorted, "What's wrong with romance, pray tell?"

Millie snatched her hand and arm free, almost tripping on a large stone. He could have at least reached out to help her, she fumed; but, no, he was too intent on some inner thought that was setting his profile into rigid lines and his long legs into a faster pace. She never had said she did not believe in romance. Why couldn't he just accept her as a friend and let her be herself—whoever that was—as she was doing with him?

"I never said anything was wrong with romance, I just said—"

"I know perfectly well what you said," Millie interrupted angrily. She had to walk faster to keep up with him. "Just because you don't seem to find any need of romance in your own life, you don't have to put down the idea for everybody else."

"Me?" Woods snapped. "Who says I'm the only one who isn't looking for romance? It seems to me that you've got your own flighty ideas mighty set about how you don't need a man in your life. What's the big difference?"

Millie raised her chin. "Flighty? I never have flighty ideas, Woods Sanders." She glared at the big yellow dog trying to lick her hand and waved it away, almost cursing

under her breath when the hurrying heels of her button tops
kept sinking in the gravel.

"No, by damn, you don't, come to think of it! You have
everything so neatly worked out in your mind that nobody
could dislodge one of your ideas if he set dynamite to it. Not
that you'll ever let anyone get close enough even to plant the
dynamite. You won't even let a friendly dog trot along beside you without waving him off." He heard her suck in a
deep breath. "You'd likely not recognize romance if it was to
knock on your door."

"If it *were* to knock," Millie corrected with deliberate
coldness. God! His obvious disdain for her was slicing her
insides into ribbons. She had to strike back or be maimed
forever. What did he mean, that she wouldn't even let a dog
get close to her? He was stark, raving mad. "Use subjunctive
mood, not 'was,' since such a thing as romance knocking on
a door is literally impossible."

How else, Millie agonized, could she defend whatever
was aching deep on the inside but to revert to the role of
teacher, the one in charge? Being the man, *he* was the one
who had said he'd had no intention of asking her to marry
him after they made love in the cave, and *he* was the only
one who could make such a proposal. Not that she would
have listened. . . . Men had everything going their way, she
decided with the same feminine reasoning that had made her
correct his grammar.

"Lord! but you're sanctimonious," Woods replied. Giving
her a so-there look, he added, "And you're incorrigible, to
boot!" He scolded himself for having imagined all evening
that she, too, had enjoyed the looks from the crowd that
seemed to be approving the notion that Millie and he *might*
be sparking. Until now, he had half entertained the idea
of. . . . His temper and torn pride took over again. "I don't
know why I try to have any kind of relationship with you
other than teacher and pupil—or teacher and board chairman."

"Neither do I!"

They were on the edge of the schoolyard then, with Millie
almost running to keep up. No doubt some of the people had
lagged behind for visiting, for there were still horses and

vehicles in the schoolyard and some just then moving off into the night.

Both Millie and Woods slowed then. Each was glad in his own way that the dispersing groups of chattering people paid the couple little attention and settled for brief "good nights" as they drifted away toward their homes.

Millie saw Henry Stevens inside the schoolroom, dousing the lanterns. By the time Woods and she reached the steps leading up to the teacherage—in silence as frosty as the night air—they heard Henry close the front door and leave.

A night breeze riffled Millie's curls then, and Woods caught a whiff of jasmine. A disastrous feeling of tenderness mixed with desire rushed over him, despite his ruffled temper. And, he thought with awful clarity, had he not become angry because the old hurt from her rebuffing him back in the cave had erupted again? Great balls of fire! A woman did not have the right to turn down a man's proposal when he never had made one. It was demoralizing, he reasoned; that's what it was.

Woods jammed his hands in the pockets of his breeches and tried to ignore the tantalizing smell of her perfume. Millie would never see him as anything but a friend. His earlier plan to visit with her in her living room after the hoedown and hear her laughter—and maybe steal a kiss or two—fell dead among the dry leaves rustling around her doorsteps.

"Good night, Woods," Millie said after she turned her doorknob. Still short of breath—from the near race in trying to keep up with the maddening man, she reminded herself— she dug deeply for a normal tone. Doubts assailed her and pricked her conscience. What if her temper and tart tongue had changed his mind about seeking her help? She could think of nothing she wanted to do more than help Woods become the most qualified candidate in next year's race for state representative; or if she could, she was not letting it surface right then.

From her doorstep Millie looked down at the handsome mountain man, not surprised that no special twinkle reached toward her from his blue eyes. The temptation to smile and hold out her hand almost overcame her, but something unrecognizable, white-hot and oozing with pain, slapped down the notion. "I'll be expecting you on Monday night . . . as usual."

"Right." A thought glimmered in Woods's mind. "Would you throw me my hat?"

Millie made no reply, just stepped inside and brought out his hat.

"Thanks," Woods replied. He knew then that he had been hoping she might invite him inside to get his hat.

Clearing her throat and wishing she knew how to patch things up between them, Millie said, "You're welcome, and thanks for taking me to the hoedown."

Woods let out his imprisoned breath when Millie wheeled around and closed her door with little noise. Until that moment he had not realized how much he was hoping that she would not slam the door in his face. At least, he temporized, she was not kicking him out of her classroom.

Millicent Monroe, the beautiful red-haired woman from Little Rock, probably never would belong in Freeman or the Ouachita Mountains, Woods reasoned after he mounted Major and rode toward the road. Earlier that evening, as well as several times since the hayride, he had imagined that maybe she did.

Woods's troubled thoughts galloped on, right along with Major after the horse turned at the crossroads and headed toward home. It must have been because he had wanted it to be true that she had seemed happy to be appearing with him at the hoedown, happy in a way that went beyond friendship.

All he could do, Woods rationalized on the long ride home, was hope that when he saw Millie again, both of them would have cooled off enough to let bygones be just that. Even though she already had helped him tremendously in his search for mastery of reading, writing, and ciphering, and she was the most fascinating woman that he had ever been around, Woods faced up to the wracking truth as he saw it: Millie Monroe was one puzzle he might not ever solve.

From far away the mournful notes of a lone dog's howl floated on the cold night wind.

"You and me both, boy," Woods muttered.

· *Chapter Eighteen* ·

Before he slept that October night after the hoedown, Woods Sanders leafed all the way through his mind and soul. He did not consciously omit a single page as he rode homeward. Somehow, though, two or three pages stuck together and glossed over a few segments in the true story of the man who had declared himself immune to women.

The arrival of Millie Monroe six weeks ago was the beginning of the current vexing chapter in his life, Woods thought, shifting his weight and not even hearing the familiar, protesting squeaks of his saddle. Now that Freeman was behind him, he let the reins play out loosely from his hand, knowing that Major would set a good pace over the six miles to his home beside Iron Creek.

Ever mindful of the beauty of his birthplace, Woods watched ghostly beams from a curving slice of a moon probe the dark forest up ahead. Mystery now bathed landmarks that had been familiar in the sunlight on his ride into Freeman, and he felt a strange longing to be sharing the piercing loveliness of the night with Millie. Through the overlapping branches of soaring trees, the hardwoods bare of leaves now, he could see the stars pulsing with countless bursts of light. The frosty night was nearing its zenith. The sounds of forest creatures were stilled, or at least concealed by the rhythmic clip-clop of Major's hurrying hooves on the rocky road.

How often, Woods wondered, had he traveled this portion

of the winding road from Freeman to the heart of the Ouachita Mountains and spent that hour pondering a million subjects all at once—or, more recently over the past two years, only one at a time? In the same way that his master gave his mind freedom to roam and bump into myriad thoughts, Major cantered along with ease, a horseshoe striking a spark from a sharp-edged rock every once in a while and casting the rock into a noisy spin. An occasional pileup of dead leaves on the road added a muffled, rustling sound to the staccato beats of the gaited horse's hooves upon the rocks and gravel.

Who was this Millie Monroe who kept popping up in his life in the most unexpected ways? Woods questioned what he assumed was the objective part of his mind. Yes, he mused when an answer came, she was, indeed, a beautiful, desirable woman, but one with the most unorthodox ideas he had ever heard about in his thirty-five years.

Why did it bother him—not the beautiful, desirable part; he was not ready to think about that yet—that she had such unusual notions about life? Like an earthworm held captive against a flat piece of ground by an eager fisherman's forefinger, the raw truth about why the new schoolmarm affected him as she did squirmed and blindly sought freedom. And with as little success.

Woods chose to think about less baffling aspects of his life. He recalled how he had begun dreaming of better conditions for Freeman and other communities in the mountains long before a solution for helping the dream come true dawned on him some two years ago. As pieces in a jigsaw puzzle make no clear pattern until they're fitted into their proper places, his vision remained no more than a segment of an unidentified whole until he had faced up to a jolting fact: He, himself, seemed the most logical one to set into motion the changes that he envisioned.

Once Woods recognized himself as a man of vision, he allowed what had at first seemed vague dreams to crystalize in his mind. For some time now, he had been seeing the automobile as the thing—what was the truer word that Millie had used one night in the classroom? he wondered. *Catalyst?* Yes, he told himself as he struggled to get his thoughts straight there on the ride home, he viewed the growing automobile industry of 1911 as the catalyst for the changes he longed to see take place.

Woods, the visionary, saw decent year-round roads and bridges for Lexington County and for the surrounding counties forming his area's new legislative district. He saw a workable system by which severance taxes paid into the state treasury would be returned in part to the area from which the earth products came. Such funds could provide more and better schools, both in small and large communities.

As he rode on into the night, Woods thought about how he and others had worked diligently throughout the past two years to build the school at Freeman.

Had he gone wrong, he wondered, when he planned to let his own education dovetail with the overall plan? Maybe he was off base. Maybe he was not the one to master the finer points of reading and writing and then carry his message to the voters next year. Encouraging him was the thought that countless others already had let him know it was their message, too.

A conversation among Woods and some of his staunchest supporters as a potential candidate for the legislature next year came hurtling back to him there on the road from Freeman. Several men had lingered after a political meeting in the schoolhouse over at Murfreesboro, only a week ago. The talk had been candid, even blunt, but designed, however casually, for one purpose: victory for their group's candidate at the polls in the coming year.

Henry Stevens had ridden over to Murfreesboro with Woods on the past Saturday night. The congenial, grayed owner of Freeman's general store had listened to the other men talk, but he had interjected his own ideas, too.

"I don't think people will be too concerned with the fact that Woods isn't a married man," Henry stated when the talk centered on that one glaring negative aspect of Forrest "Woods" Sanders, potential candidate. "After all, he'll be only thirty-six by election time next summer." With the bowl of his pipe cupped in his palm and the stem moving in emphasis as he made his point, he added with a smile and a twinkle in his eyes, "Fact of the matter is, Woods might rate high from being a bachelor. My daughter, Annabelle, tells me that he's a right handsome fellow to the fairer sex. Women can't vote, but wives and daughters can influence a man in lots of ways."

"That may be true," remarked Theo Stewart in his drawling way, rearing back against his chair and stacking one long leg across the knee of the other. He brought two fingers up to his lips, puckered, then spit a narrow stream of tobacco juice between the fingers. As usual, his aim was good and a small "ping!" sounded from the little brass cuspidor that his brother-in-law, Hiram Neal, always carried along to meetings not held at the bank. "But again, a married man just naturally comes across as more settled, more reliable, somehow."

Though he had parroted the thoughts of his brother-in-law so often over the years that few paid attention to what he said any longer, Hiram Neal added, "Theo's right, by God!"

Deferring with a thoughtful nod to Theo, who was the president of the local bank and one of Murfreesboro's most influential citizens, Travis Watson spoke up then. He narrowed his eyes and fixed them on Woods. "Theo's got a strong point there, Woods. Don't reckon you got any plans on marrying between now and next summer, when the politicking gets hot and heavy, do you?"

The ten men gathered around Woods in the schoolroom chuckled and made little asides to whoever was sitting nearest. Hiram Neal tittered, then shushed when Theo fixed him with a sour look. All were from five to twenty years older than Woods, and all were married or were widowers.

"No, I have no plans to marry." Woods felt a smidgen of surprise when he had not added the word "ever." Until that moment, it had gone with the statement every time he had uttered it in the past ten years. He exchanged glances with Henry Stevens, the only other man present from Freeman. What was bringing that smug look to Henry's normally placid face? Had he also noticed the omission of "ever"?

Woods continued. "I've been telling you gentlemen for the past year that I might not be the candidate to win this race, but that I'm going to work for whichever man can get the job done best." He cleared his throat and switched the way he had one leg resting on the knee of the other. Nobody but his good friends, Henry Stevens and the Reverend Fred Tate—and Millie, of course—knew of his limited ability to read or write, or that Millie was now helping him to remedy that shortcoming. Maybe he was letting false pride seep into his decision to keep the matter private, but still and all. . . . "There's always Sam Staples from Mt. Ida."

"Aw, shee-it!" drawled Theo, drawing out the crude word into two syllables in such a way as to suggest its smell. He may have been completely out of character now as the town's banker, but he was clearly at home in the one of mountaineer. All eyes riveted on him. "All of you know that I grew up in the back hills without a pot to piss in or a window to throw it out of, but I can spot a loser a country mile by the way his eyes sit in his head.

"Why, Sam Staples ain't worth the horseshit on your boot, Woods, and you mighty well know it. Think about how his eyes got all beady and even closer together tonight when we talked about all the graft going on in Little Rock. He can't wait to hold out his grubby hands over there in the city. We got our sights set on you, boy, and you might as well hold still."

A general rush of agreeing voices rose there in the room, and Woods listened then to several persuasive statements. It was not his way to ignore the opinions of others, not even those of nervous little men like Hiram Neal. The way Woods saw it from his years of observing people, Hiram was not a lot different from others who seemed to feel the need to sit in the shadow of a much stronger person. That Hiram had chanced to marry Theo Stewart's sister had little to do with the way Hiram was. Had the man he aped not been his brother-in-law, Woods reasoned, Hiram likely would be looked upon as a devoted and helpful friend to a forceful man.

"I take it kindly that you gents agree with me that Woods can get the vote and do a fine job for us in Little Rock," Henry Stevens said after the talk calmed down. He went to the wood-burning heater, flipped open its door, and tapped the ashes from his pipe onto its smoldering coals. "Let's shelve the problem of his being a bachelor and go ahead with our other plans."

Shrugging into his coat, the owner of Freeman's general store went on. "Woods will deliver his first big speech before the dancing begins at our Harvest Festival. If he comes across as well as I think he will"—several men interjected brief agreements with Henry's expectations—"then all of us can make the final decision afterward about whom we'll support for the election." He winked at Woods, then said in a joshing way, "Who knows? Some pretty gal might have lassoed our boy by that time. His bachelor days may be numbered already without his even knowing it."

Then, shaking hands all around and making sure that all of the men, along with their families, received personal invitations to the Harvest Festival in Freeman on the third Saturday in November, Woods and Henry mounted their horses and headed toward Freeman.

As he rode Major home from the hoedown, Woods let the events of the past Saturday night in Murfreesboro rattle around in his head. Funny, but he had not questioned or chided Henry about his remark as to how his bachelor days might be numbered. Instead an absurd idea had begun circling widely in his brain. At times during the past week, it revolved right before his eyes. He always shoved it out of view. Until tonight.

More than once during the hoedown while Millie looked so happy just being with him, Woods had found himself playing around with the farfetched idea: Marriage to Millie Monroe might be a damned fine thing.

Since Woods knew that far more married men than unmarried ones filled the legislative chamber in the new Capitol, he could not argue against the fact that, as a bachelor, he might have two strikes against him if he did decide to run for representative. Millie was so beautiful and got along so well with people that he had no trouble counting her as an asset to a husband. He refused to let his mind wander further and dwell upon what a heady armful of woman she was. He was determined to be logical about the matter.

The thorn in his lopsided reasoning kept cropping up all evening during the hoedown, and now, as Major was loping closer to home: Millie had said plainly that she did not plan on getting married. Back in the cave—God, how he hated dredging up that blow to his pride—she already had as good as turned him down, when he had not even asked her.

Quickly Woods pushed away memories of his time with Millie in the cave, returning to the present. Tonight, after she got all riled at him for laughing at her romantic musings about Selma Bordeaux and Willis Turner, Woods recalled with mixed emotions how he also had given in to impulse and lashed out at her. When was he going to learn that giving in to his quick temper never did anything but put him in an even worse light than before he blew up?

After he reached his bed and stretched out underneath the patchwork quilt, Woods flipped back through the evening's musings. Nowhere did he find more than that one big reason—the vast differences in their upbringing—not to get busy sparking Millie Monroe and trying to change her mind about marriage. Maybe in the next few weeks he could reach acceptable levels in reading and writing that would help him erase the feeling that their differences were insurmountable.

If Clive Durham, scamp that he was, could hang around Freeman's new schoolmarm with the obvious intent to court her, why couldn't he do the same? The thought of the pink-faced man bringing her the box of candy still rankled. Already he had asked Henry Stevens to order something special for Millie, but it had not arrived yet. He decided that on his next trip into Freeman he would ask the storeowner to order another surprise, a box of candy twice as big as the one Clive had given her.

Not sleepy, not when his brain was whirling at such a dizzying rate, Woods tried analyzing his reasons for not trusting the easterner.

From the first meetings held with Clive a few years back, about leasing the Sanders property to Southern Bauxite Mines, Woods had been suspicious of the company's representative. Easily some of the main details of those meetings surfaced.

* * *

"The bauxite is not doing you or your family any good just lying in the ground, Mr. Sanders," the man from Buffalo, New York, had explained to Woods as the two men sat on the porch of the Sanders home. "If you lease to the company I represent, you can expect a nice income for years to come, maybe for the rest of your life. That can mean much security and a far finer way of living, you see."

Woods noticed the nervous, flighty way that Clive Durham perched on the rocker, as if he might be afraid to relax and let the real person inside show. "I may not be looking for a finer way of living, but a man does have a need to look to the future. I want to keep your contract and look it over, maybe get a friend of mine to read it."

"There's no need for bringing in a third party," Clive remarked quickly. "I like dealing with a man who runs his own affairs, you see. My advice is for you to sign today so that we can begin mining. Remember that the mine will be offering jobs to your friends and neighbors, as well as to you."

When Clive's gaze slid around the porch and never met the penetrating one from Woods, even when his glasses did not hide his eyes, Woods became even more certain that there was a caginess about the man that boded no good for him, the landowner. Right then Woods knew that he would not meet again with the easterner unless his friend, Reverend Fred Tate, sat in on the meeting—after Fred had read the contract and explained the details to Woods.

When the minister appeared alongside Woods at the other meetings, Clive barely concealed his anger and frustration at having Fred present.

After some telling questions from Woods at their final meeting, Clive explained unctuously, "Of course my company will pay the landowner his royalties, just as soon as the initial cost of constructing the mine and buying equipment is recovered." Though a tight smile barely creased his round face, he seemed particularly outdone with the minister, who did little but sit, listen, and watch every move the fidgety Clive made.

"How will I know when that cost is recovered, Clive?" Woods asked now that almost all of his other questions had been answered to his satisfaction. They had reached first-name basis by then.

"Good point," Fred Tate said. "Would Forrest have access to your books?"

"Certainly not. I'll be making oral reports to him from time to time as I hear from the head office in Buffalo." Clive replied defensively. "Southern Bauxite is a reputable company. Forrest will get his money. In the meanwhile he will be earning a generous salary as general overseer of the mine on his property."

Woods pondered as he lay on his bed rehashing those early meetings with Clive Durham. It appeared that it might be another year before he would receive any money from the ore mined on the Sanders farm over the past two years.

From having read the contract only a few nights ago, haltingly but thoroughly, Woods knew that monies should have begun coming in last year at the latest. He suspected that his former inability to read and understand the dratted contract was what had kept him from pushing Clive harder than he had already. He figured that he was being a mite testy about the matter, but Woods had no wish for the arrogant easterner to learn that only now was he truly learning to read and write. The man found opportunities enough to let Woods know that he found all of the hill folk lacking.

Suddenly Woods recognized a new hitch in his half-formed plan to spark the beautiful woman from Little Rock. He had very little money, other than his monthly salary as overseer. All that he owned was land and livestock, and all was mortgaged to the Landowners' Bank of Little Rock. If he had not counted so heavily on that doctor in St. Louis being able to restore his mother's eyesight, he reflected, he still might not have any money to speak of, but he would not also be in debt.

Woods flopped over in his bed and lay facedown, his mind still working. How right it had seemed two years ago to withdraw his savings, mortgage the farm that Agatha had long ago deeded over to Woods, and escort Agatha to St. Louis. The doctor performed his operation for a hefty fee, but Agatha remained blind. Woods accepted as reward enough his mother's cheerful reassurances that at least he had tried his best to help her get back some of her vision. Too, it helped a tad to recall that it was in St. Louis that he had found the trained dog, Shep, to serve as Agatha's aid.

At the time of the loan from the bank, Woods reasoned, he had expected to be receiving a considerable monthly income within a year from the bauxite mines. And for years to come. His old anger at Clive Durham for having thwarted him—and other uneducated landowners as well—by withholding monies due rose like bile in his throat. The man was rotten.

Woods, before giving in to his need for sleep, promised himself to study his contract again and have a real showdown with Clive. If he won, as he meant to, then he could advise other landowners. Time was running out: A new junior officer from the bank in Little Rock seemed to be stepping up his recent threats by letters to foreclose on the Sanders farm unless the loan was paid back before the end of the year.

Soothed at the thought that Millie's teaching him was making it possible for him to cope better with people like Clive Durham, Woods relaxed and let sleep take him over. When he dreamed of the beautiful new schoolmarm, though, it had nothing at all to do with her being a teacher.

"Uncle Woods," Marty Clegg called right after noon the next day when Woods was seeking some privacy from the relatives overflowing the Sanders home. "I wanted to talk with you today."

Woods paused on the bank of Iron Creek, not completely displeased that his oldest sister's son had found him. Usually he enjoyed every aspect of the frequent visits on Sundays from one or more of his older sisters and their families. Somehow, he had felt out of sorts ever since waking up and remembering his dream about finding Millie in his arms again.

"What's going on with you up at Mt. Ida, Marty?" Woods looked back toward the house on the ridge. He smiled when he saw that one of his younger nephews was playing chase with a couple of his coonhounds in the fall sunshine; another

was idling in the chain swing hanging from a limb of the big
oak in the side yard, the same swing that had served Woods
and his sisters when they were children. "I'm glad to see that
you're still bringing your pretty girlfriend along when you
come down to visit. Where's Shirley now?"

The younger man blushed, but he returned his uncle's
teasing smile with one of fondness. "She's helping clean up
in the kitchen."

The two ambled down the bank of the creek, both of them
tall and dark-haired.

"Shirley seems mighty nice," Woods said after a spell. He
suspected from what he had been hearing his sister, Gladys,
say all day that Marty wished to talk about Shirley. "And
she's as pretty as a speckled pup, as your grandpa used to
say about the really good-looking girls."

"Shirley's pretty, all right. We want to get married on New
Year's Day and come live here and farm on the family
place," Marty said all in one breath. When Woods looked at
him sharply but made no comment, he went on. "Mama says
that you're too busy now overseeing at the mine to do much
farming, and that you're likely going to be spending lots of
time next year running for office. Then after you get elected,
you'll have to be in Little Rock —"

"Hold up, Marty. I haven't even decided to run yet, and
here my sister already has me elected." Woods chuckled and
laid an arm across his nephew's shoulders. "How old are you
now?"

"I'm twenty, and Shirley's eighteen. Papa's place isn't big
enough for me to farm with him, and I've always loved it
here. If you'd not mind, that is, until we could get us a place
of our own. Mama told me that Grandma deeded the place to
you a long time ago."

Woods dropped his arm and studied the earnest young
face that closely resembled his own. For a moment he wondered if he might not be feeling more than a little envious.
Marty might be terribly young, but he had a firmly fixed
goal in mind, one that seemed within his grasp.

His deep voice full and warm, Woods said, "The farm is
Mama's so long as she lives, Marty, no matter whose name
shows on the deed. I've no objections to the two of you

coming here to live and work the land, even if I don't run for office. In fact, I'm pleased that you want to. Lord knows we've got bedrooms to spare and a hall down the middle to give lots of privacy. I expect Mama and Aunt Glovina will be tickled at having somebody around all of the time, now that I'm gone so much more than I used to be."

Soon the two were talking about crops for next year and hurrying toward the brown fields to inspect fences.

Later they returned to the house, where a blushing Shirley told of her eagerness to make her home with Marty beside Iron Creek. As Woods had predicted, both Agatha and Glovina liked the idea of having the young couple move in with them after the first of the year. The more Woods thought about it and listened to the excited talk going on in the large living room, the more he decided that the idea was solid and right for all concerned. He had a strong feeling that his father would have approved heartily.

What Woods could not figure out, after Gladys and her large family left to return to their farm near Mt. Ida, was why the news of an upcoming wedding in the family left him feeling a bit depressed. As soon as Agatha and Glovina announced that they were tired and going to take naps, Woods saddled Major and rode into Freeman.

"I hadn't expected to see you until tomorrow night," Millie said after ushering Woods inside the teacherage. She brushed at the curls hovering untidily about her face. There was nothing she could do about her suddenly skipping heartbeat. Was he still angry at her?

"You're mighty dressed up for some reason." Woods thought about how her dark blue skirt and blue-striped waist set off the deep red of her hair in an extra nice way, then wondered why he couldn't say it out loud. He was not surprised that he could not read much from her face; was she still mad at him? He sank onto the sofa after she did and turned toward her. "You look mighty pretty, Millie." The words did not match his thoughts at all, and he despised himself for holding back. What was he afraid of?

"Thank you."

"Did I interrupt something? Were you going somewhere?"

"No."

Woods glimpsed a cape of the same blue as her skirt lying across the side chair. A scarf and a pair of dainty gloves lay there, too. "You must have just come home from somewhere."

"Yes, I did." Millie jumped up, evading his eyes. "I'll put on water for tea, if you'd like some. Or do you prefer coffee?"

"I'm far better at working the cookstove, remember?" Woods asked, rising and motioning for her to sit back down.

Why, Millie wondered while Woods put the kettle on, didn't she go ahead and tell that she had ridden with Clive to look around at the Huddleston farm near Murfreesboro, the farm where diamonds had been discovered lying in a field some five years ago? When the easterner appeared at her door that morning and invited her, she had accepted in a moment of despised weakness. True, she did want to see where the Arkansas diamonds were being found, but it was more than that.

A wild notion that she was feeling hemmed in had seized Millie and led her to go with Clive, prompted no doubt by her restless night—which was itself brought on by the unnerving ending to the delightful evening with Woods, she acceded grimly. Caught up in her thoughts, she sat on her sofa and listened to Woods puttering around in the kitchen corner. Ever since their first meeting in Uncle Fred's living room, the forceful mountain man seemed to have become all tangled up in her life in ways having little to do with plain friendship.

Millie sent a testing hand to the back of her neck, fingering the short hair and recalling how when she had cut it, she had felt she was stepping into a new phase of her life. Well, she had not been wrong. Everything was new, all right, and not just her surroundings.

Sending a sidewise look at Woods, Millie thought of the new her, the one who had a passionate yen for Woods Sanders that bordered on near insanity when she tried to rationalize it. The thought that she might be falling in love with him kept sneaking into her mind more and more lately and leading her to wonder at the truth of her declaration that she neither needed nor wanted a man in her life. Maybe she had been wrong, though one-sided love seemed no kind of love worth considering.

"What's this?" Woods asked from where he stood near the cookstove, staring at the kitchen table.

Startled from her thoughts by his deep resonant voice, Millie glanced toward him. She had not realized that the sun already was dipping behind the mountains beyond her kitchen window. A pinkish light was coloring the teacherage. The questioning, perplexed look on his face brought a little smile to her own. "That's a bouquet of feathers. The curly ones are from the ostrich farm near Hot Springs, and the others with the lovely colored 'eyes' are peacock feathers."

Woods caught the amusement in her voice. "Where in the world did they come from?"

"Clive Durham brought them to me."

"I didn't know you liked old feathers, or I would have brought you some from our chicken yard." He hoped that his voice showed his intention to sound teasing. On the inside he was seething with resentment that Clive must have called on her that day and brought her another present. He hated himself for having to know more. "Have you been with Clive today?"

"What difference does it make if I have?" Was he, perhaps, a tad jealous? For a second she wished that he was, then chided herself for getting her hopes up that maybe he was feeling more than friendship. Maybe he was still upset with her over last night's tiff.

"None, except I thought you had more horse sense than to waste your time with that banty rooster."

"Woods Sanders, you love meddling in my life, don't you?" She felt her temper stirring and commanded it to be still. "I don't have to explain to anyone why I rode over to the diamond farm near Murfreesboro with Clive today."

"You're right. You don't." Despising the images he was getting of Millie and Clive together for most of the day, Woods reached to pour the boiling water into the teapot. "Hell's bells!" He slammed the kettle back down and rammed his hand into the water bucket sitting nearby.

Instantly Millie was rushing toward Woods, her face contorted with compassion. "How awful! You forgot to use a
lifting pad, didn't you?" She peeked over his shoulder at his
hand still resting in the bucket of water. "Is the pain terrible?
I'm so sorry. What can I do to help?"

Woods slid a look down at the beautiful red-haired
woman. With her fingers clutching his arm and her mouth
rounded in sympathy, she was leaning against him staring at
his smarting hand. He could hear the little warm compas-
sionate sounds deep in her throat. Up close like that, he
could smell far better the wonderful jasmine fragrance of her
hair and skin. He could see the rapid pulsing of a vein in her
neck, and he itched to touch it and release some of the surg-
ing passion heating up his blood.

"Now that you've asked me," he teased, "I guess you can
kiss my hand and make it well." Smiling upon seeing her
lovely face flush in the soft pink light coming in the window,
he lifted his hand from the water and examined it.

"I don't see any red marks now," Millie said, leaning to
look more closely. He really did have nice manly hands, she
thought.

"I reckon I'm going to live after all."

Both Millie and Woods seemed entranced there in autumn's gentle twilight. She still rested her hand on his arm.
He still held her gaze with his. For a pulsating moment or
two, the only outwardly visible movement came from the
drops of water sliding down Wood's hand and plopping back
into the water bucket.

And then, without their even wondering how or exactly
why it happened, Woods's arms enfolded Millie with a gentleness that belied the storm of passion flooding his body.
With a movement as natural and imperceptible as the changing of the hues of the light coming through the window, he
pressed her slender body against his solid strength. His
mouth found hers and made a tender claim on its trembling
softness. His heart thudded unmercifully at the womanly feel
of her in his arms, at the heady smell of her face and hair so
close to his own, and at the sudden sense of power that
holding her brought. *Why,* he thought with utter amazement,

there is nothing in the world that I can't do with this beauti-
ful woman beside me.

To Millie's surprise, her body skipped over those remembered delicious fits and starts of getting all fired up from
Woods's kiss. She wondered if she might not have imagined
that his past kisses had set her on fire, so rapidly was this
one enflaming her every cell. Like a whirlwind of delectable, tingling sensations, she thought. She knew for certain
then that her attraction to Woods Sanders not only was still
very much alive, but also was growing. Never had she
wanted to get lost in his arms as much as she did at that
moment.

It made no sense, Millie thought in a kind of mindless
panic. Nothing about her reaction to the man had ever made
any sense. The texture of his mustache against her skin, the
feel of his broad chest beneath her suddenly aching breasts,
and the remembered manly fragrance of him stormed her
sensibilities. Who was she when she was in his arms? She
entertained the idea that maybe she belonged there. She
struggled to free her mouth while she had the strength to
resist.

"Why do you affect me this way, Woods?" She did not
care, as she would have once, that her voice was ragged.
This time Millie heard the inner voice suggesting that maybe
she was falling in love with Woods. But she disregarded the
one that said she already had done so.

"I was thinking about asking you the same question." He
was no longer immune to women—or at least not to the one
in his arms.

Her brown eyes questioned his blue ones in desperation,
but she found no answers.

An alien sound gradually became a familiar one. Someone
was knocking on the door of the teacherage.

Millie stepped away from Woods's arms, unaware that the
back of her blouse was wet from where his hand had rested
during their kiss. While she moved on weak legs to answer
the knock, Woods remained beside the window and watched
her skirt sway above her slender ankles encased in button top
shoes. Lord have mercy on his soul, he agonized with a

hollow feeling in the pit of his stomach. Even the way she walked across a room was driving him crazy.

Lucas Milstead stood at the door, and within a brief time, he had accepted Millie's invitation to come inside. The three exchanged pleasantries as though it was not unusual for them to be together there in the living room of the teacherage.

"I guess you're wondering why I'm here," Lucas said, his gaze shifting from Millie to Woods. "Annabelle saw you ride into town not long ago, Woods. Right off she got the idea that I ought to come over and ask both of you to join us for supper. Henry and the boys are out tending to the horses now while she mixes up biscuits."

Subdued by their recent kiss and her soul-searching question, Millie and Woods exchanged half-shy looks.

"Annabelle is very kind to invite us. I'd like having supper with all of you," Millie said, turning to where her cape lay on the chair. She suspected that she was being rescued from something threatening, yet she felt no gratitude. "What about you, Woods?"

"Sounds fine to me, too," Woods answered. He could not figure out what was bringing an amused look to Lucas's face. Right off he had told Lucas about his scorched hand, figuring that might explain the obvious tension in the room. Did he guess that he had interrupted a kiss?

Lucas watched Woods reach for Millie's cape to drape around her shoulders and went outside to wait for them near the porch. A huge grin creased his face as he rammed his hands in his pockets and spoke under his breath to the darkening sky. "Yessir. That was the print from Woods's wet hand on Millie's blouse. Annabelle is right. There's more than friendship between Millie and Woods. Wonder how long it'll be before they recognize it?"

· *Chapter Nineteen* ·

Annabelle and her father, Henry, welcomed Millie and Woods to their home when they appeared with Lucas. After supper the Milstead boys, Faron and Steven, excused themselves and went upstairs. Not until the five adults had finished their coffee in the living room did the talk get around to more than light topics, for the evening had proved one of easy frivolity.

After the three men discussed a few details about the upcoming Harvest Festival, Annabelle said, "Selma came to the store late this afternoon when Papa opened up to let somebody get a new rope for a well." Plainly showing her delight in at last having accepted Lucas's proposal, she slid an adoring look at him as he sat beside her on the sofa in the living room.

Not having missed how Lucas Milstead's dark sturdiness seemed a complementing contrast to Annabelle's womanly blondness, Millie said, "That's grand news. She must have gotten braver after she played for us at the schoolhouse Friday afternoon and saw that nobody seemed to notice the scar on her face."

The four plied Millie with questions, and she fended them off by saying with a small laugh, "I didn't deliberately keep quiet about it. I assumed the youngsters had said something about the beautiful music, and the topic just never came up."

Woods looked thoughtful as Millie told more about Selma playing her violin. Had Millie been going to tell him about it the night after the hoedown when she brought up the question of a possible romance between Selma Bordeaux and Willis Turner if the two ever got together again?

After offering cigars to Woods and Lucas and then settling

back onto a big arm chair, Henry said, "You did a fine thing, going to see Selma and asking her to play for your pupils, Millie." He struck a match and held the flame to his pipe, drawing on it and getting the tobacco lit before going on. "Selma's daddy, Horace Witherspoon, was a mean old coot. He was cantankerous from the day he moved to Freeman with little Selma and his housekeeper. He reminded me of a horse with a cocklebur lodged underneath its saddle blanket, ready to lash out at anything simply because he couldn't get at the real root of the pain.

"There's no telling how much cruelty that old man inflicted on those two young people before Willis ran off in the night and Selma got shuttled off to school in Memphis. It wasn't anybody's business but theirs, I don't reckon, but it seemed mighty strange that Selma never was the same the few times she came home after that."

Woods, sitting on the other side of a lamp table from Millie and listening to Henry, found himself fascinated by the way the lamplight danced in Millie's red curls. Having clipped the end of his cigar, he returned his pocketknife to his pocket and reached for the box of matches sitting nearby. Even when he was not looking directly at her, he was still thinking about how pretty her profile was. He could feel her gaze washing over his face as she turned to watch him light his cigar.

Annabelle sighed and smoothed back the blond tendrils escaping from her stylish pompadour caught up in a topknot. "Millie, everyone from around here already knows so I guess it's only fair that you find out more about Selma, too." She glanced at her father who was drawing gently on his pipe and squinting through the smoke out into space. "From what we've heard, from Mabel mostly, Selma's father didn't approve of Mabel's brother as a suitor for his sixteen-year-old daughter. Papa isn't the only one who saw Mr. Witherspoon had a mean streak, but nobody believes he meant for his punishment to his child to produce the scar that it did. Who knows what led him to do what everyone believes he did? Selma seems to have come to terms with her past, thank goodness."

Woods spoke up then. "I wasn't much more than a grasshopper back when Fern, Annabelle, and all of us kids used to run and play in your pasture behind the house here, Henry, but I remember what fine horses ran in Mr. Witherspoon's pastures next to yours."

It dawned on Woods that for him to speak of the past and name Fern Stevens as a part of his growing-up years was new. A sidelong glance at the dead woman's husband sitting on the sofa showed him that Lucas Milstead was also at ease with the casual statement of fact.

Feeling strangely freed, Woods continued. "After I moved to Hot Springs and began working around different stables, I heard a lot of talk about what went on at the racetrack. A goodly number of the winners at Oaklawn had come from Witherspoon's stock." Caught up in musing, he added, "It seems a shame that the Witherspoon pastures never have been put to use since the old man died and Selma sold off all the horses."

Lucas asked, "Do you reckon Selma might rent out the pastures, now that she has obviously decided to get out among people? I wouldn't mind moving some of my horses down here after the first of the year. That might be a good way to help Ransom get set up with his own horses when he gets grown."

"That ought to tickle both Ransom and Warden since they're getting to be such good friends," Henry said. "Ransom can't stay away from horses, and Warden is always looking for animals to doctor. Mabel was by the store this afternoon, saying she was feeling lonely since Annette had ridden off with Warden. Somebody came by and told him about a rare breed of dog—rare for these parts, anyhow—having given birth to a litter somewhere near Dierks." He chuckled. "That Warden is deadset on learning all he can about animals before he even gets to a vet college."

Then Millie, saddened upon learning the source of the scar on Selma's face, initiated a brief discussion on the sterling qualities of Warden Marks, the student, adding how she hoped to assist him in getting a scholarship to the University of Oklahoma. It pleased her to learn that the others felt the young man was as commendable as she did. Their fond accounts of some of the boy's childhood pranks surprised her, and she found herself laughing indulgently along with them.

It occurred to Millie that Freeman was more than a small town: It was also one large family of caring people. They did talk about each other with relish, but she realized that she also had fallen quickly into the little habit of indulging her curiosity about her neighbors. Now that she thought about it, none of the talk, and certainly not hers, seemed designed to be malicious.

His angular face wreathed at intervals by the smoke from his cigar, Woods seemed more intent on watching her than in adding to the conversation, Millie mused. Several times during the exceedingly pleasant evening he had sent her looks of open approval. Each time she had felt inexplicably warmed.

Annabelle returned to the subject of Selma Bordeaux. "Do you think Selma will play for the pupils again?"

"Yes," Millie replied with enthusiasm, "she plans to come for the last thirty minutes of each Friday and do more than play. She says she'll gather some materials she used to use and teach the basics of reading music."

"You're some fine teacher, Millie Monroe," Woods said. "Here you've charmed a woman who hasn't stepped outside her fence in years and gotten her involved in our school. I wonder what your secret is?"

Millie laughed, her face feeling hot from the unexpected praise coming from Woods and then from the others. "Thanks for the nice words, but Selma had to be ready to take this step on her own." Wanting to tease the serious-faced Woods as he studied her through his cigar smoke, she added, "Besides, if I have a secret and told it, then it would no longer be a secret, would it?"

"I'm ashamed that the rest of us gave up on Selma," Annabelle said, not missing the teasing look Millie was giving Woods. "Other than you, Mabel Marks is the only other adult she has allowed in the house in years, and I'm sure that's because Mabel and she were childhood friends."

"Plus the Widow Marks doesn't let anything or anyone stop her from doing what she sets out to do. She sees all and knows all—and is quick to tell all," Woods added with a gentle chuckle. He had liked the way Millie slid her gaze his way from behind half-lowered lashes.

"But she's got a heart of gold," Henry said stoutly, puffing away at his pipe.

Remembering the way Mabel had sidled up to Henry on that first day she had visited his store, Millie smiled to herself while talk flowed from the others about the many good deeds done by the talkative Mabel Marks. Even though it appeared that Henry Stevens was not interested in taking up the buxom widow's obvious invitations, Millie reflected, he must have a tremendous amount of respect for her. Too, there was the unresolved question in Millie's mind of who had bought Mabel's supper box at the social. And during supper on the night of the hayride, Annabelle had told of Mabel threading the chunks of meat and vegetables on Henry's roasting stick. . . .

Try as she might, though, Millie couldn't recall having seen Henry and Mabel eating together at the box supper. And no wonder, she mused with exasperation. That was the night that Woods had allowed Clive to step into her life.

Not allowed, Millie corrected to herself as everyone else in the Steven's beautifully appointed living room chatted, but invited, as if she did not have sense enough to run her own affairs. An awful indignation claimed Millie, brought on by the thought that Woods must have believed he had the right to choose the new schoolmarm's friends. She had a feeling Clive Durham was friend to nobody in Freeman. Somehow she welcomed the little flare of buried anger at Woods; it was far easier to deal with than her compelling attraction to him.

The clock on the mantel struck ten, and Millie rose. After giving heartfelt thanks to Annabelle and Henry for a delightful evening and bidding Lucas good night, Millie and Woods left.

When Woods tried to keep his hand on her arm after they left the Stevens home behind, Millie deliberately stepped away from him. She walked in the ruts of the road so as to avoid pileups of gravel and perhaps stumble. She was in no frame of mind for him to touch her and turn her back into a quivering, unrecognizable mass of emotions.

Millie could not forget that back in her kitchen when she had questioned Woods after their jolting kiss, she almost had let her vulnerable side show. How he would have laughed if she had told him about her infatuation with him, her growing attraction to him. Lucas's knock on her door truly had been a giant blessing.

Remembering how Woods had accused her of being so afraid of someone getting close to her that she refused to let even the town's dogs follow her closely, she spoke to the three dogs that came from the shadows and began tagging along. She was unprepared for the reward of their doting looks. Had they really recognized their names? My, she thought with wonder, but she was picking up knowledge in Freeman about all kinds of things . . .

Breaking in on Millie's reflections as they walked in front of Selma's home, Woods said, "I enjoyed our visit with the Stevenses. It's good to see Annabelle and Lucas happy about their wedding, isn't it?"

"I wouldn't dare answer for fear of being ridiculed as a foolish romantic woman."

Uh-oh! Woods thought. He had played the devil in some way since their kiss back in the teacherage. But when? For the life of him, he could not recall having brought up anything controversial. All evening he had basked in her good-natured banter that usually included him in the nicest kind of way. A time or two he had suspected she was sending him secretive little smiles and looks and his heart had expanded beyond reason. He would give an arm and a leg to know what Millie was going to say to him when Lucas had knocked on the door. Determined to keep the earlier sweet mood between them if possible, he dropped the subject of Annabelle and Lucas.

"Do you ever ring the bell?" Woods asked when the squat little belfry over the porch of the schoolhouse came into view. Their footsteps on the rocky road rang out in the chilly darkness, but he noticed that she seemed intent upon keeping her distance.

"Every morning and after the noon hour. Most of the pupils go home to eat."

"Does it work all right?"

"Yes."

"How are the Hobbs children? Are they still coming to school regularly?"

"Yes." She pulled her cape closer against the cold of the October night. "Gladys told me last week how happy they were that you'd brought by some cough syrup for the baby. Your mother's formula must be very good, for it has already helped the child's night coughing and allowed all of them to get more sleep." She slid him a sideways glance, admiring as always the easy, straight way he carried his tall body. "She said you told her father how badly you needed a driver over at the mine and that he took the job. Those were fine things to do."

Woods wriggled his shoulders and cleared his throat, easing a hand inside the pocket of his breeches. "No finer than what you did." She jerked her face toward his, then seemed to notice the way his jacket hitched up over the hand in his pocket. "Before James came in from the barn that day, Mary Lee told me about you getting that church in Little Rock to send clothes for the whole family. She said that if James hadn't been so impressed by your interest in their children, he likely wouldn't have allowed them to wear the clothes."

"That was the least I could do. The family needed help." Her tone matched the frosty night air.

Woods grinned in the darkness. Millie apparently didn't like being thanked for doing things for others any more than he did. At least she had talked to him in words of more than one syllable. "Is school attendance good, in general?"

"Yes."

Giving up then on drawing Millie out further, Woods saw his horse lift his head in their direction. His white front stockings were blobs in the pale light coming from the stars and the silver of moon. From where he stood staked behind the teacherage, Major whinnied. Hell's bells! Woods thought. He was getting more attention from his horse than from the redheaded woman striding along beside him.

"Would you like me to bring in some wood for your heater?" Woods asked, searching for some legitimate excuse for getting inside the teacherage again. They reached the three steps leading up to the door then and Millie climbed them. From where he stood on the ground watching her, the sway of her slender hips and the sound of her rustling skirts intrigued him. He could not help but wonder if underneath she was wearing the red garters.

"No, thank you. I can manage fine on my own."

"It was just a friendly offer."

Unable to put aside her earlier angry thoughts about how Woods had let her down on the night of the box supper, Millie read messages that were not in his words. Was Woods perhaps overly eager to reestablish their relationship as being no more than one of friendship? she wondered as she felt inside her skirt pockets for her door key. He likely wanted to make sure that she not interpret his unsettling kiss in her kitchen as anything of consequence. Maybe he had kissed her on impulse or maybe out of some misguided sense of duty—the same one that apparently had led him to back out of the bidding for her supper box and turn her over to Clive Durham a few weeks ago.

Woods hated it when he saw Millie inserting her key into the keyhole and heard her turning the lock. The sound grated on his nerves. It was so final. He had come over to Freeman earlier that Sunday afternoon searching for something elusive, and he was not eager to leave without finding it. An inner voice warned him that he was even less eager to identify what it was he had thought to find.

"Good night, Woods," Millie said. "It was a lovely evening."

"Like hell it was," he growled, reaching out and grabbing one of her hands with both of his. Hers struggled, then lay still. "What happened tonight to change you, Millie? Why are you shutting me out?" He swallowed hard, for the words spilling forth seemed wrong for easing whatever was punishing him on the inside. "We're still friends, aren't we?"

"Of course."

Millie considered the way her body refused to go along with her mind and lock Woods out. The aroma of cigar smoke still lingered about him, contributing in a maddening way to the tantalizing aura of raw virility that always seemed to exude from him. His touch on her hand was shooting warm desire throughout her racing pulse. And the secretive humming had kept her charged up all evening.

Unaware that she was gazing into his face with wonder, Millie thought about how she would give her eyeteeth to know what was making him look up at her so soulfully. "I really should go inside now."

Woods released his captured breath. For a moment he had thought that her eyes were saying something vital, something coming from within. No, he reflected, Millie Monroe so seldom let down her guard and revealed what went on inside that the action probably was downright scary to her. The few times that he had seen it happen were the ones he cherished and longed to enjoy again. Maybe in good time. . . .

"Couldn't you at least give me another kiss?" he drawled in his deep-voiced manner, emboldened by the devastating thought that he was not going to see her again until the following night. When she stood as if transfixed on top of the third doorstep, still gazing down at him, he went on after sending his free hand to smooth his mustache. "It's a long cold ride over to Iron Creek. A kiss from you would keep me warm all the way home." Smiling, he tugged on her hand, tickled beyond reason when her feet moved down one step.

"Woods, ours is the strangest relationship I ever heard about." *It has to be love. No, it cannot be love; I've known the man less than two months.* She wished the darting night breeze would sweep away her inherent need to rationalize everything as swiftly as it had blown away her earlier anger at him over . . . she could not remember what, not when he was holding her hand and looking at her as he was. His low voice seemed to be pulling her toward him as surely as his hand was.

"How's that?" He gave another gentle tug on her hand, not letting his expression show that he knew she had moved down on the lowest step. He could feel and hear her skirt blowing softly against his breeches, the sound almost like a seductive whisper. "What's strange about an unmarried woman and man liking each other's company—and kisses?"

"For one thing," Millie said breathlessly, aware that she

was standing on the ground then, his hand still holding hers and imperceptively inching her traitorous body closer to his, "we've only known each other a few weeks and—"

"Six weeks today, to be exact."

Surprised and somehow flattered that Woods knew what she herself knew but had not uttered, Millie went on in a voice unsteady but brave. This was uncharted territory for her. "People can get . . . confused by trying to know all about people too soon."

"Oh, yeah?" Woods asked, his face so close to hers then that he could feel her breath touching his skin and smell the tantalizing fragrance of her hair. Her lifted face revealed her puzzlement; her eyes were wide and searching. In a tone barely above a bass whisper, he said, "If I'm confusing you, I apologize. I don't think it's confusion that you're causing in me. A better word might be fascination." In the pale light from the partial moon and the star-filled sky, he watched her lovely lips tremble and her eyes shut him out.

"No, I didn't mean you confuse me. I meant I confuse myself about—" Millie stopped abruptly. She already had revealed too much about her deep feelings for him, she thought with a kind of panic. Always when she had bared her heart and soul to a man—she had known only two: her father and her fiancé, who, strangely, no longer had a name or face—she had been hurt, had found her very words being hurled back at her like poisoned arrows.

"About me?" Woods asked, willing her to look at him, then pleasured when she lifted her dark eyelashes and granted his unvoiced command. Starlight brought a devastating sparkle to her brown eyes, devastating to his teetering composure, he thought. "What's confusing about me? I seem to be about the most uncomplicated man I know. I'm just looking for a sweet kiss from you to warm me on the way home." *Oh, yeah? You're more than a man no longer immune to this woman's charms. You're a man—*

Halting the unwelcome inner voice as quickly as it had crept up on him, Woods swept Millie into his arms then and bent his head to kiss her sweet, willing lips. As he had anticipated, the fire fueling his blood ever since he had grabbed her hand increased tenfold. Throughout the warm, moist kiss, he pressed her slender body ever closer. He loved the way her arms clung to his shoulders, the way her hands caressed the back of his neck, the way her lips came alive underneath his. The smell of jasmine completed his total enchantment.

Woods confessed that it was a man-size task to make himself free Millie's mouth and settle for one last look at her beautiful face in the pale light. Even more challenging was his allowing her to climb the doorsteps again. "Good night. I'll see you tomorrow night in the classroom."

Millie mustered no more than a weak smile and an inane reply that she had already forgotten by the time she went inside the teacherage.

What a week, Millie thought when Friday afternoon rolled around. All week she had given silent thanks to Woods for having fallen back into the role of student when he appeared for lessons. Had he continued in his attempts made over the weekend to peek into her mind and heart, she doubted that she could have kept back any longer her need to talk about her attraction to him and how it seemed constantly in her mind.

As if a weight was pressing down on her, Millie had suffered from the tension building inside during each hour spent with Woods. She had welcomed his announcement on Wednesday that a political meeting would keep him from coming on Thursday night. After she waved her pupils off to their homes on Friday, the thought that the handsome mountain man was coming that night loomed uppermost in her mind.

"You're early again," Millie said with little enthusiasm when Woods appeared at her door that Friday night. She found dealing with what his presence did to her was far easier in the classroom. Oh, she agonized, he was all spick-and-span as usual and smelling to the heavens with that spicy fragrance of bay rum. Also as usual, his presence filled the room, even when he still stood at the entry. He gazed down at her in a lazy manner that set her heartbeat into the dizzying pattern she had come to expect. She had hoped that she might be over her tendency to stare at the cleft in his chin, but she found that she was not. Looking anywhere but into his blue eyes seemed a safer course, though.

"Don't wear yourself out showing you're tickled to see me. A simple curtsy will do."

Millie smiled and heard it turn into a half giggle back in her throat. She blamed it on the way that Woods was looking at her, as if he might be thinking she was somebody nice to look at, a comparison that tickled her when she realized she likely was giving him the same look. "I didn't mean to sound rude. Come in."

Woods peered around the room, but he did not step inside. He should have been prepared for how beautiful she looked and how good she smelled, but he was not. Would he ever get used to the way that seeing her up close after even a brief absence set his pulse into a gallop? Her long-sleeved waist of wide coppery stripes matched up with the rich tones of her hair and eyes. "So old Clive didn't make it over to bring the payroll and spark you tonight, huh?"

"No, he didn't." Millie had already warned herself not to jump off into a frenzy if Woods brought up Clive's name tonight. The week had been too long and taxing. She was eager for a light mood, the kind she had enjoyed so often in his company. "I won't mention his name if you won't."

"That's a deal." Looking and feeling terribly pleased with himself, he said, "I brought you something."

"Well," she asked, "where is it?" His hands were empty.

"Aren't you supposed to act surprised and tell me that I shouldn't have?"

"That hardly seems my style."

Woods tossed back his head and laughed, the deep bass sound bouncing around the room. "You're right, Millie. You have your own style." He stooped and lifted something resting on the ground beside the steps. "Here you are, pretty schoolmarm. Something you've been wishing for."

Millie's hands flew to her opened mouth. She gasped, then felt her face flushing. "A bathtub? You've brought me a bathtub?" Her round-eyed gaze swung between the shiny copper tub with its high, rounded back and the black-haired man who was placing it on the floor near her heater. With her knees drawn up, she thought, she could lie back and soak when she felt the need. "Now I can figure out why Henry Stevens kept putting me off about the delivery of my order for a bathtub."

"Yeah, he told me when I asked him to order it that you had made the same request—but for one of tin. I convinced him to cancel that order."

"The copper is beautiful." She fixed him with a considering look, her eyes crinkling at the corners. "I've never before heard of such an outlandish present in my life."

"That's all right. I've never before met such an outlandish woman." Woods beamed down at her. He could tell she was pleased but that she seemed to be battling with some inner conflict. "You amaze me, Millie Monroe. One minute you're making announcements that you have the freedom to be yourself, and the next, you're acting embarrassed over receiving a bathtub. Which is the real you?"

Millie slid the handsome mountain man an appraising look before kneeling to examine her gift. She felt not the least embarrassed. She was thinking that Woods had no idea how close he had come to stating her own views about herself, she reflected while her hands ran across the polished copper surfaces. She did not know who she was either, not anymore, not since having met Woods Sanders.

"Thank you, Woods. You're a thoughtful man. I know I'll enjoy using the bathtub."

Millie stood then, her face no longer warm from anything except pure happiness. She felt curiously light-headed. She looked up, expecting to see Wood's familiar handsome face with the black mustache above the wickedly sensuous mouth, expecting to see his dancing blue eyes and the intriguing cleft in his chin.

What Millie saw made her breath catch and her heart turn over: No longer was there any doubt. She was looking into the face of the man she loved. Yes, her heart and mind combined to shout over her crashing pulse, she was truly in love with the mountain man! She was in love in a crazy way that made no sense, in love in the magical way that lyrical poems

sang about, in love as that secret inner voice had been suggesting for weeks.

"What's wrong?" Woods asked. Her eyes seemed full of
far more light than could be reflecting from the lamp sitting
on the kitchen table. What was causing her lovely lips to
part in such tantalizing wonderment? He sensed that something newborn stretched out between them and that it might
be rooted in a secret corner of his heart. His breath hung
back in his throat.

"Nothing's wrong. I've just realized . . . what a wonderful
man you are." Millie wanted to shout her marvelous discovery, wanted to throw her arms around him and kiss him, but
she knew that she could not even whisper love, unless
Woods also loved her. Unless he released his locked-away
love for Fern and fell in love with her—and told her so—
Millie reasoned with all the facts that her newly swollen
heart allowed, then her knowledge would have to remain
secret. The only kind of love she could voice would have to
be reciprocated.

Even so, it was a joyful moment for Millie. Not a fleeting
physical attraction but robust love lived inside her heart, she
exulted. And it did not matter that she had met Woods not
quite seven weeks ago. She felt wise in a manner sublimely
provocative. At least one facet of the puzzling new Millie
had revealed itself.

Though he was far from being convinced that things between Millie and him were exactly as before, Woods put
away his questions. Her mysterious smile quite stole the
moment, and, if he would but admit it, stole a bit more of
his heart.

Maybe his bringing Millie the bathtub had shown her he
had meant it when he told her that it was fascination drawing
him to her and that he honored their friendship, the baffled
Woods told himself when they went into the classroom and
began the evening's lessons. Whatever had brought about
the change in the beautiful redhead, he was all for it. He
could not remember feeling so fine in ages.

"You've outdone yourself this week, Woods." The fire
was burning out in the big heater, and the classroom was

becoming chilly that Friday night. Millie hated seeing the evening come to an end. Being with the handsome mountain man, even when he was engrossed in working an algebra problem or poring over maps, was bringing her even greater pleasure, now that she knew what it was that drew her to him. She had fallen more deeply in love all evening, only this time she had understood what was happening and had not fought it. "I like the way you're reading further into the books than you have to. You must spend a lot of time on your studies."

"I do." *And a lot of time thinking about you.*

"Have you given any more thought to the speech you said you would make at the Harvest Festival? I'd like having you try it out on me."

"Maybe I'll work on it next week."

"You'll have to make up your mind pretty soon about whether or not you'll be a candidate, won't you?"

"So everybody and his dog tells me."

"Are you still uncertain that you're the one to run for representative?"

"Not as uncertain as before you got me started reading and writing. I thank you for that, Millie." When she smiled and looked flustered, he added with a deliberately dramatic frown, "Of course there's still one major drawback to my possible candidacy, or so I've been told."

"What in heaven's name could that be?" Indignation sharpened her voice. Why, Woods Sanders was perfect! He had everything going for him—looks, voice, manners, ideals.

"That I don't have a wife."

Millie swallowed and sat up straighter. What would she do, she agonized, if he announced that he was planning on getting married? She had never forgotten Annabelle's account of Woods's seeming disinterest in sparking any of the unmarried women in the area after his return from Hot Springs. She also recalled his defensive tone in the cave when he announced that he had no plans to propose . . . at least to her. "What difference does it make if you aren't married?"

"My backers say that a married man gains more respect."

"I never heard such bosh!"

"Really? I value your opinion . . . as a good friend."

"A single man can make as good a legislator as a married one, especially one with your ideas and personality." She panicked at the thought that he might rush out and marry one of those society women that he had taught to ride horseback when he lived in Hot Springs. Maybe he had loved one that Annabelle had not known about and—

"Supposing that I can't get enough backers unless I have a wife. A fine platform is no good without supporters." Woods fidgeted with the chalk in his hands, tracing little squeaky patterns on the slate lying on his desk. Words began to form there.

"You can tell them that they're wrong, that marriage isn't for everybody." Millie heard her words and sensed that they assaulted her freshly opened heart. She stared at Woods's head as he bent over his desk. The light from the lantern hanging above them lent extra luster to his black hair. More than once that evening she had recalled how crisp its texture was and how she had loved ruffling it while they kissed.

Woods passed his slate over to Millie's desk then, turning it so that she could read what he had written.

Millie licked at suddenly dry lips, then read aloud, her voice faltering and then dying, "Will you . . . ?" Her heart threatened to race into oblivion. She lifted her eyes to meet his, her lips forming a disbelieving "O."

". . . marry me?" Woods finished his written message for her. "Will you marry me, Millie?"

Millie's initial elation in reading the unexpected proposal had faded the moment she realized Woods was not following it up with a declaration of his love for her, or any kind of special feeling. At least he could have told her again of his fascination. He was looking merely for a woman to fill the gap beside him when he became a candidate and then a legislator. Hesitantly she shoved the slate aside.

Millie knew from having read the *Arkansas Gazette* through the years that at the elegant parties in Little Rock, where legislators and other politicians were frequently entertained, people moved about in couples of Mr. and Mrs. Yes, she thought, she knew how that level of society functioned.

When a politician went to church and tipped his hat to one and all, Millie reflected, he needed a wife on his arm. Having children attend Sunday school helped, too. In his home when guests came, a man needed a wife. And at night when all the lights were out, a politician needed a wife in his bed, for it would be imprudent for one in the public eye to be seen frequenting houses of low repute. Not any of those wifely roles required the one splendid aspect of marriage that Millie deemed vital: mutual love.

The silence in the classroom grew heavy. Sounds of a dogfight out in the schoolyard went unnoticed. Woods wished that Millie was not such an expert at hiding her thoughts. She might not be looking for a husband, but surely, since they were friends and had such good times together—whether making love or arguing or just plain talking—she would consider his proposal. Her face was a beautiful study of calm. He felt as if his own face had broken out in hives.

"Well," he said after swallowing and licking his dry lips, "will you marry me, Millie?"

"You're asking me to marry you so that if you run, you'll not be the only unmarried candidate, aren't you?"

Millie's question sounded to the nervous Woods mighty like a challenge. His pulse thundered in his ears. He locked up his already scarred heart even tighter. "So what if that's the case?" Why was he having to search for a light tone? She was right, wasn't she? "All I want to hear is your answer."

Millie rose, wrapping her pride around herself as securely as she did her cape. Joy and sadness were having a free-for-all in her whirling brain. "I need more time to think about it. You know how I have no plans to marry."

"Is that fair? I didn't have any such plans myself until recently," he grumbled as he took down the lantern and blew out the flame. She could make him mad enough to spit buttermilk, he fumed. He might have known that she would react to his proposal in some damnable, farfetched way. At least she could have smiled. Was she not the one who always said she wanted them to be friends? A true friend would have smiled. "I can't wait around very long for an answer."

Millie was at the side door of the classroom by then and

stepping rapidly toward the doorway into the teacherage. Woods hurried until he was only a step behind her. If he had not known better, he might have suspected that she was running away from something frightening.

"Hang that part about telling me good night out here," he growled right next to her ear as she opened her door. "I'm coming inside."

"No problem," she replied airily. My, she thought, but her head was still spinning. No matter that Woods had not said that he loved her, she could not ignore the nice little humming inside that his presence always created. She turned before going to put away her cape in the bedroom. "After you take off your coat, you might like to put the percolator on for coffee."

"Do you have any milk? I'd like to have some hot chocolate."

"Mabel brought some milk over this afternoon, but I detest anything with chocolate in it. I never keep chocolate around." Wasn't that just like him, to try taking over every aspect of her life, even choosing what she served from her own kitchen—and deciding that she would do nicely in the role of politician's wife? Yet she was madly in love with the man just the way he was, she admitted. Upon seeing Woods's thoughtful expression, and unaware of what she was revealing, she went on. "And it makes me sick to smell it, too."

Woods grinned, and his eyes twinkled devilishly. When Millie's expressive face showed that she realized what she had told, his grin stretched wider and evolved into the deep cackle that always delighted her with its manly sound. "Then old Clive didn't make any points with you when he brought the candy and made you sick?" He laughed harder.

"As a matter of fact, he didn't," she agreed after her own laughter died alongside his.

Leaving Woods on his own in the kitchen, Millie went into her bedroom and shed her cape. For the first time since their lovemaking—five weeks ago tomorrow night, she mused—Millie parted the curtains covering the window. Moonlight was too scarce for her to make out the shape of Promise Ridge, but her dreamy thoughts brought the cave into focus. Had some secret part of her known that rainy afternoon that she already was in love with the mountain man? If only he had fallen in love with her at the same time, she thought with a sigh at the perplexities facing her in dealing with his proposal.

Determined to allow herself just to enjoy being with Woods, Millie peeked into the mirror over the chest then and fluffed up her red curls. She had noted how during the past week they had begun to stretch from the added weight of new growth. Her hair now fell into natural patterns of both waves and curls that, thought still short, framed her face in a soft red cloud.

Had it been only seven weeks since she had lopped off her long hair back in Little Rock and started in search of her new life? Millie wondered. It seemed to have happened a hundred years back and to someone else.

Part Six

Yes, he kissed her hard and stroked her hair
And asked her to follow him anywhere.
Her heart nigh breaks: She loves him dear,
But it's words of love she aches to hear.

Black deeds descend, around her do swirl;
She's sucked up into a frightening world.
Her heart is paining; her mind goes dizzy.
Her mountain man is what he seems—or is he?

· *Chapter Twenty* ·

Millie wondered if Woods might not have forgotten about his proposal by the time she returned to the living room. They drank coffee and laughed a lot, though neither could have said about what. As had become their wont when together, they talked of sundry things.

Once, when Woods spoke of the bauxite mining companies and their dealings with the landowners, Millie detected a sharp edge to his tone.

"You'll think I'm just mentioning Clive Durham to rile you," Woods said, "but I'm not. He and I haven't seen eye to eye about matters pertaining to the mines and landowners since the start. Southern Bauxite Mines might be a fine company, but it makes me wonder when its representative takes the attitude he does toward all the landowners and workers."

"Even I have wondered if Mr. Durham might not show too little regard for people around here," Millie confessed, remembering her earlier suspicions that trouble brewed between the two men and that it was neither new nor connected with her. "He seems to have a pompous air, even when referring to his superiors in his own company."

"Then why do you let him keep calling on you?" Woods had deliberately kept his place at the end of the sofa where the two sat, not wanting Millie to think he was trying to take advantage. He turned his entire upper body toward her then, too eager to hear her answer to stick to his resolution.

"His calls might not be my idea, you know. Besides, he hasn't been here all that much," Millie replied defensively, aware that Woods no longer assumed the relaxed pose of a man at ease. She figured it was not the time to bring up what seemed to her a glaring fact: Clive Durham likely would not have called at all had Woods not sicced the man on her at the box supper. Her earlier decision to inform Clive politely, if he called on her again, that she did not care for his visits seemed her own business. The evening was too special to mar with even a slight misunderstanding.

Sensing that they were drifting into dangerous territory, Woods said, "Forgive me for bringing up the subject of mines and old Clive. Just as on that first night when I was visiting with you, I'm getting all het up and talking your ear off."

"I think your being a talker is one reason I'm so . . . fond of you, Woods. And you're a good listener, too." Millie flushed at her near slip of tongue and slid him a look from behind half-lowered lashes. Probably she should not have mentioned anything about her feelings for him. Though she wished he would, he had not hinted at any he might be holding for her, had not even repeated what he had termed fascination.

"Oh, yeah?" Woods liked her statements.

Millie guided the conversation to safer topics. She disliked the idea that anyone might have bad feelings toward the man she loved, but she especially hated the thought that Clive Durham might harbor ill will toward him. She fought down a shiver of apprehension trying to race up her spine.

During the talk about the mining company, Millie had seen again the momentary blaze of the fiery temper that had flared the day Woods had learned that the new schoolmarm was a woman.

Millie already knew why Woods had not welcomed a woman, not when he had counted secretly on the new teacher to help him overcome his deficiencies. In a world dominated by men, the thought of asking a woman for help must have deflated him terribly, she reflected with compassion. That Woods had overcome his petty grievance and forged ahead with his plans to become thoroughly literate proved to her that he was, indeed, a brave, rugged individual. A true mountain man, just as she had sensed on that first day.

Hearing Woods's resonant bass voice and frequent hearty

laughter warmed Millie in the way she had come to love. An hour later she was wishing that the night would go on forever and that the fascinating man did not have to leave. When he left, she was going to have to deal with what kind of answer she might give to his heart-shattering proposal. With a repressed sigh of resignation, she watched him move near the door.

"I may not see you again 'til Monday night in the classroom," Woods said. He could not remember when he'd had such a stimulating talk with anyone, even Millie. She had seemed as eager as he to discuss the details of his plans for creating a better place for the people of the area. Since she had made it plain that she would give her answer in her own good time, he guessed she might have welcomed any topic to talk about other than his proposal.

Millie tried to hide her disappointment that Woods was leaving by brushing briskly with her hand at a streak of chalk dust on her skirt.

Only from his willing that it be so had Woods been able to keep back his urgent need to know what Millie's answer might be. He knew how she liked to mull things over in her mind, though, and he guessed he owed her the chance to do so. A startling question rose in his mind: Was he, maybe, sparking her . . . just a little? "There's a big meeting of voters in Sampson tomorrow night. It's a long ride, and I expect I'll spend the night with a cousin over there."

"I'll be hoping that things go well."

Woods kept watching her beautifully sculpted features. He doubted that he could have moved his gaze had he been ordered to. Something led him into a devilish boldness that he had not mustered in a long time. "Come here and give me a good night kiss." His pulse pattered in heady anticipation. What would she do?

Millie tilted her head and looked up at Woods, loving the way that his voice seemed to reach right out and pull her close. He was only three steps away. No man had ever before issued her such a command. No man had ever looked at her in the way that Woods was looking, either. Her heartbeat revved up, and her words came out jerkily. "Are you trying to influence my thinking about . . . certain things?"

"Hell, yes," he replied with a flirty wink and a partial smile that sent the left side of his black mustache higher than the other. "I figure a wife might be handy in lots of ways outside lending me respectability as a candidate." If Millie took so much as one step toward him, Woods thought as he smiled down at her, he would be the most surprised man in Lexington County. But she had not backed away . . . or told him to go to hell. In a half whisper he urged, "Come let me show you what a hug and a good night kiss can do."

"I think I already know, so I'm offering only one." She shivered a little, for his velvety voice was sending goose bumps feathering up and down her spine. Her face warm from Woods's irresistible wink, Millie went into his open arms. His mouth upon hers, hot and wet and stirring up all kinds of longing, almost wrecked her tenuous composure. It demolished outright her regular breathing pattern.

Millie returned Woods's kiss with matching fervor, her newly discovered love for him snipping away any remaining threads of restraint. She suspected that had she been in Woods's arms when he made his unromantic, businesslike proposal, she likely would have swooned and gushed "yes" before she could think about something so essential to a good marriage as mutual love.

At first Millie had wondered why Woods dropped the subject of marriage after she returned to the living room. Then when they became engrossed in talk, she guessed it had something to do with his all-fired interest in campaign issues. After all, she reasoned with a mind going to mush from his sizzling kiss, his stated need for a wife was merely one part of the planned campaign. She was not jealous of Woods's ambition; she was, in fact, almost as enthralled with it as he seemed to be. The man was a born leader. But she did wish that he had asked her to marry him for some other reason than to. . . .

The feel of Woods's arms pressing her body closer to his erased Millie's recognizable thoughts then. Her arms tightened around his neck, and her blood raced at a more thrilling speed. She needed no rational reason to be opening her mouth to his and reveling in the tantalizing assault of his tongue upon hers. She loved him.

Millie could not seem to settle down after the sound of Major's hooves faded into the night. The kiss might have been a single one, she reflected with awe at the tinglings still alerting her body, but it set her every cell on edge. Not interested in getting ready for bed, she wandered aimlessly around the living room, reliving the evening. Yes, it had happened, she reassured the doubting part of her mind. There sat the copper bathtub, right where Woods had set it near the heater.

The memory of Woods's proposal rose up. A burning need to read his words again spurring her on, she sucked in a breath and headed for the classroom. The slate must still be lying on her desk where she had dropped it after reading his startling question.

Not forgetting her last foray into the classroom in the middle of the night when she had discovered Woods as the "thief," Millie stuck her head out her door and listened before slipping through the side door into the darkened schoolroom. Only the barks of several excited dogs from somewhere up near the crossroads reached her ears. Probably they were barking at each other, she reflected with false bravado.

No, Millie corrected when another sound intruded after she reached the classroom. Those were the hoofbeats of a racing horse. Her heart hammered. Were they coming down the road toward the schoolhouse? Clutching the slate to her bosom, she hurried outside. There was little light from the crescent moon, and she had to squint to see the road clearly. It must be Woods returning, she rejoiced as she hurried toward the road to meet him. He was coming back to amend his proposal. She shivered in the cold night air. This time he would tell her he had discovered that he loved her and—

Millie allowed the sight of white stockings on the legs of the racing horse to mislead her. It seemed to her that the entire pack of dogs in Freeman was in clamoring, earnest pursuit of the horse galloping at breakneck speed down the

road. Leaning low over the saddle horn, the rider was indeed
a man wearing a black hat, and he did have a dark mustache.

Millie was halfway across the large schoolyard before she
could see the man's face and body well enough to realize
that though there seemed to be something familiar about
him, he was not Woods. He was not turning into the schoolyard. She had been a silly goose: Why, Freeman's dogs
wouldn't be chasing Woods and Major.

The man did not sit his horse at all like Woods, Millie
reasoned. Neither was he as lean, though the mustache
would have fooled almost anyone at a distance and in the
ghostly light, she reassured herself. And how could she have
forgotten that Major had white stockings only on the two
front legs, not on all four? She had made mistakes all
around.

How asinine she had been to rush out toward the road,
Millie scolded herself as she watched the rider and horse
disappear down the shadowed road toward the Gooseneck
River, the dogs still giving noisy chase. Had the man seen
her there in the pale moonlight? He had appeared to glance
her way, but he had been traveling so fast that she could not
be sure. She looked across the road at the several houses
sitting back underneath their sheltering trees. No light softened any window.

No matter that she had given in to a foolish impulse, Millie thought as she returned to her living quarters and locked
her door. She had done nothing wrong—except to get her
hopes up that it might have been Woods returning with declarations of love. Suddenly weary, she got ready for bed
while her thoughts ran down. Wanting the slate to be the first
thing she saw upon awakening, Millie placed it on top of her
chest of drawers.

Annette Bordeaux surprised Millie the next morning by
appearing at her door. The pretty black-haired girl extended
an invitation from her mother to join her and a few other
women for tea that Saturday afternoon.

After Annette left, Millie wondered if she should have
insisted that the girl stay. It might have been a perfect time
for counseling her about her relationship with Warden

Marks. Somehow the thought of offering advice to anyone that day about affairs of the heart held no appeal for Millie, not when she was not handling her own any better than she was.

As she went about doing laundry and other household chores saved for Saturdays, Millie pondered Selma's invitation. It proved a far better subject for thought than the surprising developments of the night before. She already had spent far too much time that morning gazing out of her bedroom window toward a noticeably jagged peak on Promise Ridge where she had determined the cave lay.

Millie pinned her wash to the clothesline running across the back of the schoolyard, sneaking looks at Promise Ridge rearing up, according to Woods, no more than a couple of miles away. Her knees got weak when she thought about how glorious it had been to lose herself in his powerful arms. She thought again of the remarkable idea that even then her mind-boggling feeling for Woods must have been love and not a mere physical attraction. Had she known so little about herself then?

In desperation Millie ran her fingers through her short hair and shook her head. If only she could set her thoughts in tune with her heart, she reflected with a sigh as she picked up the empty washtub and returned it to its nail on the back wall of the teacherage. The smart whipping sound coming from her wet garments fighting against the autumn winds reminded her too vividly of her inner turmoil. Nature had a way of winning all battles. What about human nature?

Determined to keep her body and mind busy with other thoughts, Millie went to the general store around noon. Maybe Annabelle would be there putting up the mail. She was not ready to confide in her new friend, but she felt the need to escape the teacherage.

As Millie approached the store, accompanied by two openly admiring dogs with which she had carried on a lively one-way conversation about the weather, she noticed several horses hitched to the rail outside Booth's Livery. Perhaps Edgar was late in dispensing the payroll from the bauxite company, she mused. She recalled being at the store around noon on previous Saturdays and noting how the workers already had gotten their pay and were leaving the livery stable.

Just then, from where they played upon the wheeled hay rake in front of their father's huge barn, Francine and Noble waved at their teacher. Millie paid the children back with smiles and waves of even greater magnitude.

"What's going on over at Booth's Livery?" Millie asked Annabelle when she found the pretty blonde ensconced behind the little barred window marked U.S. Mail. Henry was engrossed in conversation with several men up near the front of the store.

"Oh, Millie," Annabelle said, her forehead wrinkling and her blue eyes signaling distress. "Someone surprised Mr. McBee over at the livery in the night and made off with the company's payroll. Whoever it was clobbered the old man over the head. He says he stayed knocked out until right before dawn. When he came to, he went to Edgar's house and waked him."

Millie's face showed her shock. Violence and robbery in Freeman? Her mind spun until she placed the name: Spooner McBee, the nightwatchman whom Edgar hired to guard the livery on Friday nights when the payroll was stored in his safe. "How horrible! Is Mr. McBee going to be all right? Is there something I can do to help him? I can hardly believe such a thing happened here in Freeman." She shivered and drew her shawl closer about her. "I remember our talking when I first came here about the dangers of having everybody know when the company payroll stays overnight in the livery safe." Vaguely she recalled that Edgar had introduced her to the wiry old man that afternoon when she had rented the horse and buggy and called on the Hobbs family.

"This is the first time it's happened since Edgar hired a nightwatchman. It's probably a miracle the man's alive, but he's going to be fine. Both Lessie and Edgar insisted that he not go home until he gets some rest. Lessie bandaged his head and put him to bed in their guest bedroom. He came to the community only last year to live with his married daughter a few miles from here, and his biggest concern was that she might worry when he didn't return this morning."

"Does anyone have any idea who could have done this

dastardly thing?" Millie asked. "Did Mr. McBee get a look
at the robber?" Automatically she took the letter that Annabelle slid across the window ledge to her and dropped it into
the pocket of her skirt without looking at it. Mail was the
farthest thing from her mind. Her brain was flashing memories of the racing horse and rider that she had seen about
midnight. Such a fact should not be treated as idle gossip,
though, and she doubted that she should tell it first to any
but officials, not even to Annabelle. She realized that she
could tell Woods, if he were in Freeman and not on his way
to a political meeting in Sampson. "Has anyone notified the
sheriff?"

"Somebody rode into Elmwood to fetch Sheriff Crumpler.
He ought to be getting here before long."

"Annabelle," Millie said lowly, leaning closer and glancing up toward the front of the store where Henry and the
men still huddled in private talk. "I need to talk with the
sheriff when he comes. I don't have any certain knowledge
about what happened last night, but I feel that the sheriff
should have some information that I can give. Do you think
he'll be coming here to the store when he gets in town?"

"Yes, he always comes by here when he's in the area,
though he's not likely to arrive in town 'til after noon, even
on a fast horse. Josh Crumpler has been sheriff for years. He
and my father are bitter political enemies, but they manage
to be civil to each other." Annabelle studied Millie's concerned face. "Can't you tell me what you know?"

Millie felt embarrassed that she was going to refuse, but
she could not forget the many times that her father had railed
about how people should not go around blabbing things that
could sorely affect the lives of others. And too often, she
recalled, her father's beliefs had proved accurate. "Trust me,
Annabelle. If what I tell the sheriff proves helpful in finding
the thief, as I suspect, you'll hear about it from your father
or him. Please go along with me on this and send the sheriff
to the teacherage when he gets here."

"I will." Annabelle nodded and smiled in understanding
then and came from behind the postal window.

"I was planning on having tea with Selma Bordeaux this
afternoon. Do you suppose the sheriff could send a message

there if he gets ready to talk with me before I return to the teacherage?"

"I'll leave word with Papa if he hasn't come by then," Annabelle assured her. "Don't worry. Sheriff Crumpler will come for your statement when he's ready for it, even if it's not until after dark. He probably will be spending the nights at Mabel's until this thing gets settled."

Annabelle looked more pleasant then and added, "I'm going to Selma's for tea, too. I was never so surprised as when Annette invited me. Her good experiences in your classroom must have set her to thinking. Everybody is talking about how wonderful it is to have Selma getting out and renewing old friendships. Somebody told me she has agreed to attend church with Annette from now on."

"It's grand hearing good news about her," Millie replied.

Back in Millie's mind rose the thought that likely everybody was talking about how much time Woods was spending at the schoolhouse, too. Frequent visits from Annabelle, Mabel, and Lessie never produced outright prying, but Millie could tell they wanted her to talk about Woods. Though she had come to terms with the way people in the small town, including her, talked about each other, she did not like that the talk about Woods and her might contain out-and-out falsehoods. As a possible candidate, his reputation must remain unsullied. Of course now that he had proposed to her. . . .

When the sheriff had not appeared at the teacherage by mid-afternoon, Millie assumed he was not yet ready to speak with her. She tried finishing up her chores after returning from the store and had almost succeeded when the time came for her to get dressed for her visit to the Keyhole House.

The slate with Woods's now familiar scrawl across it lay on the chest of drawers in Millie's bedroom, tantalizing the besotted schoolmarm. What was she going to tell him? The thought of living the rest of her life with the mountain man was exciting, mind-boggling, and terribly tempting. But the thought of marrying a man who did not love her in the same passionate way in which she loved Woods negated the numerous positive aspects. Now that she was entertaining ideas of marriage—and after she had been so certain that she had embraced a solitary way of life—Millie was struggling to dig and delve for answers outside her love-filled heart.

Eyeing the slate from time to time and still finding Wood's proposal incredible, Millie slipped into a fresh white waist and her navy skirt. She brushed her freshly shampooed hair into a red cloud of curls and waves and blithely ignored the pile of clean clothing lying on her bed, telling herself that she could get her ironing done that night.

Several pleasant surprises awaited Millie at the Keyhole House that afternoon. The first came when she reached the gate in the picket fence and saw that drapes no longer shut out the light. Only sheer curtains hung behind the huge windows. The house appeared far more inviting.

"How kind of you to join us, Millie," Selma said after pouring tea and handing around delicate cups of exquisite Sevres china to Millie and her two other guests: Mabel Marks and Annabelle Stevens.

"Lessie sends her regrets," Annabelle said, "and asked for a rain check."

"I understand," Selma replied. "I'll remember to invite Lessie next Saturday when I ask my neighbors farther down the road to come for tea. Today I wanted to invite my closest neighbors."

Mabel sent a doting look at their hostess. "I'm right proud of Selma for gettin' a hold on herself again. I may be fine company"—Mabel chuckled to show she was poking fun at herself—"but Selma needs to see more than ole gossipy me. Everybody knows it wasn't easy for her to come back here bringin' the corpses of both her daddy and her husband to bury—and her pregnant with Annette at the time, too."

Annette came in the living room then and spoke to everyone before taking away the gleaming brass kettle with a promise to return later with more hot water.

Now that sunlight filtered into the room through the delicate lace curtains, Millie could see that the furnishings were even more beautiful and elegant than she had suspected from that first visit. The earlier dank, musty smell of the house had become a sweet, spicy fragrance suggesting potpourri and sunshine.

After Annabelle made a polite comment about Selma's obvious trials, Millie said, "I guess all of us have to deal at one time or another with problems we think are insurmountable. When we look back later, we discover that they were not."

Selma smiled directly at Millie. "Sometimes it's a small instance that tips the scales in our favor. Your enthusiasm for life spilled over on me, Millie, and I guess it was what I needed. From your first day here, I peeped at you from my music room upstairs as you walked on the road going about the business of becoming acquainted with your new world. The rather shocking sight of your lovely red hair cut short told me that you are unique—as did your afternoon walks."

"You're being kind." Aware that all eyes were upon her, Millie shifted about on her chair and managed a weak smile. She recalled her suspicions on several occasions those first weeks that someone from the Keyhole House watched her from behind a curtain.

At the time it never had occurred to Millie that the secretive watcher might be sending looks of benevolence or, perhaps, envy. Then she had viewed them as prying intrusions into her privacy. A painful knot rose in her throat. How little she had truly understood what can go on inside a house or the reasons for some of the actions of its occupants. And how much more she had to learn, for the Keyhole House was only one!

"Here she was," Selma said, looking at Millie but speaking of her as if she was not sitting in the room, "an unmarried woman from the city finding a place for herself in our village when I couldn't seem to do that in sixteen whole years. I should have been the one calling on her, as all of the other women in town did sooner or later."

Sending a gentle look toward the pink-faced schoolmarm, Selma went on. "But *you* called on *me*, something nobody but my old friend Mabel had dared do in years because of my rudeness. After your visit, Millie, I couldn't settle back into my rut with ease. Your invitation to play for your students stirred up my old itch to share my music. One reason I wanted this small group here this afternoon—yes, I still watch out my window and I know who does the most visiting back and forth—was so that I could thank you in front of your closest friends for jolting me into realizing that I have a daughter and friends who are very much alive and who need me—and are needed by me."

While listening to her hostess and feeling a tad flustered upon recalling that curiosity seemed to have been what prompted her to call that Sunday afternoon at the Keyhole House, Millie noted only incidentally that the pretty woman had a scar on her left cheek. Curving over Selma's cheekbone as it did and being larger than a silver dollar, the puffed-up scar was easily seen upon first glance, or if one happened to be looking for it. The woman's lovely voice and manners vied ably with the disfiguring mark, Millie decided as she had when Selma had appeared at the schoolhouse with her violin.

At Selma's pause, Millie said, "Thank you. You have done me a great favor by agreeing to come on Fridays and teach my pupils and me about music as you know it."

Annette returned then with the kettle of hot water and poured it into the silver teapot. "Mama's right," she said to Millie. "She really has changed since your visit. Her attorney in Hot Springs has been after her ever since our housekeeper died last year to let him send somebody to take her place, and she finally answered his letter and agreed the week after you came."

The announcement brought agreeable comments from both Mabel and Annabelle and allowed Millie to look more closely at her hostess. She was delighted to see that Selma had foregone the unbecoming loose hairstyle, apparently adopted in an attempt to cover her scarred cheekbone, and now was wearing it caught up at the crown with pearl-encrusted combs. The warm gleam of the pearls seemed to accentuate the blackness of her overly curly hair, leading Millie to think again what a lovely woman Selma was, both on the inside and the outside. Of course she did not believe for an instant that she herself had had nearly so much to do with Selma's reentry into life as Selma had said.

"My attorney wrote this past week that he will be bringing over a widowed woman and her young daughter around Thanksgiving. He has known the woman and her family for years and says that due to misfortune they need a place to go. I'm looking forward to having some help around this neglected place. Both Annette and I like the idea of having another girl around, too."

"Then I'll be getting a new student," Millie said, pleased at the thought.

"Yes," Selma replied. "One of the woman's main concerns was about her daughter's education. I was happy to report how well the year is going for Annette."

Then talk rolled around to the robbery at Booth's Livery.

"Hearing about the robbery just about ruined my day," Mabel said, her round face troubled. She accepted another cup of tea from Selma and, with a rueful look down at her hefty middle, helped herself to a second slice of apple cake. "I can't get it out of my mind how Edgar asked Warden to fill in one Friday night for old Spooner. Lord sakes, I don't want nobody hurt, but if that had been my Warden last night—"

"Well, it wasn't Warden, and all of us are glad," Annabelle consoled. "The nightwatchman is going to be fine. Before I came over, Lessie ran into the store for a few things. She said she was unable to have tea with us because she wanted to keep McBee in bed' till he felt clearheaded. She figures he can go home with his daughter before dark."

"What else has happened?" Millie asked, setting her cup on its saucer and returning both to the nearby tea table. "Has Sheriff Crumpler gotten here?" She sat very still for Annabelle's reply.

"Yes, the sheriff was over at the livery, along with practically everybody in town." Annabelle sipped her tea. "Papa said the sheriff seems to have tall suspicions that the robber is someone from around here. Mr. McBee told him that it was right at midnight when he was attacked."

"Someone—?" Millie began and stopped. Why, the sheriff was out of his mind. It was midnight when she saw the man race by the schoolyard, and he was not from Freeman. "He says that someone from around here is guilty? I find that hard to believe."

Mabel exchanged quick but knowing looks with Selma, then with Annabelle before saying, "Talk is that the nightwatchman has identified the man who hit him over the head with a shovel—"

"Haven't we talked enough about such upsetting things while we're supposed to be having a good time?" Annabelle interrupted with uncharacteristic rudeness, leaning forward and holding out her cup toward Selma for a refill. "Let's talk about the Harvest Festival coming up next month."

After refilling cups all around, Selma said, "I'm looking forward to attending the festival. Annabelle, I was thrilled when Mabel told me that Lucas and you will announce your wedding plans that night."

"I've already gotten started on your gown," Mabel volunteered with a warm smile reaching across to Annabelle. "It's goin' to be a humdinger! And your attendant's is goin' to be purty, too." She included Millie in her smile then.

Millie watched Annabelle blush prettily and murmur her appreciation, but she found herself thinking more and more about the robbery. To her way of reasoning, the sheriff needed her testimony before he went off half-cocked in his theory about the robber being from Freeman. She might be the newest citizen, Millie reflected, but she knew that the people of Freeman were not the kind to commit such crimes as had been described, and she had a strong suspicion that the man on horseback might be the culprit.

When it was time for the women to leave, the subject of the robbery never had surfaced again.

· *Chapter Twenty-One* ·

After Millie and Annabelle left the Keyhole House and reached the road that Saturday afternoon, Millie looked toward the crossroads. "Do you suppose the sheriff has been

looking for me?" She glanced overhead. "It'll be dark soon.
I want to give him my statement."

Annabelle also looked toward the crossroads where her
father's store sat, with the livery beyond. "I don't see any
strange horses from here. Maybe he already has his stabled
at the livery for the night." She asked, "Do you want me to
go with you to the teacherage and wait until he comes?"

"No, thanks. If you see him, be sure to remind him that I
have something vital to say about last night's robbery."

Annabelle's forehead wrinkled prettily, and she seemed
about to say something of apparent importance. Instead she
clamped her lips together, waved a casual farewell, and
turned toward her home.

Once inside the teacherage, Millie had a fight with the
Monster and almost gave up on cooking herself a hot supper.
Finally coaxing a steady flame and setting on a pot of stew
made with the nicely dressed rabbit brought by little Junior
Blackstone early that morning, she gave in to her wish to
think about Woods without interruption. She knew that her
thoughts had little to do with needing him to work on her
cantankerous cookstove.

No, Millie admitted as she touched a match to the wick of
the kerosene lamp on her table, she was thinking of the
handsome mountain man because she loved him. She missed
him, too. She could hardly wait to hear all about the political
meeting . . . and to tell about the robbery at the livery.

Millie brought in an armload of wood from the rick behind the teacherage and stoked her heater before she set her
flatiron on the heater's smooth top to get hot. While she
awaited the visit from the sheriff, Millie thought with a new
efficiency gained since coming to Freeman and finding her
free time diminished, she could be getting her ironing done.
There was no telling what tomorrow might bring. If nothing
out of the ordinary happened, she wanted to pay another call
on the Hobbs family and inquire about the baby.

Not caring that she might be acting like a fool, Millie read
Woods's proposal from the slate, then parted the curtains in
her bedroom for one last look at Promise Ridge before complete darkness set in. The blackness of the ridge blended too
well with the night sky, and she could not make out the—

Millie's lips parted in surprise. She was unable to distinguish clearly the outline of the cave where Woods and she had made love, but in that spot, a flame flickered. Could it be that some hunters were seeking refuge there against the cold of the night and had built a fire?

Craning her neck at her bedroom window, Millie peered at the horizon in search of a full moon. There was no moon up, and she recalled that it had been far from full on the preceding night when she had tried to make out the features of the hurrying rider. From what she had heard, coon hunts took place on nights of full moons when the trees were bare and the moonlight gave off enough light to see even in the forested areas.

Millie looked back at the small glow in the distance. Whoever was in the cave was likely no coon hunter. Well, she thought as she closed the curtains, no doubt there were other kinds of animals to hunt than coons. For personal reasons she did not like the idea that someone apparently was using that particular cave.

It was past ten o'clock when Millie smoothed out the last of her dampened tablecloths on her ironing board. Impatiently she had puttered around the teacherage that evening while waiting for the flatiron to heat up at intervals upon the heater and allow her to finish her task. For the linen tablecloth, her best one, she needed her iron almost red-hot.

Millie allowed she was miffed that the sheriff had not called upon her and taken her statement. Whatever could have kept the man? Annabelle had told her after Selma's tea party that the sheriff had received her message. Surely the man would know that she, a schoolmarm, would not be volunteering a statement about a crime if she did not have something fairly important to report. She would have to rise early and see if he was at Mabel's, she decided.

Wonder why she had not heard Clive's Model-T clattering into town? Millie's thoughts ran on. Maybe the company representative was in Hot Springs for the weekend and had not learned that the weekly payroll had been stolen. Judging from Clive's past criticisms of the mountain people, she had no wish to hear his comments about the robbery. She shook her head in quandary. She knew for certain that she would refuse to accept any more of the man's unwelcome attentions, no matter that he might think she was being rude.

Millie had just lifted the newly heated iron from the heater when a knock came upon her door. "Double damn!" she said underneath her breath. She had heard no sounds of an approaching horse; the sheriff must have walked across from Mabel's where Annabelle had said he likely would spend the night. Aggravated that the sheriff had waited so late to come, she hurried to unlock her door and fling it open.

"Well, sir, it's—" Millie began, then swallowed her next words. She did not have to be told that the man standing at the bottom of her steps was not the sheriff. He wore a black hat pulled low over his forehead. In the pale light coming from her lamp across the room she saw that the expression on his face was grim. Her pulse leapt, but her legs refused to back up. She had seen that face before.

"Lady, you better forget you saw anythin' last night," the man snarled in a gruff voice, "or you'll be sorry."

A broken front tooth drew Millie's horrified gaze to the man's mouth and his black mustache. It was almost identical to the one Woods wore. Nothing else about him even remotely resembled Woods, though. His skin was pocked, and his eyes appeared to be black and full of venom directed toward her.

Millie realized that she was looking into the face of the man who had raced by the schoolhouse the night before and that he, indeed, had seen her standing in the schoolyard. Then she saw the gun in his hand. Before she could shut the door, he stepped on the middle doorstep, sticking the toe of one boot into place at the base of the door and holding it wide open. He was pointing his gun toward her, his face screwed up threateningly.

Sucking in a noisy breath, Millie clutched harder at the handle of the forgotten flatiron. The sudden increase of warmth through the lifting pad surged against her fingers.

Without thinking beyond the moment, Millie let the hot iron drop down on the hand holding the gun. The man gave a terrible scream and lost his balance. The gun fell onto the threshold of the door and skidded into the room. Everything was happening lightning fast, but before Millie slammed the door shut and turned the lock, she saw the groaning man toppling backward from the top step. The putrid smell of burned flesh almost nauseated her.

Wild with fear, Millie dashed over to the table and blew out the lamp. Only the glow coming from around the air vents below the door of the heater gave out any light then, and, on unbelievably weak knees, she tiptoed into her bedroom and leaned against the door jamb. Her pounding pulse was punishing her, and she heard her breath coming in painful spurts.

After what seemed an eternity, Millie detected noises from outside that sounded as if the man might be cursing under his breath and getting to his feet. Where were Freeman's dogs when she needed them? she agonized. How had the man arrived at the teacherage without them in hot pursuit? And where was his horse?

More immediate questions surfaced then. Would he try breaking down her door, or coming through a window? Millie knew that the iron had been almost red-hot and that when she let it fall on his hand, it had created a sickening, sizzling sound. She could still smell burned flesh, and her squeamish stomach almost revolted at the thought of what the man's hand must look like. Maybe he was burned too badly to try breaking in on her and killing her with his gun—

Millie breathed out a silent but fervent prayer of relief as recollection came: Her flatiron had fallen outside, but the man's gun was in the corner of the living room near the door. Tears came, and Millie wished for Woods. She wished for the sheriff. She wished for someone to appear and comfort her. She wished that she had not had such a grueling day and night. Her last improbable wish was that she had never heard of Freeman, Arkansas.

Later Millie might wonder how long she leaned weakly against the door into her bedroom, but for the moment, she welcomed its reassuring solidity and clung there long after she could discern no alien noises coming from outside. No matter that she wanted to dash across to Mabel's for help, she was too afraid that the man still lurked nearby to think of leaving the teacherage.

Daylight wandered into Millie's bedroom and stabbed her

consciousness. She became aware that she was lying fully clothed across her bed, wrapped partially in a quilt. Her normally befogged morning brain struggled to make sense of her predicament. In an unbelievably brief time for her, she became alert. Shivering, she jerked up to a sitting position. It must be cloudy outside, she reasoned, and far later than the weak light indicated.

With a haste she had not known she could summon so soon after waking, and without even the benefit of coffee, Millie made her ablutions and dragged her brush through her curls. There was no time to change into unrumpled clothing.

Cautiously she peeped through the curtains all around and made sure that the man was not outside before opening the door and dashing across the schoolyard toward Mabel Marks's house on the other side of the road. The sheriff *had* to be there, she kept telling herself all the way. The pistol, wrapped in a towel, weighted down her coat pocket.

"Yes," Mabel said when she opened her door to the trembling, wide-eyed Millie and heard her question. "Sheriff Crumpler spent the night here, and he's settin' down to breakfast back in the kitchen." Her knowing gaze took in Millie's unkempt appearance and the unsightly bulge in her coat pocket. "What's wrong, Millie? Come in and have some coffee and a bite of breakfast. You look like you done seen a ghost."

Millie followed the plump friendly woman into the kitchen, liking the welcoming aroma of freshly brewed coffee in a warm room on a brisk morning.

As soon as Mabel made the introduction, Millie started talking and laid the weapon on the table. The only boarder at the table that Sunday morning, Sheriff Josh Crumpler, his face showing little concern, took the towel-wrapped gun and removed its bullets before laying it on the floor. Once he returned to eating, he never missed a bite of the grits, eggs, and biscuits on his plate during Millie's account of the bizarre happenings.

Exasperated and angered at the fat-faced sheriff's apparent lack of interest in the pistol and what she had told, Millie said in a barely civil tone, "I can't believe that you never came to hear what I had to report, especially since you admit that both Annabelle and Henry told you that I wanted to see you. I might have been killed last night."

"From what you say, Miss Monroe," Josh Crumpler replied in between hefty bites of biscuit and syrup, "you've been threatened by some unknown man in the middle of the night, and you want me to believe that you saw that same man riding like a banshee down the road late Friday night."

"I most certainly do want you to believe me," Millie retorted. "Where do you think I got the pistol?" She glanced at Mabel who, after fetching a cup of coffee for Millie, had eased onto a chair at the end of the table. Fortifying herself with a sip of coffee, Millie went on. "Mabel, or anyone in Freeman, can tell you that I'm the teacher here—"

"I know all about you, Miss Monroe," the sheriff broke in with a smug tone. "I also know that you don't make a very reliable witness when it comes to clearing Woods Sanders. You could have gotten the pistol almost anywhere, even from Woods."

Millie leaned back against her chair and stared at the man, then down at Mabel. Why was Mabel avoiding her eyes? "What does Woods Sanders have to do with what I've been trying to tell you?"

Sheriff Crumpler buttered another biscuit and poured more syrup onto his plate, then fixed watery eyes on Millie. "Old man McBee told me yesterday afternoon that the man who knocked him out and robbed Booth's safe was Woods Sanders. The only reason I haven't already pulled him in is that I'm waiting for him to get back from Sampson. He's the culprit."

"That's a lie!" Millie could hardly believe her ears—or her eyes, for the sheriff was calmly eating again. She watched Mabel's fingers flick imaginary crumbs from the spotless white tablecloth. "Woods would never rob anyone, much less hit an old man over the head with a shovel. Tell him, Mabel. Tell him about Woods."

A rap on the back door followed by the sound of the door opening prompted the plainly nervous Mabel to jump up. Henry Stevens walked into the kitchen, his usually pleasant face solemn and showing his surprise upon finding Millie sitting at the table with the sheriff from Elmwood.

Within moments, Millie had told Henry of her anger at the sheriff for what she viewed as his false accusations against Woods. "How can anyone believe this lie? Sheriff Crumpler seems to have neglected his duties here, and I think everybody should know how he ignored my request to give him a statement that could have prevented this damnable lie from being spread about Woods." She was close to tears. "He doesn't believe the man I saw on horseback on Friday night showed up at my door last night and threatened me with the gun that I brought here."

Sheriff Crumpler slowed down on his eating then. "Miss Monroe, from what I've heard from the folks in Freeman, you ain't a reliable witness when it comes to Woods Sanders. It stands to reason that a woman who's bein' sparked almost every night by a man ain't gonna count for much when it comes to gettin' the facts straight. That's why I didn't waste my time comin' over to the teacherage." When Millie gasped and turned red, he went on. "Now you can't argue with that kind of thinkin', can you?"

"I can, and I do!" Millie retorted. She was aware that both Mabel and Henry seemed curiously reluctant to join in the conversation; both sat and stared into their cups of coffee. "What's wrong with you two? Double damn! You know that Woods has no reason to steal and that—"

"Calm down, Millie," Henry cautioned. He stirred his cup of coffee and brought a spoonful up to his mouth and swallowed it. "There's not much we can do until Woods gets back from Sampson later today. None of us believes for a minute that Woods is the thief, but the sheriff has to check out all statements, especially the one from Spooner McBee. After all, he was the one who got conked with the shovel."

"Annabelle told me that Mr. McBee moved here only last year. Couldn't he have been mistaken in the darkness, just as I was at first? Even I thought the man looked like Woods when I first saw him on the horse the other night," Millie explained, eager to get the frightening incident cleared up. Why weren't Mabel and Henry kicking up a fuss? She did not care what people said or thought about her. Woods's reputation and future were at stake, maybe even his freedom.

In a panic-stricken voice, Millie went on. "Woods hadn't been gone but a short time when I heard the hoofbeats, and I thought it might be him coming back to see me. I started out to the road to meet him after I saw the white stockings on the horse. The moon was pale, and I was almost to the road when I realized that the rider wasn't Woods. Then I recalled that Major has front stockings only on the front legs, whereas that horse had them on all four. And the dogs were barking and chasing after them. Everyone knows that they're familiar with Woods and his horse and pay them little attention."

Turning then to include the sheriff in the story that she already had related to him, Millie continued. "I didn't tell anyone what I had seen before this morning because I thought it should be told to an official first. I was wrong. I should have shared it with Annabelle at least."

With Henry's piercing gaze added to those of Mabel and Millie, Sheriff Crumpler seemed a bit more interested in what Millie had to say than he was a little earlier. Also by that time he had cleaned his plate and removed a toothpick from the stoneware holder on the table in Mabel's kitchen.

Millie went on, her words tumbling out. "The man did have a black mustache, though, and he wore a black hat like the one Woods wears a lot. When he showed up at my door, I saw again that the mustache and the hat were the only things that truly resembled Woods. The man had pockmarks on his face and a broken front tooth—"

"Glory be!" Mabel interrupted loudly with an I-knew-it look toward Sheriff Crumpler, who was idly picking his teeth. She folded her arms and plopped both elbows down on the table. "She's describin' that no-account Jep Logan what come stragglin' into Freeman back in the summer lookin' for work in the mines. He stayed here a night or two before he found himself a place in the hills."

In a quarrelsome tone, Mabel spoke loudly to the now wary sheriff. "Now you can see, Josh, that what Henry and all of us kept tellin' you yesterday is true. Woods wouldn't steal even if what you've heard about the bank in Little Rock threatenin' to foreclose on his place is right. We've all heard about that from his blabby Aunt Glovina, and we figure

Woods will take care of it without robbin' anybody. Besides, I'm like Millie in thinkin' that Woods wouldn't hit that old man from behind with a shovel. McBee ain't got eyes in the back of his head, so how can he be sure who snuck up on him? He probably ain't been around Woods more'n twice since he moved here."

"Yes," Millie exclaimed with a huge smile of relief. She paid scant attention to what else Mabel had said after identifying the man. "Jep Logan. That's the man whom Annabelle and I saw fighting with Lavelle Landeen one afternoon over at the livery stable. I knew that his face looked familiar, but I—" Millie stopped in mid-sentence. She had not been close enough to the fighters that afternoon to see the men's faces, yet she was certain that she had seen Jep Logan's before. She recalled that he had looked familiar, even on the afternoon of the fight. Her mind whirled. "I know now where I saw that face, Sheriff Crumpler."

Millie gloated as she announced to the three watching her with open interest, "Jep Logan's face is on a wanted poster in the post office in Little Rock. The name over it wasn't Jep Logan when I saw it in September, but I'm almost positive that the face is the same. He's being sought for robbing a bank in St. Louis earlier this summer, if I'm remembering correctly."

While Henry wondered aloud why Sheriff Crumpler wasn't familiar with the current set of wanted posters, Millie recalled with horrifying shame how upon first meeting Woods, she had compared him to the likeness of the mustachoied outlaw. Oh, she had been so blind and so judgmental, she agonized. And now she had fallen in love with Woods and was desperate to clear his name.

As soon as the men were quiet, Millie said, "One way you can check my story about Jep Logan threatening me last night, Sheriff, is to find him and look at his right hand. It's likely one huge burn from my flatiron."

Sheriff Crumpler pushed back from the table, retrieved the pistol from where he had laid it on the floor, and rose. His watery eyes cloudy with thought, he pulled the toothpick from between his front teeth and said, "It don't make a lick'a sense that the man could come to town last night on a horse and not be seen or heard, what with everybody kinda nervous. I never heard no big dog ruckus, myself, and I was sleepin' in the Widow Marks's front upstairs room. Likely Edgar can tell me if anybody from these parts has a horse with four stockings. That would be rare."

Millie repeated what she had said earlier, her words sharp as thorns. "I heard no horse before or after the man knocked at my door."

The sheriff nodded. "I can check out 'most everything you're sayin', Miss Monroe, if Widow Marks can tell me where I might find this Logan feller."

"I'm purty sure that he took to staying in that old cabin close to Lavelle's . . . place of business," Mabel said, clamping her mouth shut afterward, as if she might have already said too much about the community's moonshiner.

Rising, Henry chimed in then with helpful directions to Lavelle's place and volunteered to ride along with the sheriff. Despite Sheriff Crumpler's obvious dislike of the suggestion, Henry left with the round little man.

After the men left, Millie, though she was tempted, refused the solicitous Mabel's offer to fix her some breakfast or to let her nap in a spare bedroom. She doubted that she could get food past the aching lump still filling her throat. Until she saw Woods again and felt his arms around her and heard his deep voice assuring her that all was well, she would exist in her current state of misery.

Anyway, Millie thought as she started back to the teacherage on that cloudy, cold morning, she figured she must be in the middle of a nightmare. The events of the past twenty-four hours stretched credibility and robbed her of her appetite, she mused fuzzily. First there was the robbery and the nightwatchman getting hurt, then all the scary business with Jep Logan and the false accusations against Woods. And whoever heard of eating during a nightmare?

· *Chapter Twenty-Two* ·

"Millie, let me in," came Woods's voice that Sunday night.

Millie struggled in her dream world. Was someone at her door? Opening her eyes when another knock sounded, she found her bedroom dark. How could it be night when she had lain down only a few hours ago, after Annabelle, Mabel, Lessie, and Selma left for her to get some rest? Her brain balked. She didn't want to be disturbed—

"Millie!" Woods's voice came loudly that time. "Let me in. It's Woods."

In a flash Millie discarded the earlier thought that she didn't wish to be disturbed. "I'm coming," she called, jumping up from her bed and retying the belt on her green wrapper. Fighting to shed her usual grogginess upon awakening, she fumbled with the lapping front panels of the garment so as to cover her cleavage. To hell with lighting a lamp and searching for slippers. Her eagerness to see Woods was conquering her drowsiness right and left.

Millie had not dared hope that Woods would come into Freeman before tomorrow night's lessons, much less drop by to see her. What time of night was it, anyway? she wondered.

"What took you so long?" Woods grumbled good-naturedly when she flung open the door and stood blinking at him sleepily. His breath caught low in his throat at the sight of her in the green silky garment. He had thought the moonless night was dark, but he had no trouble seeing her lovely face or the form-fitting garment billowing out above her slender ankles and bare feet. "Not that the wait wasn't worth it. I'm sorry to have waked you, but I wanted to see you."

"Oh, Woods, I needed you," Millie said with such relief in her voice that she barely recognized it as her own.

Before she could wake fully and talk herself out of the impulse seizing her, Millie threw herself against Woods when he shut the door behind him. Ducking her flaming face against his broad chest and letting her arms fit underneath his own and hug him close, she felt and heard the war being waged by her erratic pulse. She breathed in the essence of the man so close. His coat smelled of cold night air and leather and pure mountain man, the man with whom, even at that moment, she was falling in love more madly.

Millie burrowed closer, delighting in the feel of his strong arms tightening around her. The fire in the heater must have burned out, she thought, for she was trembling. "You're here and all right. I'm so relieved."

"Henry and Sheriff Crumpler told me that I'm here mainly due to your efforts, and I came to thank you. I've spent the past few hours with Edgar and them over at the livery. I know it's too late to be calling. I'd ridden a mile down the road toward home when I realized that I couldn't leave without seeing for myself that you're all right."

Woods savored the feel and smell of the sleep-warmed Millie in his arms, and his mind reeled from the shock of her being so openly happy to see him. Careful, he warned himself when an aroused part of him urged him to kiss her breathless there in the dark room. The gloriously feminine smell of her was everywhere, jasminey and tempting as hell. A soft glow from the star-filled sky seeped through the curtains. He dropped a light kiss on top of the saucy red curls resting against his chest, not eager to jar the obvious happiness in her welcome by presuming too much.

In spite of his uneven heartbeat, Woods said in what sounded to him like a fairly normal tone, "Tell me you're all right, and I'll leave and let you go back to bed." When she didn't lessen her hold around his chest, he asked, "If I'm going to stay a few minutes, don't you think it might be wise for me to light a lamp?"

"Yes," Millie said, moving back a step or two and peering up at him. His eyes seemed unfathomable pools of silver in the near darkness, and she shivered again. It must be be-

cause she had nothing on under her wrapper and the room
was chilly, she thought. She had bathed in the copper bathtub he had brought her, then stretched out on her bed to nap.
That must have been hours ago, she realized. "I was so worried. I was afraid something might happen to you."

Woods found his way to the kitchen and felt for a match
from the holder attached to the wall near the cookstove.
When he struck it and got the kerosene lamp going, he replaced the chimney and turned back to face Millie. "Does
your sweet welcome mean that you've come up with an answer to my proposal?"

"No," she hedged, wishing that his tone had not been so
playful. The hurt from his not having mentioned love when
he spoke of marriage two nights ago—or now—rose up and
sliced at her wounded heart. "But we *are* friends, you know.
With the strange turn of events around here while you were
gone to Sampson, I wasn't sure when I might see you again
—if ever."

"You said you needed me?" She never before had said
that, he reflected with surprise; too often she had told him
how she needed no one—especially a man. Walking over to
the heater to keep from snatching her into his arms and kissing her, Woods held out his hands. Little warmth came. He
knelt and fed a few sticks of wood from the nearby wood
box into the little iron heater. The resounding thuds of wood
settling upon the bed of coals and the clanking of the cast-
iron door when he closed it helped bring him to his senses.

"I did?" Millie studied her bare toes sticking out from
underneath her green wrapper. She should not have confessed that she needed him, she scolded herself. He might
guess how she felt about him and view her as a woman not
nearly so self-sufficient as she once had claimed . . . and believed.

Woods smiled to himself. Why had he thought Millie's
words might hold some special meaning? And why did it
smart, now that he learned that they didn't? "Are you having
problems with the cookstove? Henry gave me your message
by way of Annabelle that the Monster needs a taming."

"Yes," Millie replied, able to move away from the door
then and settle upon the sofa. "I needed you to see about the

stove." She tucked her bare feet underneath the full skirt of her wrapper. Thank God there was something to talk about until she could conquer her runaway heartbeat. "The wicks keep getting caught down in the little grooves."

"I'll see about the cookstove later," Woods said, shedding his coat and walking over to the sofa where she was sitting and watching his every move with wide eyes. "Are you truly all right? I could kill that sorry Jep Logan for threatening you. I never wanted to hire him back in the summer, but one of my men spoke up for him."

"I'm so glad Henry and the sheriff found Jep in that cabin near Lavelle's place and that his burned hand proved my story," she said after he sat beside her and told some of the details. "Annabelle, Mabel, Lessie, and Selma came over to keep me company this afternoon and told me about it."

Woods cocked his head in surprise. "And Selma, too? She must really be feeling better about herself."

They moved into the kitchen area where Millie told about the tea party at the Keyhole House and what she had learned about the possibility of gaining a new pupil soon. Meanwhile, Woods examined the cranky cookstove, and from time to time, in keeping with what she was telling, he shook his head in disbelief or in aggravation and added appropriate comments.

After he trimmed the round wicks and got a flame burning, Woods put on the coffeepot without even asking her if she wanted him to. He turned then to where Millie sat at the kitchen table drinking in his every movement with a noticeable air of contentment. "Did you have something to eat tonight?"

"Yes, Mabel brought some yeast rolls and a mold of butter. Lessie brought some blackberry jam. She asked me to go blackberry picking with her next summer."

"Why don't you take better care of yourself?" he scolded with an edge to his deep voice. "If you didn't keep yourself involved in the affairs of everybody in Freeman, you could take the time to master the cookstove and cooking." When she angled her chin and sent him a haughty look, he added with a devilish grin, "I know. I'm one of those making demands on your time. You ought to say you'll marry me just so you'll have someone to cook a meal every once in a while."

"I do quite well for myself, thank you, considering I don't have a decent cookstove," Millie replied. "I live my life the way I choose." There he went, trying to take over again. But seeing him safe and well brought too much happiness for her to remain miffed for long, and she sent him a forgiving look from behind half-lowered eyelashes.

"Is it true what my callers told me this afternoon?" Millie asked. "Did Sheriff Crumpler take Jep Logan to Elmwood to lock him up in jail? Did he confess to robbing the safe?"

"Not really, though after Spooner McBee came and admitted that he had made a mistake and that Jep was really the one who knocked him out, Jep stopped yelling his denials. When he left with the sheriff, he made a bold statement that he wasn't doing anymore talking until he got a lawyer. They didn't find the money in his cabin or in his saddlebags, so they don't have much to go on except what Spooner and you told them. You'll probably have to testify at the trial."

"Does the sheriff seem convinced now that I was telling the truth?" Millie asked. She had no wish for Woods to know the sheriff's tacky insinuations about her unreliability as a witness.

"Yes, but he can't figure out where the money is. There are a million places where the rascal could have hidden it, not that he'll be out of jail any time soon to be spending it."

Looking even grimmer, Woods added, "When old Clive gets back from his weekend trip to Hot Springs, he's going to have a conniption fit. He'll likely be driving over tomorrow with another payroll. Edgar isn't looking forward to hearing another of Clive's lectures on the stupidity of the people in the Ouachitas. Poor Edgar lost some of his own money, too, money he had on hand to take to a horse auction he had planned on attending yesterday."

"I don't see how Clive or anybody else can class Jep Logan with the rest of us here. The man was an outlaw before he ever drifted to Freeman," Millie pointed out with what seemed perfect logic to her. Neither Woods nor she noted at the time that she put herself in the category of citizen of Freeman. "I'm sure that when the sheriff checks his wanted posters, he'll find the man is wanted for bank robbery in St. Louis."

Millie heard the coffee perking faster and thought about how cozy and natural it seemed for Woods to be in her kitchen talking with her about the happenings during the weekend. The memory of hugging him at the door still fed the little inner humming that had gotten off to a fine start during their embrace. Her world seemed to be centered right there in her kitchen. She sniffed at the good smell of coffee ready for serving. She doubted that she would ever get over how special it made her feel for Woods to do the little things for her that women usually did for men—like making and serving coffee or tea.

While searching for cups in the overhead cabinet, Woods commented on Millie's alertness in placing where she had seen Jep's face.

Relieved that Woods could not read her mind, Millie tried to forget how she once had compared him to the grim-faced outlaw on the poster. She fingered the little curls feathering in front of her ears, then attempted to smooth those at the crown of her head into a semblance of order. A half-formed thought that had danced in her mind earlier that day reappeared.

"Woods, maybe you ought to shave your mustache."

"Why in hell would I do that?" He was pouring their coffee, and he paused, the percolater in midair. She could come up with some of the damnedest ideas. Was she, perhaps, comparing him to some clean-shaven man—like Clive Durham—and finding him lacking?

"Well," she hedged, deciding from the stormy look in his eyes that she had broached a subject for strong debate, "look how both Mr. McBee and I thought at first that—"

"That's something I wanted to talk to you about—the way you were traipsing around at midnight in front of the schoolhouse." Woods set down the percolater with a loud bang and brought their cups to the table.

"So what? It's not your business what I do." Millie jumped up to get spoons, not wanting to think about how she had been outside Friday night because she had gone to fetch the slate with his proposal on it. And never did she plan on confessing to him that she had thought he might be the rider in the night, on his way back to see her.

Woods might be able to master the cookstove and make better coffee than she, but he wasn't perfect, the look on Millie's face seemed to imply when she returned with the spoons.

"It is, too, my business what you do."

"Why?" She stirred the sugar in her coffee with far more force than necessary. She was determined not to let her temper flare out of control, but she resented his dictatorial tone. "Because I'm the schoolmarm and your tutor?"

"Hell! You know better than that." Woods took a sip of coffee, then made a face. It was still too hot. Anyway, he hadn't remembered to put sugar in it. Millie had a way of throwing him off kilter, he reflected irritably.

"Oh, I suppose it has to do with your image of me as a wife to lure the voters."

"You're incorrigible!"

"If you came here to quarrel, you're off to a good start."

Woods huffed and dropped a spoonful of sugar into his coffee. Stirring the dark brew then, he became aware of how childish their show of short tempers was. Hadn't he promised himself to avoid such little displays of temperament?

Willing himself into calmness, Woods looked across at Millie in the circle of light coming from the lamp. Her eyes were dark-framed brown pools touched with sparkles. Her red curls framed her pretty face in charming disorder.

Millie recognized and welcomed the unspoken truce. "The coffee tastes good. Thank you." She felt it was her turn to bring up some topic to talk about. "Will the men get their pay tomorrow when Clive comes over?"

"If he can figure out a way to keep from paying them and hold on to the money, likely he will. He acts as if the company's money belongs to him, judging by the way he ignores what he owes landowners."

His harsh, almost bitter, tone led Millie to consider what Mabel had said that morning about Woods's having mortgaged his farm and being short of cash to pay off the loan.

Did Clive's reputedly holding on to company monies have anything to do with Woods's alleged financial predicament?

Millie did not welcome the sudden thought that if and when Clive did drive over from Elmwood, he probably would be calling on her. How could she get rid of the pesky man without seeming rude?

If Clive would only pay attention when they were together, Millie agonized, he could figure out that she never did anything to lead him into believing that she found him attractive—well, she confessed, not since that night after the box supper when she had believed there was something going on between Woods and Annabelle. It had seemed vital at the time to show Woods that a man did find her attractive and that she had not needed him to encourage Clive to lavish attention on her. Now she despised herself for having been so vain and so hungry for Woods's approval.

"You're beautiful, Millie," Woods said, jolting her from her reverie. The little silence while they drank their coffee had soothed him and set him to thinking about how nice it was to be with her, even without talk. He still could not get over how he had been unable to return home that night without seeing her, despite the late hour—and how he had ridden an entire, punishing mile before facing up to his need to see her and turning Major around.

The way his blue eyes were assessing her face and hair brought a warmth to Millie's cheeks. One word reached deep inside her heart and lodged there. Beautiful? Woods had said it as though he might have coined the word just for her.

"You're just being kind," she murmured, dropping her eyes and letting them admire the manner in which his large fingers cradled his coffee cup.

Little habits of Woods's that she had come to know, Millie realized, like his forefinger half tracing the lip of the cup in between swallows, seemed etched permanently in her mind. She saw the dark hairs on his wrist and the contrast of his crisp white cuffs against the tan of his skin and remembered how that curiously masculine sight had moved her in some strange way that first time they had sat together at the kitchen table. There was no doubt now that she must have been falling in love with him a little, even then.

"No, I'm not just being kind," Woods insisted. He loved the way her eyes hid behind her eyelashes and gave her an adorable look of shyness. Millie Monroe shy? he questioned with a start. The memory of her delight in their lovemaking in the cave was stealing upon him and playing the dickens with his pulse. The rise and fall of her breasts underneath the silky green fabric caught and held his gaze, and he could think of nothing but how those warm mounds of flesh had felt beneath his hands and mouth. His tongue wet his lips before he added, "I mean it. You're beautiful."

"Then maybe it's true that beauty is altogether in the eye of the beholder." Her heartbeat faltered. She lifted her gaze, and it stumbled into his as it made its way back to her face.

"That line sounds like Shakespeare," Woods replied, his mind searching. A forefinger smoothed at his mustache, and his forehead wrinkled. "But it's from Lew Wallace, right?"

Millie smiled across at him. "You're becoming better read than your tutor, Woods Sanders." Her pride in him added extra force to her smile. "How was your meeting in Sampson?"

Woods launched into an energetic account of his meeting with the men of the next county, barely slowing down until all had been told to his interested audience of one red-haired woman. Coffee and talk ran out at about the same time.

"The strangest thing happened," Woods said after both sat in companionable silence, mentally totaling up all that he had related. "They asked me to speak about my plans if I became representative, and I found that the speeches I had read and practiced flew out the window. I talked as if I might be discussing my plans with you. It didn't seem to matter that my words were ordinary and not very different from what I would have said before I learned to read and write decently."

"That's the way it should be," Millie exclaimed, her hand reaching out, as if it might have a mind of its own, to rest on his there on the table. "You had nothing to be ashamed of, Woods, before you came to me. Mastering reading and writing merely satisfied some yearning inside you and gave you the confidence to speak before others. You had it all together in your mind long before you began studying with me. If you've gained confidence, I'm glad, but you were already a born leader when I first met you. Now you can be a more effective one."

Woods drank in Millie's words as if they were some magical elixir. Could she be right? He felt that he might have reached a mountain peak when he had not known that he was climbing. What was there about the beautiful woman from Little Rock that fired him up to such heights? His locked-up heart expanded and tried to send him a message, but his brain took over.

"I must be leaving now," Woods announced as he rose and walked to get his coat.

Millie stood and watched him, wishing that he would stay, not caring that it was midnight and that tomorrow was a school day. The thought of the teacherage without his presence almost destroyed her composure. In order to survive, was she going to have to accept his proposal without its sorely desired declaration of love between them?

The absurd thought struck Millie that she was addicted to Woods Sanders and that the addiction was for all time. She might as well try to understand the cleft in his chin as to try to make sense out of her love for the mountain man, especially when she was with him. Already she had learned that there was no assuaging her passion for his presence.

"Are you going to come give me a kiss?" Woods asked.

"You're not giving orders tonight, I see." She loved it when he acted so cocksure and flirty.

"Get over here, woman," he growled, sending her a wink and a smile along with the mock command.

Unaware that her eyes were flirting outrageously and that she walked with the assurance of a woman certain of her sexual attraction, Millie went into Woods's waiting arms. Their kiss broke the tenuous composure she had struggled to maintain ever since his arrival. In a moment of pure fancy, she felt that she was no more than mercury imprisoned within a thermometer and that whether she soared or fell or remained static depended at the moment on the whims of her beloved handler.

Roaring passion shot upward without pity, and Millie's trembling mouth and body transmitted the message to Woods without words. Her body was alive and crying out for more than the hot wetness of his mouth and tongue on hers. When he moaned and crushed her thinly clad body closer, her hands met behind his neck and interlocked inside the collar of his shirt with the fierceness of a captor. Her contact with the warmth of the bare skin covering the tensed muscles of his neck sent her already overheated senses into a frenzy. She marveled at the texture of his skin, then sent her hands onto separate paths through his thick hair.

Woods scooped Millie up into his arms and carried her into the bedroom. It seemed to him that nothing so everyday as a brain controlled him as he lay her on the bed and cradled her against him. Her mouth and body pressing against his had released an inner force of far more telling persuasion than a brain can muster under such circumstances, he confessed.

The furious racing up and down of his heated pulse reverberated in Woods's ears, driving him to give Millie more sensuous kisses, the begging, telling, no-backing-out kind that seemed mere echoes of the ones she was returning as they lay entwined upon the bed. If his hands sent tremors within Millie when they parted the green wrapper and exposed her breasts—and they did—her fingers sent ones of equally hot sensation all over Woods when they unbuttoned his shirt and bared his chest.

"What you do to me is—" Millie hesitated, unsure of the words to describe her ecstasy as Woods kissed her pulsating breasts and laved her nipples with his tongue in a manner that set her inner humming into a chorus of longing. She knew that love dictated to her and was begging to be mouthed, but he would not want to hear of it. Her mountain man might call her beautiful and ask her to marry him to further his ambition, but he had lost his heart years ago to a woman now dead. She let the thought fade. Her hands gloried in the feel of his incredibly smooth biceps and shoulder muscles.

Smiling at her increased trembling, Woods lifted his face

and kissed her chin, using the tip of his tongue to trace its shape lightly.

"What I do to you is like . . . heaven?" he finished for her, bending to whisper it right next to her ear and turn her into an even shakier mold of jelly. "That's what you do to me." When she yet gazed at him in a kind of quivering quandary, he went on in that low husky voice that she remembered so well from their first lovemaking. "Like sugar?"

Still not completely pacified with his terms, Millie wrinkled her nose. He bit it lightly before sprinkling its saucy shape with kisses. "How about sugar and spice?"

Millie rolled her eyes in playful contemplation, letting her fingers tiptoe around the cleft in his chin. He fingered a tiny curl lying in front of her ear, then sent both hands to frame her face while his fingers got lost underneath the cloud of red curls. The heels of his hands rested on her temples, and he could feel the rapid tempo of her pulse while their eyes locked in mutual fascination. He felt that he might be holding the most precious thing in the world, right in his hands.

The old wounded part of Woods's heart welcomed the mischievous sparkle in Millie's eyes, for it jerked him back to the pleasurable, sensual playfulness of the moment. "Sugar and spice and something wicked, just for fun. How's that?"

Millie laughed back in her throat then. "I'll settle for sugar." Why not? she wondered, immersed totally now in the madness beginning when she had melted into Woods's arms back in the living room. She was settling for the moment and not giving a single thought beyond it. "You're pretty sweet."

"Leave out 'pretty,' and I'll buy that, darling girl," he said with pretended hurt to his masculinity.

His endearment for her sailed straight to Millie's hungry heart and joined the others he had given her that afternoon in the cave. Her fingers traced the beloved shape of his smiling lips and became trapped within his mouth when he sucked them inside. She almost lost her breath, and her eyes widened. A delicious spate of goose bumps brushed down her back and slithered inside, along with the hurricane of sensations racing around deep within her womanhood. How was it possible that his lovemaking was even more thrilling than she had remembered?

"And you've got spice, too, mountain man," she continued breathlessly after kissing the cleft in his chin, then dotting it boldly with her tongue.

Millie wouldn't allow herself to follow up on Woods's third term. "Wicked" brought an unwelcome memory of her earlier belief that what she felt for Woods was no more than an infatuation or a physical attraction. She did not like thinking about how naive she had been or how she had known so little about herself before recognizing her love for this handsome, blue-eyed man.

Pleased that Millie still called him her mountain man, Woods slipped off his remaining clothing then and turned back to her. With a tenderness bordering on reverence, he lifted her and got rid of the green wrapper. His gaze told her how pleasing was the sight of her slender nakedness. His words served as the perfect accent: "You're the most beautiful woman I've ever seen."

Tears formed in Millie's eyes as she studied his face and manly form. She couldn't have told if they came because of his compliment or because she was so awed by the sight of Woods's perfectly formed body. "'Handsome' hardly does you justice." She knew it was true. One had to know this man that she loved and add all his other remarkable traits to be able to describe him accurately. He was far more than what met the eye and called up the common term "handsome."

Woods leaned to kiss her then and fit her nakedness next to his. Her need to search for a new word skittered away. All that counted then was to give herself over to receiving new and wondrous kisses and fondling from the man she loved so completely. The receiving became heightened when she began giving back embrace for embrace, touch for touch, sigh for sigh. His hands and mouth worked a torturous magic, from her forehead down to her ankles.

If she were the liquid part of a thermometer as she had imagined earlier, Millie thought fuzzily, she was going to burst from its top any moment. The tantalizing thought sent a frantic haste to her own caresses on his smooth, muscled body; his labored breathing and murmured endearments told her that she was casting her own kind of spell on her beloved mountain man. She pressed her breasts closer to his solid chest, glorying in the titillating brush of the hair on his chest against her tender skin. Maybe it was because he had called her that, but, for that space of time, Millie felt that she was truly beautiful, likely the most beautiful woman in the world.

"My sweet girl," Woods whispered again and again. He could not know that Millie's heart heard each whispered endearment as clearly as though they had been giant-size yells. All he knew was that she was more delectable woman than he had recalled, more woman that he had dreamed could exist outside fantasy.

Woods gathered Millie close and made her his once more. The warm joining of their bodies without pain this time added to her rising ecstasy. She cried out joyously when his rigid manhood touched her molten center. So good and right, she thought with mindless excitement, opening herself to him more fully and bringing her legs up to hug him closer.

The heat simmering within both lovers during their earlier unabandoned caresses increased right along with his rhythmic thrusts. A magical friction triggered secret tongues of fresh flames in both yearning bodies.

With wild abandonment she clung to his broad shoulders and called home each searing thrust with frantic welcoming movements of her own. She became aware only of the exquisitely agonizing flames within her womanhood rising to greater heights from each of his tantalizing strokes. Ever higher, their sparks of passion singed and burned, then flared, until they became one scintillating, roaring blast of white-hot fury.

No longer capable of being contained, their combined fire blasted itself into oblivion, taking the lovers beyond the top of some unseen peak for the wondrous explosion. They gasped at what their frenzied union had created. They clasped each other closer, as though to meld more than cruelly fleeting passion, as though to become one in an even truer sense than the one they shared blindly at the moment.

Shaken and drained, Woods and Millie lay in the after-glow of their spent glory. Their breathing matched up in a sporadic pattern there in the bedroom of the teacherage. He kissed her swollen mouth tenderly. She smoothed back the hair falling across his forehead, leaving her fingers resting there. The silence bound them in mindless wonder.

Millie longed to peek into Wood's heart. Already she knew what hers was singing, what the gentle inner humming meant. The hateful knowledge that his heart could never echo what hers sang so joyously from memory kept her quiet. She had fallen in love with a man who had no heart to exchange. The brutal truth demanded that she deal with it. But not now. Now she would savor the afterglow of their ecstatic lovemaking. To her way of thinking, a close exami-nation of the moment or what it might mean other than utter delight, then putting it into words, might distort or diminish it.

"Millie," Woods said after he rose and slipped into his clothing with far less speed than he had shed it. His brain was trying to function. "We need to talk."

That he felt only partially himself bothered Woods. Some inner voice kept trying to nudge at his feeling of sublime satiation. After he dressed and realized that Millie had made no reply, he stooped and picked up her green wrapper from where it had landed on the floor. In the dim light coming from the lamp in the other room, he saw that she still lay as he had left her, half-curled on her side watching him. He wondered if he might not always remember her that way, beautiful and so obviously content from making love . . . so deliciously female. He held out the wrapper. "Come. Put this on before you get chilled."

Millie did as he asked, languidly, almost as if she might be in a trance. Turning her back to him, she heard the whis-per of the silk as he held the wrapper for her to put her arms in the wide sleeves. The smooth fabric was cold except where his hands touched it, and she shivered. From where he stood behind her, he leaned over her shoulders to pull the front panels together and tie the sash at her slender waist. Throughout, Millie felt as if Woods was making love to her all over again, so tenderly and gently did he cover her with the garment and his powerful arms.

Unable to resist the temptation, Millie gave in to her desire to lay her head back against Wood's chest. He pleased her when he dipped his chin to rest upon the top of her head and nudged it closer. His sweet breath fanned her tousled curls. She could hear and feel his heart beating behind her.

After a long moment of blissful silence, she forced herself to step from his warm embrace and face him. How to find a perfect ending to such a perfect joining of lovers? Millie knew that she would always think of Woods that way, as her lover. Her mountain man lover.

"We need to talk," Woods said again, catching her hand and leading her into the living room, all the while wondering at her silence. He recalled he had been more than willing to talk back in the cave. Too much.

"No, please." Millie looked up at him, seeing the cleft in his chin first, then his mouth and eyes. She saw a softness of his manly features that she never before had noticed. It must be the lateness of the hour, she reflected. "We don't need to examine happiness. Words might spoil what happened between us tonight."

Not wishing to gamble that she might be right, he murmured, "Never would I take a chance on doing that."

Woods studied her beautiful face, then cupped it between his hands and did a more thorough job. He doubted that he would ever forget the loveliness of her oval face and her large brown eyes at that moment, eyes that seemed to be seeing into his very soul without half trying. He felt curiously naked, almost detached from reality.

The lamp was burning low. The fire in the heater was dying. Time seemed to have marched ahead without his awareness, Woods thought. Perhaps Millie was right; their lovemaking was a statement all by itself. Talk could wait. Letting out a huge sigh, whether of joy or of sadness, he did not know—he kissed her pretty mouth with something akin to awe and went out into the night.

Part Seven

Blow, evil winds, whine and blow!
You may shake her, even bend her low;
What's good will sweep behind.

Never a deed so bold,
Never a voice so strong
Can drown the song of lovers.

· Chapter Twenty-Three ·

"Yes," Millie explained to her excited pupils right before dismissing them on the following afternoon, "tomorrow is the last day of October, but Halloween doesn't truly begin until after dark. Remember how we talked of its meaning— hallowed evening. If there truly are witches and hobgob- lins,"—she smiled when the younger children exchanged wide-eyed looks and sat unnaturally still in their double desks—"they won't be prowling until after the sun goes down tomorrow. We'll have a little party at afternoon recess, though, with punch and refreshments."

Shouts and applause from the twelve pupils met Millie's announcement. She beamed upon seeing that Noble Booth was beginning to overcome his shyness and act as a bright eight-year-old should. Having the precocious Francine for a little sister had almost squelched the boy's natural exuber- ance. She suspected that his growing friendship with the spirited Steve Milstead had more to do with Noble's blos- soming out than any guidance from her. Millie basked in the notable progress made by all of her students in the past sev- eral weeks, the older ones as well as the younger.

While the youngsters took advantage of their teacher's ob- vious mood of indulgence and buzzed private conversations, Millie watched Annette and Warden in the back of the classroom. Exchanging secretive smiles, they seemed ach- ingly young to be thinking of marriage in the near future. During recesses when one or the other, or both, sidled up to Millie for private conversation, Millie often steered talk to- ward the next school year. She never had made a stark de- nunciation of marriage for college freshmen, but she had emphasized the pitfalls of young students bogged down from

357

responsibilities outside the classroom by telling imaginary accounts of imaginary couples much like Annette and Warden. Whether or not her attempts to counsel the couple were successful, she had no idea.

Millie did not have to look at Gladys Hobbs, whispering now to her deskmate and best friend, Minnijean Blackstone, to recall how quickly the girl had settled into her studies after she received suitable clothing to wear and attended school regularly. Her little brother, Artis, was fast catching up with the other firstgraders in his reading and writing.

Having turned sixteen last week, Ransom Milstead was losing his earlier reticence, and Millie wondered how much of his new confidence might be coming from the knowledge that his beloved Aunt Annabelle would soon become a permanent part of his home as stepmother to Steve and him.

The two little Green girls and Francine were getting far too rambunctious, Millie decided. She couldn't help but wonder what devilment the three might be planning, guessing that likely it centered on some unsuspecting boy. Lifting the brass bell sitting on her desk and giving it a slight shake, Freeman's new schoolmarm ended the school day with a resounding clang.

Even after the last farewell had faded, the woman from Little Rock smiled upon recalling how the youngest widened their eyes and exchanged fearful looks when she talked of witches on broomsticks, while the older ones looked wise and slightly bored. What would she do, she mused, without her pupils and their inborn talent for pulling her away from her private world during the days?

Within an hour, Millie was in her kitchen admiring her handiwork: She had turned a huge pumpkin into a grinning, snaggle-toothed jack-o'-lantern. Her pupils would be surprised when they saw it at the Halloween party tomorrow.

Early that morning James Hobbs had appeared at the door of the teacherage with the beautifully rounded pumpkin. Millie's obvious delight and sincere thanks led him to share the news that he had slipped off to bring it early because he had not wanted Gladys or Artis to know what their father was doing. At his concerned question about whether or not she knew how to make a jack-o'-lantern, Millie had elevated her chin and replied stoutly that she did.

Remembering how the sad-faced James had brightened when she asked about Mary Lee's and his sickly baby, Millie promised herself that before another week passed, she would rent the buggy again and see for herself how improved the child was. James had given credit for the baby's progress to the cough syrup that Agatha had sent by Woods. For a moment she got lost in thinking of how the hill folk seemed like one big caring family.

Millie jumped up then and checked the temperature of the Monster's oven. Humming aloud because the oven seemed heated just right for baking the cookies she had made, Millie tackled the golden dough with the rolling pin. She was determined to turn out some special cookies for her pupils, in spite of her frequent past failures at baking. What Woods had said last night about her needing to learn to cook and take better care of herself had nothing to do with her decision, she assured herself. It was time to master cooking; that was all.

Twice more—and no longer humming—Millie rolled out the dough before she managed to get it thin and smooth enough for using the cookie cutters that Mabel had loaned her. It was Mabel's recipe and instructions that she had followed as well, Millie reflected with new appreciation for counting the talkative woman as her friend. Henry Stevens's words—"Mabel's got a heart of gold"—came back to her. He was right.

Millie, her lips screwed up in concentration, cut out miniature jack-o'-lanterns and set on raisins for eyes, nose, and mouth. She cut out little witches, decorating them in the same way, but adding some of Mabel's cocoa and sugar mixture to their black hats and dresses. The faint hint of chocolate rising from the sugar concoction was not enough to stir up her abhorrence to the odor.

Millie's thoughts raced on to the party and its other planned surprises: the jack-o'-lantern with a candle burning from within, and the punch that Lessie offered to make and deliver at afternoon recess, followed by games played outside. Oh, the day would be one of fun!

Keeping her mind on the party and the cookies that she continued to cut and decorate for second and third batches prevented Millie from dwelling on her apparently unrequited love for Woods. She welcomed the distraction. Ever since his departure after midnight last night, she had fought against thinking about him. Too often she lost the battle. The smell of browning cookies snatched her back to her task.

"I'm impressed, Millie, I really am," Woods said that night when he came to the teacherage early as had become his custom during the past week. His admiring gaze switched from the tin full of Halloween cookies with their raisin features back to Millie's animated face. He sniffed appreciatively once more before she put the lid back on and shoved the fat container out of reach. "It seems to me that as the one who keeps the Monster tamed, I should be given at least one cookie."

"Not on your life," Millie said. She glanced at the cook-stove. "Don't brag on it, or it might blow up. As for the cookies, I made them for my pupils."

"I don't count?" he asked in feigned dejection.

"Not one iota. Your mother and aunt and all those sisters already have spoiled you rotten."

Woods threw back his head and laughed, pleased at his good fortune on finding that Millie seemed her regular self, or what he considered her normal self—delightful spiciness and beautiful femininity threaded with a zest for all that life offered.

On the ride into town at dusk, Woods had entertained all kinds of upsetting thoughts about how Millie might treat him after their lovemaking of the night before. He already had decided that if she told him to get out and refused to have anything further to do with him, he would demand that she marry him right away. How he intended to force her to do that against her will still boggled his mind. Not having to make any kind of decision about Millie Monroe right then in the teacherage left Woods feeling high as a kite riding spring gusts of fragrant winds.

Or was his soaring mood caused merely by his being in her presence? a persistent voice asked while Woods watched

Millie bring a dog-eared book to the kitchen table where he sat.

"Here's my father's favorite anthology of poetry," Millie said, easing onto the chair next to his and sliding the book toward him so that both could see the pages. She liked watching his intelligent face take on the almost reverent expression it nearly always did when he looked at a printed page. She also liked the way that her inner humming was dancing her into a kind of breezy happiness at being in his presence. "I thought you might enjoy taking it home and reading from it. You'll pick up new vocabulary as well as find some beautiful thoughts expressed in new ways. The books in the classroom don't offer such a variety of poems."

"Thanks, Millie."

Woods leafed through the book, thinking more about Millie than the words on the pages. Her curls shone like spun copper in the lamplight as she leaned to share the book with him. The smell of jasmine seemed as much a part of the book as it did of her.

Was Millie as thoughtful and caring about her regular students? Woods wondered with a trace of jealousy that seemed downright childish when he recognized it for what it was. Recalling her sharp but effective reprimands to him when he had first begun algebra and had lagged in memorizing the formulas required, he realized that a core of steel lay at the center of her soft feminine voice and manner, even when she played the role of teacher.

Now that he thought about it, Woods mused as he leafed through the book and both of them skimmed pages, Millie had shown that quality of concealed strength in her slender body at their first meeting. And at other times, too, his thoughts ran on. He put a stop to them. He did not want to remember her expressed attitude toward marriage . . . and men as a part of her life. Not now. It haunted him too often as it was.

After Millie's passionate response to his lovemaking last night, Woods had been unable to sleep more than a few hours. He kept asking himself why it was that a woman like Millie Monroe could so plainly enjoy being in his arms but had not agreed to become his wife. No answers ever came except the one that she had given in the cave: She liked her life as it was.

How could he change her mind? Woods had wondered while lying awake most of the night. Maybe he ought to wear his suit more often and spruce up as Clive Durham and other men from cities did. Would she like him better without his mustache? he asked himself when he recalled her comment about him shaving it off. Not that he intended to do anything about it, still the question arose. Millie controlled herself with a tight rein and seldom let her emotions show, so how could he tell what she thought about anything? Even when she lost her temper, she never let it rage out of control as he was wont to do.

Woods had come to the terrifying conclusion that Millie Monroe must be the most nearly perfect woman on earth. No wonder she kept saying that she did not need a man. Damnation! She did not need anyone. She had waltzed into Freeman and charmed the hell out of the whole town—and its dogs.

Yes, Woods thought more than once that sleepless night and again now that he was with her in the teacherage, Millie was a small perfect world all by herself. He tried to see the beauty in that conclusion, for he truly admired her in every way, but, frankly, he told himself, it stank. Yes, he argued with the newly literate part of himself, *stank*, not *stunk*. It stank that Millie wouldn't even talk about becoming his wife—not even after he had offered her a true proposal.

Contentedly leaning her head near Woods's and looking over his shoulder at the flipping pages, Millie heard a noise that squelched her ebullience. No longer did the sight of his large tanned hand so near her smaller, paler one on the book claim her full attention. She stiffened and exchanged startled looks with Woods, surprised that they seemed to have moved closer without her realizing it. His face was only inches away from hers. His eyes had never seemed so blue or penetrating. She swallowed so loudly that she wondered if he might not have heard the little squishy sound.

"I might have known that Clive wouldn't show up until night," Woods said. Lord! Her lips were so tempting. He was glad that he hadn't looked up from the book before then;

no telling what he would have done. Along with the wide-eyed Millie he listened as the automobile engine revved up out on the schoolyard for a moment before dying. "Were you expecting him to call on you?"

"No."

He looked around the room. "What happened to the feathers he brought you last time?"

"I took them to Thelma Blackstone one afternoon last week. They seemed perfect for her new house."

Not bothering to wonder why Woods's questioning her about Clive's gift didn't upset her, Millie worked to keep a straight face. Thelma had seemed thrilled to get the vase of feathers. In a rush she had confided to Millie that her husband might be foreman at the Sanders Mine but that he had no appreciation for the finer things in life . . . as she did. After that, Millie had not felt guilty about giving the tacky feathers away. If Thelma thought they were beautiful—as Clive obviously had—then she should have them.

Clive rapped on the door and was soon inside, swallowing his huge smile when he saw Woods rise from the kitchen table and smile lazily in his direction. His glasses fogged up in the warm room, but he merely swiped at the lenses with his gloved fingers.

"Well, Forrest," Clive said after fidgeting with the hat he held in his hand, "I hadn't expected to barge in on another meeting between the board chairman and the teacher. Or is that what this is?"

"You can't win 'em all, can you?" Woods countered. He sat back down. "I reckon you drove over to bring the payroll that was stolen."

"Yes," the pink-faced easterner replied. "The sheriff told me about the robbery when I got back from Hot Springs last night. I gather that could have been you locked up in the county jail at Elmwood instead of Jep Logan."

"Try not to sound so disappointed," Woods said with irony. He narrowed his eyes and sent the smaller man a challenging look. "It seems that somebody went to a lot of trouble to find a horse mighty like Major. Jep Logan never owned a fine animal like the one the sheriff found near his shack."

Clive appeared undaunted and determined to control the conversation. "I left the payroll at Booth's Livery with Edgar. He's going to guard it himself tonight. I figured since I was going to be in Freeman for a while, I'd call on Miss Monroe, you see."

"I did the same figuring. Funny that we'd have the same idea. Don't believe we've done that since you first got me to lease my land to your company for mining bauxite a few years back."

Woods kept his voice pleasant, but Millie could hear tomes of double meaning. She felt jittery. Her earlier suspicions that some deep antagonism stretched between the two men slithered around in her mind, then reared up as fact.

"Won't you take off your coat and sit down, Mr. Durham?" Millie asked, motioning toward the sofa, then perching on its edge. She didn't like the way the round-faced man was staring at Woods and then at her.

"I had hoped that what I've been hearing was wrong, Miss Monroe," Clive said after he turned from his icy appraisal of Woods. His glasses were no longer fogged up, but his eyes still remained partially obscured by the thick lenses. "I don't like putting store in gossip, you see."

"Whatever do you mean, Mr. Durham?" she asked, popping up from the sofa and glaring at him. She jammed her hands into the pockets of her skirt. The stand-up collar of her blue blouse seemed to be choking her. With distaste she saw that his face was becoming even pinker. His lips formed what she could term only a prissy moue.

"I would prefer that we speak alone." Clive jerked his head toward Woods who was still sitting at the kitchen table.

"Don't mind me, Clive," Woods said breezily. "I won't tell a soul what you two say."

Clive's eyebrows shot up in obvious disdain, but he didn't turn and look at Woods. Lowly, and with his back to Woods, he said, "Surely you aren't allowing this hillbilly to call on you and sully your good reputation—as I've been loath to hear."

Millie fumed inwardly. What gave the pompous man the right to call Woods a hillbilly? Outwardly she lifted her chin and intoned quietly with dollops of venom, "Mr. Durham, it is none of your business who comes to see me at the teacherage or what he does when he gets here. Calling people names seems utterly childish. How dare you presume that—"

"How dare I?" Clive retorted in a hoarse whisper. He drew himself up to his full height, which was not very impressive, not when the tall, broad-shouldered mountain man sat in the kitchen area of the room. "You know how I've treated you with the utmost regard and courtesy ever since meeting you that night at the box supper. You must surely know that I've had nothing in mind but the proper courtship of a fine lady like you. I rarely make mistakes when it comes to judging people. I would not be calling from time to time and bringing gifts if I didn't have a proper, lasting relationship in mind for the two of us, you see."

Millie sucked in a deep breath. She did not like admitting that her mask of ladylike demeanor was threatening to slip. "Then I suggest you leave and chalk up having known me as one of your mistakes," she hissed. "I'm sorry that I'm not what you believed. Never did I pretend to be a paradigm. I have no wish to pursue our relationship, whatever it was." She felt Woods's eyes walking all over her and wondered if he was grinning. She wished he was anywhere but there in the room. That her control was fast disappearing was scaring her to death.

"Do you want me to throw this varmint out, Millie?" Woods asked. He shoved back his chair with a loud scraping noise and stood. Though he could make out few words being exchanged over by the door, he could hear tones suggesting animosity.

"No!" Millie replied, almost as angered at his venturing to jump in the half-whispered conversation as she was at Clive's arrogance. "Sit back down. I can handle this myself." She glanced at Woods long enough to note that he still stood and was sending menacing looks toward Clive's back.

"Are you allowing Forrest Sanders to remain?" Clive asked. He made no move toward the door. In sotto voce, he said, "That hillbilly is not good enough for a lady from Little Rock, Miss Monroe. He won't even own his scrubby farm much longer."

"Whoever said that I needed your opinion about anything?" Millie demanded in a voice not much louder, praying that Woods had not heard Clive's words. The thought of a fight taking place in her living room terrified her. Her hands had settled on her hips and were turning into clammy fists. "Please leave, Mr. Durham. You're no longer welcome here."

Clive sneered then and reared back on his heels. Still holding down his voice, he said, "I might have known that a redhead who would cut her hair was a tease. I can tell now that you're no better than these yokels from the hills, you see. I'll not be wasting anymore of my time courting you."

"I'm going to flatten your nose if you don't haul your ass out of here," Woods boomed. He took a step toward where Millie and Clive were standing beside the door. He had not actually heard many of the words spoken, but he had gleaned enough to be entertaining with pleasure the thought of smashing his fist against Clive's pink face.

"Hush up, both of you!" Millie yelled. She had heard more than enough, beginning with Clive's daring to refer to Woods as a hillbilly. She had taken too much, hoping all along that a facade of politeness would end the matter. The nerve of Clive to utter such bald-faced innuendos, on top of having called Woods a hillbilly, infuriated her and swept away her resolve to control her emotions. They were running wild, and she did not care. "I don't need anybody to help me say what I have to say." She gave her full attention and voice to Clive then. "You make me sick! I'm not looking for you or any other man to be courting me. Get out!"

"You'll live to regret this," Clive hissed. His eyes showed then from behind the thick lenses, steely gray and calculating as he turned to include Woods in his statement. "Both of you!"

"Why, you sniveling—" Woods began.

The slamming of the door as Clive left cut off Woods's threat. By then he was at the door reaching for the doorknob, but a desperate Millie caught his arm.

"No, Woods," she ordered, her eyes fiery. She backed up against the door, still scorching him with her gaze. "Let this matter drop. I won't be bothered by Mr. Durham again."

"The man insulted you. He—"

"I don't care," she insisted, reaching with her other hand to clutch at his on the doorknob. "I told him off well enough. This is my business, not yours." When he grabbed her shoulders as though to put her aside bodily, she raised her voice to a sound level matching his. "If you go after him, Woods Sanders, I'll not let you back inside."

"The hell you say!"

"I mean it, damnit!"

"Move out of the way! This is men's business."

"This is *my* business! I won't move, and you'd better not make me."

Woods looked at her more closely. His eyes narrowed. "I've never seen you so het up. What's gotten into you?"

Millie glared up at him, unable yet to commandeer her runaway emotions. He might not have heard Clive call him a hillbilly and a yokel, but she knew that she would never forget it. The slanted remarks about her had not smarted nearly so much as those directed toward the man she loved . . . and admired more than any she had ever met before, she realized with new clarity. He was so true, so straightforward.

In a more normal tone, she confessed, "I guess I just plain blew up. But it's over now, and for you to follow him and get into a fight won't solve anything."

"It would make me feel a hell of a lot better," he ground out with ill humor. The sound of a motor cranking up came into the living room. "The man's a scoundrel. He had no right to talk to you in that tone."

"Maybe he thought he did." Millie's conscience smote her for ever having consented to take the first ride with Clive in his car that Sunday when they went to the Sanders Mine. Her mind was whirling with condemnation for herself, for Clive, and for the devilishly handsome Woods who somehow had tempted her into wishing to appear to be more than she was. "You shouldn't have been here listening."

"What in hell was I supposed to do, leave when he came?" He moved away from the door, arms akimbo and his balled-up fists resting on his hips.

"Double damn! You're always right in the middle of my

life. I don't know what you should have done," Millie
wailed, close to tears. "I don't know anything anymore."
Her father had always condemned emotional scenes, relegat-
ing them to the ranks of the uncultured and undisciplined.
Though she had disagreed with many of Reverend Monroe's
personal postulations, they had slanted her thinking and actions in more ways than she realized, sometimes dovetailing
smoothly with her own but just as often veering in opposite
directions. Mind over matter had seemed a logical guiding
principle . . . until she had met the mountain man now
watching her with a puzzled expression on his handsome
face. "I don't even know who I am anymore."

"You're Millie Monroe, Freeman's new schoolmarm. And
a damned pretty one, at that."

Millie lifted anguished eyes to his face. "Oh, you make
me so mad!" Tears overflowed and started down her cheeks.
"If you hadn't let Clive outbid you that night for my supper
box, none of this would have happened. It's all your fault!"

"My fault?" he echoed, outraged at the way she had put
him on the defensive when he was trying to help. "Hold up,
there. I didn't 'let' him outbid me. If you must know the
truth, I didn't have more than two dollars in my pocket that
night."

With growing alarm, Woods watched Millie's face crum-
ple. Like a little girl sighting a bleeding surface wound on
her knee, she moaned a high-pitched "Oh-h-h!" and sank
upon the sofa. She buried her flaming face in her hands. She
cried hard then, no longer trying to hold back her sobs.

Cautiously Woods sat on the edge of the sofa. He fingered
his mustache. He was not sure that he was much better off
than Millie had confessed to being when it came to knowing
who she was anymore. Why was she crying as if her world
had ended? She had sounded furious when she had accused
him of always being in the middle of her life. Was she right?
He would not have been surprised had she walloped him on
his cheek and ordered him to leave also. Her collapse surprised him beyond reason.

Seeing Millie so wrenched with sorrow and tears shredded
Woods's usual calm. Had her losing control so completely
undermined her normally unflappable self-confidence? Had

she never before let fly whatever was deep inside her mind? True, she often claimed that she said what was on her mind, but he never had believed it. She told only what she chose to tell.

Compassion, or some emotion as punishing, was eating Woods up as he felt in his hip pocket for his handkerchief. He admired Millie for having shed her usual air of composure while telling off old Clive . . . and without any help from him. Damned if the rescal hadn't deserved her every word—those he had made out—and maybe a few more. For a moment, he grinned.

"Millie," Woods said as he put his arm around her shoulders and pulled her to rest her head against his chest, "don't cry anymore." Clumsily, for the awful tenderness he was feeling was unnerving, he mopped at her eyes with his handkerchief. "Everything's going to be all right. I'm sorry if my being here caused even more problems for you, but you did do a damned good job of telling off old Clive."

Her sobs having slowed ever since Woods drew her into his arms, Millie let out a tremulous sigh. She did not think she wanted to leave the haven of his embrace for a long time. Grabbing his handkerchief, she snubbed and swiped at her tears. She realized after awhile that the front of his shirt was wet. A shudder tore through her body as she sought to stop crying.

"Th-thank you," Millie murmured, her voice thick with accumulated tears and a host of emotions best left unexamined for the moment. "I've ruined your shirt"—another involuntary shudder shook her, then a hiccup— "and your handkerchief."

Woods grinned, forcing himself not to hug Millie tighter. Her eyes, limned with lashes wet and spikey, met his. He had never felt closer to her, not even when lost in the throes of making love. He had a feeling that Millie needed the time to find her own way through whatever was muddling her mind.

Gradually silence reigned. Woods figured that a lot more than losing her temper and yelling at Clive Durham in an unladylike way was gnawing at Millie. Slowly, though, she was regaining her accustomed air of being mistress of all, including herself. A second hiccup had not dared to show up, he thought with secret amusement.

"Tell me something, teach," he said in a teasing tone. "What's a 'paradigm'?"

Millie sat up then, and, when Woods freed her, leaned back against the sofa and sent him a crooked smile. Her tousled curls tumbled low over her forehead, accentuating the coppery tones in her brown eyes. "You'll have to look it up."

Though Woods saw her reddened nose and puffy lips, he heard the core of steel in her tart reply and smiled. Millie was going to be all right.

He asked in a tone that suggested no answer was needed, "I suspect tonight is lost as a time for lessons, don't you?" After she found a dry spot on his handkerchief and blew her nose again, he went on as if she had agreed with him. "I'll take the book of poetry and go. We can pick up when I come back on Wednesday."

"You'll not be coming tomorrow?"

"No, I've got a meeting to attend."

"Oh."

Woods cleared his throat. "When I come back, we have a lot to talk about."

"Oh?"

Their eyes talked at length right then, but they did not seem to be speaking in a language that either could decipher. Silence seemed a comfortable ally.

To make sure that he did not weaken and change his mind, Woods fetched the book of poetry from the table. He shrugged into his coat and returned to the sofa, looking down at her with a kind of wonder at her loveliness. She appeared both terribly young and vulnerable, and he wanted to stay. His laboring heart felt tighter than a drum.

"A good night's sleep is what you need, Millie. I'll let myself out. See you Wednesday." And Woods was gone.

Usually the sound of Freeman's roosters crowing stabbed Millie into the first stages of wakefulness in the mornings. The next day it was the peppering of rain that did the trick.

Double damn! she fretted. She had overslept. With no

heart for thoughts about anything except her pupils and the time she would be spending with them, Millie got ready for the day with more hustle than her sleep-numbed brain liked. She could tell that the day was starting off wrong. The smell of cookies permeating the teacherage, which had seemed so wonderfully tempting last evening when they were fresh-baked, seemed biting, almost bitter.

"You're in fine fettle, today, Millicent Monroe," she muttered to her image in the mirror while brushing at her hair. Ever growing, the curls, more auburn than red in the gloomy light and curling more tightly from the dampness, clung to the bristles as if they might be fighting back. She searched in her celluloid trinket box, mollified when she found little brown combs to hold her hair back from the sides of her face. "You're finding fault even with the way your cookies smell. This is no way to begin Halloween."

Millicent? she wondered. How long had it been since she had thought of herself as anything other than Millie?

Millie scolded herself when she saw her brown skirt lying in a pile of wrinkles across her trunk. Determined not to rehash last night's unsettling scenes with Woods and Clive Durham, she reached for her blue skirt. Slipping it over her head, then smoothing down the tucked white waist inside before fastening the skirt band, she heard a familiar crackling sound coming from one of the deep pockets.

As Millie pinned her father's watch chain to her belt, she recalled how she had not bothered to look at the letter Annabelle had handed her Saturday morning. The startling news of the robbery over at Booth's Livery and her sight of the man on horseback at midnight had taken precedence over anything so mundane as mail.

When Millie slipped the envelope out of her pocket and saw that it was from Louise Nipper, she lay it on the chest of drawers. She would save it for reading later when she was not rushed. Since Woods was not coming for lessons, she liked the idea of having something to look forward to that night. In fact she liked the idea of having something to think about other than Woods Sanders and her debilitating love for him.

The few letters from Louise throughout the past several

weeks had seemed like visits back to Little Rock, and Millie always read them over and over before answering them. The sight of the envelope lying on top of the slate—with Woods's proposal on the underside—brought a wry smile before she left for the classroom. What would the very proper, happily married Louise have to say about Freeman's new schoolmarm if she knew—?

Millie cut off her thoughts. It was time to ring the school bell hanging in the little belfry above the front porch and begin the schoolday.

· *Chapter Twenty-Four* ·

"Of course I'm pleased that you invited all of the other mothers to come to the party," Millie reassured Lessie Booth that afternoon at recess. "I wish all of them had come, but I'm glad that four of you did." The two women were at Millie's desk pouring the punch Lessie had brought. Mabel had sent cups with Lessie and her apologies for not being able to attend. "I'm delighted that Selma Bordeaux was willing to come. Do you think she minded that I took her up on her offer to help and sent her inside my quarters to get my tin of cookies?"

"No, Millie, she was tickled to be treated like a regular person," Annabelle said in a low voice. She had joined the two at the teacher's desk and was soon passing out cups of punch to the boisterous pupils gathered in the back of the room.

Thelma Blackstone sidled up then from where she had been talking with her two youngsters and set down a huge stoneware jar. "I hope you won't mind that I brought some extra cookies." She lifted off the lid and smiled at the surprised Millie. "They're tea cakes with hickor' nuts in 'em.

After you was so nice to bring me the purty vase of feathers, I figured it was the least I could do."

"I don't mind at all, Thelma," Millie assured the round-faced woman, returning her smile with one of equal warmth. "I'm grateful. Cookies flavored with hickory nuts are a rare treat." She buried guilty tinglings trying to surface at Thelma's mention of the feathers.

The unexpected appearance that afternoon of the four women at the front door of the classroom had rattled Millie. The pupils had been fractious all day, whether from the driving sounds of rain and wind outside or from the anticipation of the Halloween party, she wasn't sure. Millie had been so relieved that Thelma apparently had not taken time to douse herself in her smelly cologne that she hadn't noticed that the woman was clutching a cookie jar inside her rain cloak.

"I brought some apples," Lessie Booth announced. "Edgar walked over with me and slipped a sack full and a washtub on the porch. I figured the kids might like bobbing for apples after they have refreshments. We can ask some of the boys to draw water and fill the tub."

"Papa sent some peppermint sticks for prizes, and Selma brought some licorice ropes," Annabelle volunteered then, her pretty face wreathed in smiles as she glanced back at her nephews and noted what a good time they seemed to be having with their classmates. "I'm having fun playing 'mama' to Ransom and Steve a few weeks early."

"I'm happy for you," Millie exclaimed, thinking that the December wedding date for Annabelle and Lucas Milstead really was not far away. "The idea of bobbing for apples and awarding prizes is wonderful. Thanks to all of you." Oh, dear, she agonized. All that she could offer as entertainment was pin the tail on the donkey. Why hadn't she thought about planning a special game for inside in case of rain?

The party progressed into a rip-roaring time of giggles and playful shouts when Selma returned with Millie's beautifully decorated cookies. Offering smiles all around, Selma made sure that each pupil received both a witch and a jack-o'-lantern. They called out their thanks to Millie, who was busy at the front of the classroom serving punch, with some of the energy pent up throughout the rainy day.

Not a single person present appeared to pay the least attention to the scar on Selma's cheek, Millie noted with relief. The long room reverberated with the happy sounds of
youngsters having a good time and of chattering women
gathered near the front adding their share of noise to the din.
Before Millie realized it, the cookies and punch had disappeared and the apples had been captured, in a more or less
fair show of friendly competition. Annabelle passed out the
prizes of peppermint sticks and licorice ropes with Selma's
help.

Millie waved good-bye to both pupils and adults, her
heart full of a new kind of happiness. If she had entertained
doubts earlier that she was accepted in Freeman, she considered them no longer. She felt good all over.

The four women and older pupils had helped Millie place
the desks back in order and remove the clutter. With a little
wrinkle of her nose, now that she was alone, she dismissed
the water splashed on the wooden floor from where the spirited apple-bobbing had taken place. It would dry before
morning.

With her cookie tin cradled in her arm, the contented Millie was leaving the classroom when she spied a paper bag
holding what she assumed was trash collected by one of the
women and left behind. She turned back to take it along. An
inquiring look at the contents of the bag deflated her bubble
of happiness.

Inside lay numerous cookies, some of them partially
eaten. All were the ones that Millie had baked. She wished
she didn't have to open the tin and sample one of the few
remaining therein, but she forced herself to get it over with.

Remembering the strangely bitter scent she had smelled
earlier that morning, Millie nibbled gingerly. She took a bigger bite. Oh, my stars! she thought as she grimaced and spit
the awful-tasting mess into the paper bag. Yuck! She must
have put a tablespoon of soda in the batter instead of baking
powder. The cookies were a disaster. She wondered if the
most embarrassing aspect might not be that no one had told
her.

Millie hurried to her living quarters, her flushed face set

into a mask of self-deprecation. Couldn't she do anything right . . . other than teach school?

The drizzling rain and overcast skies were bringing nightfall early that Halloween, Millie reflected while getting a fire started in her heater. It was setting in to be a miserable night. Probably her pupils would be disappointed not to be out peeking at the moon and searching for signs of witches riding broomsticks. From what she had heard about some of the tricks played by youngsters on Halloween, likely it was a good thing they would not be roaming about that night hunting ways to get into trouble.

Millie had questioned Annabelle before she left and learned that no mail had come for her since Saturday. She was glad she had saved Louise's letter. She had no desire to give more thought to Woods's proposal, though she well remembered the meaningful way he had told her before leaving last night that when he did return, they needed to have a talk.

From Millie's viewpoint, her choices seemed nil. No matter how much she loved the handsome mountain man, she doubted that she ever could consider marriage to him without his falling in love with her and telling her so. And when the time came for her to turn Woods down—well, Millie hadn't lived twenty-six years without learning a lot about the male ego. Likely he never again would be her close friend . . . maybe no kind of friend at all.

Millie wasn't sure that she could tolerate losing contact with Woods completely—not that she intended allowing anymore lovemaking, even if he continued to come around for tutoring. To her sorrow, she had learned that their second lovemaking two nights ago had only heightened her love for him and created a splendid yearning afterward that hadn't yet gone away. Only when she willed it be so could she stop thinking about the handsome mountain man.

After making herself a cup of tea to go with the leftover tea cakes that Thelma had insisted on leaving behind, Millie fetched Louise's letter and settled down at her kitchen table.

From concerted effort she hadn't allowed herself to entertain new thoughts about Woods since he had left her sitting spent on her sofa last night. One skipped to mind then, though, and it had to do with how she was sitting on the chair on which he always sat, not on her customary one. How absurd, she scolded, to be feeling closer to Woods simply by sitting where he sat when he was at the kitchen table. And why was she basking in feeling closer to a man who didn't return her love? a chiding inner voice asked right before she read the letter from her longtime friend.

Millie pursed her lips in denial of the hateful question and skimmed the three-page letter quickly, reassured by Louise's familiar neat script and her response to Millie's last letter to her. Parts of Louise's letter shocked her, and she went back to those paragraphs for more careful perusal.

> ... and your replacement, Sandra Fulmer, has given notice that she will be returning to her home in St. Louis at Thanksgiving. She says she misses the life in a larger city. Millie, the superintendent asked me to tell you that if you wish to replace Miss Fulmer, you can have your old job back after Thanksgiving. Others have applied, but he prefers to have you return. Isn't that grand news? Let me hear right away when you'll arrive. I remember how your first letter told of your disappointment in the god-awful little town of Freeman.
>
> You'll like hearing that Luther Osgood and his wife have moved to Nashville, Tennessee. You won't have to be running into them. It seems that her father has found a place for Luther in his law firm. . . .

Millie forgot to drink her tea. Her mind was whirling in disturbing directions. She could go back to Little Rock! She could pick up her former life—of finding companionship with other teachers, of living in her old apartment with its little touches of refinement, even luxury, of attending concerts and lectures, of shopping in modern, well-stocked stores. . . .

Even after she undressed and went to bed, Millie thought about the many avenues that Louise's news opened up for her. She could escape all of the things about Freeman that had disturbed her in the beginning.

No more battles with the Monster. She wouldn't have to face up to her failure as a cook and do something about it. Once again she could eat her meals in the boarding school's dining room along with the other faculty members and the students. No more afternoon walks accompanied by a playful pack of dogs—not that they frightened her anymore, she conceded with a measure of pride.

By teaching only one subject to high school girls from families wealthy enough to send them to the prestigious boarding school, she would be freed of the problems that had confronted her in the one-room schoolhouse in Freeman. No more worrying about students and their personal problems concerning lack of proper clothing, affairs of the heart, attendance, adjustment to the first year of school. . . .

At the Owen Academy for Girls in Little Rock, Millie recalled, teachers did not have to serve as both janitor and teacher in the classroom. And they didn't have to draw water from a well and use outdoor toilets. There would be no need to prepare lesson plans for so many different levels of learning in all subjects. She again would have the proper maps and reference books to enrich her lessons, and—The list ran on endlessly.

But you would miss your pupils and your friends, a strong inner voice kept insisting at intervals. *You love them.* She turned a stony ear to the one reminding her about the mountain man.

Millie's dizzying thoughts ran on into her fitful sleep, evolving into dreams that mocked her, intimidated her, and kept her tossing and turning throughout the night. Unlike in her conscious state, she could not force down thoughts in her dream world of living a life where there was no Woods Sanders of the electric blue eyes and deep-timbred voice.

Still uncertain as to what she would write Louise, a tightly wound Millie opened her door the next morning to leave the teacherage and go into the classroom. She took one look at the third and last step leading down to the ground and screamed. Weak all over, she clutched the door frame. A dead buzzard lay there, its bald pink head and broken neck lolling grotesquely like those of a naked snake. The dark-feathered bird's huge claws with their long talons stretched out in silent threat in the thin morning light.

Fighting down nausea, Millie looked all around, relieved that it was unusually early and that nobody was in sight. It was plain that the carcass had been put there deliberately, for it appeared to have been dead for quite some time and had a sickening odor. Who could have put the vulture there? Why would anyone want to frighten her? She had no wish for whoever had dumped the hideous bird on her doorstep to see her reaction and gain pleasure. Should she step over it and ask the two big boys, Warden and Ransom, to take it to the woods behind the schoolhouse and bury it?

"No, don't do that or you'll be playing right into their hands," something whispered to her when she recalled the unusually high spirits and private conversations of the two boys yesterday. "Last night was Halloween."

Millie brought her hand up to her mouth, open in shock and horror. Had she not heard more than one adult laugh about Warden Marks's love of playing practical jokes when he was younger . . . and been a bit doubtful that the studious boy in her classroom was the one about which they spoke? Millie asked herself. Warden always appeared so mature, so polite.

Ransom Milstead had become an ardent admirer of the older Warden, Freeman's schoolmarm mused now that her head was clearing. She did not welcome the direction of her thoughts. Warden alone, or in cahoots with Ransom, seemed the prime candidate for having placed the dead buzzard there. It was unlikely that the younger boys would have been allowed outside after dark, what with the night being so cold and rainy. And she doubted that any one of them would have known where to find a dead buzzard, or would have touched it if they had.

Glancing toward the road and still seeing no one, Millie grabbed a pair of old gloves and a sheet and went to work. She gagged a time or two before she finally got the smelly dead vulture lying on the sheet. Never having seen one up close before, she'd had no idea buzzards could be as large and heavy as a turkey.

By the time the indignant schoolmarm started for the woods, she had gotten control over herself and was pretending that she was dragging off some discarded shoes on the sheet bumping along behind her. The tall wet weeds, dead but still standing, slapped at her skirts. Though the rain was gone and the sun promised to shine later through the fleeting clouds overhead, the ground was wet, and her shoes bogged nearly to their button tops from time to time. She thought about leaving the soiled sheet in the little gully near the edge of the woods where she dumped the carcass and kicked leaves over it, but common sense reminded her that she could wash it and that sheets cost fifty cents. Without a second thought she buried the worn gloves along with the buzzard.

Still grim-faced, Millie had to begin the school day as soon as she returned from the woods and washed her hands. If anyone so much as noticed the muddy hem of her skirt or her damp shoes—she had removed most of the mud—she would send him or her to the corner and have the youngster copy the entire Constitution of the United States, she promised herself. She was in no mood for being crossed. Little Rock was looking better with each passing minute.

The day in the classroom was a disaster from beginning to end, and Millie could say later that she shouldn't have been surprised, what with a fierce wind rising outside and, as usual, making the youngsters restless. But she was.

That she was sharply suspicious of both Warden and Ransom since classes first began probably kept the two boys on their best behavior, Millie mused. She could find no fault with them. Until morning recess.

"Yes, you may speak to Warden and Ransom," Millie told Henry Stevens when he surprised her by appearing in the schoolyard. The stern look on the storeowner's face did not seem to belong there, and she wondered if perhaps Henry had learned about the buzzard lying on her doorstep. But how?

The mystery was soon cleared up when Millie wandered over to where Gladys and Minnijean were talking in whispers near the front porch and asked them what was going on.

They rolled their eyes and jabbered at the same time until Millie calmed them and asked for a single version.

"The hay rake from over at Booth's Livery was sitting right on the top of Mr. Steven's store this morning," Minnijean said. "Papa saw it when he left for work and came back to ask Junior and me if we went out last night. We didn't, and we told him so. After he went on to work, we ran out into the road and looked." She barely suppressed a giggle. "It looked funny to see that hay rake straddling the roof."

Millie recalled having seen the mule-drawn hay rake sitting in front of the livery stable ever since her arrival. Her imagination couldn't stretch far enough for her to figure out how Warden and Ransom could have gotten the large two-wheeled implement on top of the pitched roof of the general store without help.

"How could boys have gotten the hay rake up there?" Millie asked the obviously impressed girls.

Minnijean supplied the answer, looking smug and tossing her long braids over her shoulder. "Before class started, I heard Warden telling Annette how it was his idea to rig a pulley up in the big oaks and tie ropes to the hay rake. He said he needed Ransom to help him hoist it up."

"Annette is wildcat mad at Warden," Gladys volunteered. "She told him that she didn't think the trick was a bit funny and that it wasn't right for him to get Ransom involved. Minnijean and I told her that she could eat with us at noon if she didn't want to sit with Warden anymore."

"Annette has been giving Ransom sweet looks all morning," Minnijean said. "Do you think maybe she's going to start liking him now instead of Warden?"

Millie looked over at where Warden and Ransom were talking earnestly with the still stern-faced Henry Stevens. He seemed even angrier at his grandson than at Warden, though he apparently was dressing down both without mercy.

Deciding that she had been right to suspect the two boys of dumping the buzzard on her doorstep, Millie left the all-knowing Minnijean and Gladys and went inside to ring the bell. Morning recess was over.

Millie was not surprised when Warden and Ransom asked for permission to leave the schoolyard during lunch hour.

She suspected that they spent the time removing the hay rake from the roof of the store, though she didn't ask when they returned and quietly slid into their desks.

Recitations didn't go too well that afternoon. It seemed to Millie that the four younger boys were bent on whispering and doing all manner of things to aggravate her. Only a few minutes remained before dismissal time when the proverbial straw landed on the proverbial camel's back and whisked Millie into a new and maddening tizzy.

"What's the meaning of this spate of giggling?" Millie asked Noble Booth, whose face was as red as his hair. Steve Milstead, his deskmate, became almost hysterical with laughter at her question. Across in the neighboring desk, Junior Blackstone and Artis Hobbs seemed in similar condition.

Putting her hands on her hips, Millie demanded, "Tell me what's so funny. I'll not dismiss anyone until you do."

The four little boys, none of them over nine, ducked their blushing faces then and shuffled their high tops on the floor. Some of the older students sitting farther back looked up from their work in curiosity, growing still when they saw their usually good-natured teacher looking stormy-eyed and madder than they ever before had seen her. The little girls, grouped on the side where they had been drawing with coloring crayons while Millie listened to the boys up front read aloud, dropped their mouths and listened.

"Speak up, Noble. You seem to be the one with the secret. Tell me what's so funny. Maybe I'd like to laugh, too." She sent looks at the other pupils, noting their sudden silence and keen interest. "Everyone would like to share the joke that only you four seem to know. Tell us."

Noble squirmed. Millie waited. The entire classroom waited.

In a voice barely above a whisper, Noble said, "Steve pooted."

Millie cocked her head. Only the three other little boys sitting near her desk heard the low reply. None of them looked up, but Millie could see them shaking with silent laughter and turning ever redder. Never having heard or read the word, she brushed aside common sense and asked, "What does that mean? What's so funny about that?"

Noble ducked his head lower. Steve spoke up then, his voice ringing out as though in defense of his friend. "He said that I farted, Miss Monroe. But I didn't mean to, honest."

The classroom exploded with shrieks of laughter then. Gales of laughter rocked around the room and bounced off the ceiling as Millie stood rooted behind her desk, staring at the little boy who called Annabelle Stevens "aunt" and who always seemed such a model of propriety. While studying at the Teacher's Training Institute several years ago, Millie had read Chaucer's bawdy tales with the four-letter words for bodily functions sprinkled throughout. She knew what 'fart' meant, though she never before had heard the word used.

Millie's face burned. Her stomach knotted up in anger at her stupidity in demanding an answer from the giggling little boys. She should have known better, she kept telling herself as the laughter slowed, then rose again, louder, and to Millie's way of thinking, more derisive.

Her reddening face revealing her embarrassment, Millie reached for the bell on her desk and shook it vigorously in dismissal. Some wayward part of her left over from her own school days was creating a bubble of laughter deep inside. She thought it a blessing that everybody scrambled for the door in a rush and that nobody bothered to call farewells.

"That's it," Millie said aloud in her bedroom an hour or so later. "I can't stay here."

She might be talking to herself like a loony, Millie thought, but at least she had fought and won the battle not to go running to Annabelle with her misery. How could she bear to face her pupils now that she had fallen on her face before them? First with the inedible cookies, and now the absurd business of a little boy breaking wind and proclaiming the fact to one and all was undermining her dignity. Hateful also was her cognizance of the fact that one or more disliked her enough to try scaring her with a smelly dead buzzard. Unaccustomed tears of self-pity stung behind her eyelids.

Suddenly Millie remembered that the first Sunday of November was coming up on the weekend. The Methodist minister would be driving from Elmwood to hold services. In a determined voice, she vowed aloud, "I'll go back with Aunt Phoebe and Uncle Fred in their buggy and catch the train to Little Rock on Monday. People from around here got along fine before I came; they can do so again after I'm gone."

Millie looked askance at the simply furnished bedroom, then walked to pull aside the curtains and look out the window. The shape of Promise Ridge loomed on the darkening horizon, taunting her with burning memories. As she had noticed once before—was it the night after she had seen Jep Logan riding down the road at midnight?—there seemed to be a campfire within the cave. Would hunters already be seeking shelter at dusk? Perhaps it was a trick of the lingering sunset, she surmised. The sun's rays might still be reaching the point of the ridge even though the valleys already lay in darkness.

Her thoughts returning to her miserable state, Millie wandered into the living room. Her footsteps echoed on the board floor. By this time next week, she reassured herself, she could be back in Little Rock, back where she belonged. She tried calling up all of those wonderful aspects of her former life in the capital city that she had thought upon last night after reading Louise's letter. They palled when she thought about her pupils and her new friends, all so dear to her now. They sank out of sight when she thought about Woods Sanders.

So what if the boys had become overly rambunctious and dumped a dead buzzard on her doorstep? Millie asked herself when she saw the need to be objective and sift through all that was leading her to entertain thoughts about leaving Freeman. After all, last night was Halloween. The boys' prank did not mean they didn't like or respect her, she reasoned now that her anger and repulsion of that morning had receded. Warden and Ransom had not singled her out alone; Henry Stevens probably was the most respected and best-liked man around, and they had set the hay rake on top of his store, no matter that he was Ransom's grandfather.

Millie never had gone along with her father's saying about

how boys will be boys, but now she was beginning to see some truth in it. She fired up the Monster and put on the percolator.

A half smile lifted the corners of Millie's mouth. She really should have walked out to the road and looked at the hay rake perched on the roof of the store before it was taken down. That must have been quite a sight—and likely would be the topic of conversation for weeks and years to come. Maybe next year—if she stayed, that is—she could interest the parents in planning a Halloween party for the young people to help them enjoy the night of witches and hobgoblins and prevent further trickery that could be dangerous.

Next year? Millie wondered. She heated her skillet and cooked herself what was intended to be an omelet made according to Annabelle's instructions. That it turned out to be a leathery concoction of overly cooked eggs suited her semiconscious mood admirably. Barely aware of what she was doing, she ate it and washed it down with underbrewed coffee.

Millie's thoughts veered to the episode with the four little boys at the end of the school day. When she wiped her mouth with her napkin, she realized that she was smiling, then almost giggling. So she had stepped into a little trap and fallen flat, she mused, still smiling. It wasn't the first time, now that she was being totally honest, and likely it wouldn't be the last, not if she continued to teach. In the future—no matter where she might be teaching—she would make sure not to be so dogmatic in her demands to know what caused spurts of private giggling.

What about her promise to be Annabelle's attendant at her marriage to Lucas on the day after Christmas? Millie wondered when thoughts of leaving Freeman still darted around in her mind at intervals. It could be tedious and a bit embarrassing to return for the occasion, yet she had promised Annabelle to be her sole attendant. Mabel likely would be starting soon on the apricot silk that Annabelle had chosen for Millie's gown. Millie never gave promises lightly.

According to Uncle Fred, no other qualified teacher had applied for the job of teaching in the one-room schoolhouse back in the summer. How would the people of Freeman feel toward her if she walked out before the school year had hardly begun? And, her conscience reminded her, how could she call herself a professional if she left without a proper replacement—and with no valid reason? The youngsters once more would have to leave their homes and live in Elmwood or Hot Springs to attend school. What about the new girl, the one coming with Selma's new housekeeper? Millie sighed. All of her pupils were making remarkable progress and seemed contented. And she truly loved them, even when their actions might not suit her.

Then it was time to think of Woods and the big role that he played in her decision about whether or not she should return to Little Rock. By the time Millie had washed and put away her dishes, she was facing up to the truth: She could not leave Freeman, not anytime soon. Though she never could marry Woods for the cold-blooded reason that prompted his proposal, she abhorred the thought that she might not be around to share in his life, however vicariously, as a candidate for representative next spring and summer.

The people in Lexington County, and in the surrounding ones making up the voting district, needed a man like Woods to represent their interests in the legislature, Millie reasoned. If she were to leave before he honed his skills in reading and speaking to a finer level, he might miss out on achieving his goal, and that of many others in the Ouachita Mountains. She intended to use all of her persuasive powers to convince him to become a candidate. Why, she reflected, a man of his talents and nature might well end up as governor of Arkansas.

Yes, Millie convinced herself, she was needed in Freeman. Little Rock and what seemed at the moment to be her own best interests would have to wait—at least until after the school year ended.

"Millie," came Woods's voice after a tap on her door.

Her mind made up only moments earlier that she could not leave Freeman, no matter how tempting the idea was in numerous ways, Millie rushed to greet the handsome man she loved. Her heart reminded her that all of her rationalizing might as well have been for naught: She could not bear the thought of being alive and not being near Woods

Sanders, not being able to hear his voice or look into his face.

Woods burst in with surprising news, his huge smile at Millie the only greeting she required. As usual, his presence was all that was needed to trigger the little contented rhythm of her inner humming. The crazy thought flashed to mind that perhaps cats purred from some similar reason: happiness too pure to hide. Once more she felt as if she might be the center of the universe.

"How on earth did Jep Logan manage to escape jail last night?" Millie asked when the obviously agitated Woods slowed down his tale and removed his coat. "Is the deputy hurt seriously?"

"No, Asa has a giant headache from where Jep rapped him over the head with a pistol, but he's okay. A bunch of boys were switching around signs over the stores in Elmwood—Halloween, you know—and Sheriff Crumpler had gone to make them put things back in order before chasing them home. Clive had come to see Jep earlier, and the sheriff sent Asa over to the jail to stay 'til he got the boys and the storeowners calmed down."

"Wonder why Clive would visit the man who stole his company's payroll?" Millie asked. Later she would tell Woods about Halloween in Freeman—about the hay rake and maybe the buzzard, too. She loved watching his blue eyes dance when he was excited. His manly presence and deep voice filled the room . . . and her heart.

"I just now left Henry's store where a bunch of men were talking with the sheriff. He thinks Jep might have come this way, for the horse he found near his shack Sunday and impounded was taken from the corral near the jail last night.

"He said he heard Clive and Jep talking as if they might be quarreling, but that he figured Clive had a right to be angry at the thief and never went back to the cells. By the time the deputy got there, Clive was gone. The deputy said he checked on Jep in the back and started working on reports up in the office; the next thing Asa knew, Jep was slipping up beside him with a gun in his hand. That was the last he remembered before the sheriff came in an hour or so later and found him on the floor."

"Does the sheriff think somebody gave Jep a gun, or did he take it from the jail?"

"He figures somebody must have slipped it through the bars on the cell window while all the ruckus with the pranksters was going on down on Main Street. It was raining like it was here, and a messy night with almost everybody inside, so nobody saw or heard anything unusual. What you remembered about seeing Jep's face on the wanted poster turned out to be right, so he probably has lots of outlaw friends willing to help him escape. He left a note in the cell saying that he wasn't taking the rap for a crime that was somebody else's plan."

"I wonder what that means."

"The note said that the mastermind was somebody close to home." Woods wondered what was going on in Millie's mind, but a part of him was being dazzled by the sight of her pretty red hair held back on the sides by two little combs that he hadn't seen before. He was glad that a few curls still managed to caress the tips of her ears.

Millie frowned in genuine puzzlement. "Sounds strange."

Woods went on. "The sheriff said that Clive has posted a one hundred dollar reward for the capture of Jep Logan, dead or alive. There's a bunch of men at Henry's store planning to ride out with Sheriff Crumpler tomorrow and search the foothills."

"Are you going with them?" She hated the thought that he might get hurt . . . or killed.

"I figure to. I'm wondering if he might not try harming you and Spooner since you two identified him." His voice deepened with concern for Millie's safety. She was so beautiful and so dear to him. And maybe more than dear? an inner voice asked as it had earlier when the talk about what Jep Logan might be up to had swirled back at the general store. No, he reflected, it was just that he was a man and that men always tried to protect women and children. Millie was his friend . . . and she hadn't yet refused to marry him.

"Jep Logan won't come around here again, not when he thinks about that flatiron on his hand. He's probably miles away by now."

"I wish I could be sure. The way everybody figures it, Jep

hid the money somewhere around here and will be wanting to get it before hightailing it. I'm thinking it might be best if I take you home with me tonight."

"That hardly seems necessary. How would I get back to teach tomorrow?" She was amazed at how warm it made her feel that he seemed genuinely concerned for her well-being.

"Henry and I decided that school could let out until we make sure Jep isn't around these parts. Henry will get word to the families of the pupils. Jep might show up here during school and harm some of the kids, as well as you."

At the mentioning of her pupils, Millie didn't waste any time before throwing clothing into a small bag. Woods set the damper on the heater so that the fire would burn out, then came and stood in the doorway to her bedroom watching her. He wished he wasn't such a coward and could press her for an answer to his proposal. Had she even given it another thought since he asked her to marry him five nights ago?

"You shouldn't be leaving your curtains open that way after dark, should you, Millie?" he asked.

With pretended carelessness, Millie agreed. She had no wish for him to know how she often looked up at Promise Ridge and the cave where they had first made love. Thank goodness the slate with his proposal on it was lying face-down on the top of the chest of drawers.

Walking over to close the curtains while Millie snapped her valise closed, Woods peered out through the window. "If I didn't know better, I'd think that was a fire or light up in the cave on the ridge." He squinted his eyes in thought while his fingers toyed with his mustache.

Millie replied, "I thought the same thing earlier this evening, and one night not long ago, too. I remembered what you said about hunters sometimes using the cave for shelter."

"Which other night did you see a light up there?"

"Saturday, the night you were at Sampson, the night after the robbery. It was probably hunters then, too, wasn't it?"

"Maybe." Woods closed the curtains, his face showing that his mind was elsewhere. He helped Millie on with her coat, then picked up her valise and walked with her to the door. "I've got Edgar's buggy outside—the one you call the one-hoss shay."

"You were pretty sure that I was going to go with you, weren't you?"

"Yep." He grinned and winked at her. "You were going to go with me, or else I was going to spend the night here and leave that shay sitting out front for everybody to see."

"You're terrible, Woods Sanders. You ought to be ashamed."

"I know." Feeling cocky from her assessing, flirty look at him from behind her half-lowered eyelashes, he added, "Being around a paradigm just seems to bring out the worst in me."

· *Chapter Twenty-Five* ·

The blanket of darkness still covered her, but Millie jerked awake in the guest bedroom of the Sanders home. From a ghostly distance a rooster was crowing in answer to the one in the barnyard behind the big house overlooking Iron Creek. Had she heard the sounds of hoofbeats rushing away? Remembering where she was and how safe she felt, she let sleep embrace her again.

Daylight greeted Millie when she next awakened. Looking forward to seeing Woods and to visiting further with Agatha and Glovina—his mother and aunt had been preparing for bed when Woods and she arrived rather late last night—she made a hasty toilet and got dressed. Woods and she had turned in soon after arriving, too, so she was unusually eager to get the new day started. She would be sharing breakfast with her beloved.

"Your hair is the prettiest I've ever seen," Glovina said after Agatha and she had welcomed Millie into the big warm kitchen with its heavenly morning smells of coffee, browned biscuits, and honey-cured ham with red-eye gravy. "I'm almost tempted to cut mine. Agatha, you remember what pretty red hair those Craig children had, don't you?"

When her blind sister smiled and nodded her gray head, Glovina continued without paying any attention to Millie's blushes. "Well, Millie's is twice that curly and shiny. Already it has grown so much since she was here last month that she's holding it back from her face with combs. My! but when the rest of the family meets you, Millie, they're going to be crazy about you, too. Just you wait and see."

The pleasant business of eating breakfast and catching up on news in the community filled the next hour. Though Millie loved renewing her friendship with the two women, she kept expecting Woods to appear any second. It was silly, she knew, but she missed him dreadfully. Wonder why Glovina thought that she would be meeting the rest of the family?

"Millie, if you're wondering where that son of mine is," Agatha said during a little lull in their conversation, "he left before the crack of dawn. Said he had something important to see about."

"I thought the sheriff and his posse were coming by here this morning for Woods to go with them in search of Jep Logan," Millie replied. She *had* heard a horse leaving in the dark.

"He said he'd likely be back before they get here," Glovina said. "If he isn't, we're to ask them to stop by before they go back into town. Don't worry about that outlaw coming here and bothering us. Those dogs out back and my trusty shotgun can take care of him and about six more without the help of anybody else."

Millie conceded that Woods's capable aunt was stating fact and tried to put her mind at ease. More than once Woods had told how Glovina was a hill woman with the talents and instincts of one accustomed to fending for herself. What bothered her was that Woods was off somewhere alone and that Jep Logan might bushwhack him.

When the perceptive women insisted that Millie get some fresh air, she slipped on a coat and wandered down the open hallway to the front porch. Shep, Agatha's devoted pet and guide, lay beside the kitchen door, barely opening a sleepy eye to acknowledge Millie's presence, as if she might be a family member posing no threat to its blind mistress.

Millie half expected the two huge coonhounds, Jake and Maud, to come bounding after her, but they were nowhere in sight. She hadn't seen them in the huge dog pen out back when she visited the privy earlier. They must have followed Woods, she decided. Was he hunting at this ungodly hour?

Millie saw Iron Creek down the little rise and heard the water singing its familiar song, thinking that the rippling rhythm seemed a fitting accompaniment to the crisp morning air. From the rock-dotted ridge rearing up on the opposite bank of the creek, calls of birds floated down to tease her ears, and she wished that Woods was here to share the music.

Small touches of soft pink led Millie closer to the rose bush arching beside the doorsteps. She recalled then how Woods had told her on her previous visit that the straggly bush was a winter rose and that it bloomed after all of the summer flowers had been forgotten.

Sitting down on the doorstep, the pensive Millie reached to pull a velvety blossom close enough for sniffing, only to draw back her hand in pain. Countless prickly thorns covered the stems right up to the bud, silent threats to would-be intruders like her, she reflected with a wry smile when she bent down to look closer. Small wonder, too. Now that little color showed among any of the surrounding trees or bushes, the dainty winter rose with its spicy fragrance and delicate color held a special attraction. There was no competition.

A distant muffled sound multiplied into thundering hoofbeats and startled Millie from her musings there on the front porch. Both Agatha and Glovina came from the kitchen and joined her. Sheriff Crumpler and seven other men on horseback reined up, vapor rising on the frosty morning air from their mouths as well as from those of their heaving mounts.

When he learned that Woods was not at home, Sheriff Crumpler was quick to accept Glovina's offer for the men to come inside for coffee and biscuits. Millie kept her distance, for she hadn't forgotten her anger at the pompous man for having assumed that Woods had made off with the payroll

and that she was not a reliable witness. Not until the last
scrap of ham and crumb of biscuit was gone did the sheriff
rise and grumble that he and his posse couldn't wait any
longer.

Barely missing a single stab at his teeth with a toothpick
taken from Glovina's table, the portly sheriff left word for
Woods as to the whereabouts of his men and him throughout
the day. Millie upped her chin when Sheriff Crumpler
seemed to single her out as he tipped his dilapidated hat to
the three women standing on the porch to see the visitors
off. She wasn't sure that the polite gesture was adequate as
an apology, but she assumed that it was offered as one and
inclined her head a degree in mute acceptance.

The sheriff mounted his horse and called over his
shoulder, "Tell Woods that if we don't meet up with him,
we'll stop by before we go back to Freeman."

The women returned to the kitchen then, and Glovina
went about the business of mixing dough for bread. Millie
watched with new interest as Glovina dipped up a cup of the
sourdough starter sitting on the back of the giant wood-burning cookstove and dumped it into a little well in the mound
of flour in a curved-bottom tray of unpolished wood. Before
she realized what she was doing, Millie was asking questions and peering over the warm-voiced woman's shoulder,
watching her stir the fragrant, thickening mixture with a
wooden spoon.

Without meaning to, Millie began telling about her own
failures in the kitchen and how at thirteen she had tried,
unsuccessfully, to take her dead mother's place, in the parsonage as well as in the church and community.

Business picked up then, all of it directed by Glovina and
Agatha. A huge apron smelling of soap and sunshine soon
covered Millie's brown skirt and amber-striped waist.

By noon a smiling, flush-faced Millie was taking the last
of several pans of cookies from the giant oven, not a single
bitter whiff or taste of soda to be found in various samples.
Then she floured her hands and imitated Glovina's rhythmic
kneading of the elastic mounds of bread dough, all risen now
and filling the kitchen with delectable yeasty fragrance.

All through the day, lively talk flowed and ebbed easily

among the three women, sprinkled liberally with good-natured laughter. Millie couldn't tell why it was that hearing the two older women share some of their failures at cooking made her feel better, but it did. And, of course, she treasured each fondly told story of Woods as a boy.

The sounds of barking dogs and thudding hooves broke into the cozy kitchen at mid-afternoon.

Hurrying outside, Millie and Glovina saw Major trotting toward the house with Jake and Maud leading the way. Millie's heart turned a somersault upon seeing Woods's familiar smile and one hand lifted jauntily. Agatha and Shep came out onto the porch, her hand resting on the big dog's collar. Woods was astride his horse, but not in the saddle. A puffy-faced Jep Logan sat there, his hands tied to the saddle horn and Woods riding behind him.

Before Woods could answer all of the questions fired at him as soon as he jumped to the ground, Sheriff Crumpler and his men rode up. The sheriff sent the other men to surround the handsome horse and lift down the scowling outlaw, turning then to Woods for explanation.

Woods complied, his hand rubbing the head of first one clinging, adoring coonhound and then the other, before sending both of them to the back of the house with a single command. "Jake and Maud helped me track Jep after I tied Major and took off on foot this morning. Just as I figured when I saw the light in the cave up on Promise Ridge last night, Jep was holed up there."

Before going on, Woods slid a secretive look toward the wide-eyed Millie and saw her face flush prettily. "The way I see it, he followed the Gooseneck to the ridge the night of the robbery, left the horse, then climbed up to the cave and hid the money. The reason Millie didn't hear a horse the night Jep came and threatened her was that he had come the back way from the ridge and sneaked up from the patch of woods on foot.

"Sheriff, Jep must have gotten back on the horse after he left the teacherage and ridden over to his shack to try and doctor his burned hand, where you found him on Sunday. The payroll sack was up on the ledge in the cave." Woods reached in his saddlebag and handed over a large leather bag to the bug-eyed sheriff.

Sending a knowing look at the outlaw, who stood now with bruised face averted, Woods added, "It appears that Jep went back to get his loot after breaking out of your jail. He probably was going to light out tonight for parts unknown. He finally told me that he left the horse staked near his shack, so you likely can find it there. Once I found him, though, it didn't take Jep long to figure out I meant to bring him back to you, Sheriff Crumpler, alive or dead. I think he'll ponder a spell before he threatens any more ladies."

Woods flexed his right hand then, and Millie sucked in a breath at the sight of his bruised knuckles. She didn't like thinking about Woods fighting with the surly Jep Logan, no matter that the man had frightened her out of her wits. Woods could have been the one battered, she thought, shivering.

"Reckon Clive Durham's hundred dollar reward is yours, Woods," Josh Crumpler remarked grumpily. He cleared his throat and spat off to the side, as though to rid himself of a bad taste in his mouth. Shifting his attention to Jep, he said, "What I aim to find out, young feller, is how you gotta gun and 'scaped my jail. You gotta danged bad habit of bangin' people over the head. Where you're goin', that ain't gonna be pop'lar."

"I ain't goin' to no jail, not by myself," Jep declared sullenly. "I done suffered enough over somethin' not even my idea." He stole a sharp sideways look at Millie, then looked down at his bandaged hand, tied now to the other with rope.

"Who you figurin' on takin' along?" the sheriff asked, stuffing his blousing shirt inside his baggy breeches and fixing Jep with a piercing look. "Who's this feller you're callin' the mastermind?"

"I'll talk when I get me a lawyer," was Jep's retort.

Soon the sheriff, his men, and the recaptured prisoner were on their way toward Elmwood.

Though Millie would have enjoyed staying on at the Sanders home, she knew that it was wiser for her to let Woods drive her back to the teacherage before darkness set in. Tomorrow was Friday. Henry Stevens could spread the word of her return, and she could hold classes and try catching up on what had been lost that day.

The three women agreed enthusiastically that they would get in some visiting again on Sunday, what with it being preaching day in Freeman. No amount of protesting from Millie could keep Glovina from pressing a syrup bucket full of the freshly baked cookies on her, along with a crusty loaf of yeast-smelling bread wrapped in a laundered flour sack. Agatha whispered to Woods, and he disappeared for a few minutes. When he returned, he brought a small wax-dipped round of cheese for Millie to take with her. The cold dampness of the cheese told her that it had been resting in the bucket kept suspended down in the well on the back porch for storing perishables.

While Woods got the buggy ready, Agatha and Glovina reminded Millie of the upcoming Ladies' Night Coon Hunt, saying they would be expecting her to spend that weekend with them. Millie did her best to refuse, but by the time she waved good-bye, she had agreed to accept the invitation. She consoled herself with the saying frequently recalled since coming to Freeman: "When in Rome . . ."

"I'm so relieved that you captured that ruffian without getting more than bruised knuckles," Millie told Woods when they reached the main road to Freeman. After having noted the battered cheek and darkening eye on Jep, she was relieved that nothing marred the perfection of Wood's handsome features.

Plainly not wanting to keep the talk moving about Jep Logan, Woods turned down a narrow side road right after they forded Iron Creek, the same crossing where Clive's car had drowned out that Sunday afternoon several weeks ago.

"I want to show you my favorite spot on the farm," Woods explained when Millie questioned him about his detour. "It won't take long."

Millie relaxed against the leather seat of the shay and gave herself over to the private time with her lovable mountain man. Now that he was with her again, she was feeling tuned up, in harmony with the world. When the shay slowed and she looked up ahead beside the creek, she saw a broad-based rise with only a few huge oaks and beeches scattered about. At the very center sat a large cleared area.

"It looks like a home place," Millie said. The sounds of the clear water racing over its rocky bed rose in the still twilight like remembered music. "I wonder why I didn't notice it that day Clive and I walked beside the creek to your house. It must be right around the bend."

"You're right. My home is about a half mile away. You were on the other side of the creek that day, plus when the trees are leafed out as they were then, you can barely see it from across the creek."

"Was there once a house here?"

Woods watched her lovely face in the gloaming, far more pleased than he realized that she apparently approved of the site and the view. From some underbrush nearby, a mourning dove not yet migrated southward cooed and fluttered. "No house has ever sat there, but someday one will." She raised a pretty eyebrow in question. "Mine. I used to help my papa work at clearing this spot. He talked of building a finer house on it someday. I always meant to build a house here for—" Woods voice floated away on a puff of wind.

Millie heard an unspoken word: "Fern." It couldn't have hit her harder had it been in the form of a slashing bullwhip. She stiffened and pulled her coat collar around her neck. The mourning dove flew from its hiding place, leaving behind whirring, vibrating sounds and a single feather floating to earth as the only signs of its presence.

In a tightly controlled voice, she said, "It's a perfect homesite, and I'm glad you showed it to me. I feel a chill coming on, though, and I believe we'd better get back on the main road before night falls."

Woods despised himself all the way to Freeman. Why couldn't he utter the word "wife" back there? After he saw that Millie seemed to like his peaceful knoll beside the creek, he was thinking that maybe it was time to push for an answer to his proposal. But all of a sudden he had gotten tongue-tied and couldn't find the words, like some bashful schoolboy, he chided with disgust. What was the matter with him? Then Millie had become all straight-backed and tight-mouthed, the way she did when she was determined to keep her thoughts inside and play the dignified schoolmarm from Little Rock.

Maybe, Woods reflected, Millie had sensed what he wanted to say and didn't want to hear it, didn't like the idea of having to tell him "no." She was the most puzzling woman he had ever been around. He had to admit that when her face took on that prim and proper air, he felt like grabbing her and trying to force her to spit out whatever was sailing around in her pretty head. Hell and damnation! He had been far better off when he was immune to women.

Millie's thoughts loomed as black as Woods's did. She was surprised about his showing her where he had dreamed long ago of building a house for Fern. Excruciating pangs of jealousy clawed at her still. Why hadn't she gone ahead and supplied the name "Fern" for him? Perhaps it would be good for Woods to know that Annabelle had told her of his eternal love for the young woman now dead and of his apparent incapacity to love another. Her innards shriveled at the thought. No, it was wiser to dissemble and keep the painful truth buried, just as she always would have to keep her love for him secret.

"What do you suppose is going on at the livery?" Millie asked when the shay topped the hill at the crossroads right before daylight faded completely. Both had avoided direct looks at the other for miles, exchanging a few polite remarks when absolutely necessary.

Clive's car as well as another larger one sat parked out front. Several horses, standing three-legged and half dozing, were hitched to the long rail near the blacksmith shed. A pale light gleamed through the ill-fitting logs of the shed and spilled out from the open end facing Stevens's store.

Soon Woods had maneuvered the one-seat buggy into a stopping place and tethered the horse. He walked back then to help Millie down. "We might as well find out what's going on together, hadn't we? I figure it has to do with the robbery and Jep Logan. Your statement might be needed."

Grateful for his not depositing her at the teacherage and leaving her to wonder, as she figured most men would have done, Millie smiled down at Woods and held out her hand. The pale light reflecting from the blacksmith shed was turning his eyes into a mysterious dark shade of blue, she marked with approval. His even teeth sparkled whitely beneath his black mustache as he returned her smile. She eyed the shadowed cleft in his strong chin, thinking that it likely had much to do with her ranking him the most handsome of all men.

Woods looked up at Millie in the dim light and felt as if Halley's Comet of last year might be making a return trip. A burst of uncanny light rushed upon him. When she put her hand in his, his brain reverberated with a blinding, crippling knowledge: He was in love with Freeman's new schoolmarm—wildly in love; head over heels in love as he never before had been, even when he was a green boy infatuated with Fern Stevens. Truth had tackled him at last, no holds barred.

Weak-kneed and with an uneven heartbeat, Woods helped Millie down from the buggy to stand beside him on the ground. His tongue seemed stuck permanently to the top of his mouth, as it had back beside the knoll. Had she not started toward the livery, he wasn't sure that he would have moved for another hour. He could think of nothing more important that just looking at her. The thought came that he might not ever get enough of looking at the beautiful redhaired woman and feeling her presence by his side.

". . . and you have no proof, you see," Clive Durham was saying in clipped tones to a watchful Sheriff Crumpler when Millie and Woods entered the shed. Jep Logan was slouched against a support post out in the middle of the shed with his hands tied behind him and then around the post. "It's the word of a wanted criminal against that of the representative for Southern Bauxite Mines. Besides, didn't I offer the reward for his capture?"

If Clive saw Woods and Millie ease into the blacksmith shed and stand beside Henry Stevens and Edgar Booth near the open end, he didn't let on. Millie heard a low din of men's voices coming from within the livery, but her interest centered on the three standing with Sheriff Crumpler in the light of the lantern in the shed.

Clive went on, his voice rising a notch. "This is an outrage to be accused of hiring Jep Logan to rob my own company's payroll and try to make people think he was Woods Sanders, but especially in front of my immediate superior, Mr. Will Reppond. He's here from Buffalo to see how things are going in Arkansas, you see."

Millie and Woods noticed the well-dressed stranger standing beside the sheriff, the man's countenance showing no emotion but his eyes fixed on the red-faced Clive. Woods craned his neck until he saw the face of the other man standing on the far side of the sheriff. He was not from Lexington County either, but Woods recognized him.

The second man was Archibald Pike, president of Landowners' Bank in Little Rock, the man from whom Woods had borrowed the money against his farm in order to take Agatha to see the doctor in St. Louis a couple of years back. What in thunder was he doing in Edgar Booth's blacksmith shop?

"Mr. Reppond is likely here because of my recent letter," Woods said, aware that Millie, Henry, and Edgar looked at him in surprise. He nodded meaningfully to Henry and Edgar, who sidestepped and stood on either side of Millie. After sending a questioning look at her and receiving a silent permission, he walked to where the sheriff stood with Clive and the two strangers to Freeman.

Quickly Woods introduced himself to the company man, shaking hands with him and then, after both acknowledged prior acquaintance, with the bank president. "Is there anything I can do to get things cleared up here?" Woods eyed Clive suspiciously. What he had been hearing had him mad as hell, but he was determined to keep his temper under control.

"Nobody needs you interfering, Forrest," Clive said, his mouth tightening and his glasses glinting in the lantern light. "You'll get your reward money."

Directing his remarks to Woods, Will Reppond said, "That's true about your receiving the reward, for the company is the one offering it. We're here because your letter got my attention. I checked into the matter and found that you're right. No lease monies have been paid to you landowners as stipulated. The sales of ore allowed us to recover our initial investment last year. Payment is a year overdue."

"But I can explain—" Clive began.

"Not to the company's satisfaction," his superior interrupted. "That's why we made this little trip over here this evening, remember?"

"And not to the satisfaction of my bank either, Mr. Durham," Archibald Pike added.

"This matter doesn't need to be discussed here among these..."—Clive's voice thinned with disapproval—"among these hill folk." He shot what Millie deemed a venomous look in her direction, the lenses of his spectacles reflecting from the light of the lantern overhead.

"Why not? These are the very people enabling our company to mine bauxite and have ore to sell and ship back east." Will Reppond's voice, though laced with the same nasal twang as Clive's, did not grate and sound arrogant. "I brought royalty checks for the landowners in this area, based on the ore taken during the past year. One is for Forrest Sanders. I'll return in the morning, and we'll get our business settled, Mr. Sanders. We want to continue mining on your land."

"My letter requested that you contact Mr. Pike and let him know when payments might begin," Woods said. "He knew that I was counting on the promised income from the mine to retire my debt." He still couldn't figure out why the banker had accompanied Will Reppond. It didn't matter, though. His heart was near to bursting with relief at the good news that at last the mortgage on his land was going to be paid off.

Archibald Pike spoke up. "When I looked into your file at your written request, Mr. Sanders, I found that a certain vice-president had taken it on himself to handle your loan papers. Mr. Reppond and I decided to drive over together when I informed him that a Clive Durham had been caught working secretly with one of our vice-presidents. The two planned to use the bank as a screen for seizing land from owners.

"The landowner would be notified of a bogus payment on demand; when payment couldn't be made in the unreasonable period of time stated, Clive and his partner would pay off the note to the bank and assume the mortgage for face value. As you all know, loans against collateral are always for less value than the property held as security. The two would be buying valuable property for a fraction of its market value."

Gasps could be heard, and none were louder than those coming from Millie and Woods. They exchanged shocked looks.

The bank president went on. "The loan officer agreeing to the shady deal with Mr. Durham was arrested today. Charges of attempt to defraud have been filed in Pulaski County against both men."

Clive seemed to be having trouble breathing, Millie noted. Though he had angered and aggravated her, she gained no pleasure from his present ignominious state. Clive's past innuendos about Woods and the people from the mountainous area came to mind. She pitied him for apparently being so puffed up with greed and envy and self-love that he never had seen the innate goodness and wisdom of the hill folk.

Throughout the revealing conversations, Millie had exulted over Woods having written to the two men and stated his problem in ways effective enough to gain such concrete results. Her mountain man had done that, all on his own! She could not remember when she had felt such inordinate pride in the tall handsome Woods. Her heart expanded when she thought about how hard he must have worked to master the necessary skills to do what he had done in the past several weeks. Surely now he would not hesitate to enter the race for representative.

"Another reason I came along," Archibald Pike explained, "is that Jep Logan is wanted for robbing a sister bank in St. Louis, one headed by my brother. The federal deputy marshal is inside the barn visiting with Sheriff Crumpler's men while we talk over these local matters out here in the shed."

The sheriff walked over to Clive. "You can hold out your hands or put them behind you. I gotta arrest you and handcuff you for the trip back to the jail at Elmwood, or Little Rock, or wherever you're gonna end up."

"You stupid dolt," Clive hissed at Jep Logan, who glanced at him from where he still leaned against the post, tied securely. "Why in hell didn't you go to Hot Springs and catch the train out for Chicago? If you hadn't doubled back here to get the payroll sack from the cave—"

"Nobody told you we found the payroll, Mr. Durham," the sheriff said, frowning and pulling at his ear. "For sure nobody mentioned anythin' about a cave since you got here."

Woods couldn't hold back any longer. He hadn't trusted or liked Clive for a long time, but he hadn't thought he was as low-down as the talk was showing. A glance toward Millie, standing between Henry and Edgar across the way, showed him her shock. "It seems plain who was doing the masterminding for Jep, doesn't it, Sheriff?"

"Shore does." Sheriff Crumpler sounded surprised and a bit hurt when he addressed Clive. "It had to be you, Mr. Durham. I reckon you left the gun with Jep in the jail t'other night, too, so he'd get outta town and not blab. I never figured I had to search a man of your station before lettin' you talk with Jep. When you couldn't nail the robbery on Woods—thanks to Freeman's schoolmarm and her bein' alert and dead set on settin' things right—you knew you was in tall trouble. I see now what-all you thought you'd gain by puttin' Woods away."

"You've no proof—" Clive began.

"Got witnesses to your own words. You're hog-tied," the sheriff went on, squaring his shoulders and seemingly coming to grips with the surprising news about Clive Durham. He slid a wistful look toward Henry Stevens, as if sending a silent apology to his staunch opponent in political matters pertaining to Lexington County. "If Jep hadn't come back to threaten Miss Monroe and let her get a better look at him, likely your plan to get Woods arrested woulda worked. Before he coulda got hisself cleared—if he ever could—you woulda done took over his place and gained all the money from the bauxite."

Jep sneered at Clive, his ugly teeth showing in the pale light. "You thought you was some smart findin' out I was a wanted man, then blackmailin' me into ridin' a hoss lookin' like Woods's and robbin' the livery, didn't you? It might have worked if Woods hadn't stayed at the teacherage so late that everybody else had gone to bed. There wasn't anybody to see but the old nightwatchman—and the schoolmarm who knew for certain I wasn't Woods Sanders."

"Shut up!" Clive snarled.

Jep went on anyway. "I didn't trust you to send me money. I wasn't about to leave the payroll in that cave for you to get and spend while I ran from the law. You call everybody else stupid, when you're the dumbest ass of all." He spit then, laughing hideously when the spittle landed on the lapel of Clive's fine suit.

To everyone's complete surprise, Clive pulled a small pistol from an inside pocket of his suit. He made a backward dash for the open end of the shed, almost pushing Millie, Edgar, and Henry down in his wild haste. Sounds of men's excited, protesting voices filled the blacksmith shed. Suddenly Clive grabbed Millie from behind, an arm angled across her face. The gun in the other hand was rising to point at her head.

From instinct or fear, she never knew which, Millie clamped her teeth into the wrist imprisoning her mouth and jerked her head backward at the same instant, feeling and hearing the sickening crack of her head against Clive's chin. A flash of something shiny falling to the ground told her that she had dislodged his glasses.

Kicking backward with one foot, Millie felt the sharp heel of her button top strike Clive's shin with force. By then her would-be captor was groaning and had loosened his hold on both her and his gun. Frightened at her audacity in fighting back at armed men twice within one week, Millie stepped over into the welcoming embrace of Henry Stevens. A mean headache was moving in on her.

Woods was already lunging toward Clive before Millie kicked him and found refuge with Henry Stevens. As the cursing man wheeled toward the open end of the shed, Woods tackled him from behind and knocked the gun free. When Clive continued to curse and struggled to rise, Woods, straddling him by then, landed a loud uppercut on his chin. A second fierce blow to Clive's cheek ended all resistance.

Amid the noisy confusion in his blacksmith shed, Edgar Booth was retrieving Clive's pistol. Sheriff Crumpler, his watery eyes bugging, had recovered somewhat from his shock and was hurrying with his gun in hand toward Woods and Clive. By then the two strangers to Freeman had fetched the federal deputy from inside the barn, and the deputy raced in with his own gun drawn, followed closely by those with whom he had been visiting. Everyone gathered around the two men on the ground.

Woods stood then. With a fierce look on his face, he hitched up his breeches and squared his shoulders, brushing his hands together as though ridding them of soil while glaring down at the sorry sight of Clive Durham sobbing.

Millie barely recalled the remaining events. Her head seemed a host of blinding lights. The next thing she knew for certain was that Woods was laying her on her bed and whispering soothing words. She heard his footsteps as he walked over to her chest of drawers; then the familiar scrape of a match and smell of kerosene told her that he was lighting her lamp.

"Sh-h-h," Woods said when Millie tried to thank him for putting her in the shay and driving her to the teacherage after the sheriff and the deputy marshall took control of Jep Logan and Clive Durham and left for Elmwood. He was right beside her bed then, and his deep voice fell as softly as the light coming from the lamp. "We can talk tomorrow. You need to get some rest now."

Woods waited until she closed her eyes. Tenderly he unbuttoned Millie's high tops and set them on the floor, the little plop sounding intimate somehow. For a moment he held her stockinged feet in both hands, not surprised that they were cold and tense. She had suffered shock, he realized as he caressed her feet until they felt warm and pliable. She was in no fit frame of mind to talk of all that had taken place or of anything else.

In spite of his own shock at the startling events of the day, Woods realized that he, himself, had a mind—and heart— far too full to examine without Millie's full awareness. Reaching for the patchwork quilt lying on her trunk, he covered his beloved's trembling body with it and gently fitted the soft fabric closely to her slender shape. He was not surprised that a faint fragrance of jasmine clung to the quilt. Her eyes remained closed, but her face softened and her body seemed to relax. Sitting again on the bed beside her, he leaned over and hugged her close, quilt and all.

"There, there, sweet girl," Woods crooned when Millie tried to murmur something. His hand covered the curls falling across her forehead and rested there for a few moments. "Go to sleep. I'll be back soon, and we'll talk then like we've never talked before."

Letting out a tremulous sigh, Millie gave in to the soothing blackness washing over her and easing her blinding headache.

Conclusion

Royal blood or station high does not the
  depth of love command.
The average woman and her average man
Claim the same ecstasy that the exalted can.
There's an ethereal beauty in all lovers' rapture
That is theirs alone for permanent capture.

· *Chapter Twenty-Six* ·

To Millie's surprise, she awakened the next morning with a delicious feeling of rejuvenation. Everything went right. She remembered to leave the coffee perking long enough for the fragrant brew to mellow. The loaf of bread she had helped Glovina make on the day before tasted wonderful, as did the cheese Agatha had pressed on her.

The pupils burst into the classroom early, their voices lilting with retold accounts of what their parents had revealed about Millie's admirable role in the capture of the thieves, Jep Logan and Clive Durham. If any recalled the odious little scenario played out during the final minutes of their last day in class, none made show of it. Even the four boys triggering the scene seemed to have forgotten all about it.

At morning recess Warden and Ransom sidled up near Millie beside the front porch while the other pupils played on the seesaws and swings or ambled about in the autumn sunshine.

"Ransom and I owe you an apology, Miss Monroe," Warden said. His handsome face, so smooth and soft-looking up close that it was hard for Millie to believe that he shaved at all, took on a pleading look. He seemed inclined to look everywhere except directly at her. "The bit with the buzzard was my idea, and I'm sorry. I expected you to ask us to take it off and bury it. We didn't mean for you to have to do it."

The schoolmarm's eyes met the boy's dark ones then. She marked their intelligence as well as their youthful sparks of mischief and passion for life. Calling to play her artful use of dissembling, Millie asked with apparent innocence, "What buzzard?"

Ransom dropped his jaw and looked at his friend, who

also was evidencing confusion. "The one we found dead a mile down the road and dumped on your doorstep on Halloween night."

Warden added, "You must have seen it when you opened your door the next day."

Silence camped for a moment or two among the three before Millie decided that the fidgeting youngsters might have suffered enough.

Struck by a sudden thought, Millie asked, "Have you boys gotten yourselves straight with Henry Stevens and Edgar Booth for horsing around with the hay rake that night?" She called up her fiercest look and gave each boy full samples.

"Yes, ma'am," they answered in unison.

Warden said, "We're going to split a rick of firewood for each one of them; in fact we got a lot done yesterday."

Millie pursed her lips as if in deep thought. "There's a pile of firewood in back of the schoolhouse that James Hobbs brought a week ago. He said he'd have to return and split it when he had more time. If you two brought your axes—"

"Yes, ma'am," Ransom interrupted with a huge smile. "I like that idea a lot. And we'll fill the wood box for you every day after school without your having to ask us to."

"We sure will." Warden studied Millie's still face and unreadable eyes, then hunched up his shoulders and rammed his hands into his jacket pockets. "Thank you, Miss Monroe."

"Me, too," Ransom seconded. His face, fair like his Aunt Annabelle's, lit up before he whirled and sprinted across the schoolyard to where Annette Bordeaux stood talking with Minnijean and Gladys.

Warden turned his head and watched, then looked down at his feet. "I reckon you can see that Annette likes Ransom better than me now. She thinks I acted like a kid."

Millie fought back a smile. It was good to see that Minnijean and Gladys were accepting Annette, and it was good to learn that Warden was acting his age. "I suspect that there'll be lots of different girls for both Ransom and you to get to know before it's time for either of you to get serious, Warden." When he slid her an embarrassed grin, she went on.

"If Annette and you are meant to get together, you will when the time's right—after both of you finish your schooling."

"That's what Mama keeps saying." Warden smiled then. "To tell the truth, Miss Monroe, that family from over near Dierks that sent for me to look at their new litter of pups has two of the prettiest yellow-haired girls you ever saw. Their pa said he was bringing his whole family to the Harvest Festival this month and that he might let his kids ride their horses to our school, if the board gives permission. I was planning on riding back over there late this afternoon—to check on the pups, of course."

Millie went on inside to ring the bell, pleased and feeling right with the world. Warden and Annette seemed to have awakened to the fact that they were both young and had all kinds of marvelous experiences ahead before they took on the sobering mantle of marriage. Strange, she thought, how Wood's face floated before her eyes just then.

Millie fretted when Woods didn't show up that Friday night for lessons. She recalled that Will Reppond, the man from the Buffalo office of Southern Bauxite Mines, had mentioned wanting to meet with Woods that day and get their business straight. If Woods had told her before he left the teacherage last night that he planned to travel into Elmwood, she doubted that she would have remembered. Her head had been aching unbearably.

By Saturday night Millie was becoming itchy. Having already written Louise in Little Rock and explained that she couldn't desert her pupils, Millie dragged out textbooks after supper and planned the lessons for the entire coming week. She was through with her bath and preparing for bed when she heard the sound of an automobile engine nearing the schoolhouse.

"Woods," she said when she recognized his voice and opened her door, "what are you doing coming here in Clive's car? Has something happened?" She panicked at the thought.

"That's not Clive's car," Woods replied with a cocky grin. Tossing a cylinder of newspaper onto the sofa, he reached for her and pulled her close, planting a smacky kiss upon her cheek. "Grab a coat and let me show you my new machine."

With her cape slung over her green wrapper and her feet in satin slippers, Millie rushed with the excited Woods out to the Model-T sitting not far from her door. His enthusiasm was contagious, and she shivered and joined in with his laughter. Both talked at once, her questions bumping into his explanations, until both realized that her teeth were chattering from the cold and that not much they were saying made any sense.

Woods scooped up a protesting, giggling Millie in his arms and hurried with her back inside.

"Get dressed, and I'll take you riding," he said when he made himself release her. His heart was kicking up a fuss. Never had she seemed so beautiful.

"Right now? Where would we go?" Shivering again inside her cape, she wondered why she asked. It made no difference. She would follow him anywhere—even to the Ladies' Night Coon Hunt that Annabelle had told her would be coming up at the next full moon.

Woods saw the shiver and pulled a side chair close to the heater. "We'll wait to go riding." He was guiding her to the chair by then, an arm around her shoulders. "I have something else far more important in mind." He cleared his throat, not surprised that the tightness building there hung on.

"I'm amazed that you went to Little Rock with Mr. Reppond yesterday after he gave you the overdue check. And then he helped you choose a car!"

"It seemed the sensible thing to do," Woods explained after he pulled up another chair and stretched out his long legs toward the heater. "He offered to teach me to drive, and after I got all of my business tended to at the bank, it was late. I got back to Elmwood this morning and visited with Fred and Phoebe. They're both well and looking forward to coming tomorrow for preaching." He watched her throw back her cape and settle back against the chair, then tuck her legs and feet underneath the full skirt of the green wrapper. The graceful, feminine movements fueled his already racing heartbeat. Keeping himself from smothering her with kisses from the moment she opened the door had been hellish.

"I'm happy you'll be able to get about the district easier and quicker by car," Millie said. "I hope you've decided to announce your candidacy at the Harvest Festival." All of those qualities that had endeared Woods to her were at work in full force, she thought while a sweet silence stretched between them. His deep voice and his smile. His black-fringed eyes chasing across her face.

Woods stood abruptly and walked to the sofa. When he returned, he held one hand behind him.

"What are you up to?" Millie asked suspiciously as he stood looking down at her. An unfathomable gleam sparked his blue eyes. Why was he looking so solemn all of a sudden?

Woods dropped to one knee right beside her and brought his hand from behind his back. "I'm up to sparking the woman I intend to marry, Millie." He held out a cluster of pink roses, smiling a little when she gasped her surprise and sat up straighter.

Millie recalled the thorn-encrusted pink roses blooming beside the front steps of his home and prepared herself for handling the blossoms gingerly. But, she thought as she buried her warm face in the spicy sweetness of the velvety blooms, she needn't have bothered. All of the thorns had been removed.

It wasn't fair, she was thinking with a kind of panic behind closed eyes. Woods was supposed to be a mountain man, not a man capable of playing the romantic hero. All along she had feared what she might do if he ever followed up on his proposal when her defenses were down. She wondered if a part of her might not be drowning from the wash of feeling throughout.

Before Millie could figure out what she was going to do, she received another shock, one demanding that she open her eyes and meet those probing blue ones so disturbingly near.

"Millie, please 'Come live with me, and be my love;/And we will all the pleasures prove/That valleys, groves, hills, and fields,/Woods or steepy mountain yields.'"

Burning pieces of firewood popped and shifted inside the heater breaking the silence following Wood's carefully chosen quotation. He was too nervous to note that Millie was crying and that her tears were spilling onto the pink roses held before her ducked face.

Fearful that he had not pleased her as he had hoped, he leaned closer and said in a voice even furrier and deeper, "Actually I don't need Marlowe's words to say that I love you and want you to be my wife. I want to wake up finding you in my arms every morning for the rest of my life. I want to have babies with you, hear your laughter, and see your pretty face every day. I want us to fight and make up, and grow old together, and find life sweeter with each passing year. I know your thoughts about not needing a man in your life, but won't you at least think it over?"

Woods paused, dumbfounded that Millie kept her face buried in the pink roses. He doubted that he could keep on living if she refused to give him a chance to win her love. "I was a damned fool not to have known that I was in love with you when I proposed the first time. Politics has nothing to do with my asking you to be mine. I love you and need you, sweet girl. Will you say 'yes'?"

Her pulse a medley of glorious song, Millie wondered at the magical way that Woods's words flowed over her and embraced her, mesmerizing her and making her feel a special part of something rare, maybe like the warm colors captured on a fine canvas. The closeness of his virile body and the sound of his bass voice seemed to be delineating her in the way that a frame defines a painting. Heretofore she might not have been any more than tenuous daubs of color, seeking life and form. Was that why she had felt that she hadn't known who the new Millie was . . . until now?

Millie leaned forward and pulled her beloved close, not caring that her tears still slid down her cheeks or that she was crushing the roses dropped onto her lap. With her face only inches from his, she smiled into his too-solemn eyes and replied, "I truly thought I didn't need a man in my life —until I met you. Yes, I will marry you, Woods Sanders, and be your love." Letting out a jubilant sound and hugging her tighter, Woods would have captured her mouth then with his, but she put a forefinger on his lips. "Wait. You might want to know that I love you, too."

Woods waited no longer. He stood even as he kissed her,

lifting her up from the chair to stand within his embrace. He couldn't seem to get enough of her mouth, and his heart thundered in celebration. Millie had said "yes"—and, wonder of wonders, she loved him, too! His hands raced over her silk-clad shoulders and back, the touch of her softness setting off bonfires of passion and dreams of a lifetime of loving.

"Will you run off with me and marry me tonight?" Woods asked when he could tear his mouth from hers.

Millie stared up at him, then laughed, the sound a delicious warm one coming from somewhere deep within, maybe from a secret corner of her heart. She had been right; the man was taking over her life—and she didn't even care! "Wouldn't it be better if we married in the church, with your family and our friends present?"

"No," he growled in a tone that thrilled her. "I'm selfish as hell when it comes to you." He gave her a torrid kiss that scorched her cool logic into unrecognizable trivia. "Let'em all wonder at our madness. They'll love talking about us for years to come."

"You're wicked," she whispered in mock horror. He raised a black eyebrow and grinned. "And you're incorrigible."

"Maybe that's why you fell in love with me."

Millie giggled at the thought, intoxicated from the way her breasts were tingling from being crushed against his shirtfront, and even drunker from the way his gaze drank in her face. "I don't know why I love you, but I do know that I never knew who I was until I realized I was madly in love with you. And I'm liking who I am better now that I'm learning you love me, too."

"I like hearing that. When you came here, you seemed all bottled up and half-scared." When she would have protested, he laid a gentle finger on her lips and his voice took on a tender seriousness. "Do you reckon that when you reached out to share yourself with everybody—me included —you discovered something precious that you had kept hidden away—yourself?"

Gazing up at Woods as if he might be the wisest man on earth, she nodded wonderingly. "You've taught me so much. You make me feel so . . . special and so wonderfully alive." It dawned on her that before she met Woods and came to

Freeman, she might have existed on a course parallel to life. Now she was sucked up into it, a vital part of everything around her.

"You must have sensed from the start how much I needed you, but I was blinded by old notions." His voice echoed what was coming straight from his heart. One hand moved to cup her face and he smiled the smile of a lover. "Throw on some clothes and let's get moving toward Elmwood. We'll wake up Fred and Phoebe and have him read the words."

"But aren't there things we have to do, such as figure out where we'll live and get a license and—"

"Don't be so bossy," he said after interrupting her with a light kiss. "We can live here during the week and at Mama's place on weekends until I get us a house built on that spot I chose a long time ago to live on with my wife. I guess I was too scared at the thought of admitting I had fallen in love with you to finish my sentence that day I showed it to you."

"I figured you picked that site for you and . . . your first love." She found the words despicable to utter, but she felt that they had to be voiced.

Woods shook his head. "Never did Fern and I talk about living on Iron Creek. She hated the place. It was my private dream, one I figured was dead . . . 'til I showed it to you."

Millie hugged him closer and buried her face against his chest, soothed from his words and more than a little giddy from all that was happening. She savored the feel of his strong body and its up-close manly fragrance.

"I already have a marriage license," came his voice right beside her ear. He planted a kiss on her earlobe.

Goose bumps popping up from his kiss and the brush of his mustache against her ear, Millie cocked her head back and let her eyes flirt with him in a manner totally new to her. Was she the center of the universe? she wondered when the possibility loomed with more reality than at those earlier times when she had entertained the fanciful idea. "My, but you were awfully sure of yourself."

"Not really," he replied teasingly. "I didn't fill out the name of the bride." One of these days, Woods thought, he would tell her that he had seen the slate with his proposal on it when he had lighted her lamp the other night and had gotten his hopes up that maybe she was considering his proposal more seriously than he had believed. But not now.

Millie leaned back against his arms and joined in with his deep-throated laughter. Against her thighs she felt the pressure of his arousal, and her eyes widened at the thought of all the wonders of making love that lay before them.

"What about school and your mother and—?"

"Sh-h-h," he murmured while cradling her face with both hands and letting his thumbs caress her throat. "I've taken care of everything. We'll honeymoon in Hot Springs 'til the middle of the week. There's a big advantage to being chairman of the school board, as well as having Henry Stevens on my side."

As a tiny part of her still tried to hang on to logic, Millie blurted, "Did you tell Henry about us? Is there something going on between Mabel and Henry?"

Woods chuckled, his teeth flashing whitely in contrast to his black mustache. "I'm glad you're not holding in all of your thoughts anymore. You've got the right kind of curiosity to fit in here in Freeman. And, yes, I told Henry what I hoped would happen. All I'll say about Mabel and him is that after Annabelle and Lucas get married, watch who takes over the mail window. After that, who knows?"

Millie nodded. She no longer was eager to think of anything other than that Woods loved her. Side by side then and with their arms all entwined, they went into her bedroom, both laughing when they almost got hung up in the narrow doorway. Never in her wildest dreams, Millie mused, had she expected to be eloping in the night with a wickedly handsome mountain man . . . lover. Feeling dazed, she reached up and tapped the cleft in his chin lightly with her forefinger.

"I need to make sure I'm not dreaming," she explained solemnly when he slid a puzzled look her way. "Maybe it's time you showed me your 'old razzle-dazzle.'"

"Nope. Not until I think you're old enough." When Millie smiled and kept gazing at him as though he might be the wittiest and most handsome man in the world, he murmured in a thick voice, "When you look at me like that, how can I think about helping you get packed?"

"I can't think what I'll need to take."

Woods stepped away from her enough to look down at her slender form with open adoration. "I plan to take my bride shopping in Hot Springs, so you won't need much. Be sure and take that green wrapper, though. I love taking it off you."

The half-whispered words held them both entranced. They looked at each other as if for the first time, wonderingly and with a sweet shyness. His hands, trembling and suddenly clumsy, went to her incredibly small waist and untied the sash. It was too late then for Woods to call back his original plan for them to leave within minutes. His heart almost leaped from his chest, and the burning in his groin could no longer be ignored when he opened the silky garment and gazed at her loveliness.

Within a space of time too brief to measure, Millie and Woods were lying naked on her bed, embracing and kissing with renewed fervor. A pause, and they became lost in exchanging soul-searching looks. In the pale light coming from the lamp in the other room, she could see, touched 'round with a lazy smile, his lips moving and forming the words for which her heart had yearned, would ever yearn: "You're mine, and I love you."

Millie felt the manly roughness of his palm as it molded itself to the shape of her jaw. Her heart expanded in wonder at the gentleness of his thumb nudging then at her lips and opening them as if they might be petals of a rosebud unfurling in slow motion. For a precious moment she leaned into the caressing hand and reveled in the incredibly new sense of belonging to her beloved.

"I love everything about you, sweet girl. Don't ever change."

"I love you, mountain man lover," she whispered back with barely enough breath to be heard. The kisses he was bestowing upon her swollen breasts were driving her into a frenzy.

Millie's inner humming became a permanent part of her erratic pulse, sweetly in tune with her overpowering love for the man transporting her into new realms of paradise. It piped her to private peaks of bliss again and again, as his tender mouth and gentle hands paid homage to all that she was. A host of emotions colored her every feeling with a palette both delicate and voluptuous. She submitted to the glorious sense of abandonment sucking her up into a whorled world peopled by two.

She nestled closer to his splendid nakedness, purring back in her throat when he seemed to sense her need for sharing and pull her even nearer. Never again would she need to squelch her feelings or thoughts for fear of being judged foolishly feminine, she reflected with awe. Woods had said he loved her just as she was.

Gone were Millie's fears of being forever alone with naught but memories of the taste of her beloved's tongue seeking hers, as it was doing now. The smell and feel of his skin underneath her hungry mouth as she kissed his furred chest would be hers to enjoy for more than that moment, she realized with joy. She moaned at the exhilarating touch of his hot, pulsating shaft against the moist gateway to the molten center of her begging womanhood. When he claimed her fully in the way she was burning for, she rejoiced that what was filling her with fiery, moist ecstasy right then would be a wondrous part of their lives together, not just a memory.

Woods lost himself in making love to Millie. His recent acknowledgement that he had fallen in love with the red-haired woman from Little Rock had set his entire body and mind into a new pace. Turning away from the static love of his youth, he had found his world astonishingly new and fresh. Millie's confession of her love for him was a reward that he had not dared dream of finding. So enamored was he with the thought of sharing his life with her that he had prepared himself for wooing her into learning to feel more for him than friendship.

The feel of Millie's satiny skin beneath his fingers and his lips was far more divine than Woods had remembered—which jolted him, because his memories had been heady and torturous. With thundering heartbeat, he claimed each delicious curve and hollow with the lusty delight of a man waking up in paradise after being stolidly asleep for years. To whatever fate had sent her to him, he promised, he would be grateful forever.

With passion rejuvenated from their confessions of love, Millie and Woods came together and, as one then, rode the crest of their ever mounting ecstasy. The dizzying journey enthralled them, quite stole their breaths and minds when giant rolls of fervor crashed over them and sailed them ever outward into the blissful space known only to lovers. Hoarse cries of celebration rang out when the culmination of their eager, frantic striving burst upon them. Millie wondered if she might not die from the thrilling, cleansing sensations overpowering her and hurtling her into sublimity. Woods thought that if he had to die anytime soon, this was the perfect way to leave the world.

They floundered back to reality, joined as they had been on their lofty trip. Exhausted and satisfied, they clung together in a mind-stretching discovery of self and each other.

A spell of silence, broken only by their ragged breathing and soft declarations of love, reigned there in the bedroom of the teacherage. Propping up on his elbow and resting his head on the heel of his hand, Woods looked down at Millie. She rewarded him with a tremulous smile and a worshipful look.

"If we're going to get married before daylight," Woods said, his finger tracing the shape of her straight little nose, "we'd better get going." The feeling that he could master anything with Millie beside him fed his soul, made him feel masterful and ten feet tall. Maybe a bit like a mountain man. In a musing tone, he added, "You're going to make one hell of a fine wife for a representative."

"I'm glad you've decided to run." She reached up and stroked his silky mustache playfully, thinking of the many times that she had longed to do so. "You'll win, for sure."

The thought pleased him. The touch of her fingers on his face fanned the embers of his assuaged passion. "Can you believe that the banker in Little Rock told me he's going to ask his friends in the district to support me?"

Millie watched his angular face while he talked, noticing the softness of his lips and the cleft in his chin. "I believe it, and I believe that you're apt to end up being governor someday."

"Not likely, but thanks for the confidence. Come to think of it, you'd make an even finer first lady of Arkansas." Woods leaned and planted a kiss on her pretty mouth, then lovingly fingered the curls framing her face. "We'd better get your things packed and get started for the parsonage in Elmwood."

"Do you want to know what I think?"

"Yes. I want to know everything that goes on behind those pretty brown eyes." The thought that he had felt that way ever since their stormy first meeting sneaked up on him and humbled him. It would take a lifetime with her to ferret out all that made her so fascinating. The prospect delighted him.

Millie held out her arms toward him. "I think I'd rather make love again before we ride off in your new car."

Woods threw back his head and laughed, delighted with the naked red-haired woman flirting with him so outrageously. "My beautiful Millie," he told her after kissing her thoroughly and feeling himself harden in anticipation, "I should have known you were going to hornswoggle me that first day when I saw those red garters and short drawers."

"You're being horrid to let me know that you saw, Woods Sanders," Millie sputtered, half-angered and embarrassed at the thought that he might have laughed secretly at what she had revealed in her clumsy fall from the wagon. She wanted to appear perfect in his eyes.

Woods held her fast, though, and she squirmed without success at freeing herself. Her breasts lay crushed against his huge chest, traitorously warming up and prickling with longing to be touched. She could feel his manhood throbbing against her thighs, could feel the exquisite answering coming from deep within herself. How she loved the black-haired man whose life had become interwoven with her own in such a delightful, promising way!

Millie's flare of ill humor got swamped by the far larger feeling of desire for her beloved, and she relaxed against him. Propping up enough on her elbow to rest her head against her hand, then arching an eyebrow coquettishly, she winked at Woods and inched her fingers across his flat belly, then down through the tight black curls to his swelling shaft. "We can argue later. Let's make love now, mountain man."

And they did.

Dear Readers,

Louisiana becomes an even lovelier place when I get letters from you. I enjoy finding out what you like and don't like about my books. You may write me in care of Warner Books, 666 Fifth Avenue, New York, New York 10103.

Myra Rowe
Monroe, Louisiana